# SAND, SAWDUST, AND SCOTCH

Also by Bob Christenson

*INTO THE WILD WITH A VIRGIN BRIDE*

# SAND, SAWDUST, AND SCOTCH

## A Life Loosely Based upon the Truth

## BOB CHRISTENSON

**To order additional copies of this book, contact:**
Xlibris
1-888-795-4274
www.Xlibris.com
Orders@Xlibris.com
672581

# CONTENTS

For Harold John, Ruth Fox, and Jerold Jerome
Christenson wherever you are

"Life moves pretty fast. If you don't stop and look around once in a while, you could miss it."

Ferris Bueller

# A LIFE LOOSELY BASED UPON THE TRUTH

**Someone once said,** "Our memories are abridged versions of ourselves." I don't know who said that. Maybe I did. How is it that people can share the same experiences yet have entirely different memories of them? I don't have an answer, but I suspect memory is shaped by both circumstance and personality.

What follows is neither a life story nor a memoir. (There's a difference. You can look it up.) For want of a better term, I call these selections memory sketches, stories from my life that I hope readers find entertaining. For I write to be read. I've never believed writers who claim to write only for themselves. I suspect even Emily Dickinson secretly hoped someday a person would open a dresser drawer, find her poems, and proclaim her brilliance to the world. And that, of course, is exactly what happened.

I write creative nonfiction. The stories are true. I know. I was there. However, to make them entertaining, I employ various elements of creative writing. In doing so, I feel free to enhance situations, create composite characters, and invent dialogue in keeping with the personalities and events I'm describing.

I have changed some of the names in these stories to protect both the innocent and the guilty. On the other hand, I have not changed names of those I like too much to give aliases.

Finally, to prevent readers from thinking that, in spite of my protestations, this really is a life story, I have avoided arranging these sketches in chronological order.[1] Each narrative is a separate entity, neither dependent upon what has gone before nor upon what follows. I had fun jumping around in my life when I wrote this collection. I hope you do, too.

---

[1] For readers who are uncomfortable with this jumbled approach, I have added a "Where and When" chronology to the back of the book. Using this handy chart, you will be able to fit any selection into a perfect chronological niche.

# I BUMP UP AGAINST ADULTHOOD

## I

**In my thirteenth summer,** I began a journey from the certainties of boyhood to the confusion of the adult world. In three separate episodes that summer, I came face to face with the tragic suffering people inflict upon themselves when they make bad choices in life. I also encountered the range of emotions this suffering can elicit in others—sympathy, apathy, denial, and sometimes outrage.

Vern, one of our mill hands, lived in a converted garage within a block of our home. He was an alcoholic of the worst kind, an alcoholic who sees snakes and spiders crawling over his body whenever he is deep into withdrawal. That summer Vern tried going cold turkey. He failed.

One Sunday around two or three o'clock in the morning, I awoke to the phone ringing. Vern's landlord had called my father, insisting he come over immediately because Vern was screaming in the garage behind the landlord's house. I don't know why Dad allowed me to go with him. Perhaps he was only partially aware I tagged along.

The wife of the couple who rented to Vern met us outside the garage. "I want him out of here!" she shouted as we approached. "Do you understand? I want him out of here!"

"I'll do what I can," my father replied, brushing past her.

"No, you'll do more than that," she shouted at his back. "I already have one drunk in the house. I don't need another in the garage!"

We heard Vern's sobbing before we entered the room. He lay curled in a fetal position on the bed, blankets pulled over his head, stocking feet moving, kicking rhythmically like a bloodhound deep into a nightmare. The blankets and pillows, soaked with sweat, were blotched with vomit and blood. The room had been torn apart, bottles and clothing scattered across the floor. Just inside the door, claw streaks of dried blood raked down the wall, made either by torn fingernails or splinter wounds from the rough lumber siding. Had he been trying to escape, or had he been trying to bring the walls into him, to bury his agony in an attempt to close out the world?

Dad sat on the edge of the bed, stroking Vern's hair, talking to him in a low, comforting voice. Vern began to quiet, responding to my father's reassuring touch. He lowered his legs from his chest, groaned, pulled them up, and then relaxed them again.

Turning to me, Dad spoke in a quiet voice. "I want you to go home and tell your mother I need her. Tell her to bring washcloths and dry sheets. Even if she has to take them from one of our beds. Tell her to bring some canned soup if we have any. Also some milk. Can you remember all that?"

"Sure," I replied. "Washcloths, sheets, milk, and soup."

"Oh, and also," he added as I started toward the door, "*you* don't need to be here. Go back to bed."

In the morning my father said simply Vern was okay. I sat on our steps and looked up the alleyway to the back of Vern's garage. I knew he was in there, lying in newly stained sheets. I could not escape the image of those blood streaks, five fingers wide, on the inside of his wall. If Vern was okay, then something was wrong with the world.

## II

My uncle Merv always had a new aunt whenever he visited our house. "This is your new aunt," he would say, introducing someone whose time in bars around the docks where he worked as a longshoreman was indelibly marked in her face. Usually blonde and cinched at the waist in a losing battle to compete with Betty Grable and Ann Sheridan of the silver screen. Sometimes I liked them; sometimes I didn't. But I had never allowed any of them to get close to me because I knew they were short-term.

In the middle of that summer, Merv showed up with Mae. In a few days she had broken down the barriers I used to keep these new aunts at bay. Not that most of them had ever been interested in anything I thought or did anyway. But Mae was different.

"Are all these books yours?" she asked, pointing to my collection. I nodded. "Have you read them all?" Again I nodded, a little embarrassed, certain I was being set up as a bookworm, some kind of weird kid who should spend more time outdoors.

"Wow, I'm impressed," she answered, running her fingers across the spines. "You have a lot of Hardy Boys stories. You must like them."

"I think I have them all. But they're a little young for me now. I'm moving into more adult books."

"Don't be so quick to put boyhood things behind you," she said over her shoulder. "Once lost, never regained."

"That sounds like something from a book," I answered.

"Could be," she smiled.

Mae turned toward me with my copy of *The Call of the Wild*. "Here. Tell me the story in this book."

"Oh, that one's really great! But the one next to it is even better," I replied, pointing to *White Fang*.

She pulled the book from the shelf. "Same author," she mused. "Better story, though, huh?"

"*I* think so," I nodded. "But I like them both."

"All right," she answered, handing me the books. "Tell me one of the stories tonight and the other one tomorrow night." She sat on my brother's bed, pulled her legs up Indian fashion in front of her, and looked at me, expectantly.

"Well ... okay," I replied, sitting down on my own bed. "This one is about a dog named Buck. He lives in California, but there's this gold rush in the Yukon, and he gets dognapped and . . ."

\* \* \*

A couple of nights later, my parents went to the movies with Merv and Mae. I had fallen asleep reading in bed and awoke to voices in the living room and the hall outside my door. People talked in hushed tones, but their voices carried unmistakable urgency. I heard doors opening into both my parents' bedroom and the hall bathroom.

As I stepped into the hall, I saw Merv carry someone into my parents' room. I could hear my mother's voice as he entered. Then I saw Dr. Underwood, the town physician, walking toward me, followed by my father. I started to move forward, but Dad held up his hand and motioned me back. The door closed behind them. I stood just outside my bedroom, listening to the voices, unable to make out the words.

In a few minutes, my mother came back into the hall. She took me by the shoulders and turned me toward my bed. Across the room my brother slept undisturbed.

"It's okay," Mom whispered. "Everything's okay. You need to go back to sleep."

"Who's hurt?"

"Aunt Mae had an accident, but she's going to be all right."

"What kind of accident?"

"Just an accident. We can talk about it in the morning."

"No. I want to know now."

"I'm telling you she's going to be okay."

"You keep *saying* that. What's wrong with Mae? What does she have to be okay *from*?"

Mom looked across the room to check on Jerry and then sat next to me. "I don't know if you're old enough to understand this, but I'll try. Aunt Mae felt sick in the theater and went to the bathroom."

She waited a moment and then asked, "Do you know what a miscarriage is?" I shook my head.

"Well," Mom began and then paused, searching for words. "A miscarriage is something that sometimes happens to women who are going to have babies. Something causes the baby to come before it is supposed to come, and the mother loses the baby."

"So Mae had a baby?"

"Well, not exactly. She sort of had a baby."

"How do you sort of have a baby? You either *have* a baby, or you *don't* have a baby."

Even in the shadowy light from the hall, I could see Mom smile. "You know, I don't know how you got so smart. The important thing here is Mae is sick right now, but she's going to get better. What happened to her was sad, but she didn't even know she was going to have a baby, so the sense of loss will not be as bad." She pulled me into a hug and stood up.

"Honey, I have to go back and help the others. Mae will be better tomorrow. Take my word for it. She'll be okay."

I lay awake for a long time. I didn't understand what I had just heard. There had been a baby. But there wasn't a baby. Mae didn't know she was going to have a baby. But she had a baby. Except it was only *sort* of a baby.

I didn't know what a miscarriage was, but if it was something like Verne's alcoholic seizures, saying everything was okay would not make it okay.

\* \* \*

I saw little of Mae in the next couple of days, only occasional glimpses as she was assisted down the hall to the bathroom. In the meantime the neighborhood ladies helped Mom with the extra work of a recuperating patient. As they talked for hours over their coffee in the kitchen, I sensed a change in the tenor of their conversations about Mae, a change from sympathy to pity. Then pity seemed to drain into resentment that this relatively unknown woman was taking so much of my mother's time and energy.

"You know Merv's track record," said Ida, my mother's best friend. "You're not going to see her again. She's just one of Merv's women."

\* \* \*

Five days after the miscarriage, Merv and Mae left our home for San Francisco, where he planned to look for work on the docks. She was pale and shuffled to the car with a strange, hitching gait. I held back, not knowing what to say or do. Just before she pulled herself into the passenger seat, she looked for me and smiled. She seemed about to say something but either changed her mind or did not have the strength to follow through. I watched the car as it passed the Catholic church on the next corner. And then it was gone.

I never saw Mae again.

# III

One Saturday in the dog days of August, our gang attended the movie matinee. We were all there Jerry, Harley, Kenny, and I accompanied by Kenny's younger sisters, Irene and Paula.

Emerging from the dark coolness of the theater into the blinding light of afternoon sun, we shaded our eyes and crossed the street to the Bus Depot Café, where we bought ice cream cones for the walk home.

Estacada is a tired old lumber town on the banks of the Clackamas River. The downtown businesses are separated from the uptown residential area by a hillside shaded with tall Douglas firs towering from an undergrowth of blackberry brambles and scrub brush.

Two roads run down the hillside, connecting these sections of town. Today both are paved, but when I lived there, only the main highway was hardtop. Log trucks screamed up this road every ten to fifteen minutes, having downshifted in the business section before reaching the hill. The city fathers ignored the speeds at which these trucks raced through town, knowing the drivers' livelihoods depended upon making two loads a day.

The other road, shorter and much steeper, was dirt. Once a year, a grader worked this road, pulling up loose rocks and softening the earth. In the summer it was hardpan; in the winter it was mud. In both seasons its banks were loose landslides of rock and dirt funneling into the brush and trees below.

Neither road held much appeal for our gang. We had a third alternative. A narrow path wound up the side of the hill through the trees, emerging only a few blocks from our neighborhood. It entered the woods alongside the dirt road, turned left, and sloped up the hillside. Gradual and shaded, the path was always our choice over the hot steep trudge of the graded road.

Strolling along a two-block section of vacant lots in our approach to the hill, each of us applied our individually special licking technique to our ice cream cones, sculpting patterns guaranteed to make the ice cream last as long as possible without losing a drop to the heat of the sun. The girls, neophytes in the art of hot-air ice-cream licking, ran ahead, seeking the protection of the shaded trail.

Grasshoppers erupted from dusty weeds and came to rest on the sidewalk ahead of us. We were already busy balancing our cones while avoiding stepping on cracks, a faux pas guaranteed to break our mothers' backs. Dodging the brown-tobacco laden insects added to the challenge of navigating this obstacle course. We stepped short, we stepped long, and we licked, savoring the flavor of strawberry, chocolate, or vanilla. At that time we could never have imagined a future in which people would find these three flavors ordinary. Strawberry, chocolate, or vanilla—this was a choice made in Heaven.

We had just started up the path when we heard girlish squeals ahead. Irene burst into view, summer dress high on her thighs as she ran, shrieking, toward us. Paula arrived before Irene could catch her breath. Hands on her knees, shaking, Irene looked up at us, a nine-year-old drama queen, apparently awaiting our reaction. I glanced at Kenny, who returned my look, smiling. We had seen it before. Irene, playing one of her roles.

She pointed up the trail. "There's ... there's a man up there."

"What'd he do?" asked Kenny, suddenly the protective brother. "He try to do something to you?"

"No," gasped Irene, puzzled. Then, abruptly understanding the meaning of Kenny's question, she blushed. She straightened and took a deep breath.

"No," Irene shook her head. "He's dead."

"He's dead?" Kenny replied.

"Yeah," she gasped, both girls nodding their heads. "There's a dead man up there."

I looked at the shocked expression on Kenny's face and grinned. "Right," I said. "Kenny, there's a dead man up there."

Kenny was puzzled only a moment before he smiled. "Sure. There's a dead man up there."

"Is there really a dead man?" Jerry asked.

"Well, of course," I replied. "Come on. Let's investigate."

I threw my right arm across my face, hiding behind an imaginary cape and intoned in my best Dracula imitation, "But beware. There may be more than one body. Come. We seek the blooood."

I began stalking up the trail. The other boys fell in behind, each adopting my funereal pace.

Kenny began adding sound effects: "Bump, bump, bump, BAAAULM....bump bump, bump bump!" In a few steps Jerry and Harley joined in. "Bump, bump, bump, BAAAULM ... bump, bump, bump, bump!"

"This isn't funny," Irene, protested. "I'm not lying. There's a dead man up there."

"Sure there is, and *we're* going to find him. Aren't we, guys?" I asked the string of Draculas following behind.

I expected Irene and Paula to break off this game any moment, but when we came to two ice cream cones lying in the trail, I had my first inkling of doubt. No one in her right mind would throw away an ice cream cone to play a joke.

The girls stopped ahead of us. "Okay," I said. "Where's the dead man?"

"Up there," they pointed.

At first I registered nothing. Then I saw a leg crossed over another leg, the foot on the upper leg bent at an odd angle, the shoe missing. I followed the leg down to its juncture at the crotch of a torso, the rest of the body hidden behind a tree trunk.

"Jeez," I muttered. "There really *is* somebody up there."

The gang stood transfixed, silent. Grasshoppers whined in the distance.

Finally Kenny asked his sisters, "How do you know he's dead? Did you go up and look at him?"

"We went partway up," Paula answered. "We could see his face. His mouth is open, and he's icky. You can tell he's dead."

"Let's go see him," Kenny grinned. "I wanna see him."

"I'm not goin' up there," Harley objected. "I don't wanna see no dead man."

"You don't *want* to?" Kenny turned on him. "This is probably your only chance in your whole life to see a real-live dead person just like in the movies, and you don't *want* to? How could you not want to?"

"I just don't want to," Harley replied, backing down the trail.

Kenny looked at Harley as if he were seeing him for the first time. Then he shook his head, grinning. "Doesn't matter. You stay here with the girls. We'll go see." He motioned the rest of us forward and began climbing the hill.

* * *

It was Old Man Morgan, the town drunk. He lay on his back, head downward, one arm flung to the side, the other across his chest. Dirt had cascaded over his lower foot and shin, the pants leg hiked up, revealing startling white skin blotched with purple bruises. He wore a thread-bare suit coat over khaki pants. The coat had fallen open and bunched under his armpits. His mouth gaped. Dried vomit caked one grizzled cheek.

The vomit had run over his upper lip and filled both nostrils. From there it trailed to the corner of an eye. The eye was open, but only a slit of white showed, the iris and pupil rolled upward into his head.

I looked up the bank, following the body's skid marks to the brink of the road's shoulder. The missing shoe lay partially buried just above his feet. Halfway up the hill lay his crumbled, stained hat. I had never seen him without this hat. Somehow, the uncovered wispy hair made him seem indecently naked.

Kenny squatted by the corpse, fascinated. "Man, he's really dead," he gushed. "Look at his eyes. I always heard dead people had open eyes."

My brother put his hand on my shoulder. I turned to see tears beginning to well. "I liked Mr. Morgan," he said. "He never hurt anyone. I wasn't scared of him the way some people are."

I found myself between two boys looking at what once had been life: the one seeing a corpse and the other seeing a man. I loved my brother then, perhaps more than I had at any other time.

Kenny looked over his shoulder. "So, what do we do now?" he asked.

"Well, we got to tell someone," I answered.

"Sure," he said, standing up and dusting off his pants legs. "We better go find Sheriff Halloway."

"Lots a luck doin' that," I muttered, shaking my head.

Sheriff Red Halloway was the only police force in Estacada. He spent most of his time ticketing Portlanders who exceeded the speed limit on their way to fish the Clackamas, the same Portlanders who had their breath taken away by the suction of log trucks careening by them both on the river road and on the main highway through town. He was usually in his patrol car parked in a hidey hole or perched on a bar stool in one of the two fisherman/logger restaurants in town, downing coffee and working political connections with hangers-on from City Hall.

Kenny thought a moment. "Yeah, well, what we gonna do? We got to tell *someone.*"

"How about Judge Archer?" I asked. We had walked by Judge Archer's house on our way to the trail. One of the few people who actually had a residence in the business section of Estacada, Amos Archer was our local justice of the peace. His combination home/office was across the street from the library, just two blocks away.

"Good idea," Kenny agreed, already starting down the hill.

"I wanna go home," Harley objected. "I don't wanna go back downtown."

"Good," responded Kenny. "Go home. And take Irene and Paula with you."

"Why?" Irene asked. "We can stay with you."

"Is that what you wanna do?" demanded Kenny. "You wanna hang around with this dead guy while we go to the Judge's house? Because we can't *all* go to his house, you know. He won't want a whole bunch of kids at his house. Better Bobby and me. The rest of you should just go on home.

I saw the uncertainty in the girls' eyes and what I thought was confusion in my brother's. Why was *he* being cut out of the action? But as I looked at him, I realized he *wasn't* confused. He was relieved. He didn't want to be a part of this. He wanted to go home.

"Kenny's right," I confirmed. "The rest of you go home. The two of us'll go see Judge Archer.

That was it. The voices of authority in our gang had spoken, I as the eldest and Kenny as the smartest.

I watched Jerry, Harley, Irene, and Paula walk up the path toward home. I looked up the hill at the legs of Old Man Morgan lying along the red dirt bank of the road. Then I turned and joined Kenny on the path leading back to town.

\* \* \*

Kenny and I stood on Judge Archer's porch, peering through the screen door into the darkness of his home. The front door stood open to the heat of the summer day. I had knocked when we first arrived, but no one had responded.

"Knock again," Kenny instructed.

I had just raised my hand when Mrs. Archer appeared behind the screen door. Because we stood in the glare of the afternoon sun and she stood in the dark coolness of the house, the Judge's wife was just a shadow except for the whiteness of both her apron and the dishtowel with which she was wiping her hands.

"Yes. What can I do for you boys?"

"We need to see the Judge, Ma'am," I answered.

"This is Saturday. The Judge is taking a nap. You boys come back on Monday."

"No, Ma'am," I replied, dropping my head to study the scuffed toes of my tennis shoes.

"And why not? What's so important that you have to interrupt the Judge on a weekend?"

I stared at my shoes, hesitant to respond. Kenny stepped forward. "Mrs. Archer, we don't know where else to go. We figured the Judge would know what to do."

"Do about what?"

"We found a dead body."

Kenny's abrupt answer floated in silence for a moment before Mrs. Archer cracked the screen door. The shadows parted with an inward shaft of light that revealed a smear of flour on her forehead.

"What'd you say?" she asked through the crack.

"We found a dead body," Kenny repeated.

"What kind of dead body?"

"A dead *man's* body," he answered. "Old Man Morgan. He's dead. He's deader 'n a doornail."

From the darkness of the living room behind Mrs. Archer came the sonorous voice of the Judge. "You'd better come on in here, boys."

* * *

Fifteen minutes later Kenny and I were back on the porch, waiting just as Judge Archer had instructed us. We sipped from glasses of lemonade, grudgingly provided by Mrs. Archer at the direction of her husband.

The Judge had listened to our story in the dark mahogany of his study, interrupting us only a couple of times for clarification. Otherwise, he had merely nodded now and then, encouraging our boyish enthusiasm for the drama of having found a dead man.

When we had finished, he excused himself to use the telephone. I glanced at Kenny to see if this curious comment had registered. I had never heard anyone excuse himself to use a telephone. Kenny, playing with a glass paperweight on the desk, seemed unimpressed.

"Clara," the Judge began, swinging his big chair away so that we were looking at the back of his head. "This is Amos Archer. I need

City Hall ... Yes, I know it's Saturday ... What? ... *Someone* has to be there ... Well, I need radio contact with Sheriff Halloway ... What? ... Yes, Edna Hall knows how to use the radio ... She's not there. She's home. Well, who's there who can ... Oh, I see. She has a radio in her house.

Well, do the taxpayers know that? ... No, Clara. I was just kidding ... Yes, Clara, I know it's a good thing ... Yes, it *does* save taxpayer money ... Yes, I understand ... Clara, I need you to ring her house ... Yes, if you will ... Thank you, Clara."

He swung his chair back around. "Boys, I'm going to be a couple of minutes. You might be more comfortable on the porch. Mrs. Archer prepared some delightful lemonade just this morning. Would you like some while you're waiting?"

\* \* \*

"This is *delightful* lemonade," Kenny intoned, leaning back on one elbow. "Absolutely delightful."

"What do you think's gonna happen?" I asked.

'What do you mean?"

"I mean, what do you think's gonna happen now?"

"We're gonna be famous," Kenny answered, holding up his glass to catch the sunlight through the lemonade.

"Famous?"

"Yeah. We'll be the guys who found a dead man. How many people in this town find a dead man?"

I didn't know how to answer Kenny. To him Old Man Morgan was just a dead man. I looked at Kenny, wondering how he could not feel anything for a man who had been our neighbor. He had lived just across the alleyway from Kenny's house, half a block from mine.

Old Man Morgan lived with his son and daughter-in-law, the couple who had rented their garage to Vern. I remembered her yelling at my father about having one drunk in her house and not needing another in her garage. I wondered if she would regret having said that—probably having said it more than once—or just feel relief when she heard the news of her father-in-law's death.

We sat in silence, sipping our lemonade, until the screen door swung open and the Judge stepped onto the porch. He wore old-man slippers below the cuffs of his blue slacks. I looked up at the blinding white of his shirt. I had never seen a man so dressed up for his day off.

"Boys, I was able to relay a message to Sheriff Halloway. He'll be on the hill as soon as possible. In the meantime I have a couple of other phone calls to make. What I need you to do is to go back up to the hill and meet the sheriff. Show him where you found Mr. Morgan and wait there with him until I come up."

"Yes, sir," I replied.

"Also, I want you to tell the sheriff I said not to do anything or touch anything until I get there."

"Judge Archer," I began, "uh … you're asking us to tell Sheriff Halloway what to do? You can't be serious."

Judge Archer grinned. "No, Bobby, I'm asking you to tell Sheriff Halloway what *I* said not to do. There's a difference."

"Yes, sir," I answered, "but I'm not sure Sheriff Halloway'll understand that difference."

The Judge studied me a moment, smiling. Finally he said, "I want you to promise me something."

"What?"

"When you get out of high school, don't go away. Stay here and run for public office."

I looked at him blankly and then turned to Kenny, who simply shrugged.

"Never mind," the Judge said, still smiling. "Just go on up on the hill and wait for the sheriff. I'll be there as soon as I can."

\* \* \*

The sheriff was already there. We saw his patrol car parked on the hill as we approached, no longer avoiding the cracks of the sidewalk. A mud-caked pickup was parked on the opposite side of the road.

Kenny and I debated over climbing the road to the vehicles or going up the path. We finally decided not to change our routine and entered the shade of the trail.

When we reached the place where we had climbed to the body, we looked up to see Sheriff Halloway kneeling by Old Man Morgan. Two men, easily identified as loggers in their heavy-duty denim jeans raggedly cut off shin high, leaned over, hands on knees, peering down at the corpse.

We had just started up the bank when the sheriff looked down at us and yelled, "Stay out of here. Get back down the trail."

"We're the ones who found Mr. Morgan," I answered. "Judge Archer told us to come up here and wait for him. He said … he said … he said not to touch anything until he got here," I finished in a rush.

The sheriff rose from his kneeling position as we climbed the hill. I figured he was mad to be told what to do by a couple of kids, but the sheriff was usually mad anyway as least as far as kids were concerned.

His red face glowered at us as we climbed the last stretch to the body. The two loggers were grinning. The one nearest us turned his head and spit tobacco across a boulder near a thicket of scrub brush.

"Hey," yelled the sheriff, "don't be messing up the scene!"

"Don't be messing up the scene?" the logger smirked. "You mean like the *crime* scene? What do you think, Red? You think you're investigating a murder here? Look up the hill. You can see where the old drunk slid down the bank. He probably hit his head on that big rock. I imagine he was dead before he stopped skidding. If not…," he turned his head to spit a stream of tobacco across the same boulder, "he drowned in his own puke. Look at him. His mouth and nose are full of it."

"Just don't be messing up the scene," the sheriff muttered, kneeling by the body once more.

"You boys touch anything when you found him?" he asked, looking up at us.

"No, sir," I replied. "We just went down to Judge Archer's house and told him."

"That was smart, boys," said the other logger, licking the paper of a cigarette he was rolling in his hand. "You did the right thing. Judge Archer can handle this."

"*I* can handle this," Sheriff Halloway growled, looking up. "I don't need the Judge to handle this."

"Right," the logger grinned, striking a match for his cigarette. "Red, you couldn't slap your butt with both hands in a dark room. Don't forget, I knew you when you were a cat skinner. You weren't any better at that job than you are at this." He shook out the match and flipped it toward the body.

"I was there the day that eighteen-year-old choker setter beat you half to death when you almost killed him cranking up the cables when he was under a log."

"Yeah, well, that's not the way I remember it," the sheriff snarled.

"Hell, there ain't no other way to remember it," the logger laughed.

At this point, Kenny, as if he sensed weakness in a hated bully, asked, "Sheriff, why do they call you Red?"

"What!" the sheriff snarled, turning on Kenny.

"Why does everybody call you Red? You aren't redheaded." Kenny pointed to the sandy fringe of hair below the sheriff's baseball hat. "Why do they call you Red? I'm redheaded, and no one calls *me* Red. But you're not, and everyone calls *you* Red."

"You little pissant, "the sheriff snarled, coming upright. "You gettin' smart-mouth with me?" He took a step toward Kenny, who backed down the hill.

"Get out of here!" the sheriff yelled, sweeping his hat off his head and waving it at Kenny as if he were shooing away a swarm of flies. "Get out of here! Go home!"

"Why?" Kenny pleaded. "I didn't mean anything. I need to be here. I found Mr. Morgan."

"We don't need both of you here. This one," the sheriff said, pointing his hat at me, "can tell us everything we need to know. I don't want you here. Get on home."

Kenny started to say something but was cut short by the second logger. "The kid's not hurtin' anything, Red. Let him stay if he wants to."

Sheriff Halloway turned on him. "Damn it. Whether you two like it or not, I'm running things around here. We don't need both of 'um."

Then he took another tack. Smoothing his hair before putting the cap back on his head, he asked, "If these were your kids would you want them hanging around a puke-soaked body like this? We don't need 'um both here. One, maybe, to answer any questions, but not two. I'm just thinking of the kid."

The loggers looked at each other and shrugged. "I don't believe you, Red," said the first logger. "You're just pissed off, and this kid is the smallest person here. But I think you're right in spite of yourself."

He turned to Kenny. "Boy, you better go on home."

"No," Kenny argued, "I don't want to. It's not fair. My sisters found him first. I got a right to …"

"Come on," the logger said, stepping toward Kenny. "I'll walk a ways with you. Tell you what," he added, throwing an arm around Kenny's shoulder. "Come along, and I'll tell you why we call that phony bag of wind up there Red."

I watched the logger and Kenny walk up the trail and out of sight. Then I turned to the two men beside the body. The logger was looking up the trail at the spot where the two had disappeared. Sheriff Halloway stared at me. I suddenly realized *I* was now the smallest person on the scene. Six kids had found the body. Now I was the only one left.

The sheriff took out a handkerchief, removed his hat and wiped his forehead. *Kenny was right*, I thought. *He doesn't have red hair. Funny, I never thought of that.*

He looked up to catch me staring and seemed to read my mind. He slapped his hat back on his head and, looking down, nudged Old Man Morgan with the toe of a boot. It was such a dismissive gesture that I looked away, embarrassed at having witnessed it.

When I looked back, Sheriff Halloway was watching me, grinning. He hitched his pants under a belly gone soft. Then he nudged Old Man Morgan again. I turned my back. I wouldn't give the sheriff the satisfaction of seeing my reaction a second time.

Below us, the other logger reappeared on the trail. I felt relief as I watched him make his way up the bank. He didn't like Sheriff Halloway any better than I did. I needed someone as a buffer between me and the unreasonable hatred of this bully poking his foot at the side of a corpse sprawled in the late afternoon sun of a hot August day.

I wished the sheriff had told *me* to go home instead of Kenny. I wanted to walk away to step down on the trail that would take me home. I didn't want to be there any longer. I wanted to go home.

Ants had discovered Old Man Morgan, several scurrying over his face, picking at the dried vomit around his mouth and nose. The white in his one partially opened eye had grayed, matching the pallor of his face. He had become a thing, not a person, even to a twelve year old who had been his neighbor only a day ago.

"You know," said one of the loggers, "in the old days they used to put coins on the eyes of dead people."

"I heard a' that," answered the other, rolling another cigarette. "Why'd ya suppose they did that?"

"I don't know. Maybe it was to keep the eyes from flying open."

"Whadda ya think, boy?" The sheriff asked, turning to me. "Scare ya to see this old man's eyes open all of a sudden? Maybe his head cranks around to stare at you? Wooo," he crooned. Holding up his hands in a Frankenstein pose, he lumbered toward me.

"Leave 'em alone, Red," growled the first logger. Turning to me, he added, "His eyes ain't gonna open, and he ain't gonna get up and walk." He took a drag on his cigarette.

"I know that," I answered, looking at Old Man Morgan again. His mouth seemed to have pulled down even more, giving him a feral look. "I just don't think it's right to joke about him."

I looked away, embarrassed at having openly criticized the behavior of adults. I waited for the sheriff to answer, certain he would rip into me.

When only silence followed, I turned back. No one was looking at me. Each was busy with his hands, pulling at shirt cuffs, brushing back hair, shaping a cigarette. It was a silent moment, the kind of moment I felt Old Man Morgan deserved as these men stood around his body. For at least that short time, the person-turned-into-a-thing had become a person once more.

Above us a car pulled to a stop on the hill road. A door slammed, and a moment later Judge Archer looked over the bank. He sidestepped down the soft dirt of the hillside. I saw that he had replaced the old-man slippers with crepe-soled hiking boots. I looked at the dirt-filled moccasins of the loggers, whose corks, I knew, were in their pickup, and shook my head in admiration. The Judge just seemed to do everything right.

He knelt by Old Man Morgan, looking from the body to the top of the hill and back again. "Well, what's your read on this, Red?" he asked, standing up.

"The way I look at it," drawled the sheriff, "he got drunk, fell off the hill, slid down, probably hit his head on that big rock up there, and ended up here. If he wasn't dead when he stopped sliding, he drowned in his own puke."

I looked at the two loggers, who grinned, amused at this verbatim recitation of their own conclusions. The one who had walked Kenny up the trail winked at me.

The Judge stood a moment, looking at the rock jutting from the hillside. "I think you're right, Sheriff. Mr. Morgan seems to have died from an alcohol-induced accident. See any need to call in the County or the State?"

When Red Halloway shook his head, the Judge nodded. "I don't either, so let's take care of things here."

He glanced up the hill. "I'm surprised we don't have a crowd gathering, but you can bet they'll be here when the word gets out. First thing we need to do is cover up this man. You got a blanket in your patrol car, Red?"

"Yeah, I do, but it's my own blanket, and I ain't gonna ruin it by puttin' it over that piece of crap," he growled, pointing at the body.

Judge Archer stood still, looking at Sheriff Halloway. He simply looked at him for a long moment. And that look wilted the sheriff. I suppose I should have enjoyed seeing this bully lose his bluster, but I didn't. I was embarrassed for him somehow. I can't explain why.

"Sheriff," the Judge began in measured tones, "if your blanket is harmed by covering Mr. Morgan, the city will reimburse you. Send your request to me in writing, and I'll personally okay it."

He continued to stare at the sheriff, who was unable to meet his eyes. "Red, go get the blanket." The sheriff nodded and began making his way up the bank.

Judge Archer turned to the two loggers. "Boys, I'm going to need your help here. If people start arriving, I'd like you to assist Sheriff Halloway in keeping them up on the road. Also, I'm going by the funeral parlor to ask Hank Newell to come down here and pick up Mr. Morgan. I'd be grateful if you two boys could give him a hand."

"Hell, Judge, we could carry him up there if you want," one of the loggers drawled. He pointed through the woods to the top of the hill where pilings held up the back side of the Estacada Funeral Home.

"Yeah, boys, I know you could. But I'm sure Hank'll bring a van and a litter."

The Judge turned to me. "Bobby, you live by Mr. Morgan's family, don't you?"

"Yes, sir."

"Well, I need to tell them what happened. Suppose I give you a ride home on the way to their house?"

"No, sir, Judge Archer, I don't need a ride home. I'm just fine walking."

"I know you are, but maybe I need *your* company before I talk to the Morgans."

Judge Archer didn't need me. I knew he didn't need me. I needed him. And he knew I needed him … on this long ride home.

* * *

I watched my neighborhood approach through the windshield of Judge Archer's Pontiac. I had focused on the Indianhead hood ornament most of the way from the funeral home after having waited in the car while the Judge made arrangements for picking up Old Man Morgan's body. I didn't want to talk, but I did like being close to the Judge in the comfort of his big car.

As we neared my house, the Judge looked over at me and said, "You did fine today. You'll be okay." He didn't *ask* me if I would be okay. He *told* me I'd be okay. The Judge was a man of pronouncements, not predictions. Somehow I knew this pronouncement had placed upon me a responsibility to live up to his expectations. Just as I knew I would never disappoint him.

* * *

It had been a long summer. Vern's alcoholic seizures, Mae's miscarriage. Old Man Morgan's death. Soon I would look forward to the opening of school, when I could lose myself in being just another kid playing football, flirting with girls, struggling with math. It would be time to pull back from this glimpse I had had of the adult world. I'd be a kid again. I'd be okay.

# THE BEACH

**My earliest memories** are of a house perched in the sand dunes north of Copalis Beach, Washington, its back to the sea, as if huddled to protect itself from the wind, rain, and cold blowing in from the Pacific Ocean. The house was not destined to hold out against this assault much longer. Waves methodically devoured the cut bank upon which it squatted. The single room at the back of the house contained no furniture because in high tides, water washed in through gaps between the floor and the siding. When the tides receded, an inch or two of sand remained. My mother cleared the room of sand between tides.

At least, that's the way I remember it. I was probably three years old, maybe four at the most. Likely the sea washing into the back of the house happened only once during a freakishly high tide. But I remember the room not having any furniture before the water came. And I remember my mother methodically cleaning it after the water left as if this was, indeed, a regular occurrence.

My parents had probably lived in several similar homes during my first three years. We were a nomadic family until I was seven. In the winter we lived on the coast. My father worked in the woods, felling old-growth trees. I have pictures of him and his partner standing at the butt of trees six or seven feet in diameter, trees they had cut down using double-edged axes, sledge hammers, wedges, and "Old Misery," their name for the two-man crosscut saw.

In the summer and early fall, we traveled through eastern Washington and Oregon, following the crops, picking cherries, hops, and apples. Today, we would have been called migrant workers, I suppose. At that time the term for families like us was not so politically correct. We were called fruit tramps. Living in dirt-floor tents, we were part of a migrant community that moved in and out of each others' lives throughout the season.

So, if this first house in my memory sounds like something ramshackle and dangerous, it probably was. My parents lived hand-to-mouth most of their lives together. They didn't make payments on a mortgage the first thirteen years of their marriage. In their earliest years, a house in danger of falling into the ocean would probably rent at a price they could afford.

* * *

The second home I remember was in Copalis Beach itself. Again a house nestled in the dunes, the last home before the road dropped to the beach. A much larger house, cloaked in seasoned gray shingles, its porch sloping away from the front door, the foundation a victim to the rot of sand and saltwater so much a part of our lives

I know I was four years old when we lived in this house because we were there on December 7, 1941. A couple of weeks after the attack on Pearl Harbor, army trucks rolled into our little town. Several hundred servicemen constructed a tent city across the street from us. The tents gave way to permanent barracks, Quonset huts, dining halls—a complete army installation in just a matter of weeks.

Authorities had decided that if the Japanese followed up the advantage they had gained with the destruction of the Pacific fleet, their most likely invasion would target the northern beaches of Washington. Unlike Oregon, those beaches don't butt up again cliffs and mountains. An invasion there, they reasoned, would allow the Japanese to roll directly into major American cities.

Consequently, women and children of Copalis Beach were asked to evacuate. My mother, Jerry, and I went to live for a time with my grandfather in Walla Walla, eastern Washington having been deemed safe from attack. I'm not sure how long we stayed there, but I remember how happy I was to be back on the beach when we were allowed to return.

I loved the beach, a remarkable place to spend my early boyhood. I still love the beach. Just the term "the beach" makes me feel good. In Oregon people go to "the coast." In Washington they go to "the beach." To most people these terms are probably synonymous, but to me they are not. The first is a geographic location; the second, an emotional trigger to treasured memories.

In my life I have been attracted to major bodies of water around the world. I have viewed the Atlantic Ocean from its blustery shores in

Maine to its warm, inviting beaches in South Carolina. I have stood on hillsides in Iceland, marveling at the power of the Atlantic in the north, and I have looked west across the Irish Sea from the craggy cliffs of Wales.

I have walked along fjords in Norway, where signs on village roads warn of troll crossings. I have crossed the Baltic Sea in a boatload of partying Finns going to Estonia to stock up on tax-free beer.

I have swum in the Mediterranean off the coasts of France and Italy and watched the sunset over the Aegean Sea from more than one Greek island. I have walked along the coastline of Malta, stepping into shadows of castles constructed by the Crusaders, and I have slept in a yacht on the Nile River.

I have strolled beside the Bosporus, crossing from the European side to the Asian side and back again so that I could say I walked in two continents on a single day.

I have fished the rushing waters of rivers in the Hindu Kush mountain range between Afghanistan and Pakistan and have walked along the Indian Ocean in Sri Lanka.

I have floated through the Three Gorges on the Yangtze in China and have viewed the Sea of Japan from the shores of Korea, though, of course, the Koreans reject this name, instead calling it the East Sea.

And I have played in waters throughout the tropics of the Pacific: Fiji, Tahiti, the Cook Islands, and especially Hawaii, the most beautiful of all tropic settings.

But beautiful as the beaches of Hawaii are, they are not my beach. And as exotic, intriguing, and sometimes dangerous as these other waters are, they are not the waters of my beach.

My beach is dirty and gray. In the winter it's cold with wind and rain. In the summer, sunny days give way to more wind and rain. It isn't hospitable, my beach. So why do I go there on spirit searches even now, seventy years after my family moved away? I go there because beneath its harshness, its cold shoulder, is a memory, a memory of a happy boyhood at the outbreak of a world war.

For the first seven years of my life, it was my home. And when we were allowed to return from Walla Walla, I wasn't just coming home. I was coming home to the beach.

# A PIRATE IN THE FAMILY

**Trapper ... carny ... house builder ... inventor ...** Ave was all these. Of course, I was not aware of most of this as a child. Of the six grandparents who were a part of my life through marriage, divorce, and death, Ave was my fascination. I stood next to him, sat next to him whenever allowed. And always I was drawn to the hook. The fascination that was Ave was the hook. A heavy steel-hinged leather harness encased his right arm. And where a hand should have been was the hook. Not one of those pincer things you sometimes see on amputees. An honest-to-God *Peter-Pan* Captain-Hook hook.

When we walked a street, I moved to Ave's right side and surreptitiously slid my hand into the hook. I knew every boy we passed envied my pirate grandfather. Ave recognized my fascination and played to it with histrionic flair. While I sat on his right side at dinner, he invoked the admonishment of my grandmother by reaching across the table, spearing a greasy pork chop and lifting it dripping to my plate. On Sundays I watched in delight as syrup whirlpooled into the vortex of hook-delivered pancakes.

Ave lost the hand at age sixteen, blowing stumps on a Minnesota farm. With the impatience of youth, he reached under a stump to see why a stick of dynamite had not gone off, and it did. He lost the hand, his right eye, and the hearing in his right ear. To reach a doctor, he traveled twenty miles by horse and buggy, holding the bloodied ends of the tourniquet in his teeth.

I have no photographs of Ave, and though he was a part of my life for eighteen years, I cannot clearly picture him. My obsession with his missing parts seems to have robbed my remembrance of all but fragmented images. I recall wispy hair frequently flattened with a palm; flexible wire-rims behind which his glass eye floated, constantly daubed with a damp handkerchief; and a prickly growth of gray whiskers that would have sandpapered the young skin from my cheeks if he had chosen to hug me to him as my grandmother occasionally crushed me

23

to her massive breasts. Of course, he did not hug me. Men in our family did not demonstrate affection. Wanting to hug a male of any age would have been slightly less excusable than wanting to be hugged.

When Ave lost his hand, he had already been on his own for two years. At age fourteen, he had run away, disappearing into the great northern woods of Canada. There is no record that his family ever looked for him. He was gone for nearly a year. Then one day as winter softened into spring, he appeared on the edge of a snow-covered clearing, pulling a rough-hewn sled laden with beaver, marten, and mink pelts. He had established the independence that would be the one constant in his life.

Ave was not one of my natural grandfathers. When my father was ten years old, his mother left him and his two brothers in the lobby of an orphanage. They did not see her again until they were adults. In the meantime, Ave had entered her life.

Ave was a nomad. He appeared from nowhere and disappeared without warning. When I recall evenings with Ave, I picture the musty tents of our fruit-tramping summers. As shadows cast by flickering kerosene lanterns danced on canvas, I sat on the dirt floor of Ave's tent, listening to the stories of hunting, fishing, drinking, and brawling that made up the mythology of the men in my family. As I listened, I waged a silent battle with Queenie, Ave's bird dog, over who would sit closest to him. Ave would drop the hook to his side, and I would hold it, breathing the oiled smell of the leather harness and treasuring the secret caress of that cold steel.

Ave did live in houses on occasion. I remember a short attempt to grow watermelons near Kennewick, Washington, where I spent part of a summer following him up irrigation ditches as he harpooned carp with a pitchfork or lazing beside him under a hot August sun while we fished the Columbia, catching exotic creatures neither of us could identify. We ate them all, including the carp.

Later Ave lived for a time near Sandy, Oregon, where he purchased a store that rented walk-in food lockers. While my grandmother minded the store, he built a house on an adjacent lot. The hook was threaded and could be removed from the steel plate at the end of the harness. He had a set of special carpentry tools hammers, screwdrivers, saws with threaded bolts in place of handles. He merely unscrewed the hook and inserted the tool he wanted. Ave seldom had the problem of looking for a missing tool. Whatever he was presently using was always there at the end of his arm. During the time he built the house, he moonlighted as a night watchman at a lumber yard twenty miles away. He constructed the house almost entirely of lumber stolen from the yard.

The summer after my father was killed in our sawmill, I returned from my annual two weeks of National Guard duty to find a grimy, rust-streaked trailer squatting by our house, electric lines and water hoses like umbilical cords connecting the two. Ave, my grandmother, and Emily, Ave's pet weasel, had come to stay for a time. Animals were attracted to Ave, and when he wasn't killing them, he returned their affection. Emily would stretch across his lap, her belly turned to the caress of his hand like some kind of furry keyboard.

I was working for the Forest Service that summer, and one weekend I took Ave with me on my fire patrol. As we bounced through the high-rock country, he pointed to one of the golden-mantled squirrels that infested the area.

"You know, you could make money on those."

"You'd have to kill a bunch to make a coat."

"Pets, Bub. People would buy 'em for pets."

"They'd die in captivity."

"Everything dies, Bub."

"Are you telling me you'd spend time chasing those squirrels around these rocks? Aren't you getting a little old for that sort of thing?"

If I struck a nerve, he didn't show it. Leaning back into the seat, he looked over at me. "I got twenty bucks says I can make more money trapping these squirrels than you make driving around telling people to put out their cigarettes."

"I don't have twenty bucks."

"Make it five," he answered.

"You got a deal."

Ave's routine for the next month consisted of camping four days a week in the high country and then delivering squirrels on Fridays to pet stores throughout Portland. They took all he brought at a dollar a head. At first he was bothered by having to reset the traps every time he caught a squirrel. But in an afternoon with wire cutters, his special tools, and some apple crates, he invented a perpetual-motion trap with sliding doors activated by the weight of squirrels lured to the back recesses of the traps by the aroma of apples. They sneaked into corridors with doors closing behind them and found themselves in holding bins with the unfortunate others who had preceded them. Ave put out the traps each morning and fished or lazed in the sun until evening, when he returned to collect his squirrel-laden treasures. At the end of the month, he added my five dollars to his profit.

Along the way he worked his con games with other kinds of animals. "God gave us the animals, Bub," he told me when I laughed at a pair of raucous blue jays he had caught with birdseed and string, "but we gave 'em the names. We can't change the animals, but we sure as hell can change the names." He sold that pair of Blue Mountain cockatiels for twenty dollars.

Having discovered a family of pack rats living in a miner's shack, Ave told a pet owner with whom he had become especially friendly that he was going to trap and sell them.

"Nobody's gonna buy pack rats."

"Why not? They don't look like rats. They have Mickey Mouse ears and furry tails."

"Nobody's gonna buy pack rats."

"I got twenty dollars says they will."

"Make it five."

"You got a deal."

A week later Ave stopped by the pet store with two plump pack rats to show the owner how cute they were. The owner was out, but his affable wife was in. Ave took one look at her and announced, "I got the pair of desert squirrels your husband ordered."

"Desert squirrels?"

"Yeah. If I'd known how hard they are to catch, I wouldn't have agreed to twenty bucks. No wonder these things are so rare."

"Well, I don't know. Mac didn't say anything to me about any desert squirrels."

"Hey, don't worry about it. Like I said, I know I can do better than twenty bucks with these."

"Well ... if Mac said he wanted 'em ... I guess ..."

The next week Ave returned to collect the additional five dollars.

* * *

That summer was the last time I saw Ave. The next spring he abandoned my grandmother in The Dalles, Oregon, leaving town with a blonde thirty years his junior. Ave was a temporary resident all his life. And that included the time he spent in our family.

# JERRY'S SLED

**The summer our gang** found Old Man Morgan's body, I was the nominal leader of the group. Gangs in those days were a *good* thing— no colors, no boom boxes polluting the air with offensive lyrics, no guns—just a group of boys who hung out together, making the most of weekends in the school year and lazing the time away in the dog-day heat of summer.

I was the oldest at twelve. The other three—my brother Jerry, our closest friend Harley, and redheaded Kenny—were one to two years younger. Occasionally Kenny's two younger sisters tagged along with us, as they had that fateful day we found the body. But the girls were allowed to accompany us only on hot summer days when we didn't have the energy to shoo them away. In the winter our activities were strictly boy stuff.

Harley was a weak, pale boy, just a few months younger than I. He was afflicted with all kinds of ailments, the kinds that attracted bullies. For a while he wore glasses with one lens blackened because he had a "lazy eye." Another time he suffered an infection that caused a yellow-green discharge from his ears. This infection cost him a year in the Oregon State School for the Deaf. As a result, Harley was a timid, frightened boy, always on the alert, like a mouse that has just been dropped into a snake's cage, instinctively aware of imminent danger.

Kenny might have weighed ninety pounds if he filled his pockets with rocks. As the youngest in the gang, he never took an overt leadership role, but, somehow, we always did whatever Kenny wanted. He was smarter than the rest of us, more manipulative, sly. He was also unpredictable and a little explosive at times. We never quite knew what Kenny was going to do.

Jerry and I were the fighters. When necessary we fought others, but usually we fought each other. As far back as I can remember, we were exactly the same size. When we were very young, our mother dressed us in identical clothing, reveling in comments from strangers about her cute twins. *I* did not revel in those comments. I needed to protect my position as the number-one son.

Jerry, on the other hand, enjoyed being as big as his older brother and somehow realized at an early age that at some future point in time he was destined to outgrow me. Until that time, we fought. We fought over anything and everything. Of course, we didn't allow anyone else to pick on either of us. We protected each other's back when we weren't pounding each other's front.

That was our gang: two brothers who frequently bloodied each other; a timid, browbeaten boy whom God seemed to have forgotten; and a redhead probably destined to be either a politician or a psychopath. Or both.

For two years, my brother and I had made money picking up bottles along the Mount Hood highway. My father could not bring himself to stay away from his sawmill, and on those weekends when the mill was shut down, he drove up the mountain to work on minor repairs or simply check on things. Since those were short work days, he often took Jerry and me with him, dropped us off along the highway with gunny sacks, parked a mile or two up the road, and made his way back with his own sack. This was before plastic bottles, before Tom McCall, before the bottle bill. We did quite well picking up beer and pop bottles along this highway, famous for its drunk, exhausted, or, in many cases, *both* drunk and exhausted drivers. At the end of the day, we cashed in the bottles at Sandy on our way home to Estacada.

I don't remember what I did with my money, but Jerry, a notorious hoarder all his life, saved his. He had fruit jars filled with coins and small bills. Those jars came in handy when Estacada had one of the worst winters in the memory of the local old-timers, the keepers of all truth and fiction in the town's history. Snow fell for two weeks. We missed so much school that the strawberry harvest in late May, dependent upon teenage pickers, was threatened with an extended school year.

For those two snowy weeks, the town leaders closed one of the roads between the upper and lower sections of town the steep, dirt road where the gang had found Old Man Morgan. Now covered with packed snow, the road had been surrendered to sledders. During the day young people played on the hill. In the evening older teenagers and young adults gathered to sled and drink beer around two fifty-gallon drums blazing with warming fires.

For a short time, our neighborhood gang joined in the jostling for starting positions at the top of the hill. But we had a secret, a secret that we protected as we protected all our secrets. We had built our own sled run, a run unknown to those who gathered to flirt and drink beer around the blazing barrels. Our run was longer and more challenging.

Behind the schools a steep, brush-covered hill rose to a grove of Douglas firs. A cat road plowed diagonally across the hill. A rusty barbed-wire fence paralleled the upper side of the road. Midway across the hill, a gap left by a missing gate in the fence marked the entrance to a path leading upward to the grove of trees.

Vegetation along the road was as demarcated as the town itself. Above the road grew springy Scotch broom, beautiful in the summer with its bright yellow flowers. Below the road a thicket of sharp, interwoven blackberry bushes offered succulent berries in later summer to anyone tough enough to brave its raking, bloodthirsty thorns.

From the gateposts, the path headed straight up at a steep angle until it reached a ridge on the face of the hill. From there the incline leveled a little, the path twisting through the field of Scotch broom to the grove of trees above.

In good weather this grove was the scene of all kinds of teenage decadence: smoking, drinking, sex. But in this hard winter, the hill was ours. We packed down the snow, turning the path into a challenging, serpentine run through the Scotch broom. At the drop-off ridge, the sled became airborne before plunging straight down and through the gate, where a hard right took the sled down the cat road until momentum slowed to a stop. It was a beautiful run.

Keeping the run secret had been almost as difficult as building it. We didn't want to share it or, worse, run the risk of being pushed aside by older boys. We each pledged a sacred oath that no one would bring outsiders to the run. But that created a major problem. None of us owned a sled.

We had managed a few trial runs by borrowing a sled from a younger boy in the neighborhood, promising him an adventure on the best sled run in town, a promise we never meant to keep, of course. However, when his mother discovered he had loaned his sled to older boys, she took it away from everyone. We had a run. We didn't have a sled.

Then we heard of a sled for sale. And it was for sale at a price that we—make that Jerry—could pay. Jerry had his jars. Jerry knew to the penny what was in those jars. We could buy this sled.

At nine o'clock at night, we completed the sale. The rest of us watched as Jerry poured the money from the jars and counted out the proper amount. The sled, of course, was not like those we saw in the Monkey Wards catalogue, not a store-bought sled. It was a homemade wooden sled, but it was beautiful. The runners covered with strips of tin. Two handles on the front. On a Monkey Wards sled, they would have been used to steer. On this sled they were there simply for looks and stability. Place the feet on them or the hands if in the preferred prone position and look as if the sled were under command. In reality, gravity and the ability to violate the laws of inertia dictated both speed and direction. Throw the body weight left or right, and hope the sled followed. This was how the sled was steered.

As Jerry pulled the sled home that night, the rest of us walked alongside, commenting on its sleek looks, its sturdiness, its fancy tin runners. This sled was *made* for our secret run. We hoped the snow would never stop, school would never open, and we could spend the rest of our lives careening down our hillside.

\* \* \*

The next morning was crisp and clear. Crisp and clear with a major surprise. During the night we had experienced a silver thaw. Everything covered with a coating of ice. Everything. Bushes bowed to the ground. Tree limbs snapped off. Wires swaying dangerously low between telephone poles. Roads treacherous. But we weren't driving. We were sledding.

We stood at the top of the hill, sweat-soaked under our winter clothing. We had managed to make our way up the cat road by breaking through the ice to the traction of the ruts below. But once we turned through the gate and started up the hill, we fully realized the challenge of the silver thaw.

The path itself was solid ice. We struggled upward by pulling on the Scotch broom alongside our run. Two steps up, one step back. Two steps up, one step back. Scotch broom is a tough, springy plant, but even it gave way to the weight of ice and boys trying to pull their way to the top of the hill. Frequently branches snapped off, sending one or more of us sliding down the ground we had worked so hard to gain.

Finally, there we stood, looking down a crystal hillside. Had I been a poet, the sight would have inspired. I could see the tops of the fence posts along the cat road below, icicles shining from the barbed wire, frosted blackberry brambles peeking over the far side of the road. But the slope beyond that drop-off was so steep that I could see nothing else of the hill itself. Below that, the school playing fields, softened by the white of snow and ice, marked the beginning of the flat land that was upper Estacada.

In the distance the steeple of the Catholic church reached upward, its white sheen all but lost in the winterscape below me. I could make out the roof of our house a block beyond the church. Everything sparkled in the icy stillness of the morning. If I had been a poet …

But I wasn't a poet. I was a twelve-year-old realist. My attention did not remain on the flatlands of Estacada. I focused on the ice-covered hillside below me. I traced the path of our run as it wound through the Scotch broom to the ridge and then plunged straight down to the gate posts, icy sentinels marking the entrance to the cat road.

If we managed to reach the gate, we had to cut a hard right on the road, or we would go over the other side and down the blackberry-covered slope, all the way to the edge of the playing fields below. *This is crazy*, I thought. *I don't want to do this.*

I looked to my brother. It was *his* sled. By rights, the honor of its maiden voyage belonged to him. But he did not meet my eyes, and I knew he was not going. Not even glancing at Harley, I turned to Kenny. He tucked a loose strand of red hair into his stocking cap as he studied me, an amused smile on his lips. *He's not afraid*, I thought. *He's waiting to see what I'm going to do. If I don't go, he will.*

I was older. I was the nominal leader of this gang. It was my duty to go down this hill. I stepped forward and announced, "I'm going." Silence greet my proclamation. In the case of Jerry and Harley, relief. In the case of Kenny, recognition of my rights as the elder.

* * *

I stood over the sled, adjusting my hat. The other three wore stocking caps, but *I* had a special hat. My uncle, who fought with the

Marines in the Pacific Theater, had given me this hat. Though military issue, the hat was not in keeping with tropic islands. It was an Arctic hat, hood-shaped with a small bill and a large band that snapped over the chin and mouth. A beautiful hat. I had worn it every day in our recent winter weather.

But it was a man's hat, and I was a boy. Several sizes too large, it kept sliding around on my head. Slippage to the right blinded my left eye. Slippage to the left blinded my right eye. The hat falling forward blinded both eyes. But it was a beautiful hat, well worth the trouble of occasional sight loss.

I stood at the top of the hill, adjusting my U.S. Marines hat, John Wayne, through and through, steely-eyed and confident on the outside, heart hammering on the inside. I took the favored prone position on the sled. My brother moved to my side and held the sled while I settled in, adjusting my legs and gripping the pseudo-steering handles.

I flashed Jerry the thumbs-up so popular in movies about World War II pilots, and he gave me the shove that started the sled down the hill.

Kenny and Harley stood several yards below. As I swept by, Kenny yelled, "I'm going, too!" and jumped on my back. His right arm caught me under the chin in a choke hold. His left hand gripped my head, pushing my hat down over my eyes. Where before I had seen a white hillside, I now saw only military-issue brown felt.

The loss of sight probably didn't matter anyway. I couldn't have stayed on the path even if I could see. We careened down the hill, Scotch broom snapping and cracking as we bounced from one side of the run to the other, heading for the ridge that marked the drop-off point to the gate below. I could hear Kenny yelling, "Left! Right! No, left! No straight! Go straight!" I fought with one hand to uncover my face, holding a steering handle with the other as if the steering handles actually had anything to do with the direction of the sled.

We became airborne as we flew over the lip of the ridge. At that moment, Kenny left the sled. I don't know if his leaving was a conscious decision or if he was thrown off. But since Kenny was smarter than the rest of us, I suspect it was a conscious decision.

The good thing—well, for a moment it seemed like a good thing—was that as he flew off the sled, he pulled my hat from my face. Still airborne, I saw the gate posts below. They were straight ahead. I bounced once. I bounced twice. I shot between the posts, hit the middle of the road, and, airborne again, flew over the lip of the road's shoulder into the blackberry brambles on the steeper slope below.

Crashing through ripping vines, I buried my head into the sled to protect my face. The brambles were so thick that I felt sure I'd be pulled to a stop. But I didn't slow. I maintained speed as I plowed through thorns tearing at my clothing, ice cracking and snapping. *Jeez,* I thought, *I'm going to make it all the way down! I'm not going to stop! I'm going to make it all the* ... WHAM! I ran headlong into a railroad tie.

Later reports from the gang describe a perfect somersault. First my feet and legs appeared above the blackberry bushes, followed by my torso, arms, and head. Then my feet and legs disappeared into the brambles, followed by the rest of my body.

I don't know if I was knocked out. I don't know if people really are knocked out by blows to the head the way they are in movies or on TV. I *do* know they see stars. Those stars are not a comic-book convention. I *saw* stars. I may have been unconscious because the next thing I remember is hearing the gang make their way through the blackberry bushes and coming down from the top of the hill must have taken some time.

I heard footsteps crunch the ice. They stopped by my head. I opened my eyes to see my brother leaning over me, tears running down his face. *Wow,* I thought, *he really loves me. In spite of all our fighting, he really loves me.*

Jerry wasn't crying for me. He was crying for his sled. In my left hand I held one of the steering handles. The rest of the sled lay crumbled behind the railroad tie, the wood splintered, the tin strips torn from the runners and twisted into the air above the wreckage.

\* \* \*

The walk home was long and quiet. Jerry walked ahead; I, several paces behind, the steering handle still in my hand. Throwing it away seemed an insult to the corpse of the sled we had left on the hill above us. Kenny and Harley lingered behind, occasionally whispering in the low, somber tones reserved for funeral processions.

When we stepped through the back door of our house, Mom, washing dishes at the kitchen sink, smiled through the steam and asked, "Well, how'd it go?"

Jerry looked at her, lower lip quivering. Then he broke into tears and ran through the room and down the hall. When the door to our bedroom slammed, she turned to me, wiping her hands on a dish towel.

"So," she said, "what did you do this time?"

# CLOSE ANIMAL ENCOUNTERS OF THE THIRD KIND

## SNAKES

**I had no fear of snakes** until I moved to Pakistan. Oh, I had the usual intake of breath if a snake suddenly slithered across a path or through the grass in front of me. And I remember once deciding that I didn't need to fish a particular set of rapids on the Clackamas River when I discovered a large bull snake sunning near the boulder I had chosen as the perfect casting spot. But I had lived most of my life in western Oregon, and snakes on that side of Mt. Hood are relatively harmless.

Pakistan, on the other hand, is a land of venomous snakes. Over fifty deadly species exist on the subcontinent. The cobra, of course, is the most famous as well as the most common, but the most dangerous is the krait. Kraits average three feet in length with an occasional five-footer showing up. Their venom is fifteen times more deadly than that of the cobra. In fact, U.S. soldiers in Vietnam, where the krait is also common, labeled that country's two species the five-step and the one-hundred-step, referring to how far a bitten person could walk before he died.

No, I was not afraid of snakes before my three years in Pakistan. However, I returned to the States with a deadly fear of them. Even now, forty-five years later, I pale when I come across a harmless little garter snake. As for that big bull snake on the Clackamas River, if I encountered it today, I'd probably need CPR to jump-start my heart.

Don't think I spent every day in Pakistan being chased by snakes. Actually, I had only one face-to-face encounter. Usually I saw live cobras only in cages or baskets, commonplace attractions in the bazaars. Most of the snakes I saw, in fact, were dead. Pakistanis kill them whenever possible. Unlike their neighbors, the Hindus of India, Pakistanis are primarily Moslem. Because Hindus believe the snake may be a past relative in a present life, it is protected, not killed. Therefore, thousands in India die each year of snakebite. Moslems don't look at a cobra or krait as possibly Grandma come back for a visit. If a Moslem is threatened, he strikes back. There is no turning the other cheek in Islam. Still, the snakes win many of these encounters.

Cobras and kraits are nocturnal animals. Lethargic during the day, they sun themselves on rocks and ledges or hole up in the shade on extremely hot days. At night they hunt. They are especially fond of rats. Rats are especially fond of the refuse in a typical Pakistani village. Therefore, both rats and snakes are frequently visitors to the villages.

Pakistani villagers usually go barefoot or in sandals. Their villages seldom have indoor plumbing, and much of the time, the villagers sleep outdoors in the oppressive heat of the summer months. Darkness, cobras and kraits moving through the night, sleepy people walking softly in sandals or bare feet—a deadly combination of circumstances.

Contrary to the beliefs of many Pakistanis, cobras don't hunt people. We are easy to kill but too big to eat. Given adequate warning, most snakes avoid confrontation, but they don't take lightly to surprise and become especially cranky when people, stumbling into the dark to relieve themselves, step on them.

On the other hand, snakes in Pakistan are not class conscious. While they may like the crumbling walls, cluttered courtyards, and garbage heaps of the villages, well-kept houses with manicured grounds are not off limits to cobras and kraits. In the colony where I lived, people encountered them both in their homes and their work places.

I always liked going to work early. I enjoyed the quiet time before my students and fellow teachers arrived. A last cup of coffee, a little polish on the lesson plans—this was one of my favorite times of the day. In Pakistan it was also a time when I frequently chatted with a chowkidar, a security guard, who had the night shift at our school. His workday ended as mine began, and we usually had a few minutes of conversation before going our separate ways.

One morning as I entered the school grounds, he walked rapidly toward me, and I sensed he had been waiting for my arrival. He began motioning me to follow him. "Sahib! Sahib, come! Come! I show you!"

"What? What's up?"

"Come, Sahib. Come. I show you."

I followed him around the corner to my classroom. Because of the heat in Pakistan, our school had no interior rooms. All classrooms opened to the outside. He led me to the door of my room, where he excitedly pointed to the doorstep. There, stretched across the entry, lay two dead cobras. He had discovered the snakes on the steps as the sun set the evening before. The concrete held the heat of the afternoon, a natural attraction for the cold-blooded cobras. They had settled down for a nap from which they would not awaken. He had killed them with his nightstick.

The chowkidar was especially proud of himself because he had managed to kill two cobras in one setting. Pakistanis have a number of strange beliefs about cobras. In the marshy regions of what is now Bangladesh but was then East Pakistan, some believe cobras milk their water buffalo at night. They can't really describe the method the snakes use to accomplish this task, but thinking about it creates some bizarre images, to say the least.

A belief in West Pakistan, where I lived, is that when a person kills a cobra, he must hunt the area until he kills the cobra's mate. If not, the mate will seek him out, no matter where he goes, and wreak vengeance. The chowkidar had spared himself this worry by killing both cobras at once.

When I first heard this superstition from a Pakistani especially proud of his snake-killing talents, I asked the obvious question: "So you kill a cobra in the same area. How do you know it's the mate?"

"Easy, Sahib," came the reply. "The mate never come to get me. So I know I kill the right one." I couldn't argue with that.

The chowkidar and I measured the two cobras on my doorstep. That is, *he* measured them while I watched. People die from carelessly handling dead cobras. The venom doesn't depend on life to maintain its potency. In fact, even decapitation isn't prevention. The venom sacs are located just below the eyes, and pressure on these sacs forces venom from the fangs. To die from the strike of a live cobra is frightening enough. To die from the bite of a dead cobra? That's a little too Edgar Allan Poe for me.

So I provided a yardstick from my classroom, and he measured the snakes. The smaller was thirty-six inches long. The larger, forty-two inches. A young pair. The average length for cobras in the subcontinent reaches four to five feet. But these two were long enough. As far as I was concerned, we didn't need to set any records.

After the chowkidar had gingerly dropped the cobras into a canvas sack to take them home to show his family, I went to find a janitor to hose the grease and blood off my classroom doorstep before students began arriving. Later in the day, they heard about the snakes and were upset with me because I had not kept the corpses for them to see. Teenagers are teenagers the world over.

Since I encountered only one live cobra in a threatening situation while in Pakistan, why did I return to the States with such fear of snakes? Basically, I lived with that fear the entire time I was there. And that very fear is the reason I did not encounter more of them. It made me cautious, perhaps overly cautious, some might say, but I don't think so. Give me a choice between prudence and stupidity, and I'll choose prudence every time.

I didn't let the fear keep me from enjoying the country. I hiked. I fished. I explored the old crumbling forts left behind by Maharajas of ages past. But I always wore boots when I went into the countryside, and I walked with heavy footsteps in rocky or brushy areas because snakes respond more to vibration than to sound. I was on full alert most of the time.

At home I didn't pick up wood from our woodpile without using a large club to hammer the pile first. I wanted to warn snakes away, of course, but I also wanted to drive out mongooses. They especially liked our woodpiles, and some of my neighbors encouraged their residency because mongooses are deadly enemies of cobras. However, as many as half the mongooses in Pakistan are infected with rabies. I didn't like the odds of that particular tradeoff. It was my house. Both snakes *and* mongooses could find somewhere else to live.

Despite my almost paranoid avoidance of snakes, however, the possibility I would stumble upon one was always there. And finally it happened. The encounter was on a doorstep again. Only this time the snake was alive.

One of my favorite people in the colony was Phil, a fellow English teacher. Phil and his two roommates shared a house that had the singular distinction of being favored by snakes. Several had been spotted around their home.

One evening a young chowkidar observed a cobra slither into the house's shrubbery. Cobras are somewhat territorial, and there existed the possibility it would take up residence around the house. The chowkidar knocked on Phil's door to warn him. However, the young security guard had limited ability to pronounce English words.

Phil opened the door to a very excited young man, proud of both his position as a chowkidar and the life-saving information he was about to deliver. "Yes?" Phil asked.

"Snack, Sahib. Snack," the young chowkidar replied, pointing to the shrubbery.

"What?"

"Snack, Sahib. Snack. Snack."

So Phil went back into the house and returned with a peanut-butter sandwich.

This incident coupled with the other snake sightings around the home always bothered me whenever I approached it.

Sometime during our second year in Pakistan, my wife and I arrived on a warm spring evening for a dinner party at Phil's house. I had just reached for the screen door when she began shouting, "Snake! Snake! Snake!"

I shouted back in perfect cadence, "Where? Where? Where?" But I knew where because while she yelled, she pointed at my feet. In response, I performed a dance that would have made Saint Vitus proud.

Then I saw it. Beady eyes. Flicking black tongue. Head pulled back. S-shaped body weaving from side to side. My worst fear realized. Wait a minute. Maybe not so fully realized. The snake working its hypnotic sway before us was about the size of a large nightcrawler. A baby cobra.

Now before your maternal instincts kick in and you begin to ooh and ah, let me point out that baby cobras are capable of lethal injection three hours after being hatched. In fact, some think baby cobras are more dangerous than adult cobras because the adults seem to control the amount of venom they release in a strike, depending upon the threat they feel. Baby cobras, in their youthful exuberance, always deliver a full dose. I emphasize this because I don't want your condemnation for what follows.

This little guy was ready to duke it out. I turned to my wife, politely excused myself, and left the porch. Having walked around the house to the back door, I borrowed a broom, returned and beat the little sucker to death.

And *that* was my big snake kill in Pakistan.

---

# MONITOR LIZARDS

I saw my first monitor lizard even before I saw my new home. These impressive creatures are common throughout Pakistan. Looking like miniature dragons, monitor lizards average three to five feet in length, walk or run with their heads upraised and often stand on their hind feet, employing their heavy tails as counterbalance in order to use their uncommonly sharp eyesight both to spot prey and avoid danger.

When threatened, monitors assume an intimidating defensive stance. Like many animals in nature, when agitated, monitors can make themselves appear even larger than they are. They achieve this apparent increase in size because they have the ability to inhale large amounts of air, which puffs up their throats. While seeming to grow, they face off on their would-be attackers with a daunting display of aggressiveness.

Holding open large jaws lined with sharp teeth, the monitor hisses, flicks its long forked tongue, and snaps its powerful tail back and forth. A bite from those jaws injects a dangerous mix of toxic bacteria and low-dose venom. A blow from that heavy, muscular tail can inflict real damage upon the lizard's adversary.

Nevertheless, as I was about to learn, this frightening display by an animal so willing to defend itself did not warn off Pakistanis who came upon them. Man, it turns out, is the monitor's worst enemy.

\* \* \*

The superintendent of Mangla International School met my family at the Rawalpindi airport. He had arrived with two cars, his own and an additional company car with a driver. After loading our luggage into the superintendent's car, we climbed into the second for the seventy-mile drive to Baral Colony, my wife and our children in the back seat and I in the front. I was about to discover why some people in the colony called the place I now occupied the "suicide seat."

We were mostly silent for the first half hour or so. The driver had said so little that I assumed he had no English. I watched out the windows as we sped past scenes of sensory overload. Camels, sometimes singular, sometimes in small caravans, plodded along the road. Donkeys pulling carts or weighed down with unbelievably large loads trotted along the shoulder, usually under heavy-handed prodding from men or boys armed with willow switches.

Even though our windows were tightly closed in the air-conditioned car, the stench of diesel crept in as belching busses crammed with people both inside and sitting on top roared past us. Motorized rickshaws competed for space with gaudy trucks painted like circus wagons, the drivers peering through windshields nearly covered inside with golden tinfoil, pictures, and swaying tassels.

And the horns. Constantly blaring horns. No traffic cops, no stop signs, no speed limits. No rules of any kind. Every man for himself. Pakistanis, I found, drove primarily with a foot on the gas and a hand on the horn, playing a constant game of chicken on a road barely wide enough for two-way traffic.

We were traveling on the Grand Trunk Road, a major thoroughfare across the subcontinent that has existed since the third century B.C. The Grand Trunk has been the scene of magnificent history. Maharajas on elephants had surveyed their holdings from this road. The armies of Alexander the Great descended from Afghanistan through the Khyber Pass and traveled into the heart of India along the Grand Trunk Road.

We swept past villages of mud houses, sides dotted with circular, hand-packed manure, drying for later use as fuel in cooking fires. Women balancing clay jugs, baskets, and cloth bundles on their heads walked gracefully along worn paths. Children chased each other through dusty courtyards. Groups of men, engaged in animated conversation, squatted in the shade of ancient, scarred trees, I wondered as I watched all this if Alexander had seen the exact same scenes so many centuries ago.

Suddenly I was jarred from daydreaming by a torpedo-shaped gray apparition streaking across the road and disappearing into scrub brush on the banks of an irrigation ditch. "Wow!" I exclaimed, coming upright in my seat. "Did you see that!"

"Yes, Sahib," the driver replied. "You have those in America?"

"I don't know. What was it?"

"That was a lizard, Sahib."

"Well, it was a damn *big* lizard."

"Yes, Sahib. Damn big lizard."

"I just realized something," I smiled. "You speak good English."

"Yes, Sahib. I have English in school."

"Do you know what kind of lizard that was?"

"The English call it by some strange name. 'Mommy lizard' or something like that."

"Monitor lizard?" I asked, catching my breath as he turned the wheel sharply to avoid a boy pushing a bicycle loaded with large bundles of straw.

"Yes, Sahib, that is exactly what the English call that lizard."

"What do *you* call it?"

"We have several languages in Pakistan, Sahib. Each one has a different name for that animal, but they all mean very much the same thing."

"And what is that?"

"All those names mean …" He smiled before he gave me his punch line. "All those names mean 'damn big lizard.'"

Our shared laughter was interrupted as we approached a camel loaded with heavy timbers strapped to its sides. Beside the camel, swaying in its strange seasick-inducing gait, the camel driver complacently strolled down the middle of our lane. As we swung around them, a bus coming the other direction bore down on us, horn blaring. Punching both the gas and the horn, our driver took up the challenge. Just as I was certain I was going to meet Allah on my first day Pakistan, our driver cranked left, nearly taking the nose off the camel while the bus missed our back bumper by inches.

"Sorry, Sahib," the driver said, as he brought the car into our lane once more. "What were you saying when that crazy bus driver arrived?"

"Actually, I think I was praying. Doesn't it scare you to drive like this?"

"Like what, Sahib?"

"Like weaving in and out. Like barely wiping out camels, kids on bikes, busses?"

"Oh, Sahib," he smiled. "That bus driver was a bad driver. I'm a very good driver. No need to pray when you ride with me."

"Maybe, but I wonder how many people are killed on this road."

"*Inshallah*, Sahib."

"What?"

"*Inshallah,* Sahib. It means 'God wills it.'"

As I was to learn in my three years in Pakistan, *Inshallah* governed every risk. If Allah wanted you to die, you would die, no matter what precautions you took. If Allah wanted you to live, you wouldn't die, no matter what risks you took. And that explained in one word both the Moslems' fearless ferocity in their historical conflicts with the West and the reason Pakistanis drove the way they did in the twentieth century.

A few miles down the road, the driver initiated conversation once more. "I remember now what we were talking about before that crazy bus driver," he began. "We were talking about the lizard."

"Yes," I replied. "We were talking about the monitor lizard. I've seen one in a zoo, but I never thought I'd see one running loose anywhere."

"Oh, you will see many, Sahib. They are very much all around here. And when you see those lizards, you must kill them."

"Why would I do that?"

"Those are very bad lizards, Sahib. Very bad."

He gave me a minute or two to think about his proclamation before he added, "But you must know how to kill them, Sahib. There is only one way."

"And what way is that?" I asked, watching a young boy trotting along the road with a chicken tucked securely under his arm.

The driver waited until he had safely passed the boy before answering. "You can kill these animals only if you flip them over on their backs and stab them through the stomach."

When I didn't response, he waited a minute or so before he asked, "You believe me, Sahib?"

"Believe you about what?"

"Believe me about the only way to kill the lizard."

"Of course, I believe you," I answered. "Why wouldn't I believe you?"

He glanced at me, grinning. "Why not, indeed, Sahib? Why not indeed?"

I answered his grin with one of my own before returning my attention to the scenery racing by us. Looking toward a village on my side of the road, I thought to myself, *This is a land of storytellers. I'm really going to like it here.*

\* \* \*

Sometime later, we drove by another donkey cart, the driver switching the donkey with the regularity of a metronome.

"Does everyone whip the donkeys?" I asked.

"Yes, Sahib. A donkey's life is a hard life. I have a Hindu friend who tells me if I am bad in this life, I return as a donkey."

"Well, then," I smiled, "the way you drive, you'd better start practicing wearing a harness."

"*Inshallah*, Sahib," he laughed. "*Inshallah*."

* * *

The driver had been right. During the time I lived in Pakistan, monitor lizards were a common sight. On drives into Rawalpindi to the west or Lahore to the east, I'd frequently see monitors along the road. But I didn't have to leave the colony to see them. They regularly appeared on the edges of our monsoon ditches and near our outside laundry buildings.

In a desert land, rains are infrequent, but when they come, they come with an intensity that belies the term "desert land." The heavy storms filled our three-foot-deep concrete monsoon ditches to the brim with rushing water. In addition, the shared washrooms, where house servants did the laundry, were always damp from spigots left dripping.

In dry lands animals are drawn to water. Monitors were no exception. They came for the water itself or for the small rodents, birds, and insects lured to the water. Both the ditches and the washrooms provided water and food for the lizards.

Even if I had believed the driver, I would never have tried to flip a monitor lizard over. Their first response to human approach is flight, a reaction with which I was in full agreement. But like the cobras, I eventually faced off on a monitor in a confrontation from which neither of us could run.

* * *

My house in Pakistan was quiet. No TV. Only one radio, belonging to Rahjab, our bearer.[2] Rahjab loved listening to what I guess you would call Pakistani top hits.

However, I couldn't stand them. The falsetto singers sounded like a symphony played with fingernails upon a schoolroom blackboard. So Rahjab could listen to his tunes only when I was absent from the house. When I was home, all was quiet. Except, of course, when I listened to my own music on my phonograph.

Eight-track players were popular when I moved to Pakistan. Nevertheless, with my always-behind-the-times mindset, I had included in our shipment of household articles a floor-model phonograph and my large collection of vinyl records. This eclectic collection—everything from country to classical—proved to be a major draw for colony residents who had been in Pakistan for two to three years, listening to the same music over and over again.

People I had hardly met stopped by to ask if they could borrow records to copy on their tape players. I, on the other hand, could not transfer any of their music to my collection. For the first year, I was content with my records. By the middle of the second year, however, I, too, found myself wishing for something new.

Toward the end of that year, new arrivals in the colony raved about a singer who had hit the top of the charts in the States. This young singer,

---

[2]   A bearer is the head servant in a subcontinent household. When people hear I was in Pakistan for a teaching assignment, they assume I was there as a Peace Corps volunteer or some other organization that would require living in a Pakistani village, sharing the villagers' hard lives. The truth is I lived in a comfortable colony of expatriates. When we arrived at our home after that long ride from Rawalpindi, we found Rahjab waiting on our doorstep. He wanted a job. The school superintendent interviewed Rahjab and recommended we hire him. He had been the bearer in the home of one of the most important people in the colony and was extremely overqualified to serve in our household. Used to large dinner parties with important and sometimes overly pretentious guests, Rahjab must have been disappointed with our quiet needs. Nevertheless, over time Rahjab became a member of our family. Our children loved him, and he both loved and spoiled them. The hardest thing about leaving Pakistan at the end of my contract was leaving Rahjab behind.

they claimed, was destined to become a permanent fixture in the ranks of America's favorite entertainers. Her name? Barbra Streisand.

\* \* \*

My second summer in Pakistan, Phil and I traveled in the Middle East.[3] Our last stop before returning home was Beirut, a beautiful, cosmopolitan city of modern buildings displaying wares from around the world. Fortunately, we experienced Beirut a decade before civil war tore it apart.

In a music store, I found Barbra Streisand's debut album. Our new arrivals had been right. Once back in Pakistan, I almost wore out that record.

\* \* \*

On an ordinary afternoon the autumn following our venture into the Middle East, I returned home from school, dropped books and papers on my desk, kicked off my shoes, put Barbra on the phonograph, and leaned back in my overstuffed chair. A Scotch, having been silently delivered by Rahjab, rested on the end table beside me.

The perfect ending to a day of teaching school in Pakistan.

Barbra had just begun "Cry Me a River" when an irritating scratching, scrapping sound from the window over my chair interrupted my perfect moment. I turned toward the window, its lower half filled with our in-window air conditioner. I tried to shut out the noise, but it became more and more insistent.

*Damn it*, I thought as I pulled myself up from the chair and stepped to the air conditioner. *What's wrong with this thing?*

I twisted the dials left and right; however, the scratching, scrapping sounds not only continued but increased in volume. Finally, I realized the noise was not from the air conditioner. It came from outside the house. Standing on tiptoe and peering over the top of the air conditioner, I found myself face to face with a highly agitated monitor lizard.

---

[3] See "Stranded in the Nile Valley"

Swinging its head from side to side, mouth gaping, forked tongue flicking, the lizard saw me at the moment I saw it and shifted its frantic motions into high gear, spraying my window with saliva.

I fell back into the room, ignominiously landing on my backside. After catching my breath, I crawled forward to the wall below the window and slowly rising on tiptoe, once more peered outside. Nothing had changed. I stared at the lizard as its head rose and fell in what appeared to be a frenzied struggle to crawl onto the top of the air conditioner. Was this creature actually trying to climb into my house? The time for action had arrived.

Armed with my weapon of choice—a broom, of course—I slipped out the front door and crept to the corner of the house. Slowly I peeked around the corner. The lizard swayed side to side as it struggled, clinging to the air conditioner with its front feet, its back legs scrambling against the brick siding, ripping the wall in deep strokes as it attempted to tear itself from the side of the building. The monitor was not trying to climb over the air conditioner. It was trying to escape *from* the air conditioner. The lizard was stuck.

Remember those in-window air conditioners? They always dripped water. In the States, the puddle of water under them probably didn't attract the visitors our puddles in Pakistan did. Like the monsoon ditches and laundry houses, these puddles brought thirsty creatures to our homes, and those thirsty creatures included monitor lizards. This one, seemingly not satisfied with the puddle, had decided to climb to the water's source.

Monitors have long, curved claws. My visitor had hooked its claws into the vents of the air conditioner and could not get them out. The bothersome noise drowning out Barbra came from its equally long hind claws dragging down the side of my house as it fought for traction.

I studied its dilemma for a short time. "Sorry, buddy," I offered before stepping closer. "This is better for the both of us." I lined up on the lizard in my left-handed batting stance, pulled back the broom and, aiming for what would be its front armpit if it were a human, stepped into my swing with a powerful follow-through like Ted Williams going for the right-field wall.

CRACK! The monitor flew through the air, fighting to right itself, and with the agility of a cat landed on its feet. Running even as it hit the ground, the lizard dove through our hedge and raced out of sight around the nearest laundry building.

I returned to the house, put the broom away, freshened my drink, and settled into my chair once more. Then I reached over, lifted the tone arm of the record player, and placed the needle into the outer groove of the record. "Now, Barbra," I said, leaning back into the chair, "Where were we?"

The perfect ending to a day of teaching school and liberating monitor lizards in Pakistan.

## MORTAR-EATING ANTS

Including ants with cobras and monitor lizards in a discussion of close encounters with the animal life in Pakistan may seem anticlimactic. But these weren't merely ants. They were creatures-from-outer-space science-fiction ants.

I realize ants are omnivorous with a taste for almost everything, but these black large-jawed creatures had unusually voracious appetites and an uncanny ability to find their way into our home. Especially annoying was their weird craving for an unidentified ingredient in the mortar used to construct the brickwork of our house. A favorite target was our fireplace. On a number of occasions, bricks suddenly dropped, crashing to the floor. In the newly opened space, a swarm of these giant ants, reacting with alarm as great as ours at their sudden introduction into the open space of our home, scrambled, racing back into the dark recesses of their tunneled life.

One morning, I discovered a stream of ants entering the living room from behind a loose plate on an electrical outlet, trailing along the baseboard and turning into the kitchen. I followed the stream as it continued into the pantry. There I found the target of their invasion: a torn package of sugar. A returning stream, loaded with grains of their reward, retraced their passage along the baseboard to disappear behind the outlet.

I removed the sugar package and waited for their onslaught to break down once the message reached headquarters that their gold mine was no longer in play.

On another morning, however, they tested my patience. Barely awake, I left the bedroom in a quest for some much-needed coffee. As I turned the corner into our home's entry hallway, I came upon a startling scene. I needed a couple of moments before really comprehending what lay before me. Looking for all the world like a heaving, living black rug, a mass of wall-to-wall ants covered the floor the entire length of the hall.

I gingerly tiptoed through the heaving mass, shuddering at the crunching beneath my feet, and made my way into the kitchen. There I brushed off the ants clinging to my lower legs and entered the pantry once more. However, this time I wasn't looking for a broom. I was looking for a way to eliminate them. I needed to upgrade my weaponry. I emerged from the pantry with our vacuum cleaner in hand. Well, didn't I say the ants filled the hallway like a heaving black *rug*?

Almost humming, I made my way down the hall, vacuuming up ants. Twice I went outside to the common grounds to empty the vacuum bag. Finally, however, the hallway was free of ants.

Smugly satisfied, I put the vacuum away and puttered in the kitchen, making coffee and toast. I have to admit, however, that every half hour or so I checked the hallway for any signs of the ants' return.

They didn't, and I'd like to report that I had taken care of the problem to everyone's satisfaction. But I had not. Two weeks passed before Rahjab quit complaining about ants spewing from the vacuum cleaner every time he used it.

---

## THE UNIDENTIFIED

Cobras, kraits, mongooses, monitor lizards, mortar-eating ants. Was that it? Was that the sum total of what I encountered in Pakistan? No. There was the lizard Rahjab cornered in our fireplace one afternoon and speared with the poker. Carrying the two-foot-long squirming, hissing creature out the front door, Rahjab held it at arm's length in front of him, obviously fearful of the creature spraying blood and saliva as it frantically fought for its life.

When he returned, shaken and sweat-soaked, I asked, recalling the words of the driver on my first day in Pakistan, "That was a bad lizard, Rahjab?"

"That was a very bad lizard, Sahib. A very bad lizard. You don't want that lizard around Kip and Cassy. Never, Sahib. Never."

To this day, I don't know what kind of lizard it was. I have described it to a few people familiar with reptiles, but they merely shake their heads. All I know is that it was dangerous.

Rahjab had lived with all these creatures from his birth. He took most of them in stride. But the sight of a shaken Rahjab holding a bloody fireplace poker and admonishing me in tones he would never use under less than dire circumstances confirmed that this lizard was indeed "a very bad lizard."

* * *

Among the unidentified was a black cloud of beetles the size of golf balls that one day targeted my house, crashing with a suicidal frenzy into the western brick wall, the wall containing the same air conditioner assaulted by the monitor lizard. I watched fascinated as the beetles' runny remains streaked down the window.

After the beetle storm had subsided, I walked by the shattered corpses heaped along the foundation of my home. *Just another creepy-crawler episode*, I thought to myself. *You didn't come here to find a second Oregon, did you? And these, along with all the other exotic creatures in this land, are part of the world you* did *come here to experience. Besides,* I continued counseling myself as I returned to my living room, *think what great dinner-party stories these encounters are going to make.*

I looked down at the ever-present stack of student papers on my desk. Ironically the assignment before me concerned a giant insect. I had read the opening paragraph of Franz Kafka's "The Metamorphosis" to my students and asked them to use this paragraph as a springboard into stories of their own. It was one of my favorite assignments. But today it seemed especially appropriate. *How fitting,* I thought, *to have been interrupted in the midst of a huge cockroach's nightmare by a bombardment of giant beetles.*

However, even though some of my best students had produced shining results, I couldn't concentrate on their stories. Giving up, I fixed a Scotch, sank into my easy chair and turned on the phonograph. Soon Barbra brought back a world devoid of cobras, kraits, mongooses, monitors, mortar-eating ants, two-foot long lizards not to be allowed around children, and large suicidal beetles.

But that was the world I had left behind when I took the job in Pakistan. A world I had exchanged for an exciting experience halfway around the globe. I had sought a challenging adventure in an exotic, age-old land. And now I was experiencing the adventure.

*Still*, I thought, turning away from the beetle-splattered window above my chair, *for the moment, at least, I need a little respite.* And when Barbra began singing "Happy Days Are Here Again," I found it.

# ZIPPER

**Zipper wasn't my dog**. He wasn't my brother's dog. And he definitely wasn't my mother's dog. Zipper was my father's dog. I suspect Dad and Zipper hooked up before Mom entered the picture. Otherwise, she probably wouldn't have allowed Zipper to stay. You see, the two of them competed for Dad's affections, and because Zipper's love was unconditional, he had the inside track

Zipper and Dad were almost inseparable. Everywhere Dad went, Zipper tagged along. In those days—the early '40s—cars had wide rear decks, the platform spaces behind the rear seats, much larger than those of today, where some people barely have room to display their baseball caps, stuffed animals, bobble-head dogs, or swaying hula dolls. These early cars had decks large enough to accommodate a big long-haired red dog like Zipper. Dad would open the back door, and Zipper would bound onto the back seat and up onto the deck, where he'd assume a regal position, casting disdainful looks at mere roadside dogs as the car went by.

Usually when Dad drove anywhere without Mom, Zip went along. The only exception occurred when Dad left the house to work in the woods. Falling old-growth timber was dangerous enough without a dog underfoot. However, this was a fact Zipper never understood or accepted.

In those early morning hours when Dad left for work, Zipper scratched at the back door and whined, but no matter how much he begged, he wasn't allowed out until the car was safely gone. Otherwise, he would have chased it until he could run no more.

But too many other times as my father drove away, Zipper watched me through the back window, clearly enjoying his superior position in Dad's world. Oh, I was allowed to ride along sometimes, but, more often than not, I heard, "Not this time, Bobby. Maybe next time."

I don't know why Dad allowed Zipper to accompany him when I couldn't. Maybe he wasn't comfortable leaving me in the car when he made his tavern stop on the way home. If so, it must have been because I was only five years old. I could have gone into the taverns, you know. There was no law against children in taverns at the time.

Only a few years later, after we had moved to Oregon, Jerry and I spent Saturday afternoons in taverns with Dad and Mom, watching them compete in shuffleboard tournaments while we ate greasy hamburgers washed down with various flavors of sugared soda.

As a matter of fact, we learned to roller skate in a tavern, an establishment owned by friends of my parents. These friends had two daughters who were whizzes on roller skates. The family lived in quarters at the back of the tavern, and in the morning before they opened for business, the sisters skated through the tavern, performing intricate maneuvers while coasting around chairs and tables, spinning in cleared spaces, and occasionally daring to skate on the bar itself. The sisters gave Jerry and me lessons in roller skating among other things. But that's another story.

At the time Zipper was part of our family, we lived in the weather-beaten old house in the sand dunes of Copalis Beach. Zipper had one special place in our home, a ragged blanket behind the big woodstove in the kitchen. He retired to his blanket when the rest of us went to bed. But not until then.

My parents spent each evening sitting around the potbellied stove in the living room, usually quiet time since both liked to read after dinner. Zipper curled up as closely as possible to Dad. Since Mom wouldn't allow Zipper on the furniture, as closely as possible meant at my father's feet. He'd rest his head against Dad's leg and pretend to sleep. If Dad said something to Mom or moved in any way other than to turn a page, Zipper would raise his head, and Dad would drop a hand to rub his ears. When Dad returned to his book, Zipper lowered his head and once again feigned sleep.

In the winter with the Pacific winds and rains assaulting the house, going to bed was a nightly challenge. The two bedrooms were shut off from the rest of the house to preserve heat in the kitchen and living room. Unlike most people who prepare for bed by undressing, Jerry and I *dressed* for bed. We'd strip to our winter long johns, weird one-piece, armless underwear with legs that cut off just above the knee. We'd then pull heavy sweaters or shirts over our heads and stuff our feet into wool socks. Looking like padded gremlins, we readied ourselves for the dash into that frigid room.

Mom preceded us, switching on the bare light bulb that dangled from the ceiling and turning down the pile of blankets on the bed. With a yelp we'd dart through the door, leap onto the bed and pull the covers over our heads. Assuming fetal positions, we'd shiver, teeth chattering, until our cocooned space warmed with our combined body heat.

Later, I'd hear Dad and Mom go into their room. For a while, Zipper would whine at the door, his nightly vigil never rewarded. If Mom wouldn't let him on the living-room furniture, he had no chance at all of sleeping on their bed. If I had been a little older and a little braver, I might have asked if Zipper could sleep with Jerry and me. We could have used his body heat. However, I doubt Zipper would have settled for that compromise. He didn't want a bed. He wanted Dad.

Finally, I'd hear Zipper give up and pad away toward his blanket. And sometimes when I dared to move a little and venture into an unheated area of the bed, I'd envy Zipper his warm place behind the stove.

So where did Zipper spend the days he couldn't go to the woods with Dad? He spent them in the same place Jerry and I spent ours. We went to the beach.

Don't get me wrong. Zipper didn't spend his time *with* us. Jerry and I usually met our friends at the beach, and while their dogs stayed with us, Zipper went his own way. He had his own agenda: driftwood logs to christen, sandpipers to chase, and dead crabs or piles of rancid seaweed to sniff and paw.

At the end of the day, Zipper, Jerry and I returned home, the three of us wet, sand-crusted, hungry and tired. Zipper usually investigated his bowl to see what table-scrap leftovers Mom might have deposited there before retiring to his blanket.

But no matter how asleep he seemed to be, sometime in the early evening, he'd lift his head, listen and then rise, stretch and move to the kitchen door. He'd always hear my father's arrival before we did. The car door would slam, Dad's footsteps would approach the door, and then he'd enter, reaching down to rub Zip's head as he stepped around him to hand his lunch bucket to Jerry or me, whoever had read Zip's lead and managed to be second in line at the door.

Mom packed the same lunch for my father every day: two bologna sandwiches, a crème-over, and a thermos of coffee. Each evening he returned with half a sandwich. And each evening Jerry and I argued over whose turn it was to have that soggy prize. Zip, in the meantime, contented himself with that pat on the head.

Those were the best of times the beach, the bologna sandwiches, the red dog who loved my dad as much as I. Those were the best of times.

* * *

We lost Zipper somewhere in the Columbia Gorge.

On our way fruit tramping into eastern Oregon, we had spent the night in a motor lodge on the outskirts of a town on the Oregon side of the Columbia River. I don't remember where exactly—probably Hood River or The Dalles.

A motor lodge was a luxury for our family. For the coming summer we would live in our tent as we followed the crops before returning to Copalis Beach in the fall. Motor lodges were the precursors of today's motels. Stand-alone cabins with small bedrooms and kitchens, they offered road-weary travelers a touch of home. Our family could not afford more than one or two stays in these over the picking season. We went to bed happy, looking forward to a summer of sun, dirt, and cricket-chirping evenings.

In the morning, Zipper was gone.

* * *

"When I got up, he was at the door," Dad said as we stood in the parking area in front of our cabin. "I let him out to do his business and left the door open for him. Probably twenty minutes or so had gone by before it dawned on me he hadn't come back in. I came outside and called him, but he didn't come. Then I walked through the place, looking for him, but he wasn't here. He was just gone."

"Oh, Harold," Mom replied, taking his arm, "when you're at work, he has the run of the beach. He's used to taking off. He probably saw another dog or a squirrel or something and chased after it. He'll be back."

"I don't know," Dad said, shaking his head. "This isn't like him."

"Usually whenever I have to go to the beach to bring the boys home, he's either never around or pays no attention to me," Mom insisted. "He always comes home when he's ready."

"Maybe," Dad replied, "but that's when *I'm* not on the beach. You want to find me on the beach, you look for Zipper. You find him, and you've found me."

"Harold, I know how close you are to him, but he's a dog, not a person. He's a dog. He *can* be distracted."

"Yeah," Dad said, "Zipper *is* a dog. But he's not just any dog and as much as we're family, he's not the kids' dog, and he's not your dog. Zipper is my dog."

He stepped back and toed an *X* in the gravel. Pointing to it, he said, "That's where Zipper would be right now under normal circumstances. Right *there*. Don't tell me something's not wrong."

Mom studied him for a moment and then replied, "Okay, maybe something *is* wrong. So what do we do now?"

"Get the boys some breakfast, and then start packing up our gear. I'm going to look for him, starting with the manager of this place. Maybe someone complained about Zip or figured he was a stray. Chased him away with a stick or something like that. I don't know, but I'm gonna find out. If the manager doesn't know anything, I'll go door to door asking if anyone else has seen him. In the meantime, leave our door open because if you're right and he just took off, he'll probably be back before I am."

Dad's search radiated outward in an ever-widening circle. First he made the round of the other cabins. Then he walked through the neighborhood, having enlisted the help of a couple of teenage boys who had suggestions about vacant lots and wooded areas. Finally he returned for the car and drove through the town. But Zipper was gone.

"I left our home address with the manager," Dad said as we finished loading the car. "I also gave him the telephone number of our first job. We can't wait here any longer. If we don't show up today, we'll lose a day's wages and maybe the job itself.

"The manager's a nice guy. He said he'd contact vets and people like that around town. And his son is one of the boys who helped me look for Zip. He and his friends will keep looking. The manager says if Zipper shows up, they'll keep him here and contact us."

\* \* \*

Our drive that day was a quiet one. And that was not like us. We were usually a noisy family on the road. A noisy family that especially liked to sing. The first song I remember learning was "You Are My Sunshine," and I learned it on one of our road trips. But on this day, there were no songs. Instead a deadening silence filled the car as we drove eastward, a silence finally broken by Mom.

"You know, Harold," she began in a soft voice, "I maybe have an idea about what happened with Zipper." When he remained silent, she continued, "You know how he jumps into the car whenever you open the back door? Well, what if someone packing up this morning left the back door of their car opened and he jumped in."

"Why would he do that?" Dad asked, not turning his head toward her.

"Because it's something he loves to do. Because he's always been rewarded for doing that."

"But wouldn't the people just make him get out? It's not like they wouldn't see him."

"I don't know," Mom shrugged. "Maybe they thought he was a stray looking for a family. Maybe they just liked him … I don't know. But if that's what happened, they drove off with him, and we can only hope they love him as much as you do."

None of us bought that last comment. No one could love Zipper as much as my father did. But over time her suggestion became the official explanation for Zipper's disappearance. He didn't run away. He didn't become lost in a strange town. He jumped into someone's car, and a family that would love him *almost* as much as Dad loved him simply drove away.

\* \* \*

My father talked about Zipper only one time over the summer. My grandparents had already set up their tent and reserved a space for us in our first campground. When we arrived, Dad had to explain Zipper's absence. Ave's Birdie was as close to him as Zipper had been to Dad. So he understood, and my grandmother understood. They respected Dad's silence on the topic of Zipper the rest of the summer.

* * *

Upon our return to Copalis Beach, Dad sifted through the pile of mail held for us at the general store. We knew what he hoped to find. But there was no letter from the manager of the motor lodge. And with continued silence, we acknowledged the fact that Zipper was gone from Dad's life.

* * *

Nine months later we moved into Aberdeen. A few weeks after the move, Ave and my grandmother dropped by unexpectedly. In her arms snuggled a tiny black and white puppy. "We thought we could keep him, but we can't," she explained. "Maybe you can." She held the puppy out to Dad. He took it from her and, barely glancing at the squirming body, turned and handed the pup to me.

Mom understand what my grandparents were doing. "Sure," she smiled. "We'd love to have him."

But if my grandparents thought this puppy would take Zipper's place in my father's heart, they were mistaken. As soon as they drove away, he looked down at the tiny puppy sitting at his feet, staring up with eager eyes as if he knew the opportunity of success in this family depended upon the approval of the big man standing over him. Dad studied the pup for a moment and then turned away. "That's a rat terrier," he said. "Nothing but a lap dog." And from that moment on, he paid no more attention to the puppy.

As it turned out, the puppy *was* a lap dog, and denied my father's lap, it sought another, the lap of someone willing to sit on the floor, legs extended because the puppy liked to drape himself over those legs and sleep, sleep occasionally punctuated with whining and squirming as he chased or evaded the demons of his dreams. The owner of the lap wouldn't move until forced by legs gone to sleep or bladder threatening explosion. Only then would he gently ease from under the pup with a promise to return.

You see, Bucky wasn't my brother's dog. He wasn't my mother's dog. And he definitely wasn't my father's dog. Bucky was my dog. But like the roller-skating sisters, that's another story.

# TEENAGERS-GOD LOVE 'EM

**Near the end** of my third year in college, I switched my major from pre-law to humanities. Changing the major was a relatively easy decision. Deciding what I would do with a degree in humanities proved a little more difficult.

My pre-law courses, heavily freighted with political science and economics, were much too plodding and regimented. From the beginning, I had fought this curriculum by stepping away from the prescribed courses as often as possible, looking for classes that piqued my interest. Invariably these classes were in the humanities.

In part, this wandering into other fields resulted from my first experience with a college professor, in this case my pre-law advisor. As soon as I entered his office, he motioned me to a chair by his desk, opened a college handbook to the page on pre-law directives and pointed to a neat layout of my next three years. I would take this and this and that, with an occasional opening for an elective of my choice.

"Register for these classes," he said, tracing his finger down the first-quarter list. My only optional choices would be a class each in P.E. and humanities. I'd need two years of the former and one year of the latter along with a math or science course to fulfill my requirements for a degree. Then he made a slight adjustment, an adjustment that revealed the man before me.

"You're supposed to take this class," he said, pointing to a course title on the first-year list. "But this," he added, moving the finger to the second-year list, "is a much better course. Granted it's a sophomore offering, but it doesn't require prerequisites, and you'll like it better."

When I entered the sophomore class a week later, I had difficulty finding an empty desk. *Wall-to-wall students*, I thought to myself. *Must be a great course to be so popular."*

Then my pre-law advisor, dressed in a plaid sport coat and bow tie, entered the room and welcomed us to his class. Looking around, I wondered how many other freshmen pre-law majors had been conned in order to pad his numbers.

In the next couple of years, I realized that most college teachers fall into three categories: those who genuinely love teaching, are approachable, and excite their students with challenging material; those who have been there too long and are merely going through the paces; and those who glory in their positions with no real interest in the art of teaching. This last category is a collection of pompous egocentrics who demand respect without earning it.

Oddly enough, I enjoyed both the first *and* the third of these. The first because they were genuine teachers in the finest sense of the profession, and the third because they were uniquely odd characters who entertained me. I didn't realize it at the time, but oddballs like these would be fodder for narratives I would later write.

However, my pre-law advisor didn't fit any of the three categories. I'd like to place him in the middle group, the beaten-down, tenure-protected teachers who simply cruised through classes, using yellowed notes and relying upon multiple-choice tests and student aides to do their grunt work. But my advisor wasn't washed-out. He was simply boring. He had a captive audience without a clue on how to engage them in his material. It didn't take me long to figure out why he had to pad his class numbers with shanghaied first-year students.

I never returned to his office. Plodding through my first year, I followed the path he had traced with his finger in the college handbook. My sophomore year, I counseled myself. After a year in his classroom, I figured I could read the pre-law page as well as he could. But once I embarked upon self-counseling, the change in my life's direction began.

Upon his advice, I had elected that first year to fulfill my humanities requirement with a class entitled *Survey of English Literature*. "As a pre-law major, you can't get too much stuff about England on your transcript," my advisor proclaimed. "Our laws are based upon the English model, and those law-school moguls love seeing this kind of thing on your transcript." True or not, registering for that class changed my future.

Professor Ford mesmerized me. He combined a love of literature with the ability to engage his students in an exploration of magnificent writing from that small island across the sea. For the first time in my life, I realized the power of a truly inspired teacher. He both entertained and challenged us, all this with a deceptively casual teaching style.

Through that year I looked forward to only two classes: my PE basketball class and this "Get-some-stuff-about-England-on-your-transcript" elective. I was hooked, both on basketball and literature.

The next year I took another class offered by Dr. Ford: *Survey of American Literature.* Unable to pass it up, I added the class to my already heavy schedule. On the list of second-year pre-law requirements was a class in English history. Looking longingly through the literature offerings, I found a course in Shakespeare. *Well,* I rationalized, *Shakespeare has a lot of English history.* I substituted Shakespeare for the history of England. And so it began.

Over the next two years, I also discovered philosophy and world-religion courses. They, too, made my list of classes, either augmenting or substituting for my prescribed pre-law curriculum.

As I entered my third year, the time to begin applying for law school arrived. However, I put off the decision, unable to force myself into this commitment. By the middle of the year, I still had not applied. Torn between what I was supposed to do and what I wanted to do, I finally faced reality. I had to make a choice. The decision was both easy and freeing.

* * *

"You understand if you make this change, you may have to take as much as an additional year of classes to fulfill your graduation requirements?" Dr. Ford asked. We sat in his cluttered office space, books stacked randomly on shelves behind him, papers haphazardly scattered across his desk.

"I know. And I'm willing to do that. But I don't think it'll take a full year. I've carried fifteen or more hours of classes every term. And I've taken so many courses from the humanities department that I think I can graduate with just another term or two."

Dr. Ford tapped his cigarette on the edge of a glass ashtray, then leaned back in his chair. He studied me for several long moments, enough to make me self-conscious. I glanced at the teacher who shared his office space. She seemed to take no notice of us as she worked through a stack of student papers.

A stark contrast existed between Dr. Ford's cluttered half of the office and her meticulously organized side of the room. Books neatly arranged on the shelves, a desk clear of everything except a stapler, pens in a round ceramic container, and the papers before her. Later I would learn just how much this contrast illustrated the differences between the two.

"Well, Mr. Christenson, you seem to have given this decision serious thought. I have no doubt you are capable of making this work. But I do have one important question." He crushed out his cigarette and leaned forward, both elbows on the desk. "What do you plan to do with this degree?"

"I think I'd like to teach."

"Really. College, I assume."

"No, I was thinking high school."

"High school? What on earth for?" Glancing at the his officemate, he added, "Sorry, Helen. No offense."

"No offense taken, Phillip," she answered without looking up from her papers.

"But seriously," he said, returning to me, "why high school?"

"I'll admit I'd like to teach literature in college someday, Dr. Ford, but I simply don't want to go on to graduate school right away. For the past two years, I've worked four days a week for the Forest Service while carrying a full class load the other three days. The only breaks in this routine have been summers, when I've worked full-time, and a couple of months in the winter when my job closes down."

I picked up a pencil from the clutter on his desk and idly rolled it between my fingers. When he didn't respond, I continued. "Frankly, I'm tired. I want to get out and put my education to work. Hopefully, down the road I'll make the move from teaching high school to teaching college. I'd like to think so. But I'm not ready now."

Dr. Ford brought his hands up and rested his chin on interlaced fingers. He said nothing for a moment, making me nervously wonder if I had said the wrong thing somehow. Then he leaned back again. "I can appreciate what you're saying. However, it has been my experience that relatively few people in our English Department started out in high school. I think statistics show those who go into high-school teaching usually do one of two things. They either drop out of teaching within five years, or they stay on in high school for the rest of their careers.

Even those who get their advanced degrees normally continue working at the high-school level."

He swirled his chair toward the other desk. "Do I have that right, Helen?"

For the first time since I had entered the office, she looked over at us. "As usual, Phillip, you are well informed. However, you seem to be suggesting that teaching high-school English is a dead-end job. Is that really your intent?"

"No, Helen," Dr. Ford smiled. "I would never say something like that. Especially in your presence."

"I didn't think so, Phillip. Now I have work to do. Suppose you leave me out of your conversation while you clarify to this young man what you really meant to say."

Dr. Ford swirled back to me. "What I meant to say was if you want to teach in college, you should not waste … Oh, excuse me, Helen … not *spend* your time teaching high school. You should go right on to graduate school."

"I appreciate your advice, Dr. Ford, but I think I'd like teaching high school."

"Really? Aren't you forgetting something?

"What?"

"Teaching in high school means you'll be teaching …" He paused as if he couldn't bring himself to complete the sentence. "You'll be teaching … *teenagers*."

\* \* \*

I left Dr. Ford's office with the promise I'd take a couple of days to think over our conversation before making my decision. I had walked only a short way down the hall when I heard a voice from behind. "Excuse me. I'd like to talk to you." I turned to find Dr. Ford's officemate hurrying to catch up with me. At least it seemed like hurrying. After I came to know Helen Browne, I realized that all but the very fit were challenged to keep up with her usual pace.

"Of course, I couldn't help listening in on your conversation," she began as she slowed to a stop. "It's one of the many drawbacks to sharing office space with Dr. Ford. Oh, don't get me wrong," she smiled. "I love Phillip. But I find him a little messy, both in his housekeeping and in his way with students. I hope you didn't take his comments about teaching high school seriously. That was more for my benefit than yours. You see, if you make that decision, you'll become one of my charges, and then he'll have to listen in as the two of *us* work together."

I must have looked confused because she smiled and extended her hand. "I'm sorry. I'm Helen Browne." Her grip was firm, and her gaze steady. "I'm a member of the English Department, but I'm on permanent loan to the Ed. Department. I'm in charge of all candidates who plan to teach high-school English. As such, I'm responsible for the methods classes as well as supervising their student-teaching experience."

"So when I told Dr. Ford I was considering teaching high-school English and he acted as if I'd be better off working in a leper colony, he was really having fun with you?"

"Exactly," she smiled. "But don't think he wasn't serious when he counseled you to teach at the college level. Phillip thinks that's where the very best teachers belong. In a way, what he said to you was a compliment. But enough about Phillip Ford. To tell you the truth, I suspect you had already made up your mind when you came to see him. You were actually looking for affirmation. Am I wrong?"

"No, but after talking to Dr. Ford, I may be back to square one. I really need to think through this."

"Yes, you probably do. But if I may, teaching in high school can be a rewarding experience for the right kind of person. And as for Dr. Ford's comments about teenagers, I'd like to point out they'll not only challenge you. They'll entertain you as well."

She studied me for a moment before adding, "I really hope you come back to the office, having made the right decision." With that, she turned and walked back up the hall, several students stepping aside as she brushed by them in her take-no-prisoners pace.

* * *

Over the next couple of days, I was drawn again and again to Dr. Browne's final comment. Teenagers would entertain me. That might have seemed an odd statement to some, but I had had experience with teenagers, and, yes, I found her comment remarkably accurate. Teenagers can be both challenging and entertaining.

For the past two years, I had supervised weekend tree-planting crews in the spring and fall. The crews consisted of teenagers, mostly Estacada boys with experience in the woods. However, each season a few boys from Portland landed jobs on the crews as well.

Estacada boys who ventured into Portland would probably have been treated as uncouth rednecks. City boys who ventured into the woods suffered reverse prejudices. They knew little about life off the pavement and, consequently, became targets of practical jokes.

As foreman, I found myself protecting these Portland boys even though I often had trouble choking down my own laughter at the pranks played upon them. In most cases, the jokes were harmless enough. Also, the local boys usually went out of their way to sooth hard feelings.

As I considered Dr. Browne's comments, I recalled some of these experiences, zeroing in on a few of my favorites.

\* \* \*

One spring on the first day of the job, we broke for lunch at the top of a steep clear-cut we had been planting all morning. Heavy fog hung over us, obscuring the upper mountain ridges and laying a dampness over everything.

As we made our way to the rig, one of the new boys from Portland approached me. Red-faced from the strain of a hard morning's work, his shirt soaked through from both sweat and the damp fog, he looked anxious and a little confused. I thought to myself, *He's going to quit. We've been here half a day, and he's going to quit.*

"I was wondering," he began. "Where's the supermarket?"

"What?"

"The supermarket. I wondered where it was."

Behind him members of the crew, squishing as quietly as they could through the mud, closed in on us.

"You think there's a supermarket up here?" I asked. "Look around you. How could you possibly think there'd be a supermarket up here?"

"Well, this morning I was carrying my lunch from the car when one of the guys asked me what it was. I told him, and he laughed. He said no one packs a lunch. Everyone buys things at the supermarket up here. That's what ..." Seeing me look over his shoulder, he turned to discover the crowd of Estacada boys, some grinning, others bent over in mouth-cupped laughter.

He turned back, embarrassed at first, and then he began to grin as well. "I guess they got me, didn't they?"

"I guess they did," I smiled. "You want to point out the one who told you there was a …" I couldn't help it. I began to laugh … "there was a supermarket up here?"

He shook his head without looking at the boys grouped behind him. "No, I don't think so. But I really fell for a good one, didn't I?"

*The kid's going to be all right*, I thought to myself. I put my arm around his shoulders and turned him to face the group, who were looking a little sheepish at the moment. "So," I asked, "who's going to share his lunch with this guy?"

The kid probably had the best lunch on the crew that day. Everyone offered him something from sandwiches, oranges, and apples to Twinkies and homemade pie. In taking the joke so well, he had been secured his place on the crew. No one who could believe that logging roads into the interior of the Mt. Hood National Forest would lead to a supermarket could ever be comfortable in the woods, but the local boys got him through the planting season.

\* \* \*

There's a geological oddity along the Clackamas River Road. A cut bank exposes several rows of round rocks the size of cannon balls. These rocks appear to be neatly stacked in columns. The columns look man-made, but they're not. I suppose geologists could explain this phenomenon, and, of course, their explanation would take all the romance out of the mysterious stacks of stones. All I know is that my eye is drawn to the bank every time I drive by.

One day it caught the attention of one of the Portland boys as well. "Wow! Look at that!" he exclaimed.

A local turned toward him. "Look at what?" he asked.

"Those rocks. Did you see those rocks in the bank?"

"Oh, those. Yeah. We call them the spirit stones. The Indians stacked them there."

"Really? When?"

Without missing a beat, the answer came. "Yesterday."

\* \* \*

One morning while we were loading gear into our rig, a city boy noticed a double-bitted ax hanging on the wall of the warehouse. He tugged my shirtsleeve as I walked by.

"Excuse me. How come that ax has two blades?"

Before I could answer, one of the Estacada boys stepped in. "Bob, let me explain this." He turned to the Portland boy.

"That, my friend, is one of the most functional tools ever invented by man. Its use guarantees twice as much work done in half as much time."

"It does? How?"

"Well, let's say you're on a trail crew and you're brushing a trail. With a single-bladed ax, you have to brush one side of the trail for a distance, turn around, and brush down the other side. When you reach your starting point, you have to hike back up to the place where you turned around and start over again. Follow me?"

When the city boy nodded, the local continued. "But with this remarkable invention," he said, pointing to the double-bitted ax, "you brush both sides of the trail at once. See what I'm saying?"

"Uh, maybe, but could you explain it a little more?"

"Sure. Have you ever seen a blind man walking down the sidewalk, waving his white cane from side to side?"

"Uh huh."

"Well, it's like that. You go up the trail, swinging this ax from side to side and cut the brush from both sides of the trail in one trip."

"Really!" the city boy exclaimed.

"No," the Estacada boy shook his head. "Not really."

And because we were in the warehouse, the local boys' laughter seemed magnified as it bounced off the planked walls.

\* \* \*

But the best prank I ever witnessed was played on one Estacada boy by another. And because the target of this joke was my brother Jerry and the plot so intricate that in my position as crew foreman, I was forced to become an unsuspecting co-conspirator, this particular incident still makes me laugh whenever I think about it.

A week into a spring planting season, Oliver, the District warehouseman, approached me with a concern about my crew. "You know, Bob," he began, "those boys are banging up my hoedags pretty bad. I spent all morning yesterday scrapping dried mud off them and filing down the dings in the blades. I got other things to do with my time."

The hoedag, a heavy tool used for planting trees, is built for punishment. With its long, slightly curved hardwood handle and its brass brackets holding the foot-long steel blade in place, the hoedag is an expensive tool. Today it costs nearly seventy-five dollars. In the late fifties, its replacement cost ten dollars. Only eighty cents less than members of my crew made in a day. Since tree planters are easier to replace than hoedags, abusing the tool was a bad idea.

I liked Oliver. Even though he was nearing retirement, he worked every day as if it were his first on the job. If he had a concern, I needed to listen. "I'm sorry, Oliver," I apologized. "I'll make sure the equipment comes back in the same shape it went out."

"I'd appreciate that. But remember, you're dealing with boys, not grown men. I know a thing about boys, having raised three of them. So let me give you some advice. Telling them the hoedag is worth more than *they* are ain't gonna work. You tell a boy something, and that's one thing. But you get him to think the idea is his, and that's a whole other thing. Somehow, you need to make them *want* to take care of their hoedags. Out of pride or something like that. Least to my way of thinking, that's what'll work best."

\* \* \*

On the drive back to Portland that night, I thought about what Oliver had said. I was paying big bucks to take classes in courses like philosophy, and Oliver, a man with an eighth-grade education, could give me better advice than most of the college professors I knew. *You're right, Oliver,* I thought. *Those boys have to be finessed. But how in the world am I going to tie in their sense of pride with something as mundane as a hoedag?*

\* \* \*

The following Saturday morning, after the crew had packed trees into their carrying bags and picked up their tools, I told them to gather around. Passing a box of permanent markers, I instructed them to write their first names and last initials on the handles of their hoedags.

When the box returned to me, I pointed out how clean their hoedags were. "They weren't like that when we left them in the warehouse last Sunday, were they? You can thank a guy named Oliver for the way they look today." I went on to tell them about Oliver's concerns over the condition of the hoedags. "Basically, guys, we have to do a better job of taking care of these tools."

I could see the resistance setting in. Heads drew back. Arms folded across some chests. I must have sounded like their mothers telling them to clean their rooms. The time had come to try the pitch I had rehearsed all week. It might work, or it might become a complete joke.

"I had you write your names on the handles because from now on, you'll be responsible for the same hoedags every day. You'll handle them with care and clean them at quitting time." I could see eyes glazing over. *Okay*, I thought, *Here I go. If they find this hokey, I'll lose them.*

"How many of you have heard of the U.S. Marine Corps' Rifle Creed?" No one answered. I went on. "The Creed was written by a Marine officer during the Second World War. Since that time all Marines going through basic training have had to memorize it. Like so many things the Marines do, the Creed is designed to reflect a sense of pride in the Corps." Arms began to unfold. I had their interest, even if they were merely wondering where all this was going.

"What the Creed does is instill in each Marine a sense of responsibility and pride in his relationship with his weapon. It describes a connection between man and rifle, each responsible for a part of their shared job. You may not have heard of the Rifle Creed by name, but I'll bet some of you have heard the first two lines. They go like this. 'This my rifle. There are many like it, but this one is mine.'

"Well," I continued, picking up a hoedag. "This thing doesn't fire bullets, but it gets the job done. And the better care you take of it, the easier it'll make your day. From now on, you're going to care for this tool as if it were your best friend."

I waited for a moment before raising the hoedag upward and shouting, "Now repeat after me! THIS IS MY HOEDAG. THERE ARE MANY LIKE IT, BUT THIS ONE IS MINE!"

Stunned silence lasted a moment before someone starting laughing. Soon others joined in. *Is it going to work?* I wondered. *It could still go either way.*

Then Jim, my brother's best friend, stepped forward and, turning to face the crew, lifted his hoedag over his head. "THIS IS MY HOEDAG," he shouted. "THERE ARE MANY LIKE IT, BUT THIS ONE IS MINE!"

"THIS IS MY HOEDAG," came the answering shout from the crew. "THERE ARE MANY LIKE IT, BUT THIS ONE IS MINE!"

"Okay, then," I grinned, stepping forward. "Let's go to work."

\* \* \*

As the day went on, I worried that the novelty of the Hoedag Creed would wear off. But it didn't. Every once in a while as we made our way toward the bottom of the setting or back up the hill, one of the boys in front would climb onto a stump or a downed snag and, waving his hoedag overhead, shout, "THIS IS MY HOEDAG. THERE ARE MANY LIKE IT, BUT THIS ONE IS MINE!"

At quitting time, even though the boys were tired, they shared a box of rags as they carefully cleaned their hoedags before loading them into the back of the rig.

I had won the day partly because I gambled on the fact that this particular crew was made up exclusively of local boys, most of whom came from homes with rifles in them, boys who hunted every fall with their families and friends. I thought the Rifle Creed might strike the right cord, and I had been right.

\* \* \*

But I learned early in my teaching career that victories over teenagers often came with undesired side effects. Yes, the boys took pride in how well they cared for their hoedags, but this sense of ownership led some to newfound opportunities for pranks, the most popular being the sudden disappearance of another's hoedag. Before, this would have caused little concern. But now this wasn't just another hoedag. It was "MY HOEDAG!"

Invariably after we had taken a break at the bottom or the top of a setting, someone could not find his hoedag. The frustrated search would last until I threatened an extended day to make up for lost time. Within minutes, one of the boys would miraculously discover the missing hoedag, and we'd go back to work.

Because most of the crew learned to keep their hoedags with them even during the lunch break the frequency of missing tools diminished over time. But woe to anyone who, like my brother Jerry, could fall asleep anywhere for any length of time, even over a ten-minute break. And double woe to anyone who fell asleep alongside a devious instigator of intricate intrigue like Jim, Jerry's best friend.

\* \* \*

I hated Rocky Spur. In my years with the Forest Service, it was the only setting that had to be replanted. Not once, but three times. And I had been on that unforgiving rock-strewn monster all three times. Twice as a teenager and now as foreman of yet another crew. Rocky Spur was well named. Outcroppings of boulders hovered over a gully-streaked mountainside that challenged the crew as they worked their way down into the steep canyon and back up again.

If I could assign malignancy to an inanimate object, I would assign it to Rocky Spur. Most experienced tree planters learned to read soil the way sailors read water. But Rocky Spur could not be read. A stretch of dirt that looked soft often covered a large rock only a few inches below. Swinging his hoedag in a three-sixty arc in order to drive the twelve-inch blade into the ground, a planter hitting one of those rocks felt the impact from his wrist to the fillings in his teeth.

\* \* \*

The boys sprawled in various positions of fatigue at the top of the setting. We had been battling Rocky Spur all weekend. Now on a cold Sunday afternoon, we had struggled to the top of the canyon once more.

Normally I would give the crew a ten-minute break before we lined out and made another pass to the bottom of the setting. There we'd take another break before working our way up the steep hillside once more.

I checked my watch. Three-thirty. Since our eight-hour day included travel time, we needed to leave Rocky Spur at four-fifteen. But each pass into the canyon and back up again had been taking us nearly two hours. I had a tired crew. Another pass would probably take longer, and accompanying it would be the careless planting that exhaustion brought on.

"Guys," I began, "we face two choices. We can make another pass, in which case we'll probably give Uncle Sam over an hour of unpaid time, or we can take a forty-minute break and get back to the warehouse by five o'clock. I say we take the break."

Relieved, the boys settled more comfortably into their sprawled positions. Some began conversations. Others rested quietly. I looked to the far side of the canyon, watching fog creep up from the river below.

In the mountains, cold comes fast once the sun drops behind a western ridge. Some of the boys began pulling on sweatshirts or jackets. Jerry, however, whose body temperature registered only a few degrees below that of a well-fed woodstove, folded his sweatshirt into a pillow and lay back for a nap. In minutes he was asleep.

Because this was an early spring planting, patches of snow remained in areas protected from the afternoon sun. We had taken our break near a snowbank with enough size and shade to last for at least another week or so.

Shortly after Jerry had fallen asleep, Jim, who had been sitting next to him, stood up, reached for his hoedag, and carried it to the snowbank. There he began digging what appeared to be a long trench in the snow. The crew watched him without asking what he was doing. We were all used to his strange antics at times.

Seemingly satisfied with his trench, Jim returned to his place by Jerry and nudged him awake. "What?" Jerry asked, opening his eyes. "Is it time to leave already?"

"Nope," Jim answered. "I just get tired of watching you sleep all the time. You need to stay awake and enjoy life a little more."

Jerry stared at him for a moment and then said, "And you need your head examined."

"Maybe," Jim agreed. He stood up, took the hoedag from Jerry's side, and walked toward the snowbank.

"Where you going with my hoedag?"

"Well, as a matter of fact, I'm going to bury it." With a theatrical flourish, he dropped the hoedag into his trench and began dragging snow over it.

"Don't bury my hoedag."

"I'm burying your hoedag," Jim answered, continuing to scrape snow into the trench.

Standing up, Jerry moved toward him. "Don't bury my hoedag."

Jerry's size could be intimidating. At seventeen, he was nearly six feet tall and weighed close to two hundred pounds. Broad-shouldered with long arms and ham-sized hands, Jerry cast a big shadow.

However, those looks were deceiving. Usually he was easygoing with a soft heart for animals and people in need. But he did have a short fuse. Lighting that fuse was not a good idea.

As Jerry neared Jim, who by this time was smoothing snow over the buried hoedag, the crew remained silent, sensing that something dramatic was about to happen.

"Dig up my hoedag."

"No," Jim answered from his kneeling position as he patted the final touches over the buried tool.

Jerry leaned down and ripped Jim's hoedag from his hands. "If you don't dig it up, I'm throwing this into the canyon."

"Go ahead," Jim smiled.

"I'm not kidding," Jerry warned.

"I know you," Jim said, coming to his feet. "You're all bark and no bite."

"Oh, yeah?" Jerry yelled.

"Yeah," Jim taunted. "All bark and no bite."

Jerry turned to me. "Bob, if I throw this hoedag into the canyon, who has to go after it?"

Seeing the opportunity to support my brother without breaking my rules or showing favoritism, I answered, "Everyone is responsible for his own hoedag. If he lets you throw his into the canyon, he has to go get it."

Smiling, Jerry turned to Jim, lifted the hoedag, and begin circling it overhead. "Last chance, buddy. Dig up my hoedag."

"No, I'm not digging up the hoedag."

"All right, then," Jerry shouted. A collective gasp from the crew accompanied the sight of the hoedag sailing into open air before dropping out of sight. Moments later, we heard the clattering of the tool as it hit the rocks below.

All eyes turned to Jim as he stood up and walked toward the crew. Reaching down, he picked up the hoedag of the nearest boy. "Mind if I borrow this?"

"Why?" the boy asked, making a grab for his hoedag. "You going to bury that one, too?"

"No," Jim answered, holding the tool out of the boy's reach. "I need it to dig up the one I already buried." He turned and begin walking toward the snowbank.

"Too late," Jerry smirked. "You have to climb down and get your hoedag. Since we're going to be late enough already, you'd better get started."

"I don't think so," Jim replied, as he began digging snow from the trench.

"What do you mean, you don't think so?"

Jim, having reached the hoedag, pulled it from the hole. "I don't think so," he smiled, brushing snow from the hoedag's handle, "because *this* is my hoedag. See here," he pointed to the name on the handle. "*Jim C.* I believe that's *my* name."

"No, it's not . . ." Jerry started. "I mean it's your name, but how could …" He stopped as realization came to him. "No. You didn't …"

"Yes, I did," Jim smiled. "I switched them when you were asleep, and you just threw your own hoedag into the canyon. Have a nice trip."

Jerry turned to me. "That's not right, is it? That's not fair. I shouldn't have to go down there."

Cornered by my own rules, I answered, "Everyone is responsible for his own hoedag. If you threw yours into the canyon, you have to go get it."

* * *

As we waited for Jerry to retrieve his hoedag, one of the boys remarked to Jim, "You know, he's liable to tear your head off for this."

"Naw, Jerry can take a joke, If he couldn't, he'd have torn my head off years ago."

With the night cold setting in and the realization that Jim's joke meant we'd be getting in to the warehouse at least an hour late, time seemed to slow down as we waited for Jerry to reappear. "That thing must have gone clear to the bottom of the setting," one of the boys growled.

He had just finished his comment when a ghostly voice rose from the swirling fog below. "THIS IS MY HOEDAG. THERE ARE MANY LIKE IT, BUT THIS ONE IS MINE!"

We looked at each other for a moment before laughter erupted. "See," Jim grinned. "I told you Jerry could take a joke."

\* \* \*

Two days after I had left Dr. Ford's office, I returned. The chair behind his cluttered desk was empty. Dr. Browne looked up from a book she had been underscoring with a felt pen.

"I'm afraid Dr. Ford won't be in this morning."

"That's okay. I came to see you."

Smiling, she motioned me to a chair by her desk. "I assume you've made your decision. I hope it's the right one."

"I want to teach high school."

"Good. I'm glad." She marked her place in the book and placed it aside. "Mind if I ask what convinced you?"

"*You* did, Dr. Browne. I thought over the last thing you said to me. You know, that teenagers would not only challenge but also entertain me."

"So you think that's true?"

"Believe me, Dr. Browne. I *know* that's true."

# I LIKE BEING SINISTER

**I stop by my local Starbucks** for a latte. My local Starbucks is located in my local Safeway. What is that joke going around? Someday there'll be a Starbucks inside a Starbucks? Anyway, as the barista rings up my order, I pull my wallet from my right pocket and, holding it in my right hand, extract a ten-dollar bill with my left hand. Having taken the bill from me, she counts my change, which she then holds out to my right hand, the hand holding my wallet.

I prepare to do what I usually do in this case: switch the wallet to my left hand, take the change in my right hand, awkwardly return the wallet to my right hand while simultaneously maneuvering the change to my left hand, and put the bills in the wallet. If the change is a combination of bills and coins, the process is even more complicated.

I am ready to do all this, but the barista does what most clerks do *not* do. She recognizes that the hand to which she has extended the change is holding a wallet. "Oh, sorry," she says and moves the change over to my left hand.

"Thank you," I smile and, having taken the change in my left hand, neatly place the bills into my wallet, drop the odd coins into the tips jar, and walk away. Instead of going through the fumbling routine I so often perform, I have experienced the ease with which the majority in our society execute this simple exchange.

Now why does the barista do what most clerks do hand the money to my right hand, the hand holding the wallet? Oh, you've figured this out already, haven't you? Most people are right-handed. They hold their wallets in their left hands and operate from the right side. I, of course, am left-handed. As such, I make my way through a world designed for right-handers, a world where I am expected either to change my ways or suffer the consequences of being in a minority whose differences are looked upon with attitudes ranging from amused apathy to outright hostility.

"Hostility?" you ask, smiling. "No one cares if you're left-handed. You're making a mountain out of a molehill."

"Well, if I am," I reply, "I'm making it with my left hand."

\* \* \*

I'm exclusively left-handed. If you cut off my right hand, I probably wouldn't miss it for a week. According to my mother, when I was in the crib, she would hand a toy to my right hand. I would drop the toy and pick it up with my left hand. She would take it from my left hand and place it in my right hand. Once again, I would drop the toy and pick it up with my left hand.

I had no trouble being left-handed in the first grade. Miss Pencil, my first grade teacher,[4] seemed not to notice I was left-handed. But in the second grade the reality of a right-handed world crashed down upon me.

Mrs. Wolf was at least one hundred years old. Gray hair in a bun, patterned house dresses, heavy shoes, Mrs. Wolf was certainly not going to let me bring my left-handedness into her right-handed world. I have read of nuns in Catholic schools associating left-handedness with the devil. Other lefties recall teachers who told them left-handers were more likely to become Communists, those godless plotters with their leftist views. Mrs. Wolf never mentioned her religious or political propensities to me. In fact, I don't remember her ever talking to me. But I *do* remember the ruler in her right hand.

We practiced penmanship in the Palmer Method, a system involving page after page of ovals and push-and-pulls. Sheet after sheet of wide-lined paper filled with ovals and push-and-pulls, ovals and push-and-pulls that were never to go outside the lines.

We had quotas. So many lines of ovals and push-and-pulls, or we could not go to recess. Pages didn't count if any ovals or push-and-pulls extended outside the lines. Those of us who could not fulfill our quotas

---

[4]   Her name was probably something like Miss Pensell, but I remember "Miss Pencil." I was struck with the fact that she had the same name as the writing utensil I was learning to use. Throughout my scholastic career, I have been amazed by the way teachers' names often reflect my memories of them. See, for example, the name of my second-grade teacher.

were tortured by playground sounds from open windows as we labored at our desks attempting to catch up on our ovals and push-and-pulls.

I could not do ovals and push-and-pulls—at least not with my *right* hand. But Mrs. Wolf was adamant. I *would* do them with my right hand.

Among definitions of *left-handed* in the dictionary are "awkward," "maladroit" (a fancy word used to describe people who are physically clumsy or mentally lack perception and judgment), and "of doubtful sincerity" (as in "a left-handed compliment"). In addition, the word *sinister* comes from the Latin for "on the left" or "unlucky." [5]

Awkward, lacking in judgment, insincere, sinister—Mrs. Wolf did not allow such nonsense in her classroom. She would save me from the unholy ranks of the left-handed. She insisted I angle my paper to the left, place my right arm on the paper, and perform my ovals and push-and-pulls without bending my wrist. The hunched-over, bent-wrist, upside-down posture of a left-hander was an obscenity to the

---

[5] In times of the Roman Empire, men meeting on the street held each other's right hands, their weapon hands, to prevent sudden attacks while they spoke. Hence, the development of handshaking as a friendly greeting. However, some Romans discovered the hard way that when they held the right hand of a left-hander, they were still vulnerable to a sudden dagger thrust. Therefore, the word *sinister*, originally simply a word for the left, took on a more malevolent meaning.

right-minded Mrs. Wolf. I would do my ovals and push-and-pulls with my right hand, or I would *never* experience recess.[6]

I never experienced recess.

I held the pencil like a dagger in my right hand and stabbed at the paper. I pushed and I pulled. I drew ovals that would have swept Dorothy and Toto off to Oz in a minute's notice. But I couldn't stay inside the lines.

So whenever Mrs. Wolf drifted to another part of the classroom, I switched the pencil to my left hand and got in as many lines as possible. Invariably, however, just as I was really getting into my penmanship masterpiece, a shadow would loom over my desk, and, try as I might, I was never fast enough to pull back my hand before hearing the whistle of the Wolf's ruler as she brought it down on that offensive Satan's appendage.

Fortunately my family moved from Aberdeen to Oregon in the middle of my second year of school, or I probably would have been maimed for life by the lightning-quick one-hundred-year-old Mrs. Wolf.

\* \* \*

Three facts made Estacada a paradise: teachers didn't seem to care that I was left-handed, they didn't teach the Palmer Method, and Estacada kids played baseball. They lived for baseball.

---

[6] Left-handers do not by instinct turn over their hands and write from above the lines. If elementary teachers would recognize that some of their students are holding their pencils in their left hands and help them turn their papers to the right instead of to the left as these teachers have instructed the entire class to do, the little lefties would lay their arms comfortably on the paper and write with the same ease as right-handers. Instead, with their papers angled to the left, they cannot force their arms around to lay them on the paper. Eventually, they do what they will have to do for the rest of their lives: find a way to accommodate the demands of a right-handed world. They will improvise until they find something that works. In this case, they will write from the top, turning their wrists and dragging their left hands over their written work, taking the hunched, crimped, upside-down position assumed by the right-handed majority to be a genetic flaw of left-handers.

By the third grade, baseball consumed me. Every recess and every lunch period the game between the third grade and the fourth grade picked up wherever it had been cut short by the bell calling us back to class. The score, the inning, the batter, the count we didn't write anything down. There was no need. We knew exactly where we had left off. There was life, and there was baseball. In a perfect world the two were one. Estacada was a perfect world.

I needed a glove. My parents drove into Portland and spent an entire day searching through one sporting-goods store after another, trying to find a glove for a left-handed boy. Finally, they settled for an adult's glove, a huge glove. I was nine years old. The only way I could make it fit was to put my first two fingers in the first finger of the glove and my second two fingers in the second finger. I caught in the web, a small two-strap arrangement between the thumb and the first finger. The rest of the glove hung down like a discarded miniature mattress, waving uselessly below the functioning thumb and first two fingers.

Today, most baseball players don't even use the first finger of a glove. They place their first finger on the outside of the glove. I used this same glove through high school, still with two fingers in the first finger of the glove, two fingers in the second finger, and the rest of the glove uselessly hanging down.

However, in high school, I learned another brutal lesson for left-handers. While right-handers can play any of the nine positions on a baseball team, left-handers cannot play catcher, second base, shortstop or third base. Because the bases are run counterclockwise, left-handed infielders have to pivot to throw to first and second base, an extra move not required of right-handers. The same is true of catchers. In addition, because most batters are right-handed, left-handed catchers have to throw through the batters to catch runners on second or third base.

In elementary school I had loved playing second base. But when I turned out for baseball in high school, my choices were pitcher, first base, or outfield. I was not a pitcher, I didn't like first base, and I found the outfield boring. I wanted to play second base. But I was not allowed to try out for second base. I was left-handed.[7]

Of course, there's a simple solution for this. Left-handers could play all the positions if the bases were run clockwise. On the other hand, right-handers could not play catcher, second base, shortstop or third base. Now I know that idea is heresy for baseball purists. But how about a compromise? Maybe every other year we could run the bases in the opposite direction. First a right-handed year and then a left-handed year? No? Oh well, it was just a thought.

I was a three-sport athlete in high school. However, most of my energy went into football and basketball. Baseball had become a sport I was expected to play, not a sport I enjoyed playing. This was a far cry from the days when I had first moved to Estacada and discovered baseball, those early days when I could play any position on the field. I could play all these positions because my teammates and I had yet to learn that left-handers were allowed only a limited role in America's game.

* * *

"Oh, quit whining," you sniff. "So you had your hand slapped in the second grade. So you couldn't play every position in baseball. All that was over sixty years ago. And this superstitious malarkey about left-handers' being sinister and everything. Just words, that's all, just words.

"No one really buys into all that stuff about left-handers being evil. *Awkward*, yes, but evil? No. Not in today's politically correct world. And you know what? I doubt anyone *ever* took such notions seriously. Sounds like a bunch of old wives' tales to me."

"Most superstitions are exactly that—old wives' tales," I point out. "But old wives' tales that denigrate a group of people simply because they're different should never be accepted in what you're calling a 'politically correct world' especially when those beliefs become so woven into the basic fabric of a society that no one even questions them."

---

[7]    When I lived in Pakistan, I played second base on a softball team. I had no problem throwing out runners. Left-handers *can* play second base. I was sure of that when I was a teenager, but I didn't have the nerve to challenge the conventional thinking of right-handed coaches.

"And *I've* said I don't think they are," you reply. "Not only that, I don't think they ever have been. Not seriously. Give me some specific examples of superstitions about left-handed people. And I mean specific, not that same old hash about God on the right hand and the devil on the left."

"Well, my friend, where do I start?"

---

Marriage is big in the news today. Everyone seems to have an opinion on what should define this union between two people who want to commit themselves to a life together. Let's start with marriage.

Ever heard of a morganatic marriage? No? Well, a morganatic marriage is a union between a person of royal birth and a person of lower rank. In a morganatic marriage, a legal document declares that no titles or estates will pass through inheritance to the partner of inferior rank or to any offspring of the marriage.

What does this have to do with left-handedness? Traditionally, people in a morganatic marriage hold their partners' left hands rather than their right hands to signify a less-than-perfect union.

In India, where rural brides move in with their husbands' families, the new daughters-in-law suffer painful harassment if they are left-handed. They are not allowed to use their left hands for cooking or serving food. If they do, their hands are beaten and sometimes even burned.

In Japan until a few generations ago, left-handedness in a bride was grounds for divorce.[8]

As for the wedding rings brides and grooms so lovingly exchange, the tradition of wearing the rings on the left hand—the sinister hand—originated from the belief that such a placement would serve as a talisman to ward off evil spirits that might haunt the marriage.

---

[8]   The younger generation in Japan seems to have rejected this prejudice against left-handedness. They have formed clubs for Japanese lefties through several sites on the internet. And one of the ten top country songs in Japan several years ago was a little number called "My Boyfriend Is a Lefty."

And I should quit whining about having my left hand whacked by Mrs. Wolf? Well, I'm probably lucky I grew up in America.

In ancient Egypt left-handed children had their offending hands buried in hot sand until they were maimed enough to insure right-handedness.

Until a few decades ago, Indonesians tied babies' left arms to their bodies to force them into being right-handed.

And in that same India where young left-handed brides suffer the abuse of their in-laws, left-handed boys frequently have their offending hands tied behind their backs or wrapped in bags. If they continue using their left hands, the hands are sometimes burned and sprinkled with hot chilies.

And, my friend, here are some additional random facts about superstitions concerning left-handedness:

Among Eskimos every left-hander is viewed as a potential sorcerer.

In several parts of Africa, a sorcerer's left hand is considered capable of such evil power that he has to keep it hidden for the safety of others.

On the Guinea coast of West Africa, some believe that touching the left thumb to a beer mug will poison the beer.

In New Zealand Maori women weave ceremonial cloth using only their right hands because the left hands would profane and curse the cloth. At one time the punishment for using the left hand in weaving this cloth was death.

---

"Big deal," you protest. "Eskimos, Indians, beer drinkers on the Guinea coast, Maoris in New Zealand? How many people you know have contact with those societies? You're really reaching. The fact is, you live in America. For every right-handed baseball glove today, there's a left-handed glove. You even have your own scissors. And I'll bet the same is true for everything else. I'm sure someone has come up with a left-handed model for everything right -handed."

"A left-handed model for everything right-handed?" I ask. "In the words of Elizabeth Barrett Browning, 'Let me count the ways.'"

"The next time you see me tooling down the road toward you in my SUV, shifting the gears, dialing in a radio station or shoving in a tape or a disk, adjusting the defrosters, turning up or turning down the heat, programming the cruise control, changing the speed of the windshield wipers or adjusting their intermittent pace, punching in a destination on the GPS system, opening or closing the sun roof, remember that I'm doing all this with the hand that I don't normally use, the hand that I wouldn't miss for a week if you cut it off.

"Also, I'm left-footed. I do anything that requires footwork with my left foot. So what is my left foot—my dominant foot—doing when I drive? Well, at least when I drove vehicles with manual transmissions, my left foot worked the clutch. But today with automatic transmissions? My left foot serves absolutely no purpose. My right foot my weak foot is busy stepping on the gas pedal to increase the speed with which I'm hurling toward you or hitting the brakes to keep from turning you into a pulpy mass of road kill."

"Why don't you move to England?" you ask, grinning.

"Okay," I reply. "I'm not going to argue with you. I'm just going to give you some specific examples of things designed strictly for right-handers. I'm not even going to prioritize them. I'm going to pitch them at you in a totally random, rapid-fire way that I hope overwhelms you. I want you to feel what a left-hander feels as he realizes how much of the world is designed for right-handers, how much adjusting, how much reprogramming, he is expected to achieve in order to function.

"Some of what I'm about to describe will be of little consequence, merely irritations to the left-hander. Some will be of great consequence, perhaps even life-threatening. Don't interrupt. Don't come up with exceptions. Just listen. Listen and learn, my right-handed friend."

---

The following are a few of the objects in this world designed primarily for right-handed people:

*Power tools*: Left-handers have a remarkably higher percentage of serious accidents on jobs in which they operate power tools. Some work-site managers off-handedly attribute this higher percentage to a left-hander's notorious awkwardness. Others, however, recognize that a left-hander using dangerous tools designed for right-handers is in increased danger of injury.

In one of my father's sawmills, the trim saw was right-handed, its handle on the right of the belt-driven saw. One day the worker at this station must have been daydreaming or lulled by the hypnotic whir of the saw or the monotony of his job. For whatever reason he reached across the front of the saw with his left hand and pulled it toward him, cutting through the board he was trimming and halfway through his left arm as well. Fortunately my father was able to get him to a hospital in time to save the arm.

*Folding knives*: Pocket knives, Swiss Army knives, fishing knives are right-handed because the slots used to open them are on the left side of the blades. A person holds the knife in his dominant hand—the hand with which he plans to use the knife—and opens the blade with the other hand. When a right-hander opens the blade, it's pointing outward, ready for use. When a left-hander opens the blade, it's pointing directly at his stomach or chest in a perfect position to commit hara-kiri.

*Manual can openers*: There is no adjustment that allows these to be turned with the left hand.

*All pouring containers with numbers to indicate quantities*: Items like pitchers, measuring cups, and coffee makers are right-handed. When left-handers hold these containers in their dominant hands, they cannot see the numbers.

*Corkscrews*: Like can openers and other devices that have a clockwise movement, corkscrews are difficult for lefties. Right-handers pull the handle toward them to insert the cork. Lefties have to push it away. Most left-handers have learned to insert the corkscrew into the cork and hold it tightly while turning the bottle with the right hand.

*Stringed musical instruments*: Violins, guitars, banjos—all right-handed. Turning them over doesn't work. A serious left-handed musician has to restring his instrument.

*Playing cards*: When a left-hander fans his cards in his right hand, freeing his left hand to draw or play cards, the numbers on the cards disappear.

*One-armed student desks*: Yes, there is a model for left-handers but lots of luck to the leftie who tries to find one when he needs it. During my first two years at Portland State, I never saw a left-handed desk. By my junior year, there were a few in each building. Not each classroom. Each *building*.

Every quarter at the change of classes, I searched any building in which I had a new class to find a left-handed desk. When I located one, I commandeered the desk and carried it to my new class, no doubt annoying the crowds on the stairs or in the elevators as I pushed my way into them with my treasure in my arms.

Why this obsession with left-handed desks? For two years I had watched right-handers take lecture notes and sit through two-hour exams with their right arms extended comfortably on their desks. In the meantime, *I* had taken notes and labored through the two-hour exams with only my left wrist on my desk, my arm hanging uselessly and painfully into open space. No wonder a common description of the left hand during the Renaissance translated as "the tired hand."

*Automatic and semiautomatic rifles*: The empty shell casings eject to the right, no problem for right-handed shooters but into the face of lefties.

When I was in the National Guard, I qualified as a sharpshooter with a semiautomatic carbine while shooting right-handed. I was proud of my accomplishment in light of the fact that I usually cannot do *anything* right-handed, but I could not help thinking I would have qualified as expert with a left-handed weapon. Also, I was sure that if I ever found myself in combat, I would revert to left-handed shooting in spite of the expelled shell casings ricocheting off my battered face.

*Measuring tapes*: The case with its release-lock button is held in the dominant hand. The tape is pulled with the other hand. When a right-hander does this, everything is fine. When a left-hander does this, the numbers are upside down.

*Manual egg beaters*: I know this seems like a strange item, but nothing is more entertaining than seeing a young left-hander try one of these seemingly innocent devices for the first time. When a right-hander cranks the handle, the egg beater goes away from him. When a leftie cranks the handle, the beater comes straight for the leftie, pushing the contents of the bowl ahead of it in a tidal wave of egg yolk, cake batter, or whatever else the recipe has dictated.

*Cameras*: The shutter button is usually on the right of the camera. Therefore, a lefty has to try holding the camera steady while negotiating the tricky shutter button with his weak hand.

*Cups with logos, clever sayings, or pictures*: The handles are on the right. Right-handers hold the cups and read the printing or look at the pictures. Left-handers look at the backs of the cups.

Sue and I have a set of cups with little kitten figurines on the handles. When Sue, who is right-handed, drinks from one of these cups, she looks into the face of a cute little kitten. When *I* drink from one of these cups, I look into the—well, let's just say it's not the *face* of a cute little kitten.

*Chained pens at supermarkets:* Here's a special pet peeve of mine. These pens are always anchored at the far right of the writing surface. Convenient for right-handers, hell for left-handers tugging at a rigid chain to pull the God-help-you-if-you-try-to-steal-me sacred pen over far enough to do the required signing.

*Zippers hidden under overlapping strips of materials:* Impossible to open or close with the left hand.

Mothers of young male lefties, when your sons feel grown up enough to start wearing underwear briefs, be sure the boys are completely potty-trained before putting them into these insidious inventions of the right-handed world. And don't tell me to turn them inside out. Inside out, they are *still* right-handed.

Okay, that last item was probably more information than you needed. I'm going to stop now, not because I can't go on with more examples, but because I'm sympathetic to the glazed look creeping into your eyes.

––––––––––

"You're right," you sigh. "You're a member of an oppressed minority. I give up. I give up mainly because I don't see any reason to deny what you're saying. As a left-hander you have to adjust to things we righties just don't realize are a problem.

"Except for the power tools, however, I don't see anything on the magnitude of a civil-rights cause. I'm still not ready to run out and burn my ... burn my ... what *do* right-handers burn when they see the errors of their ways? Do they throw a right-handed glove on the fire? What exactly do you want from us?"

"You know what?" I answer. "I don't want anything. I wouldn't change anything. I like things just the way they are."

"Then what was this all about?"

"Remember the title of this piece?"

"Oh, okay," you reply. "I see. So what's the answer? *Why* do you like being sinister?"

"I like being part of a minority that has to adapt, to show ingenuity, to overcome obstacles."

"So all this was just an intellectual exercise. You were merely yanking my chain?"

"No, not really. I wanted to educate you, to smack you alongside the head for your supercilious know-it-all attitude. But, basically, I wouldn't give up being left-handed for anything in the world.

"I love it when I'm signing something and hear, 'You're a leftie.' I love it because I know the *speaker* is a leftie. Only lefties notice other lefties. It's a special club. You can become a world-class golfer, a renowned writer, the President of the United States. But how many people *become* left-handed. We're special. We're sinister. We're gauche. We're the unrepentant left."

---

And how many of us have survived a history of suspicion, of accusation, of condemnation? The following are but a few of the many left-handers in the rolls of our world's history:

Benjamin Franklin

Hans Christian Anderson

Clarence Darrow

Harpo Marx

Edward R. Murrow

Alexander, the Great

Albert Schweitzer

W.C. Fields

Helen Keller

Charles Chaplin

Harry S. Truman

Gentleman Jim Corbett

Steve McQueen

Charlemagne

Cary Grant

Greta Garbo

Joan of Arc[8]

H.G. Wells

Raphael

Shoeless Joe Jackson

Babe Ruth

Michelangelo

Judy Garland

Tiberius

Julius Caesar

Sid Caesar

Sergei Rachmaninoff

Pablo Picasso

Leonardo da Vinci

Henry Ford

Queen Victoria

Johann Sebastian Bach

Napoleon Bonaparte

Cole Porter

Mark Twain

Albert Einstein

All these amazing people were sinister … Like me.

---

[9] There have been suggestions that Joan of Arc was not really left-handed, that this characterization merely added weight to the charge she was a witch. Personally I hope she *was* left-handed.

# THE STOVE AND I

**The Copalis Beach house** was huge. At least, to my four-year-old eyes, it was huge. Of course, everything is relative. The only home I remember before the Copalis Beach house is that small cabin overhanging a cut bank of sand methodically being devoured by high tides, a home increasingly in danger of collapsing into the ocean.

So this old weather-beaten house, firmly anchored behind protective sand dunes, offered a rare stability in my early years.

The house was typical of the homes inhabited by transients like my family. Cowering from the ocean winds, it leaned a little to the right, offset by a front porch that leaned to the left. A line of two-by-six planks laid side by side led from the beach road to the porch.

As the last house before the road dropped to the beach, our lot was nearly indistinguishable from the dunes that marked the line between private and public land, a line fuzzy at best. People, like water, found the easiest routes, the most accessible downhill slopes, to the beach. If these routes passed through neighbors' lots, they simply become public access. No one living on the beach really claimed private land. People shared space as they had learned to share other resources during the Depression.

The lot contained two buildings in addition to the house itself. On a rise behind the main building perched the outhouse. A series of sawed log sections my father had plotted between the two structures pointed the way. In later years when I saw Frank Sinatra sign off a TV performance by walking through spotlighted circles in an otherwise darken sound stage, I remembered my father's carefully spaced round log sections leading to our Copalis Beach outhouse. In good weather my mother, my brother, and I followed a trail beside the blocks because we could not comfortably step from section to section. My father, a six-footer, had laid out the blocks according to his own steps, and he had long legs.

But in rainy weather the low dip between the main building and the outhouse flooded, the reason my father had positioned the blocks along the way. I recall more than once jumping from block to block, trying to reach the outhouse in an emergency situation. And I remember that sometimes, when the sun had set and I was a dusky shadow from any window of the house behind me, I defiantly stopped, stepped to the edge of a block and added my own contribution to the waters below.

The other outbuilding was the woodshed. The dreaded woodshed. I feared that building as only a child can fear a building. It was large with a sandy floor, stacked with wood my father had hauled home from his logging jobs. Chips and splinters lay inches deep around a huge chopping block so filled with knots that even Dad could not split it. Thus, it had been spared the fate of other wood in the shed, a survivor, a Spartacus in the arena of wood destined to be consumed by our stoves. And, as such, it assumed a central position in my childhood nightmares.

Two axes dominated the scene. Buried in the chopping block was a rough, scarred ax used to cut wood for the house, and against the near wall leaned the razor-sharp two-bitted felling ax so treasured by my father. On nights when my parents set aside their books to listen to favorite radio programs, he lovingly honed that ax, stroking it with an oiled whetstone until its blades glistened in our harsh living-room light. The ax was a fearful weapon a weapon used to rape the old growth of virgin forests. And in my mind, it was a weapon that could be used on me.

"Never, never touch that ax," Mom drilled into me. "Never, never touch Dad's ax." I didn't need the repetition. Not only did I not want to touch his ax, I didn't even want to enter the woodshed where the ax held center stage.

My mother had several basic sayings, each keyed to particular kinds of events. A couple were in German, but I early understood their meanings. However, the one that terrified me was in English. "That," she would proclaim, "will lead to bloodshed."

"Will lead to bloodshed." In my child's mind the proclamation always produced a singular picture: the woodshed splattered with blood, its twin axes dripping, the chopping block covered with overflow ... Whatever the *it* was, it had led to ... *the blood shed* ... a scary, dark place in the imagination of my childhood.

* * *

My memories of the interior of the house center around two rooms: the kitchen and the living room. A large stove dominated each of these rooms: Mom's double-oven wood-cooking stove in the kitchen and Dad's large pot-bellied wood stove in the living room.

The kitchen stove heated the room while flooding the house with the aroma of baking bread, cakes, and pies. Added to these was the oiled sizzle of fried clams.

My parents were commercial clam diggers, and in digging season the warming shelf of the stove always held a heaping platter of fried clams. I'm convinced no one, before or since, has been able to fry clams the way my mother fried clams. She dipped them in beaten eggs and butter, swiped them through cracker crumbs, and dropped them into oil heated to exactly the right temperature on her fired-up stove. I've given up trying to duplicate that delicacy in seafood restaurants. Eating chewy overcooked clams from white plates on white tablecloths? Now how could that capture the delight of a young boy climbing a chair to snatch a melt-in-your-mouth, buttery clam from a warm platter before rushing outside to join his friends for a day on the beach?

Linoleum covered the floor of the kitchen, and that linoleum was cold. The *house* was cold. The dunes between us and the beach offered only token resistance to winds coming off the ocean. Those winds battered our drafty old home into submission, letting in the cold, a cold that seemed to center itself in the linoleum of the kitchen floor.

Comfort in the living room depended up the vagaries of the pot-bellied stove. Silver-streaked, brass-levered, black-sided, leering its fiery grin, it kept us warm as long as we remembered to cozy up to it, to pay homage, to feed it with piece after piece of split wood from the shed— from *the blood shed*. I'm not sure, even to this day, that what happened to me in that room was not a complicity between the blood shed and the stove.

* * *

My mother bathed Jerry and me in the kitchen. She'd heat water on the stove and pour it into a large washtub. We'd be soaped, scrubbed, rinsed, wash-clothed in and around our ears seemingly especially dirty places on the bodies of boys whose playground was sand dunes and surf. Then she'd pour more warm water over us, hand us towels, and turn away as the race to warmth began.

We'd leap from the tub and run into the living room, huddling as near as we could to the pot-bellied stove, shivering as we toweled, dancing from foot to foot in our effort to ward off the cold winds whistling around the house, the cold winds seeking those cracks, those crannies that allowed them to steal from us the warmth of tub water left behind.

And on one especially cold night, I backed up and backed up as I toweled the front part of my body, oblivious to the closeness of my back part to the pot-bellied stove. I backed up and backed up, and then I bent over to towel my legs ...

I heard it before I felt it. A sizzling sound. Yet not simply a sizzling sound. Later when I saw the roadrunner cartoons, I heard the sound almost duplicated as the roadrunner raced by: *phissssit*. *That* was the sound. The sound of the roadrunner but with a liquid undertone, something like the sound of a slab of bacon dropped into a pan of hot grease except the pan in this case was a pot-bellied stove and the slab of bacon was ... Well, you know what the slab of bacon was.

I was across the room before I really knew what had happened. In my agony I registered two faces: my brother, moving quickly from shocked fear at my outcry to snickering when he realized what had happened, and my mother, the lioness rushing to a cub who had cried out in pain and fear—in this case, a cub with a severely seared rear end.

* * *

I don't know if I have scars. If I do, they are on a part of my anatomy I never see. And, no matter how close I am to an acquaintance, I'm not close enough to ask that acquaintance to solve the mystery for me. But I do know that for the next two years before we moved into Aberdeen, I walked a thin line between the blood shed and that squatting, smirking, pot-bellied demon in our living room. If it had eyes, I'm sure it would have winked at me as I gave it a wide berth whenever I walked by.

Others may have found its warmth comforting, but *I* knew the malevolence that lurked behind that iron façade, and it knew I knew. We had a special understanding, a special relationship. After all, we had had a meeting of more than merely minds, the stove and I.

# COLLECTING BODY PARTS

**8:15 A.M., October 31, 2010. Halloween.**

**I sit at** the desk in my Tigard condo, looking out the window at a gray sky. Neighborhood trees struggle to retain red, gold, and orange foliage so glorious just a few days ago. Soggy leaves clog the gutters, evidence of a losing battle. In already leafless patches, slender branches, like skeletal fingers, reach skyward. Oregon's short, beautiful fall has begun its slide into another long, rainy winter.

Tonight urchins will haunt our streets, collecting the booty of their "trick or treats." Adults will attend parties dressed as potbellied Batmen and cleavage-enhanced Elviras. Werewolves, Frankensteins, and campy Draculas will stumble through the night.

For the serious aficionados of fright night, The Oregon Symphony will perform a special Halloween treat: the screening of Alfred Hitchcock's classic black-and-white movie, *Psycho,* while the orchestra plays the film's soundtrack.

Tension will build as Janet Leigh steps into the bathtub, pulls the shower curtain closed, and luxuriates under the spray. Of course, everyone in the audience will know what is about to happen, but sometimes the expected carries as much dread as the unexpected.

A shadow looms behind the curtain before it's yanked aside. Anthony Perkins in his own freakish Halloween costume begins slashing. Slashing and slashing while the violin section screeches *WEEEK! WEEEK! WEEEK! WEEEK! WEEEK!*

Suddenly, the music stops. Only the sound of running water accompanies Janet Leigh's slow slide down the shower wall. The camera zooms in on black bloody water circling the drain. The shot returns for a close-up of her open but lifeless eyes.

Hitchcock, master of the bizarre, has once more tapped into one of mankind's favorite experiences: the thrill of vicarious horror. But the key word here is *vicarious.* Sharing someone else's horror story while safely snuggled in a theater seat is fun. Experiencing horror directly is not. I should know. I've been there.

* * *

As a recently divorced bachelor, I downsized from a tri-level country home to a small '50s ranch-style house on a modest street in Clackamas. It had a fenced backyard large enough for Odin, my Great Dane, and a second bedroom for my daughter, who had chosen to live with me.

The landscaping needed work, especially a fenced-off area near the rear of the lot. Inside the enclosure, lurked a jungle of brambles, rank weeds, and stunted apple trees. In the center of this quarantined corner stood a moss-covered, hobbit-sized shed, smelling of mold and other less decipherable odors. "Cleaning up this mess will be my first project," I declared.

Five years later, the mess was still there, weeds higher, shed disappearing into the brambles, like some unspeakable creature slowly withdrawing into its den. Oh, I occasionally chopped back the briers to keep them from escaping into the neighbors' yards, but other than that, I seldom entered the place. As for Odin, in his exploratory expedition the day we moved in, he had shied from the unmistakable scurry of hidden inhabitants in the tangled overgrowth and never again ventured near it.

A major change had occurred on the neighboring lot south of us. When I bought the house, that lot was undeveloped, tall fir trees giving my home a feeling of being on the edge of the wild, a feeling enhanced, I suspect, by my own fenced-in bit of wilderness.

But four years after my purchase, a developer cut down the trees on the front of the neighboring lot and thinned those on the back. A large, odd-shaped modern house went up quickly, a home out of keeping with our Ozzie-and-Harriet neighborhood. However, the blue-collar family that moved into the house a long-haul truck driver, his wife, and two teenage kids seemed to fit right in. At least, I believed they did. Who could have thought this family would introduce an Alfred-Hitchcock scene into my otherwise ordinary life?

Within a year of their arrival, the family mysteriously disappeared in the dead of the night. The house seemed abandoned, filled with what appeared to be an all-American family one day and empty the next.

However, it wasn't this disappearing act that forced me to face gut-wrenching revulsion. It was what the family left behind in a collection of large trash bags piled against their side of the fence.

* * *

One evening a week or so after the family's disappearance, I leaned back in my recliner, watching a TV movie, the fireplace warming my corner of the living room. At first, I thought the noises I heard came from the movie soundtrack. But then I muted the TV and leaned forward. Leaned forward because the sounds came from directly under me. Chewing, gnawing sounds beneath the floorboards of my modest little home.

When I could stand the sounds no more, I stood up and stomped on the hardwood floor. "Stop that!" I yelled. Remarkably, the gnawer did. For a moment. Then the gnawing began again. I stomped. It stopped. I waited, holding my breath. Just when I inhaled, whatever chewed on the underside of my floor began once more.

"It's a squirrel," I said to myself. "How much damage can a squirrel do?" In a few minutes the sounds ceased. Comforted by the thought this was a one-time thing, I watched the rest of my movie and went to bed.

The next evening my nocturnal visitor returned. Again I asked myself, "How much damage can a squirrel do?" I didn't want to go down there to find out. When I had bought the place, I had unlatched the small wooden barricade that opened an entry into the crawlspace under the house.

"Crawlspace" was a misnomer for the dark depths down there. In keeping with standard construction of postwar 1950s ranch houses, a square concrete foundation bordered mounds of dirt. Construction debris lay scattered across the ground. Water pipes and furnace ducts crowded the space overhead. A person might *squirm* into that space, but he would never be able to *crawl* into it.

Have I mentioned I'm claustrophobic? I'm claustrophobic.

My inspection was cursory at best. I glanced in and backed away. Even then, I knew I would never enter that space on my own volition. And now, five years later, no wood-chomping squirrel could do anything to change my mind. "Give it time," I rationalized. "It'll get bored with this." Remarkably enough, the noises stopped after one more frustrating evening. My prediction seemed to have come true.

* * *

A couple of days later, I stepped into the garage to look for something on my workbench. Odin lay in his bed beside the bench, the backdoor of the garage open as always to allow his entry and exit. Doggy doors for Great Danes are a ludicrous idea at best.

As I rummaged through the chaos that characterize my particular style of organization, I heard a scurrying sound behind me. I swung around. At first I saw nothing. The sound came from the shelves next to the furnace. *That damned squirrel,* I thought to myself. *He's in the garage.*

I stepped toward the shelves. The scurrying stopped. I glanced to the floor, looking for any object I could use to drive the squirrel out the door. Before me lay one of Odin's favorite toys, a saliva-soaked tennis ball. I picked it up and had taken another step toward the shelves when a grey movement caught my eye. There it was, staring at me with cold black eyes, whiskers twitching, shoulders hunched, ready for flight. But it was not a squirrel. It was a rat. An enormous rat.

Instinctively I drew back and fired the tennis ball, missing the rat and knocking several jars of nuts and bolts to the floor in an explosion of shattering glass. The rat leaped from the shelf and darted around the furnace, followed by yet another rat. And another. And another. An explosion of rats leapt through the air, hitting the concrete floor in stride and racing behind their enormous leader to disappear behind the furnace.

Returning to my workbench, I reached for a crowbar. I moved stealthily toward the place where the rats had disappeared. Approximately two feet of space separated the garage wall from the back of the furnace. Holding the crowbar in ready position, I peeked around the furnace, expecting to find a pile of squirming rats fighting each other for space. Instead, the space was empty.

I spun around, fearing the rats would come from the other side of the furnace to launch a sneak attack from the rear. Or for *my* rear, as the case may be. No rats there. I looked back into the space behind the furnace. Then I saw it. A ragged hole in the sheetrock just above the concrete foundation. The case of the gnawing night invader was solved.

On the other side of the garage, I had built additional shelves by laying planks across concrete building blocks. I dismantled the shelves and wrestled two of the blocks to the furnace. Yes, they would fit. I stacked them if front of the rats' entry hole. They were trapped. Now for what Hitler and his cohorts called "The Final Solution."

* * *

A short drive took me to our local "one-stop shopping center," where all needs can be met, including, it turned out, rat poison.

On the way, I admonished myself for not having cleared the jumble of brambles and rotting shed from the back of my property, certain the rats had come from there. It was not until weeks later that I learned the truth from a real-estate agent who was listing the vacant home next to me.

"They were renters," he informed me, "behind on their rent by several months. Skipped out in the night. The ugly thing was the mess they left behind, especially in the back yard. It seems they couldn't afford garbage collection, so they piled up bags of garbage until the dad came home from his trips and carted them to the local trash dump. The guys we hired to clean up the place said that pile exploded with rats when they got near it. I'm amazed you didn't smell it."

But this revelation was weeks in the future. In the present, all I knew was rats had invaded my house and I was about to deliver a major eviction notice.

After returning home armed with special treats for my uninvited guests, I investigated the shelves in the garage, looking for what had attracted them. On the shelf where they had gathered lay a ripped and scattered bag of wild-bird feed my daughter had purchased during her Audubon phase.

Odin had not moved from his bed. "Some watchdog you are," I muttered. "Those things must have been coming in and out of here for a while." If a dog can shrug, Odin shrugged. Then he closed his eyes, not the least interested in my extermination plans.

The rat poison, packaged in little packets, proved easy to handle. No need to tear open the packets, the directions stated. The rats would rip into this stuff as soon as they smelled it.

I pulled back my concrete blocks, tossed in the entire supply of packets, and resealed the hole. "Chew on that, my little buddies," I smirked as I walked out the back door.

Carefully circling the house, I studied the foundation. I had decided while driving to the store that the rats had to have another entry into the crawlspace. Why would they chew through the sheetrock behind the furnace? On the south side of the house, I found it. Behind heavy shrubs the concrete had cracked, probably from the house's having settled. A chunk of concrete had fallen out, leaving an inviting entrance for my guests from next door.

Having returned to the garage for two more building blocks, I sealed off the crack. Satisfied that no more rats could enter my home, I went back inside.

I scrubbed my hands, poured a glass of Scotch, and retired to my recliner. "And that, my friends," I said to no one in particular, raising my glass in salute, "takes care of that."

As I celebrated my victory, I remained blissfully unaware of the fact that there are two kinds of rat poison: the old-fashioned kind that simply kills them and a newer kind that not only kills them but also mummifies the corpses, eliminating the stench of rotting rat flesh as they decompose.

Unfortunately, I had trapped that horde of rats in my crawlspace with the old-fashioned kind of rat poison.

* * *

Have I mentioned this rat invasion occurred during an unusually hot summer for Oregon. In little over a week, the smell of rotting rats began percolating upward through the floorboards of my house.

Another trip to our local "one-stop shopping center" and a conversation with a clerk in the garden section educated me on the difference between old-fashioned and newer rat poisons.

On the drive home, the chagrin over what I had done was overshadowed by the dread of what I now had to do.

Rationalizing that I would need morning light for the ordeal ahead, I put off the worse part until the next day. However, I did manage to accomplish some prep work

First, I cleared a space of brambles and weeds in my fenced-in wilderness area. Then I dug a rectangular hole deep enough that marauding animals like raccoons or possums wouldn't dig up what I intended to bury. I wasn't really worried about Odin, who stood outside the gateless entry, watching my labors. But, still, he *was* a dog. No use taking chances.

When I had finished, I jammed the shovel into the resulting mound of dirt and studied the hole. It looked a little like a burial plot for a midget. *Appropriate*, I thought as I walked back to the house, Odin following behind.

* * *

The next morning, I skipped breakfast. Considering what I had to do, having a full stomach didn't seem like a great idea, nor did I have much of an appetite. Dressed in a ragged pair of jeans and a t-shirt that should have been discarded years ago, I stepped into the garage, my hiking boots in one hand and Odin's breakfast bowl in the other.

He ignored the bowl and, tail wagging, began excitedly circling me. The boots normally signaled a hike on one of our favorite trails along the upper Clackamas River.

I took my rain gear from its hook by the door and stepped into the pants, pulling the suspenders over my shoulders before sitting on the kitchen step to pull on my boots. I put on the raincoat as I walked to the workbench, where yesterday I had placed the rest of the items I'd need: a blue naval watch cap, a pair of brown cotton gardening gloves, a large red bandana, a flashlight, and an extra-large black trash bag.

Odin watched, still hoping, as I pulled the cap over my ears, tied the bandana Western-bandit style around my neck, worked my hands into the gloves, picked up the flashlight and trash bag, and headed out the door.

He followed, bumping me off balance as he pushed past to scratch at the backyard gate, eager for me to open it so that he could race me to the car. "No," I said, turning away and walking toward the south end of the house. "Knock it off. I have other things to worry about."

I knelt before the barricade in front of the crawlspace, unlatched and opened it. Recoiling from the smell, I pulled the bandana over my nose and mouth. "Oh, man," I uttered. "I don't want to do this."

Beside me, Odin whined, shifting from foot to foot. Then he backed off, sat down, and cocked his head in the way dogs have of seeming to say, "I don't know what you're doing, but I find it quite entertaining."

"Listen," I said. "If I were you, I wouldn't be so smug." I held up a gloved hand with the first finger and thumb an inch apart. "I'm this close to trading you in for a rat terrier."

I turned and, moving before I could change my mind, pushed my way into the crawlspace. There was more light than I had anticipated. The small screened ventilation openings allowed dust-mottled shafts of sunlight to filter through the shadowy interior.

I'd still need the flashlight, but not being in near darkness lifted my spirits a little.

As I had suspected, the low beams, water pipes, and furnace ducts made crawling on hands and knees impossible. With the flashlight in one hand and trash bag in the other, I had to pull myself into the space and squirm forward on my stomach, elevated only by my elbows and the toes of my boots.

I moved several feet inward before switching on the flashlight. I had swung the light over the ground ahead of me several times before I saw my first rat. It seemed to have partially burrowed into the ground with only its long tail and hindquarters showing.

Tugging at the trash bag, I pushed forward.

As I drew near the rat, I stopped, surprised by what lay before me. Scattered over the ground were large grains of rice. *What the hell?* I thought. *Where'd that come from?* Suddenly I realized that some of the grains were moving. It wasn't my imagination. They were moving. Squirmy, squishy blobs of white movement all around me. *Oh, no! Not rice. Maggots!*

They were everywhere. Their numbers ranged from individuals scattered over the ground to large wiggly piles, piles of maggots squirming over the bodies of dead rats I had to collect in my trash bag. Choking back a gag reflex, when I realized I would have to crawl over and through the maggots, I pulled myself forward.

When I was within arm's length from the semi-buried rat, I reached for its scaly tail and lifted the corpse from the dirt. This time I was not completely successful when I tried to keep from gagging. What I had lifted from the ground was not a rat. Well, not a complete rat, that is. Half a rat dangled from my fingers. Only a spear-like inch or so of backbone remained of the front half. Had decomposition happened this fast, or—I shuddered as I had this thought—had the trapped rats been cannibalizing their dead?

I dropped the half rat into my bag and squirmed forward.

\* \* \*

Nearly two hours later, I emerged from the crawlspace. Resisting the urge to brush the living and mashed maggots from my raingear, I carried the bag of rats and rat parts to the hole I had dug the day before and threw it in. Then, leaning over the pit, I brushed the maggots from my chest, arms, and legs and shook them from my boots.

I returned to the patio and cranked the faucet connected to my garden hose to full-blast position. Beginning at the top of my head, still covered by the naval watch cap, I poured the water over me, slowly working the spray down my raingear to the toes of my boots. Then, twisting and turning, I did the best I could to direct the spray down my back.

Next, I unlaced my boots, stumbled around on one leg and then the other as I pulled them off, and shrugged myself out of the raincoat and pants. I removed the watch cap, gloves, bandana, and socks and began the head-to-foot spray job all over again.

Finally I stripped to my boxer shorts and performed yet another open-air ablution. Then I stepped back into my boots, gathered the soaked clothing, and carried it to the gravesite. After dropping everything in the hole, I pulled the shovel from the dirt mound and buried the entire maggot-encrusted mess.

I walked back to the house, stepped out of my soaked boxer shorts, kicked them across the patio, opened the sliding glass door to my kitchen and stepped inside.

A few minutes later, I stood under a steaming shower, exhausted, not so much from the physical workout of dragging myself through the crawlspace as from the psychological strain of what I had endured there. I stayed in the shower until the water turned cold.

Then I stayed a little longer.

\* \* \*

Reliving that experience as I sit in my condo, I realize for the first time that the horror movie prompting this memory—Hitchcock's *Psycho*—and my own creepy story share a similarity: shower scenes. Naturally, my writer's psyche cannot help but blend the two into one.

I'm standing in the shower, head bowed, shoulders hunched, in a state of complete exhaustion. A shadowy figure slides into view behind the shower curtain. It's yanked aside, and there stands Norman Bates in his mother's clothing, knife raised above his head. But before he can begin slashing, cueing the WEEEK! WEEEK! WEEEK! soundtrack, I look over and say, "For crying in the beer, Norman, knock it off. I've had a tough enough day without having to deal with *you*. Put down that knife, take off that silly wig, and get back up the hill to your house."

Norman dejectedly turns and leaves the bathroom. I step from the shower and shout to his hunched back as he lumbers up the hall, "Hey, by the way, you probably have a few rat problems of your own in that spooky old place. If you ever need some help in that department, come around and see me. Because, boy, do I have the perfect rat poison for you."

# I FLUNK VALENTINE'S DAY

**Miss Pencil, my first-grade teacher**, invited the class to circle her desk as she demonstrated the three steps in our holiday project. First she folded a sheet of fibrous art paper, aligning the vertical edges, and creased the folded side. Next she drew what she called an angel's wing on the folded edge, a line that began at the fold, circled upward, and then narrowed downward. She picked up her scissors and cut the angel's wing from the folded paper. Smiling, she unfolded the wing. There before our eyes was a perfect Valentine's heart.

We returned to our desks, upon which we had placed our supplies of art paper, pencils, and scissors, and set out to produce our own perfect hearts. The best hearts would be used on our Valentine Day's bulletin board. Others, inscribed with our names and the names of favored classmates, would be dropped into a decorated Valentine box for later delivery.

Of course, Miss Pencil, being right-handed, had folded the art paper from the right to the left, and then, having drawn the angel's wing, cut along the lines with her right hand. All the little right-handers were able to imitate these movements, producing—if not perfect duplicates of Miss Pencil's heart—at least recognizable little hearts of their own.

I, however, being left-handed, struggled from the start. First, I had to reach across the sheet of paper and pull the right edge over to the left. Then I had to draw my angel's wing on that far side. Finally I managed to cut my way across the paper, left to right, until I reached the outline of my wobbly angel's wing. There I scrunched my left elbow against my ribcage to cut upward and then pointed the elbow toward the ceiling to cut downward. All the while using right-handed primary scissors, of course. You know the ones I mean. Stubbed-nosed scissors with cutting edges so dull that slicing warm butter would be a challenge. So what's the problem left-handers have with right-handed scissors? Because the upper blade is on the right side, left-handers cannot see the lines they are supposed to follow.

Having performed my acrobatic maneuvers with the right-handed scissors, I triumphantly unfolded my heart. What I held in my hands did not resemble Miss Pencil's pristine heart. It only remotely resembled the right-handers' less-than-perfect hearts. I looked with dismay at the ragged clump of art-paper pulp in my hands. My heart wouldn't be pinned on the bulletin board. It wouldn't be slipped into the Valentine box to be delivered to that cute blonde in the next row over.

I had flunked Valentine's Day.

If I accepted the idea that the heart is the center of emotion, I'd have to say my little seven-year-old heart had been broken. But I do not believe the heart has anything to do with emotion.

I've been called unromantic a number of times in my life because I take little interest in Valentine's Day. I'm sure my experience in Miss Pencil's class had something to do with my attitude, but I really have to say that thinking the heart does anything other than pump blood through the body is ludicrous. I know this because I have given an inordinate amount of time to researching matters of the heart.

I began questioning all we are told about our hearts when I discovered that the actual organ has only a slight resemblance to the Valentine version. It's a chunky, pear-shaped blob with rounded edges top and bottom. A collection of tubes obscures the top, and the bottom doesn't come to a neat point. In other words, my first-grade heart came closer to the real heart than Miss Pencil's oh-so-perfect cutout.

I had been duped.

I began a quest to discover why this organ has such a hold on romantic dealings, why we consider the heart the center of our emotions. What I discovered is that the heart has held this position since earliest man. I can understand how the idea started. Picture a Neanderthal, armed only with a spear, stalking a woolly mammoth. As he nears his prey, he feels his heart begin to beat faster, and he thinks his fear or his courage is being fueled by the heart. The earliest lovers felt their pulses race in the throes of passion. Surely love springs from the heart.

Well, no, it doesn't. The real control center of the body is the brain. The heart races in times of anxiety, fear, anger, or passion because the brain gears up the body's systems to meet the demands of the moment. We've known this for a long time. Yet we refuse to let go of the quaint romantic concepts of the heart. Why?

The answer seems to be that the brain simply isn't romantic enough. In fact, we usually separate the brain from emotion. To think with the mind seems coldly analytical. To think with the heart seems dramatically endearing. But the fact remains that the heart cannot think.

Okay, the heart can't think, but can it feel? How many times have we heard someone say, "Think with your brain, but feel with your heart"? Underlying that statement is the subtle suggestion that truth comes more readily from the heart. Through the ages, otherwise brilliant people have held to this belief. Aristotle, for example, flatly denied the importance of the brain, claiming the heart the seat of both reason and emotion.

The ancient Egyptians revered the heart but dismissed the brain as useless trash. When they prepared a body for mummification, they carefully removed all but one of the internal organs. They used their special salts to dry the removed organs and then either reinserted them into the body or placed them in pottery to be left in the burial vault.

The single organ left in its original position? The heart. All these organs were necessary for the deceased person's journey to the afterlife, but the heart was most important. They considered it the essence of a person, including his intelligence.

On the other hand, Egyptian scholars thought the brain existed only to produce mucus. Therefore, in preparing the body, they shoved a long hook up the nose and into the brain. After using the hook to scramble the brain into a liquid mush, they drained it through the nostrils and threw it away.

For the last couple of centuries, we've been aware of the brain's significance. Yet in our everyday language, we have relatively few idioms expressing admiration for it. In the meantime, we flood that same language with so many sayings related to the heart that we are nothing less than brainwashed.

What can the heart do? Here are a few of its accomplishments:

* It can change texture. A person who dismisses the plights of others is hardhearted. A person who loves puppies is softhearted.
* The heart can divide. Some people believe wholeheartedly in something. Others take a halfhearted approach.

* It can multiply. How often have you heard someone say, "I believe this in my heart of hearts"? This comment always makes me wonder how many hearts one person can have.
* The heart can be misplaced. Lovers claim to have lost their hearts to others. Tony Bennett croons about leaving his heart in San Francisco. Do you see how much more accepting we are of the heart than we are of the brain? What if he sang about leaving his *brain* in San Francisco? Doesn't seem reasonable, does it? Unless, of course, he was in the Haight Ashbury district in the '60s. Then it makes perfect sense.
* The heart can grow. Generous people have big hearts. The rest of us simply have regular-sized hearts, I suppose.
* Some people's hearts are more valuable than others. One can have a heart of gold, and another, a heart of stone.
* It can change weights. Some people are lighthearted, and others, heavyhearted.
* The heart can suffer seemingly major damage yet escape unscathed. Someone left at the altar is brokenhearted. Liberals are bleeding hearts. Taking an arrow through the heart is a good thing. Yes, I know. Cupid and all that. Still, I've always felt sending someone a picture of a heart pierced with an arrow seems more threatening than romantic.
* The human heart can become an animal heart. Cowards are chickenhearted. Heroes are lionhearted.
* It can move around inside and outside the body. A disappointed person feels his heart sink. Another wears his heart on his sleeve. Sometimes, however, the heart stays put. In that case a person has his heart in the right place.
* The heart has attached strings that express strong emotion. A person witnessing something sad feels a tug on his heartstrings. Frank Sinatra, feeling especially giddy, sang, "Zing went the strings of my heart."

Okay, that's enough of that. You get the picture. And I know what you're thinking. It's unfair to attack figurative language with literal interpretation. But that protection only extends itself to fresh, vivid figures of speech. When a figurative expression is so overused it becomes commonplace, it is merely a cliché.

As someone who loves clever language and has a built-in prejudice against Valentine hearts, I propose we junk all these hackneyed references to the heart. To do so, we will have to appoint some other organ as the figurative center of our emotions.

I know the brain won't be considered even though we understand that regulating emotion responses is one of its functions. Because we have assigned cool reasoning to the brain, using it to describe the heat of emotions would be difficult. We couldn't accept someone declaring he knows something in his brain of brains. And Frank would never have sung, "Zing went the strings of my brain."

Fortunately, throughout the ages, various scholars have championed body parts other than the heart as the center of emotion. I have worked my way through these possibilities and settled upon an organ I believe is the best candidate for the job.

I'd like to present a case for making this switch. If we do, we'll adopt figures of speech that are fresh, imaginative, and entertaining.

But what I like best about replacing the heart with this organ is that no little first-grader—not even a left-hander using right-handed scissors—will ever flunk Valentine's Day again.

So which organ have I chosen? Among the variety of body parts these scholars have identified as the center of emotion, the most common have been the stomach, the liver, and the bowels.

The stomach makes some sense to me. When our stomachs are full, we are content, even laid-back. But when our stomachs are empty, we often become irritable, edgy. Certainly these moods affect our emotions.

Also, like the heart, the stomach has slipped into the figurative language we use to describe emotions. When facing a decision, people are told to go with their gut feeling. A person who refuses to undertake a risky venture is denounced as not having stomach enough to do it. Nervousness is described as having butterflies in the stomach.

Nevertheless, I don't think the stomach is a good candidate to replace the heart as a symbol of affection. Too many of us dislike our stomachs. Otherwise, why would we pull them in whenever we're on public display in bathing suits? Also the stomach seems to threaten us at times. When we haven't placated it with food, it growls at us. No, we have too many negative feelings about the stomach to make it romantic.

As for the bowels, I'm not even going there.

But the liver? Ah, now we're on to something. In the first place, the liver is mysterious. How much do we know about our livers? Normally, we think about them only when they malfunction. Otherwise, they quietly go about their work without fanfare. We know little about them. But what we do know is that mystery and romance go hand in hand.

Go out on the street and ask ten people selected at random to draw a heart. You'll get ten identical stylized hearts. Those hearts that turned me against Valentine's Day when I was only seven years old. But ask ten people to draw a liver, and I suspect you'll get a collection of weird elliptical shapes, each only remotely resembling the others. Little left-handers could cut out these drawings with no problem. I suspect if I had been cutting out a Valentine liver instead of a Valentine heart, I very well could have pinned mine on the bulletin board or dropped it into the Valentine's box for delivery to that cute little blond in the next row over.

Also, I would not have hesitated sending her a liver with an arrow through it. When it comes to livers, let Cupid take his best shot. The liver is the only internal organ that can regenerate itself. A person can lose three fourths of his liver in an accident, and the remaining chunk will eventually grow into a fully functioning liver. Liver transplants don't necessarily involve dead donors. A slice of a living person's liver can be transplanted into a recipient, and both the donor liver and the slice in the recipient will regenerate. Now that's a body part that deserves elevation to a position of respect.

Imagine how switching from the heart to the liver will bring life to our language. We would really think about those idioms we use so carelessly when we refer to the heart. Substituting the liver into those expressions would startle and amuse. They would be entertaining.

* A young man doesn't propose to his sweetheart. He proposes to his sweet liver.
* A heart-to-heart talk becomes a liver-to-liver talk.
* People no longer memorize something by heart. They memorize it by liver.
* Someone facing a jealous person doesn't say, "Eat your heart out." He says, "Eat your liver out."
* An emotional person doesn't pour his heart out to another. He pours his liver out.

And on and on.

This change will be so much fun because it replaces washed-out clichés with fresh language. When a rejected boyfriend whines that his heart has been broken, we simply assume he is romantically depressed. But when he claims his *liver* has been broken, now that jars us a little, doesn't it?

And singers? Tony Bennett leaves neither his heart nor his brain in San Francisco. He leaves his liver there. Billy Ray Cyrus can whip his mullet around while singing about his achy breaky liver. And then there's Elvis, who could have sung:

> "Well, since my baby left me,
> I found a new place to dwell.
> It's down at the end of Lonely Street
> At Liverbreak Hotel."

And now we come to something that really annoys me. The worst thing the heart did to our language was the substitution of its stylized image for an actual word. After 9/11 we reached out to New York with compassion. Then the merchandisers got into the act, and soon people all over the States wore sweatshirts with Valentine hearts serving as the verb *love*. It symbolically read "I love New York." And I loved that shirt. I loved it until people began reading it as "I *heart* New York." I *heart* New York? Give me a break.

And then it spread. Now at Blazer games, screaming ladies hold up signs reading—well, I assume this is how they would read them—"I heart Nicolas Batum."

I blame all this linguistic damage on our obsession with the stylized Valentine's heart. It has so insidiously crept into our language that its mere picture can replace words.

Okay, the gauntlet has been tossed. Let's get the liver into the mix. I envision a sweatshirt with a big liver inserted between words above and below. Together the words and image will read, "I *liver* New York." At Blazer games those screaming ladies will hold up signs reading, "I *liver* Nicolas Batum." At least *that* would be fun.

So how about it? Have I convinced you? Will you join me in my campaign to save little left-handers the anguish of flunking Valentine's

Day and to save our language from lackluster imagery by breathing something fun and exciting into it?

If you do and we are successful in making this change, I guarantee I will join the ranks of people who celebrate Valentine's Day. No longer will I be called unromantic. On every Valentine's Day following this switch, I will bring home to Sue a bouquet of roses and a large liver-shaped box of chocolates.

I promise ... with all my liver.

# A LAUGH A DAY

**Never once during the thirty-three years** I taught high-school English did I regret my decision to change my college major from pre-law to humanities. Oh, I could have made more money in law, but I wouldn't have had as much fun. A day without laughter is a day wasted, and that is especially true in the classroom.

I enjoyed my students' vitality, their passion, their naiveté. Above all, I loved the fun we had together. I shamelessly entertained them, intermixing standup comedy with formal lecture. And they returned that entertainment in kind. They made me laugh even when they didn't intend to be funny.

Every once in a while, a student would say something or write something in all seriousness that would break me up. I'd be alone in my study, grading papers, and I'd laugh so hard that Sue would stick her head in the door and say, "Okay, what'd they write this time?"

At some point in my teaching career, I began to record these little tidbits and put them into a file. Here are some of my favorites.

---

Freshmen at the school where I taught most of my career had a demanding year-long project in which they were expected to produce a complicated, thorough autobiography. They interviewed relatives, gathered family photographs, and produced artwork. It was an invaluable experience on several levels, but it took excellent time-management skills. And they were, after all, freshmen. They procrastinated. Despite a series of deadlines from fall to spring, as the due date approached, they found themselves scrambling to finish the project on time.

One day in study hall, a freshman and a senior were talking near the teacher's desk. The harried freshman asked the senior, "When you were a freshman, did you have to write an autobiography?"

The senior thought for a moment and then replied, "Yes, but I can't remember who I wrote it on."

---

A student, writing about Shakespeare's *Julius Caesar* explained that the term *dictator* was actually a political title in the Roman Empire. In times of national emergency, a leader could assume the position of Dictator and do whatever necessary to save the Empire without regard to laws that had previously protected Roman citizens. However, until Caesar declared himself Dictator for Life, the position had term limitations. The student wrote, "In Rome the dictator could stay in office for six months. In America he can have four years."

---

The study of Shakespeare set up some nifty new definitions of staging terminology. I had described the soliloquy as an important dramatic tool because in this speech, delivered when the actor is alone on stage, Shakespeare's characters reveal their true motivations. Asked to define the term *soliloquy*, a student wrote, "A soliloquy is a speech in which an actor exposes himself."

---

In an exam on *The Adventures of Huckleberry Finn*, I asked, "What was the fate of Pap Finn?"

A student answered, "He was a Baptist."

---

Another explained the difficulty Ahab faced in Herman Melville's novel of the white whale. He wrote, "Ahab was having problems catching Mobile Dick."

---

For a time students were reading *The Cook*, a novel in which a sinister character kills people by feeding them copious quantities of very rich food. A student reviewing the book wrote, "Mr. and Mrs. Vale are found dead in bed of overindulgence."

––––––––––

And then there was the student in my Comparative World Religions class who explained this bit of Biblical history to me: "Abraham's wife Sarah was barren. But God got her pregnant."

––––––––––

Occasionally I received a new poetic term. A student, reaching for *iambic pentameter*, explained that "Edgar Allan Poe's 'The Raven' was written in "iambic contaminator." By the way, it wasn't written in iambic pentameter either.

––––––––––

One of my favorite lectures was a biographical sketch of Poe's life. At the conclusion of this lecture, I explained that Poe died under mysterious circumstances. On a business trip, he left Virginia bound for New York. However, somewhere along the way, he disappeared and was missing for several days.

Finally he was found lying unconscious in the streets of Baltimore. He was taken to a hospital, where doctors determined that he was in a coma. He remained in the coma until his death several days later. Blame for the coma has been placed upon everything from alcohol to mugging to rabies. In reality, no one really knows what happened to Poe during the time he was missing and what actually caused this death-dealing coma.

On my unit exam, I asked the students to discuss the circumstances of Poe's death. One student summed up my entire lecture in a single sentence: "Edgar Allan Poe died in Tacoma."

––––––––––

And whenever I become too full of myself, I have only to pull one of my favorites from the file. Students frequently wrote farewell notes at the conclusion of their final exams. One young man left me with the following: "I would just like to say that I have really enjoyed being one of your students, Mr. C. You are much more interesting than the other dumb teachers."

# FRITZ

**If there is a god for dogs,** he must have been drinking when he designed Fritz. Fritz had the head, body, and tail of an eighty-pound hunting dog. He had a hound's muscular legs and pan-sized feet. But the design problem was the *distance* between his upper body and his feet. Fritz's legs were the length of those found on a midsized dachshund. Over uneven ground Fritz had to suck in to keep his belly and private particulars from dragging. And belly and private particulars were two areas where the dog-god had especially blessed Fritz.

On the other hand, the god must have loved Fritz when he gave him his disposition. Fritz liked everyone, and everyone liked Fritz. And it was this reciprocal good will that allowed Fritz to exist as a free spirit in our little town.

Fritz belonged to no one, yet he belonged to everyone. He was our neighborhood dog. Fritz simply showed up one day. And he stayed. He was there when we arose in the morning, and he was there when we shut the doors at night.

Where Fritz slept was not really a mystery because the term "mystery" implies someone cares for the answer. But no one wanted that answer. To worry about where he slept—especially if that worry extended to which yard or which corner of a shed—would suggest proprietary interests. No one owned Fritz. Fritz inhabited our neighborhood because he had chosen it from various options in our town. Fritz was a given. He would be there in the morning, tail wagging in greeting, and he would take care of himself at night somewhere, somehow.

As for food, Fritz never went wanting. Neighbors kept Fritz-food by their backdoors. He visited homes according to his particular culinary desires for any given day. The Nelsons were good for ham and beans. The Sullivans frequently had leftover mashed potatoes and sparerib bones. Of course, any home with children had a surplus of cooked vegetables as well.

Sunday mornings guaranteed Fritz a late brunch of egg, bacon, and maple-flavored pancake scraps. Fritz greeted kids returning from Sunday school with a wagging tail that seemed to ask, "Did you give thanks for all your blessings? Did you put in a good word for me? Oh, and by the way, could you ask your mom not to mix in the green beans with the pancakes next time?"

\* \* \*

My clearest memories of Fritz revolve around the last couple of summers our gang had together before we fell into the monetary trap of strawberry fields, and at least two years before I began working summers in my father's sawmill.

This was the gang that found Old Man Morgan's body and demolished Jerry's sled on its inaugural run. Well, *I* demolished Jerry's sled. But the rest were there, so they deserve at least partial blame, don't you think? Anyway, we were still together. I, the eldest; Jerry; Harley, the boy who had spent a year in the Oregon School for the Deaf because of a green discharge from his ears; and Kenny of the red hair and freckles, the youngest of our group. Kenny, who pretended to be a follower but actually initiated almost every adventure successful or unsuccessful the gang undertook.

Fritz became the fifth member of the gang. Where we went, he went. Work-up games on the school baseball field? Fritz was there. Fritz chasing down balls that struck his fancy. Fritz dozing in left field. Fritz touching noses with other dogs and giving chase to orange cats along the first-base line.

A walk downtown for ice cream? Fritz was there. Big eyes pleading for a drop of vanilla, strawberry, or chocolate. Begging in his quiet way for that last little upside-down pyramid of soggy ice-cream-soaked cone.

The only times I ever saw Fritz reveal a sense of abandonment were the late afternoons when my family loaded our car for fishing trips. Every evening in the summer, we went fishing. My father would pull into the driveway, exchange his lunch bucket for his fly rod and creel, and slip back behind the wheel for the fifteen-minute drive to our favorite stretch of the Clackamas River. My mother, Jerry, and I had to be ready with our own fishing gear, or we didn't go.

No matter how thin Fritz spread himself in his duties as the official neighborhood dog, he always seemed to be in our front yard when my father backed the car from the driveway. Hounds look sad even when they're happy. But when they're truly sad, their faces fill with heart-wrenching despair. I would look at Fritz from the back window of the car, wishing we could take him with us. But my father would have scoffed at the idea. So I watched Fritz watch us, his tail no longer wagging, his red-rimmed eyes pleading, as we drove away.

Until Fritz's run as the free spirit of our neighborhood came to an end, those summer afternoons were the only times I felt sorry for him ... Except for that incident on Brady's boat dock when the gang discovered that Fritz was especially unique. For, you see, as far as I know, Fritz was the only dog in the world that could not swim.

* * *

A one-mile hike from our neighborhood took us to Estacada Lake. Like other so-called "lakes" on the Clackamas River, Estacada Lake is backed-up water from one of Portland General Electric's dams. Its deep green depths are lined with comfortable homes along the shore, houses with the obligatory docks for their obligatory boats. The gang swam off Brady's dock.

It was a hot August afternoon. After a couple hours of swimming, we languidly lounged on the planked dock, the sun warming us from the cold river water. Kenny stood apart from the rest of us, near the end of the dock, where Fritz lazily scratched one of his ears.

Fritz always went swimming with us, but Fritz never *swam* with us. Oddly this fact had not registered with anyone. Fritz was content to stretch out on the dock, to bark when we engaged in horseplay or worked on our belly flops and cannon balls. But Fritz never went into the water. Only after this day did we realize what should have been apparent: Fritz, a hound only in upper-body design, was top-heavy. Somehow, he knew this. Perhaps the dog-god had plugged a chip into Fritz's brain: "Don't go into the water. Only bad things can happen if you do."

As Fritz contorted his large upper body to reach his right ear with a stubby hind leg, Kenny remarked casually, "Fritz should take a swim." With that, he reached out with a foot and pushed Fritz off the dock.

A few moments later, Kenny looked over his shoulder at us and said, again in a casual tone as if he were commenting on the nice summer day, "He didn't come up."

The rest of us walked to Kenny's side and peered into the murky water stirred from the muddy bottom. When it cleared, we saw Fritz six feet below. He lay on his side, four feet moving methodically like Esther Williams in a slow-motion sequence. He struggled with what should have been panic but looked more like something from a pretentious foreign film: slow, dreamlike movements in a surreal world. A small stream of bubbles rose from his nostrils. And he didn't move. He didn't rise upward. He didn't inch forward. Except for the swimming motion of his four feet, he didn't move.

Finally Kenny suggested, "Maybe one of us should go in after him."

"It'll take more than one of us," I replied, staring in fascination at Fritz in that deep water, his feet moving, his left ear floating over his face.

"Right," Kenny answered. "On three?"

"On three," I agreed.

"One ... two ...," we recited in unison, "THREE!" With that, three of us dove off the dock. Harley had, of course, pulled back. He had learned early in life the dangers of impetuous action. Two older, self-centered sisters; a hypochondriac mother, who took to her bed for over two years when Harley needed her most; and a rebel father, who loved his motorcycle but not his family, a father who looked upon his sickly, frightened son as an embarrassment, a father who frequently dragged his eldest daughter into the woodshed to beat her with a club of firewood—this family had taught Harley to take the low road whenever circumstances demanded heroic action.

In the murky waters stirred by our arrival, I grabbed first an ear and then Fritz's neck, Kenny grabbed a front leg, and Jerry boosted the tail end. We rose to the surface, where Harley pulled as we lifted. At the end of our rescue operation, Fritz lay on the dock in the exact position he had displayed on the muddy bottom, his four feet moving in the same slow-motion rhythm.

The gang watched him for a minute or two. When the feet stopped moving and Fritz lay lifelessly still, Kenny suggested, "Maybe we should give him artificial respiration." Artificial respiration was all we had then. CPR with its mouth-to-mouth was a technique for future generations.

However, even if we had knowledge of CPR, I doubt any of us would have been willing to press a mouth against Fritz's heavy-tongued orifice as he lay there, bubbles oozing from his nostrils.

And then ... we heard a thump. Then ... a second thump. Then ... another and another and another in quick succession. Fritz's tail beating a tattoo on the dock. A couple minutes later, he struggled to a standing position. At first he swayed. But once he regained his equilibrium, he went into a sudden paroxysm, shaking water from his body in a violent spray that had us all stepping back as if everyone except Harley were not already wet. My brother took one too many steps, falling backward off the dock into the river. As the others stood there laughing, I knelt beside Fritz and wrapped an arm around his neck, craning my own neck away to avoid his slobbery gratitude at having been rescued.

\* \* \*

You want a happy ending for Fritz? Maybe I can give you one. A year or so after the Brady's-dock episode, a new couple in the neighbor adopted Fritz. Somehow, *adopted* doesn't seem the right word. *Confiscated* seems more accurate. They took him in and made him their own. They offered him the trappings of a family home. He had an indoors sleeping area. He had his own bowl. He rode off on excursions in their car.

There's your happy ending. But when the gang headed out for the baseball field with Fritz happily galloping by our side, we'd hear, "FRITZ. FRITZ, COME BACK HERE." We'd look over our shoulders to see the young bride standing in the street. Fritz would look up at us apologetically as if to say, "Guys, I really want to go, but you know how it is."

And we knew how it was. We would be selfish to want what we once had with Fritz. "Go on, boy. Get back there. You can come with us another time." Fritz would wag his tail sheepishly, turn, and lumber down the road.

Did I miss Fritz, the free spirit? Of course, I did. Do I blame him for selling out his freedom for security? Of course, I don't. Most of us have done that at some point in our lives. Still, I can't help but think of Fritz that day on Brady's dock.

Fritz didn't blame anyone for his near drowning. Instead he lavished gratitude upon those who had risked his life before saving it. And that innocence makes me wonder if the god who designed Fritz isn't, in some ways, superior to the god who designed man.

"One in the same," you respond. I wonder. I think of Harley's mother, whose preoccupation with her mysterious illnesses took precedence over a son so in need of affection and understanding. I think of his father, who beat his teenage daughter with a stick of firewood and trumped his wife's indifference with outright distain for his young son. I think of how nonchalantly we stood on that dock and watched our struggling friend on the muddy bottom of the Clackamas River. And I wonder.

Maybe the god who designed *man* drinks at times.

# STRANDED IN THE NILE VALLEY

**Phil stepped onto the highway** and turned north, facing the direction of Cairo. We could hear the car but could not see it. The long stretch of asphalt disappeared into a mist of heat waves above a mirage of water. The four o'clock desert sun had begun to cast shadows, but the ground was resisting the temperature change. The car sounded wound-out, pedal to the metal, typical Egyptian driving.

Fifteen minutes earlier, Phil had said to me, "I'm going to stop the next car, no matter what direction it's traveling. We have to get out of here."

"And how are you going to do that?"

"I'm just going to flag it down."

"Are you crazy? You've watched them come down this road. You'll be killed."

"I'm not spending the night out here," he answered.

"You just don't want to miss the movie."

"You do?"

I thought a moment. "You're right. Go for it."

A black dot appeared in the heat-wave mist. It became rectangular. Then it had wheels. It was coming fast, the engine screaming.

Phil raised his hands in a Richard-Nixon pose. He began waving them slowly.

The car was coming fast.

He began waving more quickly. The car was coming fast.

I ducked behind the rock outcropping upon which we had been sitting. An international incident was about to occur—two vacationing American teachers from Pakistan cause a major accident on the Nile River highway. I sincerely hoped Allah and Jehovah were, indeed, the same god.

---

How had we found ourselves in such a fix? Blame it on Sean Connery. We had been in Cairo for nearly a week. During that time the latest James Bond movie had been playing in one of the downtown theaters. Each day we had vowed to see the movie. And each night after an exhausting round of sightseeing, we had put off the movie for the next day. This was the last night of the movie's run. It was tonight or not at all.

Why were we so obsessed with an American movie when we were traveling in the land of the Pharaohs? Phil had just finished his fourth year of teaching in Pakistan; I, my second. Our colony theater showed two movies a week. Their taste ran to dry black-and-white English comedies and noisy Japanese sci-fi flicks. To this day I cannot hear the sound track of a Godzilla movie without preparing to stand for the Pakistani national anthem at its conclusion. We *had* to see this movie.

Phil and I were on a dream vacation: Kenya with stopovers in Egypt and Ethiopia. We had planned this trip for several months after signing our extension contracts in Pakistan. Kenya, land of the lions. When would either of us ever again have such an opportunity?

Our flight from Karachi had arrived in Cairo after midnight. The single customs official was asleep at his counter and not very happy to be shaken awake so that we could pass through his station.

With passports stamped and luggage inspected, we took a cab downtown, where we checked in at the Cairo Hilton. Sounds a little pretentious, doesn't it? The Cairo Hilton. Unfortunately there are two classes of travel in the Middle East: first class and no class. I have traveled throughout Europe staying in bed-and-breakfasts that charged five dollars a night. I have spent time in beautiful homes in the Greek islands for two dollars a night. But the Middle East? That's a different story.

We did cut our expenses by staying on a yacht moored at the Hilton pier on the Nile. The small cabin saved us money over the cost of rooms in the main hotel. Okay, I admit this sounds like a cop-out, but the yacht really *was* cheaper.

We had planned on four days in Cairo before flying on to Addis Ababa. However, our stay was extended because of that bane of the Middle East: the little authority figure with his hand out—not to shake, but to take. Throughout the region, it was called *baksheesh,* money to grease the wheels.

On the morning of our third day, we called the airport to reconfirm our flight to Ethiopia. In America this is a courtesy call, ignored by most travelers. But in Africa and Asia it is an absolute necessity. Not reconfirming can lead to seats being resold, a real shock when careless travelers arrive at the airport to find they no longer have valid tickets.

Phil and I were seasoned travelers. We took care of business. So when we returned to the hotel after a day exploring Old Cairo—a labyrinth of narrow, crooked streets packed with small shops and bazaars in the shadows of centuries-old fortress walls, mosques, and Coptic churches—we were surprised to find a message asking us to call the Pan Am ticket counter at the airport.

Our call was transferred to the office of a Mr. Ali. He explained in clipped, precise English that there was a problem with our tickets, a problem so complicated it required a face-to-face explanation.

"It's late," Mr. Ali said. "I was about to go home. But I live near the Hilton. Maybe we could meet at the hotel to discuss this problem."

Two hours later we sat in one of the hotel lounges, sipping bottled lemonade in deference to our Muslim visitor. Mr. Ali was a small man in a black suit and white shirt with an extremely narrow black tie. His narrow pant legs ended at the ankles. Pointy black shoes completed his ensemble.

"So, what's the problem with our tickets, Mr. Ali?" Phil asked.

Mr. Ali smiled. "You bought your tickets in Pakistan, and you paid with Pakistani rupees."

"Yes, we did," Phil patiently responded. "We live and work in Pakistan."

"Yes," Mr. Ali said, dabbing with a cocktail napkin at his perfectly trimmed little mustache. "I'm afraid the exchange rate on the rupees was miscalculated."

"What do you mean, miscalculated?"

"There are two exchange rates for Pakistani rupees," he replied. "The world-market exchange gives ten rupees for every American dollar. But the national rate of Pakistan is only 4.75 rupees for every American dollar."

I glanced at Phil, but he was as impassive as if he were hearing a dry economics professor at a very boring dinner table. I tried to assume the same look of disinterest.

"We know all this, Mr. Ali," Phil said, placing his glass on a coaster.

"Perhaps. But you must realize that you bought tickets for an international flight aboard an international carrier. That means your agent should have used the international exchange, not Pakistan's artificially manipulated rate."

"So what does this mean?" I asked.

"It means, sir, you have not paid the complete fare. You must pay the difference between the price computed by your agent and the price he should have charged you."

"And that difference is?"

"You bought tickets for half the money you should have paid, I'm afraid. The difference is approximately the price you originally paid." He smiled and sipped his lemonade, watching us over the rim of his glass.

"Let me see if I understand this correctly, Mr. Ali," Phil replied. "You're saying our tickets are no good unless we pay once again the price we already paid for them?"

"You understand perfectly, sir," Mr. Ali smirked.

Phil leaned forward, placing both elbows on the table. Mr. Ali pulled back into his chair. "Even if you are correct, we can't do that," Phil said. "We don't have the money."

"Of course you can pay it," Mr. Ali smiled. "You're Americans."

"We're *poor* Americans, Mr. Ali. We're schoolteachers."

Mr. Ali's eyes widened, and he smiled. "You're teachers!" he exclaimed, genuinely pleased. "We revere teachers in our country. You are very important people." He paused and then added, "As such, you deserve special consideration."

He looked over his shoulder, leaned forward, and said in a lowered voice, "Perhaps I can help you with your dilemma. I know some people who might be able to reduce the cost of your tickets. Maybe I should talk to these people." He waited with an expectant, eyebrow-raised look.

I turned to Phil and did not like what I saw. His face had darkened. He had that on-edge look that meant trouble. I started to say something, but he interrupted. "And those friends of yours they would need to be compensated, of course."

"Well," Mr. Ali replied, "they would be doing some things that might get them into trouble. It would only be right to pay them for this trouble. But," he continued, "I would take care of that for you. You could pass this compensation on to them through me. No one else would have to be directly involved." He smiled and leaned back as if all our troubles were solved.

"No," Phil said.

"Sir?" Mr. Ali asked, coming upright in the chair.

"No" Phil repeated. "We are not paying *baksheesh*. I have paid enough *baksheesh* in Pakistan. I don't intend to pay it here for tickets we purchased in good faith. I don't know who you are, but I know *what* you are. No *baksheesh*."

"I am insulted, sir," Mr. Ali replied with a hurt look. "I was merely trying to help you. If you do not want my help, you have only to say so. You do not need to insult me."

I leaned over to Phil. "Take it easy," I whispered. "We don't know who this guy is or how much pull he has."

"No *baksheesh*," Phil muttered, glaring across the table at Mr. Ali, who turned to me in recognition that all might not be lost.

His look became conspiratorial. "I have not even mentioned your lack of a certificate of origin."

"Now what?" Phil demanded.

"You have not provided a certification of origin for the rupees you spent on the tickets."

"Don't know what you're talking about," Phil said.

"Do you have Egyptian money now?" he asked.

"Yes, we do," I replied before Phil could answer.

"And when you exchanged your American money for that money, you were given a paper, yes?"

"Yes," I answered. "We have receipts."

"Well," he said, rubbing the palm of a hand with a cocktail napkin, "when you spend that money, you can be asked to show that paper. And if you want to exchange that money back into American dollars, you must provide that paper."

"We know all that," I answered. "So what's your point?"

"That paper is a certificate of origin. In a country like Pakistan where the official exchange is so far removed from the world market, foreigners spending rupees must be able to prove they acquired those rupees legitimately. Otherwise ..." he leaned across the table, smirking ..."otherwise those persons might be accused of something highly illegal. You have a colorful word for that in your wonderful American idiom."

Phil leaned forward again, forcing Mr. Ali to retreat into his chair. "And what is that word, Mr. Ali?"

"*Black market*, sir. That word is *black market*."

"Actually," I interjected, "That's two words."

"What?" he asked, turning to me.

"Two words. *Black market* is two words."

Mr. Ali reacted as if I had struck him. This pompous little man with his almost-perfect English and fastidious mannerisms had been in charge of the entire conversation. He was a man used to being in charge. And suddenly he was not.

He stood up. "I apologize, sir," he said, staring at me with absolute hatred. "My English is sometimes faulty. I appreciate your correction. I would like to stay for more language lessons, but I must go." He turned away and then turned back. "But before I do, I want to remind you I offered my help. You did not take it. Your tickets are invalid. I have recorded your departure date for Addis Ababa, and you may be sure I will notify the proper authorities these tickets are invalid. *Invalid*, sir. I believe *that* is one word." He pivoted and walked away.

I looked at Phil. "Now *that* was a hell of an exit speech!"

Phil laughed. "'Two words'? You had to say, 'Two words'?"

"Sorry. But he's such a pretentious little twit. And I have to admit his talking about black-market rupees made me nervous. I don't know how you paid for your tickets, but I bought mine with good old midnight rupees."

"Is there any other way?" Phil grinned.

We sat a minute or so without talking. Then I asked, "What now?"

"Well, I don't know about you," Phil answered, motioning to the waiter who had served our lemonades, "but *I'm* going to have a Scotch."

"That's what I like about you, Phil," I laughed. "No matter what the question, you always have the right answer."

* * *

At ten o'clock the next morning, Phil and I stood outside the downtown Pan Am office, waiting for them to open for business. We had decided to take a proactive approach to the problem of Mr. Ali.

"We have to do an end run around this guy," Phil had said as we discussed our situation over a second Scotch in the hotel lounge. "We really don't know how much clout he has, but he's pretty ticked off. I suspect he'll do whatever he can on his threat to invalidate our tickets."

"I agree. I think our best bet is to find someone at Pan Am to help us. I can't believe they condone people like Ali operating scams in their system."

"Sounds good," Phil said. "But I'm worried about one thing."

"What's that?"

"What if Ali's right about the wrong exchange rate for the tickets or even our need to produce a certificate of origin for the rupees we used? Won't we just shaft ourselves by bringing this to the attention of higher-ups at Pan Am?"

"Well, you could be right. But aren't we shafted either way? Who would you most prefer shafting us—Ali or ourselves?"

Phil grinned. "I wouldn't give him the satisfaction."

"Me either. So it's Pan Am first thing tomorrow?"

"First thing tomorrow," Phil agreed.

\* \* \*

"Good morning," greeted the young Egyptian at the ticket counter. "How may I help you?"

"We need to speak to a supervisor," Phil replied.

"Yes, sir, but maybe *I* can help you with your problem."

"I doubt it. Our problem is complicated."

"I'm sure it is, sir, but I am well trained."

"Okay, then. Here it is. We have tickets for tomorrow morning's flight to Addis Ababa. But when we check in at the airport, we may not have those tickets."

"You plan to lose your tickets?"

"No, we don't plan to lose our tickets. But they may not be any good tomorrow."

"You have the wrong date on your tickets?"

"No, we don't have the wrong date on our tickets. See. I told you. It's complicated."

"Listen," I said, stepping around Phil. "Here's the deal. There's this guy threatening to invalidate our tickets unless we pay him money."

"I don't understand. How can he invalidate your tickets?"

"Because he's in your system, that's how. He seems to have some pull, and he's using it to extort us."

"I'm sorry," the agent replied. "I don't know that word *extort*. What is its meaning?"

"It means *blackmail.*"

Phil tapped me on the shoulder. "*Blackmail,* Bob—would that be one word or two?"

"I believe it's one."

"Just checking," Phil grinned.

He elbowed me aside. No longer grinning, he put his hands on the counter and leaned toward the agent. "Here's a word you *will* understand. *Baksheesh.* Get it? The guy wants *baksheesh,* or our tickets are out the window."

"That doesn't sound like something I can help you with," the agent sniffed.

"Really!" Phil shouted. "Isn't that what I said when we began this conversation? I told you we have a complicated problem. You say you can't help us. At least now all *three* of us understand that. We need to discuss our problem with someone several pay levels above yours. All you have to do is get us to that person. Is that really so hard?"

The agent didn't answer. Instead he began shuffling through a stack of paperwork, indicating that, as far as he was concerned, our conversation had come to an end.

"Look," I said. "I can see you're really busy. You have an important job here, and there are people waiting." I thumbed over my shoulder at a couple who had come in behind us and, after hearing Phil's outburst, were inching toward the door. "Isn't there a supervisor, a manager, someone like that who can take us off your hands, leaving you free to help these people?"

Relieved by this offer of a way to save face, the young agent replied, "Let me call Mr. Murphy's office. I think I saw him come in this morning."

"There," Phil said in a soothing voice. "Now that wasn't so hard, was it?"

Ignoring Phil, the agent said to me, "This will take a moment. Could you please wait over there?" He pointed to a couple of chairs some distance from his counter.

"Did you hear the name of the guy he's calling?" Phil asked as soon as we sat down. "*Murphy*, that's what he said. Means we're going to be dealing with an American." We had discussed the possibility we might simply be substituting one Mr. Ali for another when we appealed our case.

"Could be Irish," I suggested.

"I don't care if he's Mongolian as long as he isn't another sleaze in pointy shoes," Phil replied.

"Hey, look" I whispered, nodding to the ticket counter. The young couple had left, and the agent was talking on his phone, occasionally glancing toward us. "We may be making some headway."

"Hope so," Phil answered. "But the way you abused that poor little guy, he's probably calling security."

"*Me*? You're the one who yelled at him."

"I never yell," Phil replied. "I talk in a somewhat forceful manner at times, but I never yell."

"Yeah, well, see if you can keep that forceful manner under control because here he comes."

The agent had hung up the phone and was heading our way.

He stopped in what must have seemed a safe distance from us and said in a carefully measured tone, "I have consulted with Mr. Murphy. He will see you. His assistant will arrive shortly to gather you and take you to his office." With that, he pivoted and walked away.

I turned to Phil. "Did you hear that? We're gonna be gathered."

"Well," Phil replied, staring over my shoulder, "Hope *that's* the person who's going to gather us."

I looked back. Just inside an arched entryway from the interior of the building stood a strikingly beautiful Egyptian woman. She took a few steps forward and then stopped, raising a hand to signal the front desk. I looked back in time to see the agent point at us and then quickly drop his hand when he realized I had seen him. Phil, in the meantime, had not taken his eyes off her. She smiled as she walked toward us.

"Gentlemen, My name is Amina. I am Mr. Murphy's administrative assistant. Unfortunately, just after he received your request to meet with him, Mr. Murphy was called away. I apologize for this inconvenience. However, he indicated he'd return shortly and asks if you would wait in my office."

When neither of us answered, she continued, "I assure you, our furniture is much more comfortable than those chairs. I hope you will allow me to show you the way."

"Thank you," I finally blurted.

As we followed Amina down a hall of closed office doors, Phil nudged me and mouthed, "*Wow!*"

"*I know*!" I mouthed back.

\* \* \*

We spend the next forty minutes relaxing in overstuffed leather chairs every bit as comfortable as Amina had promised. Across from us, she worked at her desk, occasionally looking up to smile and assure us Mr. Murphy should arrive at any time.

I thumbed through a month-old copy of the *International Herald Tribune*. Meanwhile, Phil pretended interest in a *National Geographic* while surreptitiously watching Amina.

"Look, Phil," I said, nudging him. "No blacked-outs." In Pakistan our copies of the Paris edition of the *Tribune* arrived marred by thick black lines of ink painstakingly hand-drawn through articles found offensive by Pakistani censors.

When he didn't answer, I leaned over and whispered, "Did you forget you're married?"

"That doesn't mean I can't look," he replied, watching as Amina rose, walked to a file cabinet across the room, pulled a folder, and carried it back to her desk.

"Yeah, but you're not just looking. You're ogling."

"I'm what?"

"Ogling."

"Ogling?"

"Yeah, you know. Ogling. It means looking lustfully at ..."

"I *know* what it means," he interrupted. "But it's a word that probably hasn't been used for over fifty years. *Ogling*. What are you, my grandmother?"

"Say what you want," I countered, "but you are *definitely* ogling."

"Pardon me," Amina interrupted, standing by her desk as she hung up the phone. "Mr. Murphy will see you now."

* * *

Except for being American, Mike Murphy was nothing like what I had expected. In a country where businessmen wear tailored suits, he greeted us at the open door of his office in a faded polo shirt, Levis, and scuffed boat shoes.

Mike extended his hand as he introduced himself, gripping mine with a strong American handshake. Since many Muslims consider firm handshakes acts of rudeness, I had spent the last two years experiencing one "dead-fish" handshake after another. Strange how the simple act of a good handshake could be such a reminder of home.

"Pardon the mess," Mike, said stepping aside to allow us entry into the office. It *was* a mess. Packing boxes, some opened, some not, cluttered the room. A large desk overflowed with what appeared to be framed certificates and photographs as well as loosely stacked notebooks and file folders.

"Here," Mike said, brushing wads of crushed packing paper from two overstuffed leather chairs, twins to those we had occupied in Amina's office. "Make yourselves comfortable." He pushed aside some of the clutter on his desk and leaned back against it.

"Sorry about all this. I'm not officially in today. But I needed some uninterrupted time to clear away this mess. Looking at me, you probably thought this was casual Friday or something."

"No problem, Mr. Murphy," I answered. "We appreciate your meeting with us when you're obviously so busy."

"It's Mike," he smiled. "And I needed a break anyway."

"Don't you have people to do whatever it is you're doing in here?" Phil asked. Neither of us could imagine anyone with a power position in Pakistan doing what appeared to be menial tasks.

"Oh, these are all my personal things. I was transferred to Cairo five weeks ago, and this stuff is just catching up with me."

"So you've been in Cairo only five weeks?" Phil asked. I knew what he was thinking. Mike Murphy had not been in the Middle East long enough to understand the nuances of the culture, especially something like *baksheesh* or the pervasiveness of corruption in general. We had brought our problem to a neophyte.

"Well, yes, I've been here only five weeks *this* time," Mike answered, "but I've been posted here before. Actually Cairo was my first international assignment with Pan Am. I ended up spending nearly two years here."

He hesitated a moment to let this information sink in and then continued. "Since then I've hopped around some. Spent a little over a year in Istanbul, eighteen months in Hong Kong, a cold winter and spring in Oslo and an absolutely tremendous two years in Paris. Now there's a city I could live in the rest of my life."

While Mike talked, I began to realize how really sharp he was. In a casual, off-the-shoulder chatty manner, he had actually listed his credentials, letting us understand he knew both how Pan Am operated in general and, more importantly, how they dealt with different cultures around the world. In short, we had hooked up with exactly the person we needed.

"So, you came here from Paris?" Phil asked.

"Oh, no. The company usually has us come home for a while between international postings. I spent this last year in New York. I figured to be there longer, but when this job opened, I jumped at it. I love Cairo. It's not Paris, but it's a fascinating city in its own right."

He pushed more of the clutter aside, making room to sit on the desk. Folding his arms across his chest, he said, "But enough about me. I understand you two have a problem. Tell me what's going on."

* * *

Mike Murphy turned out to be a good listener. He didn't interrupt us with questions as we summarized our encounter with Mr. Ali. After we had finished, he studied us a moment and then said, "Well, offhand, I don't know if this Ali character works for us, but if he doesn't, he knows someone who does because his information is right on."

"Meaning?" I asked.

"Meaning he's right. If the exchange rate used for your tickets was based upon Pakistan's artificially jacked-up rate, you really did get them at what amounts to an unrealistic fifty-percent discount. That's not something I can see Pan Am simply dismissing."

"It wasn't our fault," Phil objected.

"Probably not," Mike agreed. "And I'm going to see what I can do to help you, but you have to be prepared for disappointment."

Without glancing Phil's way, I could sense his sinking deeper into his chair. This trip floated right near the top of both our bucket lists, and we seemed on the verge of losing it.

When neither Phil nor I responded, Mike stood up and walked around his desk, where he picked up his telephone. "Listen, guys. I meant it when I said I'd do what I can to help. But I need to make some phone calls and will probably have to go up the hall to talk one of our number-crunchers. I suspect I'll need at least an hour before I can give you any answers. You can wait in Amina's office if you wish, or go out and walk around a little. Take in some of the local scenery."

"We'll wait in Amina's office," Phil said, standing up. "Can't beat the scenery there."

Mike seemed puzzled for a moment before he understood. "Oh, you mean Amina."

"Yes," Phil replied, smiling for perhaps the first time since we had entered Mike's office. "She's ... well, she's a knockout."

"Uh huh," Mike nodded. "Yes, she is. But flirting with her might not be a good idea."

Phil asked. "What's wrong with a little harmless flirtation?"

"Well," Mike answered, glancing at his wristwatch, "what's wrong is that her husband frequently drops in within the next hour or so to take her to lunch."

"Oh, she's married?"

"Not just married. He's a member of the Egyptian Olympic wrestling team."

When Phil didn't answer, I asked, "Whadda ya think, Phil? Still choosing Amina's office over checking out the neighborhood?"

* * *

Surprisingly, Phil's choice remained Amina's office. But as we sat in the leather chairs, thumbing through a couple of brochures extolling the advantages of flying with Pan Am, I noticed Phil had toned down his admiration of Amina.

"I'm surprised you wanted to wait here in spite of Mike's warning about her husband," I said in a low voice.

"My reason had nothing to do with Amina."

"Really? What was it then?"

"The clock's ticking," Phil replied, tossing his brochure onto a side table. "Ali's probably pulling strings as we sit here. I'm too nervous to go walking around town without knowing what's happening. I want to be here when Mike gets back from whatever he's doing. What if we fouled up by laying all this out to a Pan Am guy? Isn't that exactly what I was afraid of when we talked about coming here?"

"I think we've done the right thing, Phil. What else were we going to do? Mike seems to be on our side."

"Yeah, he does to me, too, but what if these people he's calling don't agree? And he didn't even mention that certificate-of-origin bit. If our rupees aren't any good, we might be stuck here. Has that crossed your mind?"

"No, it really hasn't. Think about it, Phil. Pan Am is a big operation, no doubt about it, but we work for an American company with major international clout of its own."

"You're telling *me* about the company?" Phil responded. "I was working for them when you couldn't find Pakistan on a map."

"True," I smiled. "But think about what the company's done. They've built a showcase community in the middle of nowhere. And our school is their pride and joy. They won't leave us stranded in Egypt. They'll bail us out if we get stuck here."

"What makes you so sure of that?"

"Think about it. We might be in some trouble, but they can't afford to lose a pair of popular, talented English teachers like us just because we engaged in the nefarious practice of spending some black-market rupees."

"You might be right," Phil grinned. "Only you forgot *handsome*."

"What? Oh, right. A pair of popular, talented, and *handsome* English teachers like us."

Phil's mood continued to lighten as he watched Amina make another trip to the file cabinet.

Forty minutes later, the office door opened, and Mike leaned in. "Hey, guys, how about some lunch? I'm buying."

I looked at Phil, who nodded. "You're buying?" I asked. "Mike, you just said the magic words."

* * *

136

A giant sycamore shaded the interior courtyard of Mike's favorite neighborhood restaurant. I leaned back from our table and looked through the light-filtering leaves at a brilliant blue sky. Several strings of small lights were woven through the lower branches.

"I'll bet this is really pretty at night," I commented, still looking up. The courtyard walls muted the street sounds—blaring horns, shouting vendors, and braying donkeys.

"It probably is," Mike replied. "I've never been here in the evening because I live across town, but most of the city's restaurants take on a special flair at night, especially those with courtyards like this. Egyptians are desert people. They love their oases, and in their homes and public places, these courtyards *are* their oases."

Mike sipped tea from a small glass in a brass container. Phil and I drank our usual bottled water. Mike had ordered for all of us, using terms we didn't recognize while he pointed to items on the menu, the waiter looking over Mike's shoulder and scribbling on a small pad.

"He's disappointed," Mike commented as the waiter walked away. "We're probably his first customers, and we're eating lightly by Egyptian standards." I looked around at the empty tables. We were the only people in the courtyard.

"It's early," Mike said, reading my look. "In an hour or so this place'll fill up. Like most people on the Mediterranean, Egyptians eat their big meals at midday and then go home or back to their shops, close the doors and sleep for a couple of hours." He added a drop of honey to his tea. "The town pretty much shuts down," he continued. "Then they go back to work until late in the evening. That's when Cairo really comes alive."

"Mike," Phil interrupted, "can we talk about our situation?"

"Egyptians don't talk business over a meal," Mike replied. "That comes with the coffee. Why not wait and enjoy our lunch?"

"We're not Egyptians!" Phil barked. But his look turned from anger to sheepishness as he realized how unwarranted his outburst had been in light of Mike's hospitality. "Sorry. I guess you're right. When in Egypt, do as . . . Well, you know."

"Good," Mike smiled. "I think you're going to enjoy what I ordered."

\* \* \*

Lunch turned out to be roasted pigeons stuffed with rice, onions, and various spices we couldn't identify. A large bowl of additional rice, curly pasta, and lentils accompanied the main course.

"Wow, Mike," I said leaning back with a small pigeon rib for a toothpick. "I can't believe you called this a light lunch."

Mike shifted from the table as three young men in aprons cleared the dishes. "Light by Egyptian standards," he smiled.

Our waiter returned with a tray of miniature cups in saucers. "Ah," Mike sighed. "Egyptian coffee. Almost as good as Turkish."

Phil picked up his cup, sipped, and returned it to the saucer. "So this is coffee?" he asked.

"Well, it's a little strong by American standards," Mike replied.

"No. I wasn't complaining. But if this is coffee, then it's time to talk about our situation."

"Okay, Phil," Mike answered. "Let's talk about your situation."

By this time the restaurant had several customers, and at Mike's suggestion, we moved to a smaller table near the courtyard wall. "Egypt gave the world two very significant products," Mike said, reaching into his briefcase and pulling out a yellow pad. "Paper is one and I have that. The other is beer. We don't have that. Want to try a local brew while we work this out?"

"No, thanks," I replied. "We don't drink local beer."

"Really? Why not?"

"Our local beer in Pakistan is called Murree beer, and it's almost guaranteed to give you a case of the Jehlum Waltz."

"The Jehlum Waltz? I assume that's your version of amebic dysentery."

"It's not just a version. It's the mother of all amebic dysentery."

"Why *Jehlum*?"

"Jehlum is a nearby village where our bearers sometimes shop for produce and meats," I replied. "Most Westerners go to the food bazaar only once. After that they're content to send their bearers. We treat everything they bring back with all kinds of stuff and cook the hell out of it, but the Waltz still hits us on a regular basis."

"This food bazaar is bad, huh?"

"When a meat seller has to sweep away a swarm of flies before you realize the black mass hanging from a hook is, indeed, a cut of meat, it's bad. The bazaar swarms with flies. They're such a basic part of Pakistanis' lives they don't even notice them."

"You might say the same thing about flies here," Mike observed.

"Maybe, but I'm not sure it's as bad. One time I was buying oranges from a guy, and I watched a fly dab at the corner of one of his eyes, move down his face, ascend into a nostril, and return to his upper lip to search for goodies in his mustache. And you know what? The guy never indicated in any way he was aware of this thing crawling up his nose.

"The standing joke," I continued, "is that Pakistan should declare the fly its national bird."

"Okay," Mike replied, grinning, "but why the Jhelum *Waltz*?"

"Because its victims walk bent over in a weird shuffling gait. You can see them coming, and you can smell them. They emit horrible gasses from both ends. A single belch can clear a room."

"You win," Mike laughed. "The Jhelum Waltz is the mother all amebic dysentery. But I've been drinking the local beer without any problem since my first assignment in Cairo. It's called Stella beer, and it's really quite good as long as it's not left out in the sun too long. Egyptians have a bad habit of that."

"Thanks anyway, but we'll pass."

"You know, guys," Phil interrupted, "I'm really enjoying this little chat about the merits of beer and dysentery, but might it be possible… *might it just be possible* we could talk about our situation!"

"You're right," Mike replied. "Sorry. I guess I've never before had an enjoyable discussion of dysentery."

Phil didn't smile.

Mike pulled his pad closer. "Okay, here's the way I figure it. Pan Am isn't going to ask you for any money back. They'll honor any flying you've already done on these tickets. But the company's not going to let you go on to Nairobi without an additional payment. And that additional payment would be substantial, I'm afraid. I think we should cash out the remaining value of your tickets at the proper exchange rate and use the balance to plan your trip home."

Phil began to slump in his chair.

"Oh, you don't have to go straight home," Mike continued, looking at Phil. "You have all this time planned for the trip, and you can take as many layovers as you want on the way back. Between here and Pakistan, you can hit several great cities."

Phil didn't respond. His disappointment pushed him deeper into his chair.

"In fact," Mike said, reaching into his briefcase for a small notebook, "I think you'd have enough to start with a side trip somewhere off the direct path to Karachi."

"What kind of side trip?" I asked.

"Well, I'm looking," responded Mike, running his finger down a page in the notebook. "Obviously, you can't go south or west without costing more money. But you could go north a ways before turning toward Pakistan." He stopped at one entry in his listing and tapped his pencil on the table as he read.

"No," he sighed. "I was hoping I could give you Rome, but I can't." Then sliding his finger down the page, he said, "But I could give you Athens."

"Athens?" Phil said, sitting up. "You can give us Athens?"

Mike looked over and nodded. "Yeah, Athens would work."

"Athens," Phil grinned. "Athens is one of my favorite cities in the whole world! I *love* Athens!" he exclaimed, turning to me. "Bob, I *love* Athens!"

"Yes, Phil, I know you do. You've told me more than once how much you love Athens."

"And we have lots of time," Phil continued. "We could do some island hopping. Get out to Mykonos. Slide over to Delos for a day."

I looked at Mike, who was grinning. *Mike*, I thought, *you certainly pushed the right button this time.*

"Whadda ya think, Bob?" Phil asked.

"I've never been to Greece. I think it'd be great."

"Athens," Phil mused as he settled back into his chair. "It's not Nairobi, but it isn't shabby."

* * *

By the time we left the restaurant, Phil was his usual ebullient self. Greece had turned the trick.

"You'll need to extend your stay in Cairo," Mike had said. "It'll take a couple of days to put this together. Besides, I suspect this Ali character is going to be lurking around your check-in counter tomorrow. In fact, I think I'll go over there just to see if I can spot him. This probably won't be the last time I have to deal with this guy. In the meantime, this'll give you a chance to see some of the valley. Most tourists spend their time in the city and Giza. These are great, of course. But they miss out by not venturing into the valley with its outstanding historical sites."

"Yeah," Phil replied. "We can go down to Saqqara. Whadda ya think, Bob?" Phil and I had talked about visiting Saqqara, the site of the famed Stepped Pyramid, but we didn't have time on our original schedule.

"Sure," I answered. "That'd be great."

The final plans worked out with Mike gave us twelve days in Greece, four days in Istanbul, and three days in Beirut. From Beirut we'd fly to Karachi, where we'd connect with Pakistan Airlines for an in-country flight home.

On the street in front of the restaurant, I extended my hand to Mike. "We really appreciate what you've done for us."

"Hey, no problem," he replied, sidestepping a couple of donkeys that had taken sanctuary in the shade of the restaurant wall. "So what are you going to do with the rest of the day?"

"We're going to Giza," Phil answered.

"Oh, you haven't been there yet?" Mike looked at his watch. "You know, you'd be better off to wait a couple of hours. That'd give you time to see everything and put you there for the sound-and light show. That's a great experience."

"Nah," Phil replied. "We need to get back early. There's a movie in town we want to see."

"A movie? You'd pass up the sound-and-light show at Giza for a movie?"

"Mike," I said, "how many Godzilla movies have you seen?"

He thought a moment. "I don't think I've seen any."

"Well, we've seen them all. The latest James Bond movie's in town. We're gonna see it."

"Okay," Mike answered after a pause. "I'm not sure I understand, but okay, I guess."

"Besides," Phil said, "a sound-and-light show? Sounds a little hokey."

"*Hokey*?" Mike smiled. "Is that a word you teach in your English classes?"

"Yeah, it is, Mike," I replied. "It comes just a couple of lessons before *ogle*."

"I'm sorry. I don't get it."

"It has something to do with Amina," I answered, nodding toward Phil.

"Oh," Mike smiled. "You didn't, did you?"

"Didn't what?" Phil asked.

"Didn't ogle."

"Of course, I didn't. Her husband's an Olympic wrestler."

"You bought that?" Mike laughed. "Boy, you two are easy. No wonder Ali picked you out of the crowd." He continued laughing as he stepped around a pile of camel dung and walked into the roadway.

"Mike!" I yelled at his back as he pushed his way through a group of young beggers. "Mike!"

"I'll have Amina give you a ring when the tickets are ready," he called, walking away without looking back. "Have a good time at Giza."

* * *

At nine o'clock that evening, we entered the lobby of the Hilton, exhausted after a long afternoon. Giza had been unbelievably crowded with tourists, vendors, and camel drivers offering both photo ops and rides around the three pyramids. Tourist busses climbed the hill, one after another, disgorging people armed with cameras and maps.

We marveled at the Sphinx while strolling around the monuments. Best of all, we sneaked into a tour group going into the Great Pyramid. Having entered through the Robbers' Tunnel, we wound our way along a maze of passageways, final reaching the royal burial chambers. Phil and I remained undetected in the musty, dimly lit interior as the tour guide recited his canned speeches in theatrically reverent tones.

When we emerged, shadows had begun to fall across the desert, the setting sun orange-red in the western sky. We walked down the hill to the city bus stop. Earlier we had ridden horses up the hill. While tourist busses climbed the remaining half mile to the pyramids, city busses did not.

Normally Phil and I would have walked, but an enterprising young Egyptian offered horseback rides for a relatively small fee. "Let's do it," Phil said. "We can tell our grandchildren how we rode horses into the desert like Lawrence of Arabia."

"Sure," I answered. "Why not?"

By the time we reached the pyramids, I knew why not. The horses were small and bony, their wooden saddles barely covered with thin felt mats. *Grandchildren, Phil?* I thought to myself as I painfully slid from the horse. *Fortunately, I already have kids; otherwise, I don't think there'd be any grandchildren.*

As we dragged ourselves into the Hilton, it's a wonder the ever-present security guards didn't confront us before we reached the interior lobby. We hardly blended with their normal clientele. I had fallen in the passages of the Great Pyramid, and dried blood coated one knee. Phil's tee-shirt had been torn by a persistent young boy who tugged on it while trying to sell a key ring featuring a dangling miniature pyramid. Our faces were streaked where sweat had channeled the dust that covered everything in Giza, including the tourists.

"What do you think about the movie?" I asked, hoping I knew the answer.

"I don't know," he sighed. "It's still playing tomorrow night. Maybe we should have dinner and turn in. What do *you* think?"

"I think tomorrow night would be just fine."

"But we *have* to see it tomorrow," Phil said. "That's the last night it's in town."

"We'll do it," I assured him. "We'll leave as early as possible for Saqqara. That way we'll beat the crowds and get back in plenty of time for the movie."

"Right," Phil replied. "Let's check at the desk for bus schedules."

A young man perfectly attired in a blazer over a white shirt and carefully knotted silk tie glanced less then discreetly at our disheveled appearance and asked, "May I help you?"

"We're going to Saqqara tomorrow," Phil said. "We need to know where we can catch the earliest bus."

"Oh, no, sir. You cannot ride the bus."

"Whadda ya mean, we can't ride the bus?"

"You are Americans, sir. You cannot ride the bus."

"The bus is forbidden to Americans?"

"The bus is not safe, sir. Americans do not ride the bus."

"We've been riding busses all over Cairo. We *can* ride the bus."

"Americans do not ride the bus, sir. You need to hire a car. I can arrange for a car with a guide. Americans hire cars."

Phil leaned over the counter. "We don't want a car. We want a bus schedule. Do you have a bus schedule?"

Shaking his head and turning his attention to papers on the counter, the clerk sniffed, "You cannot get there from here."

"Whadda ya mean we can't get there from here!" I exclaimed. "Of course, we can get there from here. I'm sure there are people there from here. I'm sure there are people here from there. If there are people there from here and there are people here from there, they must have got there from here and here from there. Of course, we can get there from here!"

A long moment of silence followed this outburst. Phil and the clerk stood frozen, open-mouthed. I looked around sheepishly at several well-dressed tourists staring at us.

"*What* did you say?" Phil finally asked.

"I don't know what I said, but I know we can get there from here."

The desk clerk had partially recovered. "Sir, I did not mean you cannot get there from here. I meant you cannot get there from here by bus."

"Why not?" Phil asked. "Busses run on the Nile Valley highway, don't they?"

"Yes, sir, but Saqqara is not in the valley. It is in the desert. The busses do not go into the desert."

"I see," Phil replied. "But there is a road to the Saqqara pyramids, isn't there?"

"Yes, sir, but Saqqara is several kilometers into the desert. You must hire a car."

"We don't want a car," Phil repeated. He thought a moment and then asked, "Can you get a map and show us the village or town nearest the road to the pyramids? If we can get to that town by bus, we'll find a way to Saqqara."

"Sir, that is not right. You could be lost. You need to hire a car. I can make that arrangement. I can have a car here in the morning whenever you need."

"Look!" shouted Phil, bringing the tourists to the alert position again. "We *don't* want a car! We *don't* want a driver! We *don't* want a guide. We want . . . *a bus*! Do you understand? We want ... *a bus*! He stared at the clerk, who slowly backed away.

"Now, do you have a map and a bus schedule?" Phil asked in a polite, quiet voice.

"Yes, sir," the clerk replied timorously. "I will be right back."

"You frightened him," I said, watching the clerk disappear into a back room.

"*I* frightened him? I wasn't the one shouting about people from here getting to there and people from there getting to here."

"You're right. *You're* the angry one. *I'm* the crazy one. Well, the crazy one thinks there's a Scotch in the bar with his name on it. Why doesn't the angry one stay here and work out the particulars with our little friend while the crazy one checks out that Scotch?"

"Okay," Phil replied. "Just don't start telling the bartender about people from there getting to here and people ..."

"Yeah, yeah, I got it," I interrupted, walking away. Then I turned back. "Don't forget to leave us plenty of time for the movie tomorrow night."

"No problem. I'm on it."

*No problem?* Now there's a statement that would come back to haunt us.

* * *

The next morning the mullah's call to prayer still echoed across Cairo as Phil and I left the Hilton and began our walk to a major depot for busses into the valley. We had decided to avoid a city-bus connection. "We'll be riding much of the day," Phil had said over breakfast in the hotel coffee shop. "We could use the exercise."

"Okay by me," I agreed. The need for exercise was simply an excuse. Neither of us wanted to take a city bus to the station. The night before, when the desk clerk had pronounced the busses unsafe, we agreed with him more than we were willing to admit.

On our first day in Cairo, we had walked to a city-bus stop, intending to visit the Museum of Egyptian Antiquities. When we arrived, we were amazed to see people lined along the curb. "Look, Phil!" I exclaimed. "They're queuing!" Queuing is a uniquely British tradition. It is polite. It is democratic. It is civilized. Unfortunately it's a practice the British were never able to introduce into the far reaches of their Empire. In Pakistan any time a door opened in front of a crowd, those with the sharpest elbows were the first to enter. Here, on the other hand, people stood in line waiting for a bus.

"Of course, they're queuing," Phil, who had an English wife, replied. "We're closer to England. We're closer to civilization." Smiling, we stepped to the end of line and waited.

In fifteen minutes or so, a bus pulled from the main stream of traffic and moved toward us. It looked like a homemade tank. Iron railings had been welded to the top and sides of the vehicle. The bus slowed as it moved by us but didn't stop. People along the curb began leaping to the bus, grabbing the iron railings and hanging on while it swept back into traffic and resumed speed. As the bus disappeared into the chaotic mix of trucks, cars, donkey carts, and motorized bikes that made up Cairo traffic, its human cargo began making their way hand over hand along the iron railing and into the open door.

Phil and I stood alone on the otherwise empty sidewalk. This had not been a queue. It had been a line of people seeking the best places to launch themselves at a moving bus. "You're right, Phil," I said looking straight ahead. "We're closer to England. We're closer to civilization."

"May I help you, gentlemen," interrupted a voice behind us. We turned to see a young Egyptian neatly dressed in a white shirt and dark slacks. He wore round rimless glasses and had the standard mustache and slicked-back black hair of the Egyptian college student. His right hand held a leather briefcase.

When we didn't immediately answer, he asked, "Where do you wish to go?"

"We want to visit the Museum of Egyptian Antiquities," Phil replied.

"Quite right," he said with an accent that could have been perfected only by a couple of years in England or hours of watching British movies. "It's a glorious collection of our country's archeological history. Everyone new to Cairo should visit it right off. But that official name is ridiculously long isn't it? What you Americans call 'a mouthful,' I believe. We who live here refer to it simply as the Egyptian Museum."

"Well, that'll make asking directions much easier," Phil responded.

"Quite right. Come with me." He turned and walked down the sidewalk as if there were no question about our following. I looked at Phil and shrugged. We fell into step behind him.

Along the way he explained that busses with railings did not stop unless people needed to exit. "Those busses are only for the brave," he said in a tone that suggested we were not in that category. "To be sure you are able to enter a bus, you need to go to major transfer points, where people leave one bus and take another. Just a few blocks away is such a place."

When we arrived, he helped us locate the right bus, wished us a good day, and walked away. "Now *that*," I said to Phil, "was Arab hospitality."

"We're closer to England," he replied. "We're closer to civilization."

\* \* \*

Our early morning walk to the depot where we'd catch a bus to Al-Badrasheim, the village nearest Saqqara, was pleasantly quiet, a rarity for the streets of Cairo. A few vendors pulled carts of vegetables and fruit to the open-air bazaars. Occasionally donkeys brayed behind clay walls, but even their complaints seemed muted as if to respect the quiet morning hour. Overhead, a purple-blue sky streaked with shafts of orange-red light promised another spectacular desert sunrise. Phil and I walked in silence as if even quiet conversation would spoil the mood of a slowly awakening Cairo.

\* \* \*

Mike Murphy had been right. The Nile Valley was beautiful. As we put more miles between us and Cairo, the stream of human traffic along the highway lessened. At first the bus had been forced to the middle of the road to avoid people walking along the way as they switched heavily laden donkeys and prodded complaining camels loaded with goods for the markets. In a few miles, however, people seemed less transient. Farmers tended rice paddies, grain fields, and orchards along the road. Children waved at the bus, at home in this green lush land, sustained with channeled irrigation waters from the Nile River.

When we had boarded the bus, we checked to make sure we had the right one by handing the driver a slip of paper on which a shopkeeper at the terminal had written our destination. He glanced at it and then, handing it back, said, "I understand English very well. I also speak French, German, Spanish, and Italian. Oh, and, of course, Arabic. How many languages do you speak?"

"We're Americans," I replied. "We barely speak English."

\* \* \*

I had been dozing when the bus pulled to the side of the road and the driver called, "Americans, this is Al-Badrasheim."

The scene outside the windows did not differ from what we had been seeing for miles. There was no village here. "Are you sure?" I asked the driver as we made our way to the front of the bus.

"Yes," he replied, pointing to a narrow road winding through the fields to our left. "Al-Badrasheim."

\* \* \*

Midmorning Al-Badrasheim was almost as quiet as early dawn Cairo. Phil and I crossed a footbridge over an irrigation ditch and entered the village square. Vendors had set up tables under weathered canvas tarps. A few elderly men, sipping coffee, sat in the shade of trees. The arrival of two Americans did not seem an unusual event in the village. They watched us a few moments as we walked down the street and then returned to their conversation with only sidelong glances as we passed.

We followed the road through the village until it ended abruptly at the edge of a grain field. "That's it?" I asked. "That's Al-Badrasheim?"

"Small, isn't it?" Phil replied.

"Small? This isn't small, Phil. This is close to nonexistent. How do we find a ride to the pyramids from here?"

But Phil wasn't listening. He had spotted a couple of young boys watching a goat herd in the next field. He began motioning to them. One of the boys hesitantly approached.

"Taxi?" Phil asked. "You know taxi?"

"Taxi?" the boy repeated.

"Yes, taxi. You know taxi?" Phil asked again, pantomiming a steering wheel, turning it left and right in his hands.

The boy's eyes lit up. "Taxi!" he exclaimed, nodding. He began turning his own imaginary steering wheel. "Taxi!" He motioned us to follow and trotted down the road toward the village. *We* didn't trot, and when he realized we didn't share his need for speed, he slowed to a walk.

We followed him down a side street, where in front of a walled building sat an aged black Buick. Two large bare feet stuck out the window on the driver's side.

"Taxi?" Phil asked the boy. "That's a taxi?"

"Taxi," he replied, nodding eagerly. "Taxi."

Phil pulled some loose change from his pocket. He extended a handful of coins to the boy, who shook his head as he backed away, hands raised in protest. Then grinning, he turned and trotted back toward the fields.

As we watched him round a corner, I said, "You know, Phil, just when I'm about to condemn the entire Middle East for its mercenary ways, we run across someone like that college student who helped us with the busses our first day in Cairo or a kid like this out here in the middle of nowhere."

"Arab hospitality, Bob. It's a civilized country closer to England, you know."

We approached the Buick and looked inside. The feet belonged to a large snoring man sprawled along the seat.

"Are you sure this is a taxi?" I asked.

"I don't know. Wake him up."

"*You* wake him up!" I said, backing away.

Phil hesitated a moment and then wrapped a hand around one ankle and began shaking it. The interior of the car exploded with a loud bark as the owner of the feet sat upright and stared at us.

Phil smiled and asked, "Are you a taxi?" The man continued his bewildered stare, dark eyes wide in a face mostly hidden in a bushy, unkempt beard. "Are you a taxi?" Phil repeated in a louder voice.

"Am I a what?" the driver asked.

"Oh, good. You speak English. I asked if you're a taxi."

"My car is a taxi. Is *that* what you mean?"

"Yes," Phil replied. "That's exactly what I mean."

We explained that we wanted a ride to Saqqara. He shook his head and made the universal Middle-East dismissal gesture with his hand, something like brushing flies from a plate.

"I have a client in this house," he said pointing to the walled building. "I wait here for him."

"Is there another taxi in the village?" Phil asked.

"There is *no* taxi in this village. I am from Cairo. My client comes to visit his parents every week. I drive him. There is no taxi in this village."

"So you wait for your client while he visits his parents?"

"Yes. You understand. I wait. I cannot take you to Saqqara."

"What if you could?" Phil asked.

"What if I could? I told you I cannot. I wait for my client."

"Maybe you could make additional money by taking us to Saqqara while he is visiting his parents."

"Sir, you would be at the pyramids for at least two hours. My client will be ready to return to Cairo before that time."

"We aren't asking you to wait for us at the pyramid. We're only asking you to get us there. We'll find a ride back on our own. It's about twenty, twenty-five kilometers from here to Saqqara. You could take us there and be back in under an hour."

"I don't know, sir. *How* will you find such a ride? Saqqara is in the desert. There are no people there."

"We've been to the pyramids at Giza," Phil answered. "There are all kinds of people at the pyramids. There are busses, taxis, private cars. We'll have no trouble finding a ride."

"No, sir," the driver answered, shaking his head. "Saqqara is not Giza. It is not the same."

"That's not your worry, my friend," Phil said, putting a hand through the window and onto the man's shoulder. "You get us there, and we'll get back."

"You will pay me for both ways even though I do not drive you back?"

"Of course," Phil replied.

The driver thought a moment. Then he nodded. "I go talk to my client. If he say okay, I take you."

"That's all we ask, my friend," Phil smiled. "That's all we ask."

* * *

Leaving the Nile valley, we followed a narrow road up a steep incline into the desert, I marveled at the abrupt transition from the luxuriant valley floor to a seemingly lifeless expanse of desert sand. It was like stepping across a threshold. Within minutes the temperature in the old Buick spiked. The road ahead shimmered in the desert heat.

As we passed one desolate sand dune after another, I began to feel uneasy. "Saqqara is not Giza," the driver had said. What if we *did* have trouble finding a ride back? I shook off this sudden loss of nerve. *Phil is right*, I thought to myself. *There'll be all kinds of people there.*

We topped another hill. Before us, framed by a turquoise sky, loomed the Step Pyramid, a monument to the excesses of a civilization so obsessed with death and the afterlife that living in the present lost value. Built one hundred years before the pyramids at Giza, the Step Pyramid had a worn look, its ledges heaped with wind-driven sand. Yet in this isolated setting, it had a quiet majesty. The first stone monument built by man, it had withstood the ravages of a harsh, unforgiving land for over four thousand years.

The driver swung the Buick around in a large parking lot. Phil leaned over the front seat to pay him. Then we stepped from the car, unable to take our eyes off the pyramid. While we stood transfixed, we heard the car pick up speed as the driver power-shifted gears in his hurry to return to his client in Al-Badrashcim.

For the first time, I lowered my eyes and looked around the parking lot. It was empty. I watched a dust swirl dance across the lot. I looked up at the sun, a sun bigger than any I had ever seen, its heat already soaking my tee-shirt with sweat. I heard a mournful sigh as a slight wind raised sand on the dunes nearby.

I looked at Phil, who still gazed upward at the pyramid. "Phil," I said. "Phil."

"What?" he asked, not taking his eyes off the pyramid.

"Where are all the people, Phil?"

"What?" he repeated, turning to me.

"The people. Where are all the people?"

He looked around at the empty parking lot and then glanced at his wristwatch. "It's early yet," he replied. "It's only ten-thirty. We did just what we said we'd do. We beat the crowds. Let's go see the pyramid. By the time we finish, the people will be here."

"Phil, I love your glass-is-half-full-instead-of-half-empty outlook on life. I really do. But the truth is you've been ignoring everyone who has said Saqqara is not Giza. What if we are here all alone after seeing the pyramid? How do we get back to Cairo?"

"Well, in the first place," Phil smiled, "we don't have to get back to Cairo from here. We just have to get back to the highway. We can catch a bus from there."

"Okay. How do we get back to the highway?"

"I don't know," Phil replied. "Let's consider our options. First, we can start walking back right now. In that case we miss visiting this marvelous pyramid we've come all this way to see. Second, we can visit the pyramid and then see if people have shown up. If they have, we hitch a ride. If they haven't, we walk."

He began ticking off his points on his fingers. "The first is a lose-lose proposition. We don't see the pyramid, and we walk. The second is a win-win proposition. We see the pyramid, and we get a ride. The third is a win-lose proposition. We see the pyramid and we ..."

"... walk," I finished for him.

I looked to the sun-filled sky. "Two hours from now, it's going to be even hotter."

"It's Egypt," Phil grinned. "Did you come here for the snow?"

I looked at him, his arms folded, the small flight bag he carried everywhere slung over his shoulder. He cocked his head, smiling as he waited for my choice of the options he had listed.

"Damn it, Phil," I finally said. "I hate it when you're right."

"The half full is *always* better than the half empty," he laughed as he turned toward the path leading to the pyramid.

From the top of another small hill, we saw below us, a mud-baked hut next to propped-up signs in both Arabic and English marking the entrance to the pyramid site. A rusty bicycle leaned against the hut. In the doorway stood a diminutive Egyptian dressed in a ragged sport coat over baggy pants and sandals. A billed police-style hat shaded his eyes as he watched us approach. I looked upon this hat with misgivings. In my travels to foreign places, the most irksome problems usually have resulted from dealing with minor authority figures in billed police-style hats.

He moved to meet us. "Sirs, there is a modest admission fee for the site." Then he added, "If you wish a guide, there is an additional fee, but the guide is very qualified." He smiled, and somehow that toothy smile won me over, billed police-style hat and all.

"And who would that guide be?" I asked.

"*I* would be that guide," he answered, tapping his chest. We negotiated a fee and walked down the path with our newly acquired guide.

\* \* \*

Saqqara was everything we had hoped to experience. The Step Pyramid dominated the scene, of course, but the temples surrounding the pyramid were, in many ways, as intriguing as anything we had seen at Giza.

"There is an additional fee to enter the temples," our guide said, "but this fee is well worth what you will see." I smiled, and Phil, amused by my obvious approval of this little man, nodded in agreement.

Brightly colored hieroglyphics covered the interior temple walls. Our guide pointed to various symbols, translating them for us. "Here the Pharaoh approaches his tomb," he explained. "Here are his wives and followers. These are the animals he will take to the afterlife." Our little caretaker put many U.S. college professors to shame.

\* \* \*

It was nearly noon when we returned to the caretaker's hut. The sun cast no shadows. Its heat drained us, slowing our steps. We shook hands with our guide and walked to the top of the hill overlooking the parking lot. Heat waves shimmered in the emptiness below us.

"Phil," I asked, looking at the road snaking from the lot into the desert, "is this option three? Do we really walk?"

"Let's talk to your new friend," he replied, turning back on the path.

\* \* \*

"No, sirs, I have no way to take you into the valley."

"When you leave here, how do *you* go home?" I asked. In answer, he silently pointed to the bike.

"Do you have a radio?"

His face brightened. "Yes, sir, I have a very good radio. I listen to music from Cairo."

"No, what I mean is do you have a radio you could use to call someone for a car?"

He looked puzzled. Finally he answered, "I don't talk to the radio. I just listen."

"Option three," I said, turning to Phil. "We walk."

\* \* \*

By the time we reached the valley floor, we had quit sweating, a sign of serious dehydration. Our tans had surrendered to the blistering heat of the Sahara sun. Burnt red, salt deposits in the corners of our eyes and mouths, we staggered into the shade of a fig tree. There we sat, exhausted, listening to water bubbling in a nearby irrigation ditch.

"Phil," I said through cracked lips, "I want that water."

"Think Jhelum waltz," he replied.

"I need water."

"You have a choice. You can suffer a little dehydration for a day, or for a week you can puke, belch, and ..."

"Okay, okay," I interrupted. "I know you're right. But let's get moving. I can't sit here and listen to that water."

As we walked, concentrating on nothing more vital than putting one foot in front of the other, several boys climbed the bank from the irrigation ditch paralleling the road and studied us. One of the boys said something to the others, and they jumped down the bank into the field.

A few minutes later, they rushed back, holding glass jars brimming with water obviously scooped from the ditch. "*Baksheesh! Baksheesh!*" they cried, offering us the jars. We didn't have the strength to answer. We simply wave our hands, shooing them off, and plodded on. Disappointed, they turned and disappeared into the field once more.

Finally we reached the intersection of the pyramid road and the highway. I looked at my watch. Two-thirty. We had walked under that merciless sun for over two hours.

We crossed to the far side of the highway, where a signpost displayed a large Arabic scrawl. "That's the sign for a bus stop," Phil declared.

"How do you know that?"

"I pay attention. That sign was there every time the bus stopped on the way out here."

"Phil, I don't want to doubt you, but all this Arabic script looks the same. That sign might very well read 'Foreigners found lurking under this sign will be exterminated.'"

Phil started to laugh and then put a hand over his chapped, bleeding lips. "You might be right, but I vote for sitting here rather than doing any more walking."

\* \* \*

An hour later, we still sat by the highway. Shortly after we had arrived, a bus came by, but the driver ignored our frantic waving. As it roared by us, I could see passengers jammed in the aisles. "He's too full, Phil. He couldn't take us."

"He *could* take us," Phil replied. "He obviously has a thing against ragged, dusty, salt-covered dregs from the desert."

"Naw," I answered. "That would eliminate half his customers."

\* \* \*

Another half hour had passed when three young boys emerged from the fields. They squatted silently, robes tucked between their legs, studying us. "They're waiting for us to die," I said. "Child vultures of the Sahara Desert."

Phil ignored my comment. Instead he asked, "You remember those melons in the bazaars? Those yellow ones with all the juice?"

In several marketplaces around Cairo, we had watched merchants cut succulent yellow melons into thin slices for their customers. Juice from the slices saturated people's clothing as they bit into them. Neither of us had ever seen such melons. They were the size of watermelons, mostly yellow with green stripes paralleling their sides.

"Phil, stop it. I don't need that kind of torture."

"No, what I'm saying is those melons probably grow right here in the valley. These kids could get us one." He stood up and beckoned to the boys. They stared. He motioned again. The biggest boy arose and walked to us.

"Melon?" Phil asked. "You know melon?" The boy watched him, unmoving.

"English?" Phil asked. "You speak English?"

The boy's face lit up with a smile. He pointed to Phil. "Engleesh," he said. "Engleesh."

"No, not me. The language. You know English language?"

The boy continued nodding and pointing at Phil. "Engleesh," he replied.

Phil turned to me. "We got any paper and a pen or pencil?"

"You gonna write a note to a kid who can't speak English?"

"No, I'm gonna draw a picture," he answered, rummaging through his flight bag.

"I have my passport," I said, "but you're not gonna draw any pictures in it."

"Never mind," he replied, holding up a Pan-Am ticket jacket and a pen. He began to draw.

"Whadda you think"" he asked, holding up his drawing. "This look like one of those melons?"

I looked at an oval with radiating lines paralleling point to point. "Actually," I answered, "it looks like a football."

"Fortunately," Phil smiled, "this is another of those countries where they play football with a soccer ball."

He showed the picture to the boy, who looked puzzled. "Melon," Phil said. "Melon." The boy continued to stare blankly.

"Eat," Phil said. "Eat." He held an imaginary piece of melon in front of his face and began chomping from side to side, like a crazed harmonica player. "Eat," he repeated. "Melon ... Eat."

Suddenly the boy jolted upright with understanding. He said something in Arabic and imitated Phil's crazed harmonica act. He repeated his Arabic version while Phil joined in with "Yes ... Eat ... Melon ... Eat ..."

"You get?" Phil asked. The boy stared at him. "You get? Melon? You get?" The boy, forehead furrowed, continued his silent stare.

Phil began running two fingers up his arm in imitation of a stick figure on the move. "You get? You get melon?" He held out his palms as if he were receiving something from the boy and then began his eating pantomime again.

The boy nodded eagerly. Phil reached into his pocket and brought out some change. The boy cupped his hands, and Phil poured the coins into them. Our newfound benefactor yelled something to the other boys and raced down the path into the fields. They jumped to their feet and followed, their robes whipping around their legs.

I shook my head as Phil, grinning over his nonverbal triumph, returned to his sitting position. "You know you're not going to see that boy or your money again, don't you?"

"Oh, ye of little faith," he answered, leaning back against a large boulder and closing his eyes.

While Phil seemed to doze, I watched several cars zip by in each direction. No busses appeared. Finally I asked, "Phil, you awake?"

"Yeah," he replied, not opening his eyes.

"I'm gonna start hitching. You ready if we catch a ride?"

"I guess so, but I'd rather wait for the melon."

"There isn't going to be a melon, Phil. If we get a ride, we could be in Cairo in an hour, drinking a cold beer in the Hilton lounge."

He opened his eyes. "Go for it," he said.

In the next ten minutes, four cars screamed past. I realized that at the speed they traveled, stopping for a hitchhiker was a remote possibility at best. Braking at that speed invited disaster. Slowing to a civilized stop would take them so far down the road they'd probably change their minds before we could get there

When a truck approached doing no more than sixty miles an hour, I thought we had a chance, but it passed without slowing, its exhausts belching black diesel smoke.

As I watched it disappear, I heard Phil yell, "Oh, ye of little faith, here he is!" The boy climbed the bank from the fields, balancing a newspaper-wrapped, grease-stained package in his hands. Phil sprang to his feet and moved to greet him.

By the time I reached them, Phil had unwrapped the package. I looked at the contents. "What *is* that?" I asked.

"Well, this is bread," he replied, pointing to several round items that resembled chapatties. "And this," he added, lifting a piece of gray matter to his nose and sniffing it, "appears to be salted fish."

*Salted fish.* Whatever fluids were left in my body dried up at the thought.

Phil knelt in front of the boy, whose excitement had drained when he realized he had not brought what we wanted. Phil, eye level with the boy, placed a hand on his shoulder. "It's okay," he said. "Everything you brought was round. I'm a lousy artist. You did better than I could have done from such a picture."

He looked past the boy to me. "You know, he wasn't gone more than half an hour. His village must be close."

He returned his gaze to the boy. Smiling, he said. "Take me to your leader." He stood and, pulling the boy by the hand, began making his way down the bank to the field below. I followed.

* * *

Phil had been right. In ten minutes, the village came into view, a collection of mud-baked huts and walls on the far side of an orchard. There were no roads. Several paths radiated from the village in various directions.

As we drew near, a group of men and boys began to gather. Several women watched from the flat roofs of the huts. Others scooped up younger children and disappeared behind the walls.

"*Salaam alaikum*," Phil greeted the crowd.

"*Salaam alaikum*," they echoed. "*Salaam.*" Then, grinning and jostling each other for position, they erupted into a torrent of Arabic.

"No," Phil answered, holding up his hands. "No Arabic. Anyone speak English?" The hubbub continued without a word we recognized.

Suddenly the crowd began to quiet and opened a path for a slightly stooped elderly man. Gray was his dominant color: gray hair straggling from under his headscarf, gray beard, gray robes. But his eyes were not gray. Dark, intelligent eyes, sparkling with curiosity. Here was a man who enjoyed a disruption of the status quo.

"*Salaam alaikum*," he said, smiling.

"*Salaam alaikum*," we replied in unison.

With a questioning look, he pointed to the newspaper-wrapped food Phil carried in his hand.

"Sorry, sir," Phil said, in recognition this was the headman of the village "We cannot eat this before we drink. We are very thirsty." He stroked his throat as if following the flow of liquid from his mouth downward. "Thirsty," he repeated.

The old man nodded and motioned us to follow him. We walked into the village, where he directed us to a rickety table and chairs under a shade tree. He pointed to the chairs, inviting us to sit.

The next few minutes were filled with uncomfortable smiles, nods, and fleeting eye contact. Then two women, dressed in black robes, their faces veiled with their headscarves, appeared, carrying trays.

The first tray contained a pitcher of water and two cups. On the second were more bread, salted fish, and some black oval objects. "What do you think those are, Phil?" I asked.

"I think," Phil answered, "those are boiled eggs."

"They're black."

"I think," Phil responded, "those are *black* boiled eggs."

I heard someone laugh and turned to see a young man about our age, holding a hand over his mouth. *Either that guy understands English, or he knows enough about Americans to appreciate our reaction to black eggs*, I thought to myself. Rising from my chair, I motioned him over.

"You know English," I said. He shook his head. "Yes, you do," I insisted. "You know English."

"Small," he answered. "Know small English."

"Small English? Oh, you mean you know *little* English."

"Yes," he replied, "little English." He seemed embarrassed, and I realized I needed to gain his confidence if we were to communicate.

"What's your name?" I asked. He stared at me blankly. "Your name?" I repeated. No answer.

I pointed to Phil, who had left his chair and was standing beside me. "This is Phil. I am Bob." When he didn't respond, I pointed to Phil again. "Phil," I said, and tapping my own chest, "Bob."

He pointed to Phil. "Phil," he said. He pointed to me. "Boob."

"Not Boob," I replied. "Bob."

"*Sometimes* Boob," Phil grinned.

I tried again. "Phil ... Bob."

"Phil," he answered. And then ... Bob."

"And you?" I asked, pointing.

He grinned and tapped his chest. "Ahmad," he said. Nodding, I smiled. Communication channels open.

"We appreciate your village's offer of food," I said. "But we are too thirsty to eat. And we cannot drink the water because we will be sick." He didn't respond.

"Phil, you have your drawing?" I asked over my shoulder. He rummaged in his flight bag and handed it to me.

"We can't eat raw foods unless they need to be peeled," I explained. "The rinds protect the food for us. If we can get a melon like this," I continued, holding up Phil's drawing, "we can drink the juice."

He stared at my mouth like a beginner in lip reading. Obviously, few of my words made any sense. I pointed to Phil's drawing. "Melon," I said. "Melon." I pantomimed slicing the melon, picked up an imaginary piece, and went into a slower version of Phil's crazed harmonica act.

He watched me intently. Then he said, "Mel-lon," sweeping his hands around an imaginary oval.

"Good," I smiled. "Can you get melon for us?"

Ahmad said something to the headman, who nodded approval. He turned back to me and held out his hand. "*Baksheesh*," he said. I handed him a five-pound note from my wallet. He stuffed the note inside his robes and walked down one of the paths from the village.

As we watched Ahmad walk away, Phil patted my shoulder. "Good job. This time we're gonna get that melon."

"I hope so, Phil, because if he comes back with more round salty stuff like … oh, I don't know … pepperoni, beef jerky …"

"Pretzels?" Phil offered.

"Yeah, anything like that, and I'm gonna chugalug that pitcher of water, Jehlum waltz be damned."

\* \* \*

For the next twenty minutes the village boys entertained us by showing off their athletic skills. First, we were taken to a nearby waterhole, where the boys took turns jumping from a low bank into water that barely reached their armpits. After each jump the adult watchers enthusiastically applauded. "That's a ten!" Phil yelled, jumping up and holding both hands above his head after one of the smaller boys had jumped, gone underwater when his knees buckled, and emerged choking on the muddied mire he had swallowed.

From there we returned to the village, where in a large circle drawn in the dirt, the boys, stilled soaked from the waterhole, wrestled Greco style. The dirt became mud as they threw each other around.

"You know," Phil said, "Amina's husband probably came from a village like this."

160

"Mike was kidding," I replied. "Amina's husband isn't an Olympic wrestler."

"But if he were," Phil mused, "he would have come from a village like this."

Our boy from the highway had just thrown his opponent when I felt a tap on my shoulder. The man standing next to me pointed to our rickety table, where Ahmad stood, holding one of the yellow melons.

By the time we made our way to the table, the melon had disappeared. The crowd gathered around us, happy about finally offering their American guests something we would actually eat.

The headman appeared, followed by a woman carrying the melon on a platter. She placed the melon on the table and retreated into one of the huts. The headman lifted a large, wicked-looking knife from the platter and plunged it into the melon. He sliced it in two and, putting the knife aside, ceremoniously held up both halves, letting the juice run down his arms. He turned the melon halves over, draining more of the liquid.

Phil and I watched in anguish as the juice soaked into the dirt. I reached for the half nearest me, but the headman pulled it back. Carefully taking his time, he began carving the melon into thin slices. Finally satisfied that the melon had been adequately prepared for his guests, he offered the platter to us.

We didn't eat that melon. We devoured it. Whenever I hear the word *devoured* today, I fully appreciate its meaning. We didn't eat that melon. We *devoured* it.

* * *

The juice that had survived the headman's preparation warded off our dehydration. Our Egyptian hosts had been unbelievably gracious. Phil and I could not imagine an experience more memorable than this. But James Bond was in town. We had to get back to Cairo.

I looked for Ahmad. "Bus?" I asked. "Bus?" He watched me, unmoving. "Bus to Cairo" I said, turning an imaginary steering wheel in the demonstrative fashion that had become a basic part of our nonverbal communication.

"Cairo?" he asked.

"Yes," I answered, turning my wheel, "Cairo … Bus … Ride."

"Bus!" he yelled. "Bus to Cairo!"

"Yes," I said. "Bus to Cairo."

\* \* \*

Ahmad, accompanied by several of the men and most of the boys from the village, led us along a path toward the highway. A car streaked by just as I stepped onto the shoulder of the road. But the car was not what captured my attention. Twenty yards down the highway stood the signpost where we had first encountered the village boys.

"Phil," I said, pointing, "we're right back where we started."

I turned to Ahmad, my arm still raised, finger pointing to the sign. "Bus?" I asked. "Bus to Cairo?"

He nodded, motioning us to follow as he walked down the road. "Cairo," he said, pointing north.

"Bus?" I repeated, wrapping my hand around the signpost.

Ahmad nodded, grinning, and began turning *his* version of our imaginary steering wheel. He pointed to the Arabic on the sign.

"See," Phil grinned. "I told you that meant bus stop."

\* \* \*

Our Arab friends walked down the highway to the path leading to their village after a farewell of handshakes, hugs and pats on the back. Moments before, a noisy crowd had been talking all at once, they laughing and shouting unintelligible Arabic, we responding with unintelligible English. Now heavy silence engulfed us. No bird sounds. No traffic. Silence. Though the sun was still hot, shadows had begun to length across the highway.

We waited thirty minutes for a bus that never came. Northbound cars streaked past, cars that would be in Cairo within the hour. Almost three hours had passed since we first stumbled off the desert road to this spot. Yet here we were once again, waiting.

Finally, Phil stood up, straightened his shoulders, tugged the strap of his flight bag, and stepped onto the edge of the highway. "I'm going to stop the next car, no matter what direction it's traveling," he announced. "We have to get out of here."

The driver of the black Mercedes zeroed in on a frantically waving Phil with the single-minded intensity of a kamikaze pilot. Only superb German engineering kept the brakes from locking when the driver finally realized Phil was going to stand his ground. The car fishtailed past, its tires screeching, the air filling with the smell of burning rubber. It came to a stop thirty yards down the road.

I looked for Phil. He was gone. *My god*, I thought, *he's impaled on the Mercedes's grill*! Then I saw his head come up from the far bank, where he had thrown himself at the last moment. He climbed to the shoulder of the road and stood there, dusting himself off, seeming to check for anything broken. Satisfied, he flashed me an okay sigh and trotted down the road toward the car.

*No, Phil*, I thought. *If he didn't kill you the first time, he will this time.*

Phil arrived at the car and bent down to talk to the driver. Several minutes later he straightened and signaled me to come. I reluctantly walked to the car.

The driver smiled as I approached. Hair neatly parted on the left, small trimmed moustache, white shirt open at the throat, he looked as if he had just stepped from a fashion magazine. Phil and he seemed to be on the best of terms.

"Dr. Hassan," Phil said, "This is my friend Bob." A manicured hand extended from the window. A soft hand. A surgeon's hand. I was careful not to give him the macho American shake.

"Dr. Hassan tells me busses don't regularly stop here," Phil reported. I stared at them with disbelief. Neither seemed concerned that a moment before, they had engaged in a life-and-death game of chicken on the Nile Valley highway.

"This is true," Dr. Hassan affirmed. "Stopping is at the discretion of the driver. You could wait here all night and not have a bus stop for you."

"But here's the good news," Phil announced. "Dr. Hassan has offered to take us to a police station where we are sure to catch a bus."

"A bus at the police station?" I asked.

"I'll talk to them," the doctor replied. "They'll stop a bus if I ask them."

"With my long legs, I'd better sit in the front," Phil said. "The back seat's all yours." I glanced at the back seat and then looked again. It was *not* all mine. Two very large ladies filled the back seat. Dressed in the black robes of the desert, they instinctively pulled their headscarves across their faces. I quickly looked away.

As we walked around the back of the car, I said, "Phil, I don't think I can fit in there."

"Sure you can. It'll be cozy, but you can fit in there."

"I don't wanna be cozy. Those are probably his wives."

"Good point." Phil replied. "Keep your hands folded, avoid eye contact, and think pure thoughts." He laughed as he reached for the handle of the front door.

When I opened my door, the women shifted a little to the left. A very little. I squeezed in, folded my hands, and stared straight ahead, acutely conscious of fleshy contact from the point of my left shoulder to the crook of my knee.

I glanced from the corner of my eye. Looking straight ahead, neither woman acknowledged my presence.

The doctor pulled from the shoulder of the road, smoothly took the Mercedes through its gears, and soon reached his cruising speed of eight or ninety miles per hour. I watched the valley streak past as Phil and the doctor engaged in small talk.

Dr. Hassan had special affection for Americans, he reported, because he had graduated from the University of Chicago. "For a while I thought I might like to become a permanent resident of your fine country, but the desert beckoned me home."

"Where *is* home?" Phil asked. "Cairo?"

"I do have a residence in Cairo, where my practice is located," the doctor replied, "but my family home is in the village where I grew up. We are on our way there for my daughter's marriage this evening. It will be a big party. Have you ever seen an Egyptian wedding?"

"No," Phil said, "but I bet it's really something."

Dr. Hassan was suddenly struck with inspiration. "Why don't you come with us? You can attend the ceremony and all the other festivities, stay in my house for the evening, and return to Cairo with me tomorrow night. You'll have a blast," he added, showing off his American vernacular.

Phil looked over the seat at me, obviously excited by this offer. What a story this would make. An afternoon in a simple village and an evening in what would most likely be an opulent Egyptian home. I was about to nod agreement when the woman next to me shifted and pinned my arm between us. My entire left side was soaked in sweat.

Phil saw my hesitation and mistook its meaning. He nodded and turned to the doctor. "Sir, we really appreciate the offer, and we are probably going to regret not accepting your hospitality for what I am sure would be a memorable experience. But we have a pressing engagement in Cairo, and we really have to get back tonight."

*Pressing engagement*? I thought. And then, *Oh the movie.* Phil thought I had hesitated because of the movie. I almost said something, but at that moment the woman shifted left, freeing my arm. *No,* I thought, rubbing circulation back into it, *let's make this ride as short as possible.*

"That's too bad," the doctor replied. "I would have enjoyed your company. But I understand obligations." Then he lifted his hand from the wheel and pointed through the windshield. "There's the police station up ahead."

We parked next to a small hut perched on the intersection of the highway and a connecting road that ran west into the desert. A single officer in a starched khaki shirt, matching shorts, white knee stockings and black ankle-high boots manned the station.

Dr. Hassan talked to the officer for several minutes and then returned to the car, where Phil and I waited.

"Everything's fine," he reported. "He's going to phone ahead to another station and tell them to warn the bus that it's to stop here for you. You should have no trouble from this point on."

The doctor gave each of us a card. "It's a rain check," he said, showing off with another American idiom. "We'll party the next time you're in Egypt." We, in turn, scribbled our Pakistan and stateside addresses on the back of a second card. "Keep in touch," he said, waving from the far side of his Mercedes. We watched him pull onto the road and disappear into the shadows now falling heavily across the highway.

* * *

Fifteen minutes later, I sat on the sunny side of the hut, watching for the bus. Phil had stood up to stretch when he suddenly dropped his arms and stared at a cardboard box near the rear of the hut. "Bob," he said, "do you see what I see?"

"I see a cardboard box if that's what you mean."

"Do you see what's written on it?"

I squinted. "The big word's *Stella*. I can't make out the others."

"Stella," Phil said. "Doesn't that ring a bell?"

I thought a moment. It *was* familiar. Where had I heard something about Stella? Then it hit me. "Stella!" I said. "That's the beer Mike told us about."

"Right," Phil grinned. "And Mike said he'd been drinking it without any problem."

"Phil, you don't suppose…," I began.

"Only one way to find out," he said and walked to the box.

"Empty … empty … empty … Wait a minute!" he exclaimed, reaching into the box and holding up a liter bottle, its cap firmly in place. He quickly dropped his arm and, holding the bottle on his side away from the hut, walked toward me.

"Phil," I whispered as he lowered himself beside me, "you can't steal beer from the police. You especially can't steal beer from the *Egyptian* police."

He thought a moment. "You're right," he replied. "But I can buy it."

\* \* \*

In a few minutes Phil returned from inside the hut. Excited, he waved the bottle toward me. "Look what he threw in," he announced, producing a church key in his other hand. He put the opener in place and started to lift.

"Phil, wait a minute!" I yelled. But too late. He popped the cap, and the bottle erupted. Foam sprayed his face as he instinctively put his mouth over the bottle. His eyes bulged as his cheeks filled. He gulped but could not stay ahead of the eruption. Pulling his mouth away, he bent over, choking. I watched in dismay as foam continued to pour from the bottle. When it finally stopped, we had approximately a fourth of the beer left.

"Here," he said, holding it out to me. "You finish it." I let him catch his breath, and then we passed the bottle back and forth, nursing the beer. Bathwater-warm, it was still one of the best beers I have ever tasted.

I had just finished the last swallow when the policeman came around the corner of the hut.

"Sirs," he said, pointing down the highway. "Your bus."

\* \* \*

At nine o'clock that night, Phil and I emerged from the lobby of the Hilton. We had showered, shaved, eaten, and drunk a couple of cold, nonexplosive beers. Somehow, though, they didn't have the personality of our hot desert Stella.

We had decided to treat ourselves to a taxi. "We've done enough bus-riding and walking today," Phil said in incredible understatement.

Having copied the movie theater's address from an English-language newspaper, we showed it to the cab driver. He looked puzzled. "What's the problem?" Phil asked. "Don't you know where that is?" The driver remained quiet for a moment, studying the address. Then he shrugged, handed the paper back to Phil, put his cab in gear, and pulled into traffic.

For the next twenty minutes as we drove through town, turning frequently left and right across traffic and into side roads, Phil and I discussed the day. "Arab hospitality," Phil mused. "We've read about it. We know it's a major principle in the Koran. But today we experienced it firsthand. That little boy so excited to rescue us on the highway. That village offering us food when you know they had so little to share. And those boys entertaining us at the waterhole and the wrestling matches."

"Don't forget Dr. Hassan," I added. "We're probably going to regret turning down his offer for the rest of our lives."

"I know," Phil replied. "I was ready to do that."

"I know you were," I answered. "I was going to say we should go for it, but I was overcome by a sweat attack."

The cab pulled to the curb. On the sidewalk, a large crowd of theatergoers elbowed each other as they sought advantage at the ticket window. I looked at the bright lights of downtown Cairo while Phil paid the driver. Across a small park, probably a city block or two at most, a large neon sign caught my eye.

As the taxi pulled away, I nudged Phil and, laughing, pointed to the sign. In bright red and blue, it read *Cairo Hilton Hotel*.

"So much for Arab hospitality," I said.

"Arab hospitality is one thing," Phil grinned, "but cab drivers are the same the world over."

* * *

Fifteen minutes later Phil and I leaned back in the soft, velvet-cushioned seats of one of the most luxurious movie theaters I have ever seen. The houselights dimmed. We waited in anticipation of those three little words that had kept us going all day. Those three magic words:

"Bond. James Bond."

# RUNAWAY MODEL A

**My father had only two years** of prosperity in his life. Using the respect he had earned running a sawmill for absentee owners, he scraped together enough credit to make a down payment on a mill of his own. This was just after World War II, and Dad cashed in on the building boom that followed. I have his bankbooks from that period. Each week he deposited eight hundred dollars into his saving account after expenses. It must have been a mind-boggling time for someone with an eighth-grade education who at age eighteen had made his way west riding the rails as a hobo.

We traveled east in our '48 Pontiac, the only new car my father ever owned, to visit his father in Minnesota. During the two weeks we were gone, the people he had entrusted with the management of the mill bankrupted our family. We returned to large unpaid bills for logs delivered to the mill. In addition, money for lumber cut in those two weeks had vanished, pocketed by those he most trusted.

Today people would say we downsized. In those days, it was called going broke and starting over. We became gypo loggers, setting up a portable sawmill in timber sales too small for the big companies. Also, at times we came in after them to clean up the windfall and small timber they left behind. In those days log trucks had loads of three to five logs. We never saw trucks like those we see today with loads of fifteen or more logs. The large companies could not be bothered with timber so small. Gypo loggers like us were brought to clean up their mess.

Dad almost single-handedly took apart the mill from one site and rebuilt it at another. By the time I was eleven, I had spent hours straightening nails pulled from the torn-down mill to be reused at the new mill.

At twelve years old, carrying gas cans and wedges, I began working with my father as he fell trees. By fourteen, I bucked behind him, limbing and cutting fallen timber into appropriate lengths with a power saw. I remember how proudly I wore my first pair of cork boots.

By fifteen, I ran the mill's rollway with the help of Jerry, barely thirteen at the time. He operated the diesel donkey, releasing cable while I pulled it to the log deck. There I set the chokers and signaled him to pull in the logs. When they reached the rollway, I cut them into proper lengths, and, using peevees, we moved them down the rollway to the mill.

The most remarkable crew member was my mother. As the offbearer, she pulled boards from the saw as the carriage pushed logs through it. Then she sent them down the rollers to the green chain. Her job was not the most physically taxing in the mill—though any job brought exhaustion in an eight-hour shift—but it was one of the most dangerous because it involved working so close to the saw.

Because we built our mill onsite, driving to it meant maneuvering over muddy, steep one-way roads, impassable for the ordinary family car. And our family cars were anything but ordinary. Dad could build a sawmill, but he could not be bothered with auto mechanics. We drove cars until they fell apart. I don't believe my father ever traded in one car for another. When we were done with a car, it went to the wrecking yard.

Had we driven these cars up the logging roads to our mill sites, they wouldn't have lasted a month. We could never afford the rugged vehicles used by large logging companies. Instead, we bought clunkers, parked them at the lower ends of the logging road and drove them up and down the mountain until they gave out. Wherever that happened became their final resting places.

I remember an old truck we used to haul slabs, the bark cuts on a log. At that time we simply threw the slabs away. We backed the truck to the end of the green chain. When it was full of slabs, Jerry and I drove it up a steep logging road to an area where we threw the slabs off the side of the hill. Then we backed the truck down the road to the mill once more.

This was trickier than it sounds. The truck had no reverse gear. To return to the mill, I had to push in the clutch and let the truck roll backwards down the hill. When we approached the mill, I used the brake to keep from slamming into it. If I didn't time this operation exactly right, I would not have the truck properly positioned at the end of the green chain. In that case, I'd have to drive the truck back up the hill and let it roll down again.

The truck was not our transportation up and down the mountain. At that time the job belonged to a four-door Model A with a functioning reverse but no second gear and no brakes.

Occasionally we worked weekends if we had stockpiled a rollway of logs at the end of our Friday shift. These extra days were pure profit since my parents, my brother, and I ran the weekend operations without our additional crew. A weekend rollway of logs was like a Christmas bonus.

One Sunday afternoon, we left the mill early, having cut our stockpiled logs. Under normal conditions Dad employed caution driving this brakeless vehicle down the road. However, on this day we came down the mountain at a good clip because we expected to meet no log trucks or other traffic on a Sunday. Mom sat up front, Jerry and I were in the back seat, he already asleep, exhausted from a hard Sunday's labor.

Suddenly I heard Dad mutter, "Oh, oh," and I leaned forward to look through the windshield. Below, a canary-yellow '41 Plymouth coupe climbed toward us on a long, straight stretch of road. The Plymouth was at least eighty yards away, but we were doing twenty-five miles an hour in a car with no brakes.

We could see a turnout halfway between us and the Plymouth. On mountain roads, there is an intricate, almost courtly protocol to using turnouts. The bigger vehicle always has the right of way. If the vehicles are of similar size, the one coming uphill gives way to the one going downhill. In our case, following this protocol was an absolute necessity because we were the one going downhill and we didn't have a snowball's chance in hell of stopping.

I heard metal on metal as Dad instinctively stomped on the brake pedal, driving it to the floor time after time. He whipped off his hat, stuck it out the window, and began waving, signaling the Plymouth to pull into the turnout.

By then we could see the faces in the little yellow car. The driver was a teenager, only a year or two older than me. Beside him sat a girl, whom I automatically assumed to be his girlfriend. I really couldn't see much of her because she held a large lime-green beach ball that obscured all but her blonde hair, eyes, and the bridge of her nose.

The teenagers smiled and waved back at us, probably impressed with the friendliness of these backwoods folks they had encountered on this remote mountain road. My father became more animated and began to honk the Model A's horn. *AH-OOGA! AH-OOGA!* The teenager smiled and honked in return. *Beep, beep. Beep, beep.* Down the road we flew, Dad waving with one hand and honking with the other. *AH-OOGA! AH-OOGA!* The teenager waving with one hand and beeping with the other. *Beep, beep. Beep, beep.*

Finally came the moment of recognition. Four eyes widened in the Plymouth. The teenager hit the brakes and stopped. *We* kept coming.

In an attempt to gain control, Dad pushed in the clutch and shifted into second gear. Since the Model A was missing that gear, throwing the car into neutral would have had the same effect. We lurched forward with heart-stopping acceleration. On our right, brush and tree roots reached for us from a rough-cut bank as we streaked by. On our left our tires threw rocks and dirt clods over the edge of a drop-off into a canyon below.

Dad tried to rectify his mistake by shifting into low gear. But we were going too fast to shift down. He ground the gears over and over, pulling the gearshift with both hands, the steering wheel left free to react on its own. The car swerved left. He grabbed the wheel and cranked it right just as we were about to become airborne into the canyon. We crossed the road and headed for the bank on the right. He cranked the wheel back to the left. Our right wheels climbed the bank. Our bodies leaned right as the car leaned left. We bounced back into the road and continued down the hill.

We reached the turnout, swerved into it, brushed the bank, and careened back into the road. The boy finally realized we weren't going to stop. He threw his car into reverse, whipped his right arm over the seat, sideswiping his girlfriend, twisted his head back and floorboarded it. I have to give him credit. He could drive. Weaving from side to side, he smoked down the hill.

But *we* were freewheeling. He couldn't outrun us. My father began swerving into the bank, hoping to slow us down. But the Model A had been built to take punishment. We kept ricocheting off the bank and picking up speed.

The Plymouth rounded a curve and whipped out of sight. When we reached the curve, we swung around it on two wheels, expecting to be right on top of the little yellow car. But it wasn't there. We were flying down another straight stretch, a stretch devoid of our little yellow Plymouth. Had he gone too far left and catapulted into the canyon?

Then we saw the hood of the Plymouth pointing into the road from the right, approximately thirty yards away. The bank on that side gave way to a marshy slope of ferns and grass. The teenager had cranked the Plymouth up the slope and managed to hold it there with brakes that actually worked.

As we streaked past, three pairs of eyes in the Model A clicked right with almost military precision to meet two pairs of eyes so wide they would have made Little Orphan Annie proud.

We swung around another curve as the road dipped to a level stretch leading to a small bridge over a creek.

We slowed ... We slowed ... We stopped.

Dad shifted into low gear and pulled into a parking area used by fishermen who worked the creek. We sat in silence.

A couple of minutes later, the little yellow Plymouth moved past us. The boy drove slowly, looking straight ahead. His hands tightly gripped the wheel, perfectly positioned at ten and two o'clock. As they passed, the girl, still mostly hidden behind the beach ball, looked at us and lifted her right hand, wiggling her fingers like a princess on a Rose Parade float. As the Plymouth pulled ahead, we could see a collection of ferns, grasses, and mud jammed between the chrome bumper and the body of the car, almost as if a primitive had decorated this float for the princess.

At age fifteen I fell in love with a mysterious girl who, carrying a lime-green beach ball, had ventured up a mountain road and, meeting a crazed backwoods family in a runaway Model A, had the grace to wave at them as she passed by.

As the Plymouth drove out of sight, Jerry rose from the seat, rubbing sleep-filled eyes, and asked, "Are we there yet?"

My mother, without turning her head, answered, "No, we aren't there yet. Go back to sleep."

And he did.

# MICKEY MOUSE IN PAKISTAN

**As a rookie teacher,** I learned a truth that all experienced teachers know: trying to conduct a regular lesson on the day before a major holiday break is an insurmountable task. The day before Thanksgiving break is difficult; the day before Christmas break is impossible. As for spring break, in the words of the Mafia, "Forget about it."

By eleven o'clock in the morning, kids have already had three classroom parties, complete with candy, cake and Pepsi-Cola. That first year they came into my classroom flying on a sugar high, and I expected them to discuss *A Tale of Two Cities*? Holiday adrenalin and sugar soon sabotaged my naive fantasy. As in most experiences for rookie teachers, I learned the hard way.

By spring break I had invented Mickey Mouse Day. My students had no down time, no so-called "free days." We worked hard every day. Because we did, I decided my classes warranted three days a year when they could play intellectual games. From the beginning I called these Mickey Mouse Days.

At first I experimented with several games, but Mickey Mouse Day eventually became the day we played *College Bowl*. I explained that while we were taking a well-deserved break, we were, nevertheless, not going to freefall into anything other than pure academic challenge. *College Bowl*, a popular TV game show in the 1960s, featured teams of college students answering questions from a variety of academic fields. I designed the game so that in the course of a single class period, every student had the opportunity to represent a team. The kids loved this game.

I collected questions from colleagues in all fields: science, math, history, geography, psychology, art, music, business. The coaching staff volunteered questions on sports trivia, and the cooks submitted questions on food preparation. Of course, the game was heavily freighted with challenges from my own fields of interest: philosophy, world religions, and literature. "Oh, no, not another Shakespeare question" became a frequent lament on Mickey Mouse Day. In a few years I had collected enough material to play the game five times a day, three days a year, and never repeat a question.

Mickey Mouse Day became an institution so popular that ex-students often asked to drop in on game days. Occasionally parents complained that kids did not want to leave school early for family vacations because they would miss a Mickey Mouse Day.

When I went to Pakistan to teach, I took the game with me. It was as successful there as it had been in Oregon. Mickey Mouse Day before Thanksgiving went by without a hitch. Then came Christmas.

Christmas in Pakistan should have been an easy holiday to celebrate. At four o'clock in the afternoon on Christmas Eve, three camels plodded through our streets, children dressed as wise men swaying in the saddles. The company had been broadcasting Christmas carols throughout the colony for weeks. But somehow all this Christmas cheer seemed a little too forced.

The cold wind blowing off the Hindu Kush had a dry, grainy feel. Sand swirled, not Christmas snow. Unless a family had connections with the U.S. airbase in Peshawar so that they could buy at the PX, the only hope for Christmas shopping lay in the local bazaars. Families could buy only so many local handicrafts before the gifts became the equivalent of Chia Pets in the States. Our teenagers were blasé. Children dressed as wise men on camels, Christmas music—to these teenagers the efforts came off as feeble attempts to create what they were missing back home.

One of the questions in my *College Bowl* game involved a recording by the Boston Pops Orchestra. The piece, entitled "Pops Roundup," featured theme songs from the TV Westerns *Bonanza, Maverick, Bat Masterson, The Rebel, Gunsmoke, Wagon Train, Wyatt Earp, Rawhide,* and *Have Gun, Will Travel.* I asked the students to identify the themes. This had been a popular question with my classes in Oregon, and I fully expected it to be a hit with American kids in Pakistan.

The question had not been drawn in our Thanksgiving game, but it came up in the Christmas game. I explained the challenge and put on the recording. Midway through the piece, I realized an unusual silence had pervaded the room. Looking up from my notes, I saw anguished faces, tears in the eyes of sixteen-year-old girls, boys with their heads down, hands shading their eyes from the view of others.

Children portraying wise men on camels couldn't affect these teenagers. Christmas carols couldn't do it. But some of these kids had been in Pakistan for three years. They hadn't seen a TV set in all that time. *Bonanza, Maverick, The Rebel, Bat Masterson, Gunsmoke, Wagon Train, Wyatt Earp, Rawhide, Have Gun, Will Travel*—these were songs of home. Songs from the living rooms of their own homes, their grandparents' homes, their friends' homes. These were songs of home.

I never again used that question on Mickey Mouse Day even after I returned to Oregon. I did not want to explain why a collection of TV Western theme songs never failed to bring tears to my eyes.

# THE BEST BEER I'VE EVER TASTED

**Oregon is known for its microbreweries**. No connoisseur of fine beers would pass up one of our local products for a bottle from a big-market brewery. And while I am no connoisseur, I, too, sing the praises of our local brewers. However, when someone once asked me to name the best beer I have ever tasted, I didn't even consider a microbrew. Instead, I found myself choosing between the Stella beer in the Nile Valley and a commonplace beer from a big-market brewery no longer in existence. Finally I answered, "When I was nineteen years old, I drank a bottle of Olympia that had to be the best beer I have ever tasted."

The summer between my freshman and sophomore years in college, I worked on a three-man slash crew for the U.S. Forest Service. Our primary job was cleaning up areas of slash, the debris from logging operations—branches dead undergrowth, chewed-up smaller trees—all the fire-hazard leftovers those operations scatter across an area.

Because clear-cuts were burned in controlled fires, the slash crew didn't do much with them. There was no need to cut or pile debris that would be burned in a wholesale fire. Most of the time we worked to clean up the mess left along logging roads leading into the timber sales.

In addition, we were an on-call firefighting crew. On days with predicted lightning storms, we were instructed to pace ourselves, to work at half speed in case we were called out when one of the lookouts reported a smoke.

We spent the summer cutting and piling slash, then covering the piles with tar paper to keep the debris dry until the first rains of fall, when the piles would be burned. It was a tedious job occasionally interrupted by long hikes into remote areas in chase of lightning fires. Loaded down with firefighting gear, cursing the storm gods, who always chose the most inaccessible areas for their lightning strikes, we griped all the way in. Secretly, however, we thanked those same storm gods for giving us this break from the drudgery of piling slash.

Yes, we put out fires. We also set them. And one of the biggest fires I fought was a fire we set.

\* \* \*

We had spent most of the summer piling slash along a main logging road into the upper reaches of the Clackamas River drainage. Because the three of us were college students, we were still working the second week of September. With one more week of dry weather, we could have avoided having to burn the slash piles. But those same storm gods who sent us on our long hikes, chasing their lightning strikes, scheduled a few showers for the week before we were to leave for school. And those showers convinced the District Office that the time had come for burning.

For three days, we torched the piles along the road. But there was one area we delayed burning, hoping a major rainstorm would interrupt the work long enough for us to escape the responsibility.

This area was a gully enclosed on three sides by a hairpin curve in the road. Above the road was a slash-filled clear-cut, scheduled for burning later in the fall. The clear-cut was not our concern. It was what lay in the gully that worried us.

When we had arrived at the area early in the summer, we found the gully full of trash logs, branches, and dried underbrush, all this debris interspersed in a stand of skinny little fir and hemlock trees. Because the timber sale did not include the gully, the logging company had not built a firebreak around it. That had not stopped them, however, from filling the gully with castoff debris.

Cutting and piling the slash into manageable piles separated by cleared ground was impossible. So we made big piles, piles of tinder-dry debris five to six feet deep, piles barely separated from each other, piles directly under the fir and hemlock trees. Beneath all that tar paper lay a disaster waiting to happen.

"You know we can't do this," I said to Del, the crew foreman, as we stood on the road above the gully.

Del reached into the cab of our pickup to bring out a thermos. Pouring himself coffee, he replied, "It's a little after eleven. Let's break early for lunch. Maybe we can figure something out."

"Better hold up on that," interrupted Denny, the other crew member. "There's a rig coming, and I think it's Tom."

Seeing the District Ranger out in the field surprised us. Contrary to what most people think, not everyone who works for the Forest Service is a Ranger. Each district office has one Ranger, the man in charge. Other employees hold titles of lesser significance. And with all his responsibilities, the Ranger is seldom out driving around the back roads. This unusual appearance made us a little nervous.

Our immediate supervisor was the District Assistant, the Forest Service's equivalent of an Army first sergeant. The District Assistant was normally someone who had come up from the ranks and understood what his crews faced on any given day. The top brass? Not so much. When they came around, we never knew what to expect. But we usually expected the worst.

"So what's the story, guys?" Tom asked as he approached us. "Why isn't this stuff burning."

"This one's a little hairy," Del answered. "You see, it's like this ..."

* * *

When Tom had heard our concerns, he shook his head. "We've had some rain. This stuff is dampened down. It's ready."

He picked up one of our drip torches and shook it to be sure the canister was full of the gasoline-diesel mixture we used. Because he was the District Ranger, we remained quiet as he lit the wick below the nozzle at the end of the torch's long spout.

He stepped to the edge of the road and, digging in his heels, made his way down the cut bank to the nearest pile. Looking over his shoulder at the three of us, he smiled. "This is the way it's done, boys."

He plunged the spout of the drip torch into the pile. Then he moved on, leaving a trail of fire behind him as he torched one pile after another. On one of the larger piles, he actually climbed to the top. With one arm wrapped around the trunk of a tree to maintain his balance, he pushed the torch through the pile several times and then jumped off as flames burst upward through the holes he had made.

Finally he reached the other side of the gully. By the time he had scrambled up the bank to the road, the fires were beginning to merge, a wall of flames building in intensity.

He walked the road back to his pickup, turned off the torch and set it on a stump. Then giving us a wacky thumbs up, he climbed into his rig, backed into a turnaround, and drove off down the road.

We watched as the fire engulfed the gully, some of the flames beginning to crawl up the spindly trunks of the standing trees.

Finally Del broke our silence. Laughing, he said, "And that's the way it's done, boys."

"So where do we start?" Denny asked.

"It'll run uphill," Del answered. "The road is a natural firebreak, but I'd better move the rig. Before I do, grab a couple of pulaskis and see if you can cut a fire line down this side of the gully. I'll check the other side after I move the rig."

A few minutes later, he yelled down to us, "Come on up. It's moving to the left. We have to work the other side."

As we hurried down the road, staying to its far side because the fire created its own wind, blowing sparks and embers through the air, Denny suddenly stopped. He stared at the clear-cut above us. "It's crossing!" he yelled. "It's jumping the road!" Smoke rolled upward from fiery circles in nearby brush. Suddenly a small snag thirty feet above the road exploded into flame.

"That's it!" Del yelled. "We need help! I'm getting on the radio right now!" He turned and sprinted for the pickup.

* * *

Six hours later, Del, Denny and I were on the upper cat road above the clear-cut, laying hose from one of the tankers below. "Hey," someone yelled up to us. We didn't recognize the voice. He was probably from one of the other districts called in to help. "Hey," he yelled again. "You guys up there. You the slash crew who set this thing?"

We were too fatigued to explain how little we had to do with this fire. After having eaten its way to the top of the clear-cut, it had jumped left into fresh timber. Before being contained, the fire would eventually consume two hundred acres. We might have had a case for defending ourselves, but we were the ones who had built the piles in the first place. We knew they were dangerous. We were due some of the blame.

When we didn't answer, the person yelled again. "Hey. You the slash-crew guys or not? If you are, someone from your District Office is down on the road. He's looking for you."

* * *

Paul Rickman, the District's second in command, was an engineer. I disliked working with engineers. They never got dirty. Even at the end of a day, hiking up trails and slogging through the woods to lay out a road or a timber sale, they never got dirty. We grunts who packed their gear and fought our way through brush, over rocks, across small streams to hold up poles with little targets as they peered at us through their transits, we got dirty.

Paul Rickman, in his matching tan shirt and pants, leaned against his Forest Service rig as he watched us work our way down the hill. He definitely was not dirty. Even his pickup, the aerial swaying a little in the slight east wind that had helped drive our fire up the hill, showed little dust from the drive up the mountain road. Everything about Paul Rickman was clean.

*We* were dirty. Our faces blackened with soot, a combination of ash and dried sweat, our shirts and jeans scorched where embers had tried to get at our skin. We carefully avoided smoldering hot spots as we approached the bank above the road.

Another problem I had with Paul Rickman was his choice in personal cars. He drove a Volkswagen Bug, the first one I had ever seen. Like most boys my age, I loved cars. I mean real cars. Chevys, Fords, Oldsmobiles, Mercurys. Real cars.

I remember the first time Paul drove his Volkswagen into the warehouse parking lot. We circled it as if we were looking at a zoo exhibit. It was ugliest thing I had ever seen. "Looks like a turtle," I whispered to the person next to me. "Bet it's just about as fast, too." How could I trust someone who never got dirty and drove a car like that?[10]

"Think he's gonna fire us?" Denny asked as we neared Paul's pickup. At this point I didn't care whether he fired us or not. I tried to say that,

---

[10]  Before I start getting hate mail, let me say that in my adult life one of my very favorite cars was a beautiful Baltic blue Volkswagen Bug.

but my throat was so parched from six hours of breathing smoke I could manage only a raspy cough.

"Hey, guys," Paul began. "Thought I'd come up and see how you're doing."

When we didn't answer, he continued, "I know what happened. You've probably been taking some heat for all this." Then he laughed when he realized what he'd just said. "I mean … Well, you know what I mean. But I want you to know no one's blaming you.

I brought you something."

He held bucket in his left hand. When he handed the bucket to Del, a bottle clinked in it. Del looked into the bucket and smiled. He reached in and pulled out a dripping stubby of Olympia, ice particles running down its side.

* * *

Three bottles of Oly. One for each of us. I was nineteen. Denny was eighteen. Paul's giving us that beer was illegal. Also, Forest Service regulations certainly were being broken. This from a man in line to become a District Ranger. Maybe I was wrong about clean engineers who drove funny-looking cars. Smiling, he handed us a bottle opener.

Nineteen or not, I had had my share of beer before that day. And I have certainly had my share since. But when I tipped that ice-cold Oly to my soot-ringed mouth, I knew then what I know now. On a logging road under a smoky sky in the upper Clackamas River drainage, a bottle of Olympia was, without question, the best beer I have ever tasted.

# SOME LIKE IT HOT

**I came home from three years** in Pakistan with two addictions: international travel and curry. Not simply curry. Pakistani curry. *Hot* curry. *Brimstone-fire* curry. Curry guaranteed to clear your nasal passages and singe your eyebrows.

Unfortunately when I looked for that kind of curry in the U.S., I found most of our Indian restaurants fear violating the American palate with anything even remotely close to authentic. In most cases the fare of Indian restaurants consists of a comfortable, non-threatening blend more representative of Southern India, where the addition of coconut milk both sweetens and cools the curry.

Eventually I found two restaurants on the West Coast willing to serve my kind of curry: one in San Francisco and the other in Vancouver, British Columbia.

\* \* \*

In the year before Sue and I married, I began slowly introducing her to my idiosyncrasies. Since Sue had never been out of the States, I thought we could start with something easy, a mini-vacation in British Columbia. We'd spend several days in Vancouver and then ferry to Victoria to explore Canada's version of nineteenth-century England. However, one of the reasons I suggested this trip involved a risky test of our budding romance. I planned to introduce Sue to real curry—authentic, mouth-watering curry.

Our second evening in Vancouver, we set out for the Maharajah, an Indian restaurant located in Gastown, one of the city's most entertaining districts. Promising Sue a life-changing experience, at least as far as her culinary adventures were concerned, I talked up the Maharajah as we strolled down a cobblestone street to the restaurant's location midway between two major tourist attractions: the steam clock with its piercing brass whistles and the statue of Gassy Jack Deighton, original owner of the first saloon in Gastown.

When we entered the restaurant, the spicy aroma of hot peppers and ginger bubbling in hot curry welcomed me home. After we had been shown to a table in a darkly lit corner, I breathed in deeply. Sue watched me with a bemused smile. "This, Babes," I intoned, "is what Heaven must smell like. Forget the seven virgins. The reward in Heaven is perfect curry."

Before Sue could reply, our waitress appeared from the dim recesses of the restaurant. She was obviously of Indian descent with beautiful dark eyes and a long black braid trailing down her back. But her attire was strictly Gastown, a blue British Columba University sweatshirt over tight jeans. "Good evening. Welcome to the Maharajah. My name is Farida," she smiled, spreading a couple of menus on the table. "Our specials for tonight are …"

"Farida," I interrupted, "we don't need to hear about the specials. We're here because I believe there are only two restaurants on the West Coast who serve authentic curries. Yours and one in San Francisco. To save time, let me explain that I've lived in Pakistan. I know curry. No specials. We're going to have a very traditional dinner."

She paused, tapping her pencil lightly against her front teeth with the attitude of someone who had heard this speech before. "Okay," she said. "Can I bring you a drink while you check the authenticity of our menu?"

"Do you have a Pimm's cup?"

"As a matter of fact, we do."

"Great. Then we'll have a Pimm's cup for the lady and a beer for me. I'd like something Canadian. The only one I know is Molson. What do you think?

"Do you drink Budweiser in the States?"

"Actually, I do."

"Then Molson should be perfect for you."

"Is that a recommendation ?"

"No, just an observation."

"Okay. If you *did* have a recommendation, what would it be?"

She looked me up and down, again tapping her teeth with the pencil. Finally she announced, "You look like a Moosehead man to me."

"Moosehead? You have a beer named Moosehead?"

"Yes, we do."

"Seems like a strange name for a beer."

"Oh, I don't know," she shrugged. "It's better than Buzzard Breath, I suppose."

"You have a beer named Buzzard Breath?"

"No, we don't. I think you can see why."

"Okay. Well, then.We'll have a Pimm's cup and a Moosehead."

"I like her," Sue smiled as we watched Farida walk toward the kitchen. "She has spunk. So what's a Pimm's cup?"

"It's a very British drink. I've found it only in English pubs and in truly authentic Indian restaurants although I understand it's popular in certain parts of the U.S. It was invented in the early nineteenth century by the owner of an oyster bar in London. His name was Pimm, and he served it in pewter tankards, hence the name Pimm's cup. It became so popular he opened a distillery and sold it from bicycles around London.

"He kept his recipe secret, but it was basically a mix of gin, fruit juices, and spices. Today, only one distillery makes it, and the recipe's still secret. Supposedly only six people know it."

"Do you think that's true?"

"I don't know about just six people knowing it, but I'm sure the recipe's closely guarded. It's a very popular drink in England. I've read that over eighty thousand pints are sold every year at Wimbledon."

"Will I get it in a tankard?"

"Probably not. It's usually served in tall chilled glasses. It's a really cooling drink. Perfect for Indian dinners because it helps offset the curry's heat."

"Sounds good," Sue agreed, turning her attention to the menu.

"Why don't you let me order for the both of us?" I asked.

"Oh, good," she, sighed. "I was hoping you'd do that. I mean, I don't really know what to expect. And," she added after a pause, "I know how much all this means to you. It seems so important and everything."

"Listen," I said, leaning over the table to take her hand. "Yes, I really want you to like this dinner, but if you don't, you don't. Curry isn't for everyone."

"Well, it seems a little like a test, you know. Who'd suppose a relationship would depend upon liking some kind of ethnic food?"

"That's nonsense. Sure, I'd like you to love curry the way I do. But I don't expect you to go fishing with me. I don't expect you to love

Woody Allen movies, and I hope you don't expect me to love cake decorating and baseball the way you do. There *is* one litmus test to this relationship, however."

"And that is?"

"You have to love Willie Nelson. Anyone who doesn't love Willie Nelson has no soul."

"As a matter of fact," Sue smiled, "I have a disk with Willie's 'Angel Flying Too Close to the Ground' in my car. I listen to it over and over again."

And at that moment, I knew I would marry this lady someday.

\* \* \*

"So," Farida asked, putting our drinks on the table, "what would you like to order?"

"We'll start with four samosas," I answered, "two vegetarian and two beef. Then we'll have chicken curry." I paused to add weight to what I was about to say. "And here's where the rubber hits the road." Farida rolled her eyes and waited.

"I want my curry hot. Understand? Hot. I don't want some watered-down version for the typical American. I want Northern curry. Hot."

"Hot," she said. "I've written *hot* on the slip. I've underlined it twice. I've added three exclamation marks. Hot. I've got it."

"That's just for me," I cautioned. "For the lady, I think medium would be best."

"Right. What else you having?"

"We'll have dal. And a plate of chapatis, of course."

"We don't have chapatis."

"What? Of course, you have chaptis. You can't serve Indian food without chaptis."

"We don't have chaptis," she answered. "But we do have rotis. If you'd looked at the menu, you'd have seen that. No chaptis. Only rotis."

"So what's a roti?"

"It's another name for chapati."

I looked at her for a moment before glancing at Sue, who was covering her mouth to keep from laughing.

"Okay. We'll have four rotis."

"Anything else?"

"No, that should do it."

As Farida walked away, Sue couldn't contain herself any longer. "I really like her," she laughed.

"I know," I replied. "She has spunk. but I wonder how much in tips she loses because of that spunk."

"I'll bet she makes more in tips than anyone else in the restaurant," Sue smiled.

"You're probably right, Babes," I answered. "You're probably right."

* * *

The samosas were delicious. Deep-fried pastry filled with potatoes, peas, and assorted other vegetables Spiced ground beef jazzing up the nonvegetarian versions. "l love these," Sue gushed, "and this Pimm's cup? Absolutely wonderful."

I sipped my Moosehead as I watched her obvious delight in the food. *So far, so good*, I thought.

"How're we stacking up to the San Francisco restaurant?" Farida asked, placing a rectangular bowl of chicken curry in front of Sue and another in front of me. A dark smiling boy who looked like a waiter-in-training stood by with a plate of rotis, a serving bowl of dal, and another of rice.

"The samosas are wonderful," Sue smiled, "and all the rest of this smells *really* good."

"So we beat out the San Francisco restaurant?" Farida asked, looking at me.

"Your food's great," I answered. "But their atmosphere's a little more authentic."

"Oh? How?"

"Well, they're a basement restaurant, so you go down a flight of stairs and through a beaded curtain into a small bar. From there, you go into the dining room, dark like this but with soft sitar music in the background."

"Sounds a little cheesy to me," Farida responded.

"Maybe," I agreed. "But what I like—what brings Pakistan home to me—is the staff wears traditional dress."

"Like what?" she asked, placing a serving spoon in the dal and spreading a napkin over the pile of rotis to keep them warm.

"The hostess wears a sari, and the waiting staff wear shalwar kameez."

"Really?" Farida replied. "And you're impressed with that?"

"Well, it adds an authentic touch to the restaurant. Do you ever wear a sari or shalwar kemeez?"

"No, but my grandmother does. I can give you her number if you'd like."

"Oh, no, that's all right."

"Well, enjoy," Farida said, turning away.

"I know what a sari is," Sue said, "but what's this shalwar whatever thing?"

"It's a pretty standard outfit, especially in Pakistan. The shalwar is a kind of one-size-fits-all pants, sort of like pajama bottoms. They're wide at the waist, pulled in with drawstrings, and narrow at the ankles. Both men and women wear them. The shalwar is a long blouse or shirt that goes down to around the knees. It sounds weird, I know, but it can be quite nice."

"The men and women wear the same thing?"

"In a sense. The basic design is the same," I answered, spooning rice onto her plate, "but women, of course, dress theirs up. They're bright colored and enhanced with embroidery. They also wear a long silk scarf. Sometimes over their heads but usually draped around their shoulders. Occasionally when they go into places where modesty demands it, they wrap the scarves around their faces so that only their eyes show. It's a little sexy, you know?"

"Well, as a fashion reporter, you lack some finesse, but I think I 've seen that outfit in movies, so I can of kind of envision it."

"I never claimed fashion to be one of my strong points," I grinned, covering her rice with curry.

"Now if you really want to be authentic," I continued, having repeated the process with my own plate, "You don't eat with silverware. You just tear off a piece of chapati and ..."

"Roti," Sue corrected, smiling.

"Roti," I repeated. "... and use it to scoop up the food and pop it into your mouth." As I spoke, I took a bite of my curry-soaked piece of roti. Frowning, I swiped some more with the roti and tasted it. "Damn! It's not right," I growled, tossing the rest of the roti onto my plate. "This isn't hot enough at all. Not even close."

"I'm sorry," Sue said. "Do you want to send it back?"

"Won't matter," I grumbled. "You can't just toss in some spices and heat it up. It has to bubble for a long time. Curry can't be rushed. When we had dinner parties, we'd bring in our bearer's father, who …"

"Excuse me. Your bearer?"

"Our bearer," I repeated. "I'd suppose you'd call him our houseboy though he was more like a member of the family. Anyway, his father was a master cook, and he'd come in to prepare special dinners for us. His curry simmered all afternoon. We could smell it for days after the party. You can't just throw in some spices to fix curry that hasn't been cooked the way you want."

"Well, again, I'm really sorry," Sue said in a low voice, trying to calm me down. "I know how disappointed you are, but I hope you're not going to take it out on Farida. It's not her fault."

"Oh, I wouldn't do that," I shrugged. "This is still good. I'm not saying it's not good. It's just not great. No, I'll eat it. Curry is curry. It's just that …"

"I'm going to use my silverware," Sue announced, changing the subject. She picked up her fork and tasted the dal. "Ooh, this is good. Curried lentils?"

"Yes. Sometimes they add peas and other stuff, but it's basically spiced lentils."

"Well it's really good," she smiled.

We ate in silence for a few moments. I served myself more curry from my bowl, and when I looked up, I was startled by what I saw across the table. Sue held her napkin to her mouth, her eyes watery, nose running.

"What's wrong? Are you all right?"

"I … I think so," she stammered. "I just didn't expect it to be *so* spicy. I mean, it takes my breath away."

*Oh, no,* I thought, *she doesn't like it.*

"I suppose it's an acquired taste," she gasped, after a moment of wiping both her eyes and her nose. "I know I'll learn to like it the way you do if I just give it a chance."

"That's all right," I said. "You don't have to eat it."

"No, we can't just leave it. I'll finish it." She took another small bite. Swallowing, she brought the napkin to her face again. "I'm sorry," she finally admitted. "I don't think I can eat it all."

"It's okay. We'll have them box it up and take it back to the motel. We have that small refrigerator in the room. We can have it for lunch tomorrow."

"It'll be cold," she objected.

"All curry's good, Babes. Hot or cold. I love leftover curry."

"Well, if you're sure."

"Of course, I'm sure. As for the rest of tonight, there's a frozen-yogurt place up the street. It's just what you need to take some of the heat off your curry."

That's what I said, but I was thinking, *She'll never like curry. If what I had tonight was the chef's version of hot curry, I hate to think how bland that stuff in front of her must be. No, she'll never like curry.*

As we stepped into the street, Sue began apologizing again. Putting my finger to her lips, I pulled her close. "Listen. You still love Willie, don't you?"

"Yes, she smiled. "I do."

"Well, then," I said, taking her hand and starting up the street, "all's right with the world."

* * *

The next morning Sue and I went for a run in Stanley Park, followed by a breakfast of small pastries and mangoes while we watched a flotilla of sailboats maneuver near the Lion's Gate Bridge. "It's beautiful here, isn't it?" Sue said.

"Yes, it is. I've often said if I lived anywhere other than Oregon, it'd be British Columbia."

"You know," Sue replied, leaning back against me, "even though that leftover curry is in the refrigerator, I could still smell it last night, and I'd swear the smell was even stronger this morning."

"Part of curry's charm is how powerful those spices are," I answered. "And, I hate to tell you this, but its heat intensifies overnight. Leftover curry is always stronger the next day."

"Oh, no," Sue laughed. "If that stuff I had last night is even hotter today, we'd better have a fire extinguisher with us when we open the refrigerator door."

* * *

We didn't have a fire extinguisher, but we made a second stop at the market where we had bought our breakfast to pick up a package of plastic forks and knives along with some paper plates, pita bread, and a small jar of peanut butter.

"What're these for?" Sue asked, pointing to the pita bread and peanut butter as the clerk checked us out.

"Bread helps cut the heat of the curry. That's another reason chapatis are used to eat it. I'm thinking if you have as much trouble today as you had last night, the pita will help."

"And the peanut butter?"

"Well, if all else fails, you can at least have a sandwich."

* * *

"This smells so good," I gushed, leaning over my plate of leftover curry.

Sue stalled, watching me as I took my first bite.

"Holy cow!" I exclaimed.

"What?"

"This is *so* hot. This *is really* hot!"

"How can that be?" Sue asked. "I mean, I know you said leftover curry gets hotter, but how can my curry from last night be so hot when it was supposed to be not so bad compared to yours. I don't mean bad, but well, you know what I mean."

"Because this *isn't* yours," I laughed, digging in for a second bite. "It's mine."

"It's yours? What do you mean, it's yours."

"It's mine. Get it? Last night I had your medium curry, and you had my hot curry!"

"Oh!" Sue exclaimed. "Now I see. And that makes everything okay, doesn't it? I can give curry another chance now that I know not all of it has to be so hot."

"More than okay," I laughed, scooping up dripping curry from my plate. "We can try again tonight if you want."

"Not tonight," Sue objected, shaking her head. "Definitely not tonight. But since you're enjoying that curry so much, how about you have it all, and I settle for this?" She began spreading peanut butter on a piece of pita bread.

"Okay, then. Not tonight. But you're not giving up on curry?"

"Willie will carry me only so far in this relationship," Sue smiled."Being able to handle curry will certainly seal the deal."

And it did.

# A FATHER'S DREAM

**I was seven** when my family moved to Oregon. Dad had been offered a sawmill job near Sandy, and he went ahead, promising to send for us once he had found a place to live. In the meantime, he would stay in Estacada with my parents' best friends, Bo and Ida Richardson, who had made the move a year before.

The call came two weeks before Christmas. Jerry and I were allowed to open our presents early. I remember how proudly I wore my double-holstered Roy Rogers pistols on that long Greyhound bus ride from Aberdeen to Portland, where Dad picked us up for the drive to Estacada.

I had no regrets about the move. I was leaving a rough neighborhood behind. Better yet, I was escaping Mrs. Wolf and her knuckle-hammering crusade against lefthanders. After eighteen months in Aberdeen, Oregon sounded like the Promised Land.

My father had rented a place for us, but it wouldn't be ready until the first of the year. In the meantime, we crowded in with the Richardsons and their three kids.

I enrolled in Estacada Elementary, overjoyed to find no prejudice against my left hand. As the Muslims say, "God is great."

Dad had held back the biggest surprise until we joined him. He hadn't rented a mere house. He had rented a farm. My mother expressed her displeasure about his unilateral decision, and whenever Mom was uneasy, we *all* were uneasy. Over the next few days, he tried to convince her living on a farm would be the best of all possible worlds.

I realize now my father was living his dream. He had grown up on a farm in Minnesota, having been taken from an orphanage by a German family. They were required by the state to provide him an eighth-grade education. In turn, he was legally bound to work for them until age eighteen.

The fact that he left their farm on the morning of his eighteenth birthday and never looked back shows how little he enjoyed life as some kind of indentured servant. But his dislike of the family didn't extend

193

itself to the farm. My father lived day-to-day with few aspirations but having his own farm turned out to be one of them.

I'd like to believe Mom accepted moving to the farm because she realized how important it was for Dad. I suspect, however, she agreed because she thought this arrangement would be temporary. We had never lived anywhere for more than two years before moving on. Also Dad was renting this farm, not buying it. In fact, the elderly owner, Mr. Grassick, insisted we understand the time would come when we'd have to leave.

The year was 1944, and Mr. Grassick's son was a soldier somewhere in Europe. "He'll be home from the war some day," Mr. Grassick said, "and when he returns, the farm is his. He grew up on the place. It's my legacy to him. Understand that, Mr. Christenson. If you're still here when he comes home, you'll have to move."

Dreams sometimes obscure reality. Dad didn't seem able to accept the possibility of our not being allowed to stay on the farm. It had stood empty for several months after Mr. Grassick and his wife moved into town. Already in deteriorating condition because the Grassicks hadn't been able to keep up with the work, it didn't merely look unoccupied. It looked abandoned. I believe my father hoped if he built up the place, Mr. Grassick would appreciate the effort and give us the opportunity to stay.

* * *

Our move-in date was officially the first day in January. Mom wanted a few days before that to make the house ready, but Mr. Grassick, a stickler for details, refused to honor her request. "The rent begins on the first of January," he declared. "That's when you'll have keys to the place."

New Year's Day was a Monday. Dad and Bo took advantage of the three-day weekend to drive a borrowed truck to Aberdeen and bring down our furniture and the boxes of personal effects Mom had packed before the three of us had taken the bus to Portland. Over the weekend, Mom supervised the unloading of the truck and the arrangement of the furniture in the farmhouse.

Jerry and I experienced none of this. While the adults performed these tasks, we had been left in Estacada to keep us "out from underfoot."

As a result, neither of us had seen our new home when Mom proclaimed Tuesday our "move-in day."

Because Tuesday also marked my return to school after Christmas vacation, I had to wait until the end of the day to finally see the farm. I was both anxious and nervous about the move. Anxious because I was tired of living with others and nervous because the day would be two firsts for me. The first time I would see my new home and the first time I would ride a school bus.

In Aberdeen I had lived within walking distance of school. Now I was not only expected to find the right bus in that collection of identical yellow vehicles parked bumper to bumper along the curb but also expected to know when to get off the bus at a place I had never seen.

Thinking back on this experience, I marvel my parents saw no problem in their seven-year-old son's managing this task. Fortunately, I wasn't alone. Mary Beth, the younger of the two Richardson girls, had been assigned to make sure I found the right bus. As it turned out, I couldn't have been in more capable hands.

Mary Beth Richardson was an older woman, a fourth-grader, and she was as tough as anyone I had ever met, including all the hard cases in my Aberdeen neighborhood. I didn't know at the time how much I would need her as we approached the line of busses. For I was about to encounter the infamous Ira Grimes.

\* \* \*

"Whoa! Hold it, boy. This ain't your bus." I hesitated, one foot on the first step and the other on the curb. I looked up into the grizzled face of the bus driver glowering down at me. Buttons strained to hold his checkered shirt over a ponderous belly. The rolled-up pant legs of his ragged jeans exposed the tops of mud-encrusted boots. He leaned to the left to spit tobacco into a coffee can and then turned to face me once more. "I said this ain't your bus. You hard of hearing, boy?"

"He hears fine," Mary Beth said over my shoulder. "He's new. And unless the number's wrong on the side of this bus, it *is* the right one."

"Yeah, well why didn't you say so?" he growled, continuing to stare down at me while refusing to acknowledge Mary Beth's presence. "You do talk, don't you, boy?" I nodded, still standing awkwardly with one foot on the step.

"I'll take that for a yes. Where do you live?"

My first words to Ira Grimes confirmed his opinion that I was intellectually challenged, an opinion that would not change for the rest of our time together. I recited what I thought I had been told to say. "I'm supposed to get off at the grassy place."

"The what! The grassy place! What the hell's the grassy place?" I stepped back onto the curb, terrified of this blustering man shouting down at me.

Mary Beth stepped to the door. "He means the Grassick place."

"Oh, the *Grassick* place. Yeah, I heard someone was moving into that dump." Returning his stare to me, he snarled, "Well, get in, boy. We ain't got all day."

As I once more started to step into the bus, Mary Beth said, "And you need to tell him when you get there."

"What? He don't even know where he lives?" He leaned toward her. "He's retarded, ain't he?"

"No, he's not. He's never seen the place. His folks are moving in today. So you tell him when you're there." She glared at him. There was no backdown in this girl.

"Yeah, well, okay, I'll tell him. Get in the bus, boy," he snapped. "I'll let you know when you're at the *grassy* place."

I found an empty seat and stared longingly out the window at Mary Beth as the bus pulled away from the curb. I didn't want to be near this man ever again. But, of course, I would be. Twice a day for the rest of this school year and into the following year as well.

I have always wondered why a man who disliked kids would drive a school bus. In my first few days as one of his captive audience, I was somewhat relieved to discover he spread his venom equally among his charges. I wasn't a special target. I was simply an easy one.

I had escaped the clutches of Mrs. Wolf only to fall into those of Ira Grimes. God may be great, but he also has a strange sense of humor.

\* \* \*

As Ira Grimes made stops along Eagle Creek Road, letting others leave the bus, I began to worry. *What if he's mean enough to let me out somewhere that isn't the Grassick place?* Finally, he pulled to a stop, cranked open the door, and announced, "Okay, boy, this is the *grassy* place." I made my way to the front of the bus.

As I stepped down, he leaned toward me. "I assume your parents have a bus schedule, but in case they don't, I'll be here sometime between seven-fifteen and seven-thirty in the morning. You'd better be standing across the road when I do. If you're not, I honk the horn twice. If you don't come bustin' your butt out that front door, I go on. And if I do that," he continued after leaning to his left to spit into his coffee can, "you miss a day of school. Believe me, boy, someone as dumb as you can't afford to miss no day of school. Know what I mean?"

I nodded as if I did and stepped from the bus, backing down the shoulder of the road as it pulled away. Turning, I saw the farmhouse for the first time.

When my father had described the farm, he mentioned the house needed a little fixing up. This comment raised a red flag for Mom because we had never lived in a place that *didn't* need "a little fixing up" and Dad had never seemed to notice. She immediately decided his preparing her for the place with that comment had to mean it was a real mess, and she was not reticent about sharing this conclusion with all of us.

Mom's warning combined with Ira Grimes's having called the Grassick place a "dump" had prepared me for the worst. But when I looked up from the gravel of the road's shoulder, I didn't see either a "real mess" *or* a "dump." I saw a home.

A dirt path led through the overgrown lawn to a four-by-two-foot slab of concrete serving as the house's front step. A narrow, tall farmhouse loomed above this step. A farmhouse completely unadorned with fussy touches. Everything had been white sometime in the past. Now the paint on the clapboard siding yellowed in peeled spots along the upper reaches and browned in mud-spattered spots along the concrete foundation.

Looking up, I saw a circular window of either an upstairs room or an attic. I had never lived in a house with an upstairs. I had never lived in a white house. *Please, God,* I silently pleaded, *let this be the Grassick place.*

The front door opened, and Mom stepped out, smiling as she wiped her hands on a cleaning cloth. As I walked up the path, I passed the strangest tree I had ever seen. I stopped, looking at it in wonder.

"Come on, Bobby," Mom called. "Let me show you our new home." She was smiling. She seemed happy. *Okay, God,* I mentally continued, *let her like this place as much as I do.*

"Mom," I asked once she had released me from a smothering hug into her apron, "What's with that tree?"

"Your father says it's a monkey tree," she laughed.

"Really? Why's it called that?"

"I don't know," she answered, stepping aside for me to enter the house. "You'll have to ask him. I'm sure he'll have an interesting answer even if he makes it up on the spot."

Mom was right. My father had a knack for explaining things, sometimes with peculiar touches. For example, whenever we saw rain and sun at the same time—the way misty rain fades into sunshine—Dad proclaimed somewhere in the world a monkey had been married. I was sure he would have an entertaining tale about the monkey tree.

As I stepped into the house, Jerry rushed up to me. "Come on, Bobby," he yelled, grabbing me by the arm. "You gotta see the barn. It's great. Come on. You gotta see it."

"No," Mom interrupted. "Bobby has to change from his school clothes before you two go climbing around in that dirty old barn. Besides, I want to show him the rest of the house."

"Aw, Mom, he won't get dirty. The barn's nice."

"Jerry," she intoned as she leveled her Mom-look at him. He looked to his shoes, and she turned to me.

"This is the living room," she proclaimed, sweeping her arm to a room filled with Mom's touches: her crocheted doilies on the sofa arms, the knitted afghan draped over the sofa back, the oval rag rug carefully centered on the floor.

The room had only two reminders Dad would share this house: his easy chair—conspicuously doily free—and his brand-new floor-model Zenith radio. My father's birthday was ten days before Christmas. Normally, he received only a token gift or two on his birthday because it was overshadowed by Christmas. This year had been different. Somehow, Mom had managed to save enough money to buy this beautiful radio encased in its mahogany cabinet. It was the perfect gift, and Dad loved it.

"What do you think so far, Bobby?"

"Mom, I think this is the best living room in the best house we have ever had."

She reached out and pulled me into a hug. "Me, too," she said softly. Then taking my arm, she added, "But you haven't seen it yet. Come on. Let me show you the rest."

* * *

The north wall of the living room had three evenly spaced doors. The first and the third led into small bedrooms. Jerry and I would have the bedroom at the front of the house. Having shown me that room, Mom led me past the middle door and merely tapped on the third door as we walked by. "This bedroom is for your dad and me. Now you have to see the kitchen. It's wonderful."

"Wait a minute," I said, tugging at her arm. What about that other door?"

"Oh, that? It's just a staircase to the attic."

"We *do* have an attic. I've always wanted to live in a house with an attic."

"I'm surprised," she replied. "As far as I know, you've never even *been* in a house with an attic."

"That's why I want to live in a house with an attic."

"Well, I hate to tell you this, but the attic is off limits for Jerry and you."

"Why?"

"Because it's filled with stuff the Grassicks have stored. They asked if it was okay if they left it there. I know you want to look, so I'll show you the staircase. But I want a promise you and Jerry won't go up there."

We returned to the door. It opened onto a narrow set of stairs barely wider than the door itself. At the top I could see the underside of a trapdoor. The staircase had a moldy smell. Even worse, there were several holes punched in the sidewalls from which sawdust had spilled into small piles on the stairs.

"What made those holes, Mom?"

"Well," she laughed, "your father says it was probably termites. They'd have to be really big termites, wouldn't they?"

"What's a termite?"

"It's a bug that eats its way through wood. But don't worry. They don't leave holes this big. Dad was just kidding."

Don't worry? I wonder how many times adults plant an image in a young person's head and then dismiss it with "Don't worry." If Mom only knew how her "That'll lead to bloodshed" had me left me terrified of the woodshed at the Copalis Beach house.

I looked up the semi-dark staircase with its piles of sawdust at the base of the walls and cobwebs strung from the slanted ceiling. All this combined with the thought of giant wood-eating bugs living there convinced me Mom wouldn't have to worry. I would *never* want to go into that attic.

Mom must have seen the look on my face. "Oh, don't worry, Bobby. There's an obvious explanation for those holes. This staircase is so narrow that when the Grassicks hauled big items up the stairs, they probably banged the walls and punched these holes. Since the staircase isn't seen by company, they just didn't bother to fix them."

"But what about the sawdust? Is something eating the wood?"

"No, the builders of this house put it there. Old houses are often insulated with sawdust."

"What does that mean?"

"*Insulated?* It's something people do to houses to protect them from the weather." She took my shoulder and turned me from the doorway. Shutting the door, she said, "Your dad can explain it if you want. Let's see the kitchen."

I looked at the closed door. I wanted it closed. I wanted it closed for the rest of the time we lived there.

* * *

Mom had been so upbeat when she stepped outside to meet me as I walked up the path to the house. I hadn't seen her this way for weeks. The stress of packing up everything on her own in Aberdeen and then taking her boys on that long Greyhound journey and the additional stress of living in such close quarters with the Richardsons had beaten her down. The final straw had been Dad's springing the farm on her. But all that seemed behind her now. I realized as we stepped into the kitchen that all by itself this room had sold her on the farm.

It wasn't a kitchen that would have made most women in today's world happy. By far the largest room in the house, it measured from the east wall of the building to the west, taking up nearly one third of the floor plan. "Isn't this wonderful," Mom gushed, holding her arms wide.

"And there's the best part," she said pointing to a large wood-burning stove, almost the twin to her stove in the Copalis Beach house. "I can cook again. I can bake again. I was so tired of that little electric stove in Aberdeen. This stove is beautiful."

But I wasn't looking at the stove. "What's that?" I asked, pointing.

"Oh," she smiled. "That's the bathtub." And it was. A claw-footed, full-sized bathtub with an oval plywood cover neatly fitted over the top.

"A bathtub in the kitchen, Mom! What's a bathtub doing in the kitchen?"

"Well, to take baths in, silly. What do you think a bathtub's for?"

"It's in the kitchen, Mom. Why isn't it in the bathroom?"

My mother waited a beat before she answered. "There isn't any bathroom, Bobby. We aren't in the city anymore."

"So we have an outhouse again?"

"Yes," she said, pulling me close again. "But an outhouse isn't the end of the world, is it?"

"No, Mom, it isn't," I agreed. Then I began to giggle.

"What?" she asked. "What's so funny."

"I was just thinking," I grinned. "You and Dad are going to have to take baths in the kitchen, too, aren't you?"

"Yes, we are. I guess we're going to have to come up with some privacy routines, aren't we?"

When I laughed, she gave me a stern look.

"No, Mom," I giggled. "I wasn't thinking about you and Dad. I was thinking about Mr. Grassick sitting in that tub while Mrs. Grassick cooked dinner."

A series of ringing sounds from behind me interrupted Mom's laughter. I turned, looking for the source. On the kitchen wall near the doorway to the living room was the strangest telephone I had ever seen, a wooden box with brass bells, a handset on one side, and a crank on the other. The rings had come in both long and short bursts.

"You like it?" Mom asked, smiling at my confused expression. "It's our phone."

"Whoever heard of a phone like that? And what's with the weird way it rings?"

"That *is* going to take some getting used to," she replied. "We're on a party line."

"A party line?"

"Yes. It means some of our neighbors share the same line with us. We each have our own set of rings. Ours is one long and three shorts."

"Sorta like Morse code or something," I said.

"It kind of is. The thing to remember is not to answer the phone unless it's our ring."

"Well, duh, Mom. Why would I want to answer someone else's ring?"

I walked over for a closer look. With the two brass bells centered below the roof-like top, the phone looked like a face staring at me. The lower portion of the phone contained a cabinet with an extended writing shelf. A small writing pad lay on the shelf, which also held a pencil in a slot just like the pencil slot on my desk at school.

"It's pretty neat," I said. "But where's the dial with the numbers?"

"There isn't one," Mom answered. She put her hand on the crank. "You do everything with this. If you want to call someone on the party line, you have to know their rings. Then you just crank long and short turns and wait for them to answer. If you want to call someone else, one long crank gets the operator. Then she puts your call through."

"Okay," I answered. "I can remember all that."

"Well, here are a couple of other things you *must* also remember. Always hold the phone to your ear to make sure no one is using the line before you do any cranking. People don't like that a bit, and we want to be good neighbors. And, whatever you do, always hang up immediately if someone *is* on the phone."

"Why wouldn't I? I'm not trying to call *them*."

"I know. It's just that some people aren't as polite as you. Some are just curious, maybe what we might even call nosey. They like to listen in to other people's conversations." This was one of Mom's clever parenting techniques. She'd slip in a compliment in such a way I'd feel I'd let her down if I didn't heed her advice.

"Don't worry, Mom. I would never listen to ... Wait a minute! Doesn't that mean people could be listening in on us sometimes?"

"That's right, Bobby. And always keep it in mind when you're on the phone. We wouldn't want the neighbors learning any of our family secrets, would we?"

I had no idea what our family secrets might be. But I knew if I ever did, I certainly wasn't going to let nosey neighbors in on them.

\* \* \*

The rest of the kitchen turned up only one other oddity. Instead of faucets, the source of water for the sink was a fire-engine-red pump.

The back door led to a screened back porch. Like the kitchen it ran the width of the house. "See those shelves?" Mom pointed to an entire wall of shelving. "By next year at this time, I'll have them full of fruits, vegetables, and meats I've canned."

She stood, studying the shelves. Then in one of the most unguarded moments I can remember, she said, "Bobby, this farm means so much to your father, and as much as I resented his making this decision without consulting me, I think he was right. As a family we might be happier here than anything place we've ever lived."

\* \* \*

After changing my clothes, I found Jerry pouting on the back steps. "Sorry," I said, sitting down beside him. "Mom wanted to show me the house. She really likes it."

"Okay, well, I like the barn."

"I know. How about showing it to me?"

\* \* \*

That night at dinner, I asked Dad about the monkey tree. "It's called that because it's the only tree a monkey can't climb," he answered.

"That's it? It's a monkey tree because a monkey can't climb it?"

"Yeah, that's it. It's leaves are like spikes with sharp edges and points. A monkey can't climb it."

"Well, that's a dumb name."

"How come it's a dumb name?"

"Why would you call a tree a monkey tree if a monkey *can't* climb it?"

"What should it be called?"

"I don't know. But a monkey tree should be a tree a monkey *can* climb."

"Wouldn't that mean all the rest of the trees in the world would be called monkey trees?"

"I guess," I muttered.

"No," Dad replied. "What would *you* call a tree a monkey can't climb?"

I thought a moment. "I'd call it a *no*-monkey tree."

Smiling, Mom leaned toward Dad. "I think he has a good point, Harold."

"Well, good or bad," Dad answered, "it's called a monkey tree because it's the only tree in the world a monkey can't climb."

I saw Mom catch his eye. She nodded at Jerry and me without breaking eye contact. "Come on, Harold. You can do better than that."

Dad looked at the two of us and said, "Well, as a matter of fact, there is another story about how this tree got its name, but it's kind of a fairy tale, and you're a little old for fairy tales."

This was more like it. I wanted a story. Jerry wanted a story. "Yeah," I answered, "I'm too old for fairy tales, but Jerry isn't."

Dad took a drink of his coffee and buttered one of the rolls Mom had baked for dinner. I knew he was stalling as he worked out the details of his story. That simply made it even more worth the wait. I loved my father's stories. I wanted this to be a good one.

"A long time ago," he began—and I noted how he avoided "Once upon a time" in deference to my advanced age—"there was a king in a faraway land who had a beautiful daughter. She was his only child, his only hope of having a grandchild. The problem was she said she would never marry. She was happy with her life the way it was. She did not want to ever be married."

Dad took a sip of coffee and continued, "In fact, she flatly refused. But the king wanted a grandchild. Finally he worked out a deal. 'I'm going to make a proclamation across the land,' he told her. 'Anyone who wants to marry you should bring a gift. When someone brings a gift you like better than any gift you have ever seen, you will marry that person.'"

Dad grinned as he came up with this next bit. "The daughter was no dummy. She figured this was her way out. All she had to say was 'Nope, don't like that' until the king finally ran out of guys trying to marry her."

Dad took a bite of his roll, using the dramatic pause to enhance his story. "Gifts started coming in. Diamonds, gold, silver—fortunes offered by handsome princes from neighboring kingdoms. But the princess just kept shaking her head, saying, 'Nope, don't like that. Nope, not that. Nope, don't like that either.'"

"But someone *did* bring in a gift she really liked, didn't he?" I interrupted, so caught up in the story I forgot I was too old for fairy tales.

"Yes," Dad smiled, "that's exactly what happened. But the strange thing was this someone wasn't a prince. It was ..." Here he made us wait with another dramatic pause. "It was a ... monkey."

"A monkey!" Jerry exclaimed, clapping his hands.

"Yes, a monkey," Dad continued. "And he held a small pot with a beautiful little tree. It had shiny green leaves with sharp edges and points. It was so beautiful the princess couldn't resist. 'I *love* this perfect little tree,' she said. And because she loved the tree, she fell in love with the monkey who had brought it to her."

"So they got married and lived happily ever after!" Jerry exclaimed, finishing the story for him.

"That's right, Jerry. They did. And ever since then they have called this tree the monkey tree."

Dad leaned back in his chair, smiling at the success of his story. I saw Mom wink at him. I smiled. I wished I could have winked at him, too.

Suddenly struck with inspiration, Dad leaned forward and said, "And guess what the weather was the day the monkey and the princess were married."

The three of us puzzled for a moment before the answer struck me. "It was raining, and the sun was shining at the same moment."

"That's right," Dad beamed. "And ever since then, rain and sun at the same time means somewhere in the world, a monkey has been married."

Laughter filled the room. Dad, Mom, and I because it was such a fine conclusion to the story, Jerry because the rest of us were laughing.

The perfect ending to our family's first evening on the farm.

\* \* \*

The next weekend my father began working on his plan to put the farm into order. Because he was employed full time in the sawmill, for the first couple of months, he had only weekends to work on the farm. But in the spring, when the days grew longer, he returned home from the mill to work until dark.

"We aren't going to plant crops," he told us. "That's a full-time job, and I'm already working one of those. But we *will* have farm animals, and I have to prepare the place for them."

"Bunnies?" Jerry asked. "Can we have bunnies?"

"Yes, we can have rabbits."

"And ponies? Can I have my own pony?"

"No," Dad answered, shaking his head. "The only horses that belong on a farm are workhorses. Since we aren't plowing, we don't need horses."

Jerry pouted only momentarily, probably realizing he had overreached with the ponies. "That's okay. We can still have bunnies. And I can feed them, can't I?"

"Yes," Dad smiled. "You can feed them."

\* \* \*

My father began his renovation of the farm by repairing fences around the animal sheds and rebuilding stalls and other features in the barn. Next he moved to the pastures, where he repaired more fences. As spring weather approached, he cut away the blackberry brambles and uprooted ragweed and other poisonous plants.

By late spring, he began bringing home animals: a flock of chickens, a few rabbits—in short time that became quite a few rabbits—and three milk cows.

He had money for the chickens and rabbits, but the cows proved too expensive. So Dad resorted to "sweat equity." He hired out on neighboring farms, working evenings till dark and every weekend, not for wages, but for the cows he needed.

His first acquisition was Daisy, a beautiful reddish brown cow with a quiet disposition. We loved Daisy.

Next came Lulu Belle, who brought with her an attitude. She had a mean streak. Largest of the three cows, Lulu Belle lorded her size over the others. Her horns extended upward for several inches and then turned forward, pointing directly over her eyes. In fact, Lulu Belle looked like those bulls you see in cartoons. You know, those glaring bulls with the pointy horns and cartoon clouds puffing from their nostrils. But Lulu Belle didn't bring any laughs to the party.

Because Daisy always occupied the last stanchion in the barn, she was the first cow my father brought in at milking time. One day Lulu Belle, the second in place, begin goring Daisy, who, wild-eyed and bellowing with terror, had no way to escape this attack because she was firmly locked in place in her stanchion. Dad, wearing rubber boots, broke his big toe kicking Lulu Belle to drive her off Daisy. It was not a good day for all three of them.

When Dad milked Lulu Belle, he had to hobble her hind feet. Otherwise, she kicked over the bucket or stepped on his toes. In addition, he had to tie a rope to her tail and run it to a post behind the stanchions to keep her from swatting his face. Lulu Belle did not enjoy the good graces of my father.

The third cow Dad brought home was Jiggs. Actually Jiggs was a freebie. The neighbor from whom Dad acquired Lulu Belle threw in Jiggs. Claiming he was so impressed with how hard Dad worked to build up the Grassick place, the farmer gave him Jiggs as a bonus. Actually, Jiggs was a problem. She had warts on her teats. As a result, she gave blood-laced milk. The farmer had a good deal. In return for my father's work, he rid himself of both a cow with a bad attitude and a cow whose milk was unfit for human consumption.

My father claimed he could cure Jiggs, and for the rest of the time we lived on the farm, he applied special salves to her warts at every milking. He never found a cure. In the meantime, we had to throw out her milk. That is, until we got the pigs.

Yes, there were pigs.

* * *

Dad came home late one Friday night after working till dark on a neighboring farm. As he walked in, he announced he had some pigs in the car.

"In the car?" Mom asked. "You have pigs in the car?"

"Well, they're little pigs. They're in a cardboard box. I'll put them in a stall in the barn for tonight. Tomorrow's Saturday, so I have the day fix up their pen."

"How little are they?"

"Oh, about like this." He held his hands apart fifteen inches or so.

"Bring them in. I want to see them."

"No," Dad said, shaking his head. "Pigs in the house? Not a good idea."

"It'll be all right. I want to see them."

"You don't want pigs in the house."

"Harold ... Bring ... Them ... In."

Whenever Mom delivered an imperative sentence with words evenly spaced and equally emphasized as if each were, indeed, a separate command, everyone in our family did what she said. And that included my father.

He brought them in.

* * *

Dad stood in the living room, holding a large cardboard box in his arms. Mom approached and carefully pulled back the flaps. "Ooh," she cooed, "they're so cute." She reached in and lifted one of the pigs from the box, her hands under what would have been the pig's armpits if its front legs had been arms.

Immediately the pig broke into high-pitched squealing, twisting and turning in a struggle to escape her grasp. Taken by surprise, Mom dropped the pig, which hit the floor running and raced for the kitchen. She chased after it, and Dad, putting down the box, ran to help her. But the flaps were still open. The remaining pigs exploded from the box and darted in different directions. Jerry and I tried to head them off, but they streaked past us.

The chase was on.

I've heard of contests where people try to catch greased pigs. I don't know why they need grease to make that challenge difficult. Believe me, catching young pigs that don't want to be caught is a monumental task. Running at full speed, these pigs could change direction on a dime.

Darting, dodging, skidding around corners, they tore through the house. Ducking behind the sofa, jetting around Dad's easy chair, jumping overturned end tables, they raced in and out of the living room. Through opened doors, they streaked into first one bedroom and then another, dashing under the beds, squirting out from under the beds, back into the living room, through to the kitchen, under the table, around the bathtub, into the living room again. Mom, Jerry, and I broke into laughter as we lunged at pigs darting past us.

*Dad* was *not* laughing.

Eventually, using teamwork, we closed the bedroom doors, cutting off the pigs' options. Then we trapped all three in the kitchen. The pigs, either tired or seeking the protection of each other, crowded under the bathtub. Dad, lying flat on his stomach, managed to pull them out one at a time while Mom knelt beside him with the cardboard box.

Standing at the back door with the box held tightly to his chest, Dad, shirt soaked through with sweat, looked at Mom and said, "Pigs in the house? Not a good idea."

\* \* \*

Our collection of farm animals now complete, we soon discovered with the animals came the assignment of chores. "When you live on a farm, you have responsibilities," Dad lectured Jerry and me. "Your mother has so much to do around this house. I have to go to work at the mill every day. You two will have chores."

I'd never heard the word *chore*, but it didn't sound good. As it turned out, Jerry and I figured we had the best of the family's division of labor.

Mom took charge of the chickens. She scattered their feed in their outside pen and collected eggs from the chicken house. At first she asked me to help gather the eggs. However, that was something I couldn't do. I could take eggs from an empty nest, but if the hen was in residence, I couldn't bring myself to reach under it to check for eggs. And even if I could do that, actually taking the eggs out from under the hen was an impossibility. You see, I was afraid of chickens. And I had every right to be.

* * *

When Mom, Jerry and I were evacuated from Copalis Beach to live with our grandfather after the attack upon Pearl Harbor, our mother warned us to be on our best behavior. Her father had been a widower since Mom was fourteen. She had five older sisters. No boys had ever lived in his house.

Our grandfather was a somewhat fussy, routine-driven man. His home in an enclave of German immigrants like himself was immaculate. His yard, neatly bordered with flowers, looked as if it had been manicured rather than mowed.

At first, Jerry and I were afraid to make noise, to pick up or move anything, to be—well, to be boys. In our family we had been encouraged to be active, to be noisy—to be boys. As things turned out, our grandfather was a gentle, quiet man who liked having us around. But at first we didn't know that. All we knew was this neat house with its picture-perfect interior décor and exterior landscaping was like nothing we had ever experienced.

Imagine our surprise, therefore, to discover the chicken pen at the back of his property. Chickens seemed too messy for my grandfather. In truth, the pen and its coop were so neatly maintained they were cleaner than some of the homes in Copalis Beach.

The hens were like family members. My grandfather lovingly spoke to them as he collected their eggs. But it wasn't the hens that were the cause of my fear of chickens. It was the rooster.

Unlike the hens, the rooster was not confined to the pen. It had free range of our grandfather's pampered backyard. I don't know why. Maybe it was too smart to be contained in a mere chicken-wire pen. Maybe my grandfather respected the rooster's take-no-prisoners attitude as it attacked snakes, slugs, even bees that had the audacity to enter its domain. For whatever reason, that rooster really did rule the roost.

And it hated me.

I learned to tread lightly in the back yard. Whenever this rooster saw me alone—it seemed to know better than to go into its macho act with Mom or my grandfather around—it would lower its head, glaring at me, fluff out its hackles, and go into an aggressive dance, darting a few steps toward me and then backing off to repeat the performance. I'm sure, like most bullies, it sensed my fear and capitalized upon it.

Then a day came when it didn't back off. It went into its dance. It darted toward me, but this time it didn't stop. Wings held out from its body, it came at me. I turned, running toward the back porch, but just before I reached the steps, the rooster hit me in the small of my back. I fell forward on my hands and knees and then flat on the ground, crying out as I reached back, trying to knock the squawking, screeching rooster off me. It dug in with its claws, pecking and tearing through my shirt.

Suddenly, over the flapping wings and manic screeching of the rooster, I heard angry, high-pitched yelling. My mother had joined the fight. Walloping the rooster with a broom, she drove it off me.

As the rooster rallied a few feet away, still in its aggressive dance, Mom threw the broom at it. The rooster with an almost dismissive sidestep evaded the broom as it flew by. Then it turned its back and strutted away.

Mom helped me to my feet and took me into the house. I could feel blood running down the inside of my shirt where the rooster had ripped with its claws and pecked with its bill. As Mom knelt beside me to check my wounds, my grandfather, having been awakened from his afternoon nap, entered the room.

Looking up, Mom told him what had happened. His eyes narrowed. His mouth tightened. He walked around us and out the back door without a word.

In a couple of minutes, the rooster began squawking and screeching again. An exceptionally high-pitched screech was followed by eerie silence.

The next evening we had chicken stew for dinner. The toughest, chewiest chicken stew I have ever tasted. And probably the best.

* * *

Mom's efforts, three years later, to talk me into helping with the egg collection was probably her version of "Face your fears, and they will go away."

Well, I didn't, and they didn't.

* * *

Jerry and I were in charge of the rabbits. I liked the rabbits, but Jerry loved them. He held them in his lap, stroking them and offering them lettuce leaves, which they nibbled as he carried on one-sided conversations.

Our rabbits were not confined to hutches. We had a rabbit shed, divided into stall-like compartments with straw-covered floors. On the outside wall of each stall, a small door, hinged at the top like a doggy door, allowed the rabbits access to a penned area where they could socialize in fresh air. At night we herded them back into the stalls and fastened the doors to protect them from nighttime predators.

Jerry and I poured special pellet-like rabbit food into their feeding trays and kept fresh water in their bowls. And when our mother prodded us, we cleaned the stalls and put in fresh straw.

Frequently we took three or four rabbits on field trips to our front yard with its patches of clover. Our assignment didn't feel like a chore. Chores aren't supposed to feel good. Taking care of the rabbits felt good.

* * *

Our father, of course, took care of the cows. In early dawn as the sun rose in the orange-red eastern sky behind Mt. Hood, he brought the cows in from the pasture for milking and then herded them back. Mom, who had left the bed when he arose, had a breakfast of hot cakes, eggs and coffee ready when he returned to the house. Thirty minutes later, his lunch bucket in hand with the lunch Mom had packed, he drove off for his shift at the mill. In the evenings he repeated the procedure, coming in this time for a meat-and-potatoes meal at the dinner table.

Our pasture lay at the bottom of a wooded hillside across Eagle Creek Road from the barn. From a gate in the fence at the top of the hill, a wide cow path led to the pasture below. Despite the cattle-crossing signs, moving cows across this road four times a day was a risky operation. Nevertheless, they suffered no mishaps unlike the suicidal possums, squirrels, raccoons, and one extremely odoriferous skunk who bit the dust at or near that crossing.

The cows were always waiting at the gate for the morning milking. But as the days grew longer, occasionally they were not there in the evening. Dad did not have to go down to the pasture and bring them up. Instead, he simply called them, not by their actual names, but by a generic name he used for all cows. He'd stand at the gate and call out this name in a specific cadence, stretching it out for a couple of long counts and finishing the call with several staccato repetitions of a shorten version of the word. *"Hey, Bosssssy! Hey, Bossssy! Hey, Boss! Boss! Boss!"* It always reminded me of the coded rings on our telephone party line. Two longs and three shorts.

He'd repeat this call only a few times before the cows appeared on their way up the path, Lulu Belle leading, Daisy coming behind, and Jiggs bringing up the rear. I was impressed that Dad could train cows to come on command. As I think about it now, however, I suspect the urgency of full udders and the promise of hay in their mangers had something to do with their compliance.

\* \* \*

The pigs turned out to be a shared effort. Dad took care of their feeding, mixing a special concoction of grains with Jiggs's milk and the contents of the slop bucket. What went into the slop bucket? Almost anything. No one who owns a pig needs a garbage disposal. Pigs are *walking* garbage disposals. Potato and carrot peelings, banana skins, watermelon rinds, table scraps—all went into the mix. Needless to say, the little pigs did not stay little very long.

In the meantime, Jerry and I took care of the pigs' socialization. Yes, pigs can be socialized. In fact, they've suffered a bad rap in our society. The general consensus is that pigs are stupid, dirty, sloppy animals. After all, Isn't being compared to a pig a major insult? A messy person's home is a pig sty. Someone with disgusting table manners eats like a pig. An obese person is fat as a pig.

Let's start at the top. Pigs are stupid? Animal researchers have identified pigs as the fourth most intelligent animal in the world. Animals ranked above pigs in intelligence? Chimpanzees, dolphins, and elephants. Animals ranked below pigs? All the rest. Dogs, cats, horses—all the rest.

Pigs are dirty? Do you know pigs will not urinate or defecate in their sleeping or eating areas? They designate a space as far away as possible from their living quarters for their toilet functions. Even piglets leave their mother's protection to seek out distant spots to do their business.

All other animals on a farm have no problem letting fly wherever they are—cows, horses, goats, chickens—all of them.

Yes, pigs wallow in mud when it's available. Does that make them stupid or dirty? Well, it makes them dirty. But stupid? No. You see, pigs have no sweat glands, and unlike dogs and many other animals, they don't relieve body heat by panting. Mud helps lower their body temperature. Also, it serves as a pesticide. And here's something you probably don't know. Pigs get sunburned. That's right. The mud is their version of Banana Boat and Hawaiian Tropic. I challenge you to name any other animal that uses sunscreen.

As for someone with bad table manners being described as eating like a pig, I'll give you that. They dive right into their food, grunting contentedly while they eat as much as possible in as short a time as possible. Reminds you of your Uncle Fred, doesn't it? The only difference is Uncle Fred wasn't born into a litter where a lack of aggression at the dinner table mean not getting to an available teat.

And "fat as a pig"? We make them that way. You want bacon for your breakfast buffet and ham for your Christmas dinner? For pig farmers, fat is money in the bank. No animal except man gets fat. That includes feral pigs, wolves, bears, porcupines, beavers—well, you get the picture. Animals like bears may stock up on fat to hibernate through the winter, but they don't *get* fat.

Of course, Jerry and I knew none of this. We simple liked those little pigs. Most farm people know better than to name animals they plan to eat. But the two of us had no idea that was the little pigs' future. Porky, Petunia, and Salomey were a part of our family.[11] We babied them when they were little and indulged them when they were big.

Their pen was large with a sleeping shed at one end and a shade tree at the other. In between they had a spacious stretch to explore and root with their snouts, looking for insects, grubs, and other tasty morsels. Pigs love to root. When not looking for food, they use their snouts to dig wallows, especially comforting when rain turns the dirt to mud.

Our little pigs made wallows almost immediately. As they grew, so did the wallows. From the time they first arrived, Jerry and I went into their pen to rub and scratch their backs. Pigs, like people, love

---

[11]    Of course, everyone recognizes Porky Pig and his girlfriend, Petunia. Salomey was the Yokums' pet pig in *Li'l Abner*.

massages. Before long the massages took place in their wallows where they'd stretch out, luxuriating in their version of a visit to the spa. In dry weather, we'd cover the pigs in dirt, rubbing and scratching as they grunted, eyes closed, in piggy ecstasy.

* * *

Life on the farm fell into a routine for each of us. But we enjoyed family life as well. I fell in love with books while living on the farm. My mother had discovered the Estacada Public Library, a converted cottage across the street from Judge Archer's home. At age seven, I had my very own library card.

Mom and I visited the library every two weeks. The front of the library—originally a sun porch—had been glassed in and served as the young people's section. I spent my time there, fascinated by the wonderful collection from which I was allowed to check out three books at once. In the meantime, Mom wandered through the main rooms, selecting books for both Dad and her.

I remember reading a series of books about animals, both tame and wild, who populated the land around a farm: Reddy Fox, Jerry Muskrat, and a host of others. Also, if I did not read the complete *Oz* series, I came close. It was a good time, a time that instilled in me the power of books, my refuge today from the demands of a media-driven society.

However, we had less quiet time on the farm than we had in our homes both in Copalis Beach and Aberdeen. We probably had small radios in those houses, but I don't remember them. Dad's new floor-model Zenith, on the other hand, captivated our family.

In the morning Mom listened to soap operas as she did her housework. Cranked-up volume sometimes allowed her to work in the kitchen. If not, she used the commercials to work on chores and then rushed into the living room to listen as Our Gal Sunday answered the question, "Can this girl from a little mining town in the West find happiness as the wife of a wealthy and titled Englishman?"

In the afternoon, Jerry and I sprawled on the floor in front of the Zenith's mahogany cabinet to listen to our favorite shows, especially the Westerns, *Red Ryder* and *The Lone Ranger*. I had saved special cereal boxes with dotted outlines forming patterns that I cut out with scissors. Following instructions for inserting tabs into slots, I turned the cutouts into cardboard buildings. These I placed in marked squares on a special map I had obtained by mailing in a specific number of box tops along with a quarter Scotch-taped to my order.

According to the promotion, I would be able to lay out the map, place my buildings in the appropriate squares, and follow the Long Ranger's adventures as he raced across the landscape. Eventually I realized the Long Ranger never came anywhere near my map. Nevertheless, I listened in anticipation for the call, "Hi-yo Silver, away!" and the final question, "Who was that masked man, anyway?"

In the evening after dinner, our family gathered for shows like *Jack Benny, Edgar Bergen and Charlie McCarthy, Amos and Andy, Blondie, Burns and Allen, Fibber McGee and Molly,* and *Our Miss Brooks.*

Occasionally, if Jerry and I were in Mom's good graces, we'd be allowed to stay up for the late-night spooky shows: *Inner Sanctum* with its creaking door and *The Shadow* with its creepy tagline: "Who knows what evil lurks in the hearts of men? The Shadow knows!"

Of course, not everything on the radio was mere entertainment. The war continued to rage in Europe and the Pacific. On April 12, 1945, our family huddled around the radio at the announcement of President Roosevelt's death. On April 30, Hitler committed suicide in his Berlin bunker. Eight days later, the Nazi regime surrendered to the Allied Forces. All this came to us on our radio.

In August we listened to reports of the two atomic bombs dropped on Japan. Five days after the second bomb, the Japanese Emperor announced in a radio broadcast his country's unconditional surrender.

The war was finally over.

* * *

As much as our family rejoiced in the ending of the war, it brought an uneasiness to our life on the farm. No one spoke of it—at least not in the presence of Jerry and me—but it had to be a major concern for our parents. Mr. Grassick had warned my father that when his son returned from the war, we would have to move. Would all the work Dad had put into the farm mean nothing when that time came?

Mr. Grassick had actually visited us a few times in the spring and early summer. A man of few words, he, nevertheless, seemed impressed with how hard my father worked to bring the farm back to life. In fact, on one visit, he delivered a pie Mrs. Grassick had baked for our family.

But after the war ended, we heard nothing from Mr. Grassick. September ran into October. Jerry had entered the first grade, riding the school bus with me. I did what I could to shield him from Ira Grimes's verbal abuse, and, except for a passing comment suggesting mental retardation seemed to run in our family, I basically succeeded.

November passed with no visit by Mr. Grassick. In December we enjoyed a beautiful farmhouse Christmas. Dad had been elevated to sawyer, the most important position in a sawmill. The mill's owners were grooming him to take over the entire mill's operation. And, of course, with the added responsibility came additional compensation.

I had never seen so many presents under our tree. Jerry and I had been up an hour before we worked up enough courage to wake our parents. Even then Mom made us wait until the two of them were comfortably seated with cups of steaming coffee before giving us the go-ahead to dive into the bonanza of presents. And dive in, we did.

We had spent the preceding Christmas with the Richardson family while waiting for our move-in date for the farm. This Christmas my parents invited them to join us. It was a nice gathering. Bo Richardson was my father's best friend. Ida Richardson, my mother's. Jerry and I had taken weak, timid Harley Richardson under our protection while we all still lived in Washington. The two Richardson girls—Mary Beth, the tough cookie who had taken on Ira Grimes my first day on the school bus, and Rita, her older sister—would probably have preferred to spent the day with their friends, but they were too polite to say so.

We had a big dinner around our table by the bathtub. Mom had cooked all morning, and Ida had brought supplemental dishes and a couple of desserts. After dinner the adults drank coffee and chatted while we five kids played our new Monopoly game.

It was a perfect Christmas Day.

* * *

The next evening, Mr. Grassick appeared at our door. When my father invited him in, he shook his head, preferring to talk outside. As Dad returned to the house, we could sense what he was about to say. "His son's coming home. We have until the first of February to move."

"Oh, Harold," my mother said, stepping forward to put her arms around him.

"I tried to tell him how much the farm means to us. I almost begged him to let me buy it. And I think he felt sorry for us. I really do. But he kept saying the farm had been promised to his son. He had to keep his promise."

"So what do we do?" Mom asked.

"What do we do?" Dad answered. "We move."

* * *

My parents found a small house in Estacada, right across an alley from the back of the Richardsons' property. It would be the first and only home they could ever call their own. It had all the modern conveniences: an electric stove in the kitchen, gas heat, a bathtub in an actual bathroom. Everything the modern family could want, according to the ads of the day. But our family had lost a home that needed us as much as we needed it. We weren't a modern family.

Over the next couple of weeks, my father sold off the animals. First to go were the chickens and rabbits. Next went Daisy, Lula Belle, and Jiggs. When we moved into Estacada, only the pigs remained on the farm.

On the day my father and Bo moved our furniture and other belongs to the Estacada house, I asked Dad about the pigs we were leaving behind. "Don't worry," he said. "I'm coming back to take care of them."

A couple of years passed before I found out what he meant by "take care of them." The day after we moved into Estacada, Dad and Bo returned to the farm with their deer rifles. They shot Porky, Petunia, and Salomey. After bleeding them out, they took them to the butcher who had cut up and packaged the deer they killed during the fall hunting season.

The day my father killed our pigs was his last day on the farm.

* * *

Mom, Jerry, and I soon adapted to Estacada life. My mother had been isolated on the farm. In Estacada she found herself accepted by a covey of neighborhood wives who spent almost every weekday in each other's homes, giving home permanents, gossiping, playing cards. Around three o'clock in the afternoon, they rushed home to clean house, wash the stacked dishes, and begin dinner before their husbands returned from work.

Jerry and I, who had only each other on the farm, now had neighborhood boys who accepted us into their circle. Of course, there was Harley, but half a block up the alley separating our home from the Richardson property, we discovered a redheaded, freckle-faced boy named Kenny. In a couple of years, this would be our gang.

As for my father, he reacted to the loss of the farm the same way he had reacted to the loss of Zipper. He never talked about the farm, as if by not acknowledging it, he could pretend he had lost nothing.

Ironically, Mr. Grassick showed up at our door in late February. His son didn't want the farm. He offered it to my father at a fair price.

The chickens were gone. The rabbits were gone. Daisy, Lulu Belle, and lovable Jiggs were gone. Porky, Petunia, and Salomey were gone. My parents had a mortgage on a house. Through the kitchen curtains, I watched my father shake his head as Mr. Grassick, in an almost fatherly gesture, put his hand on Dad's shoulder.

* * *

My father was thirty-four years old when we left the farm. He had lived his dream for a year.

I suspect many people don't do as well in a lifetime.

# THE DAY OF THE LONG SOCKS

**"Item Seven-One calling Item Seven-Three.** Over." … "Item Seven-One calling Item Seven-Three. Over."

I had been dreaming a nice dream I didn't want to leave but that raspy, static-charged voice kept drilling into my head with its annoying "Item Seven-One calling Item Seven-Three. Over." Over and over and over again.

I threw back the blankets, sat up, and, yawning, turned toward the western windows of Squaw Mountain Lookout. The panes rattled under the onslaught of wind and rain from a storm that had pounded the mountain for the past two days.

I swung my feet to the cold planked floor and sat for a moment waiting for the fog of sleep to clear before standing up and walking toward the radio.

"Item Seven-One calling Item Seven-Three. Over."

"All right," I growled, "I'm coming."

I picked up the mike and thumbed the transmit button. "Item Seven-Three. Over."

"Where you been? Asleep? I been trying to reach you for fifteen minutes. Over."

*Great*, I thought. *Bert.*

"Yes, Bert, I've been asleep. That's what people do at night, even on Squaw Mountain. Over."

"Yeah, well, it's not night. Night for you was supposed to end an hour ago. Over." I glanced at my watch. Eight o'clock. Bert was right.

When I didn't respond, he keyed back in. "What's wrong with your phone? Over."

"I give up. *What's* wrong with my phone? Over."

"It's not working. That's what's wrong with it. Lenny couldn't get you with the wake-up call. Your phone's dead. What'd you do, turn it off so you could sleep in?"

I waited him out until he was forced to come back on. "Did you hear what I said?"

"I was waiting for your 'Over.' Over."

"Some day that mouth of yours is going to get you into trouble, you know that? You better remember *who* you work for." After I waited again, he shouted, "OVER!"

"Bert, as long as you're my boss, remembering for *whom* I work will never be a problem. Now hang on while I check the phone from this end. Over."

I put down the mike, walked to the phone, took the receiver from its hook at the side of the box and held it to my ear. No static sounds. I reached for the crank, gave it a couple of turns, and listened again. Nothing. I hung up and returned to the radio.

"Item Seven-Three calling Item Seven-One. Over."

"Yeah, yeah. What did you find? Over."

"You're right. The phone's dead. Over."

"You're still stormed in, right? Over."

"Right. Over."

"Then I guess you're not gonna be seeing many smokes today, right? Over."

"Right, again. Over."

"Well, no use you just sitting around, is there? I want you to take an ax, pole pruner, insulators, and whatever else you need and work the line down to Lookout Springs. The storm probably brought down some limbs or something. The line could be broken or maybe just shorted out. Fix any problems you can. If you need a chainsaw, more phone line or something else you don't have at the lookout, we can send it up. But we won't know that until you've run the line, will we? Over." Delivering this message had brightened Bert's morning. I could hear it in his voice.

But it hadn't brightened mine. I looked at the water pouring over the lookout's propped-up shutters and beyond that the rain pounding the catwalk. A day in heavy rain and wind while working the telephone line down the mountain four miles to Lookout Springs Guard Station and then climbing back up to the lookout? Not the way I'd like to spend my time in this storm. And Bert knew it.

"Just a thought, Bert. What if Matt worked his way up the line from Lookout Springs while I'm working my way down? With both of us on the job, we'd cut the time this'll take in half at least. Over."

"Because Matt isn't at the guard station," Bert returned, his mood improving even more. "He's on his four-day break. Besides, he's not the expert on telephone lines *you* are. At least, that's what I was told when I came on the job." He waited a couple of beats before continuing, "That's right, isn't it? Aren't you the expert on fixing downed phone lines? … Oh, I almost forgot again. Over."

"Ten-four on everything, Bert. I'm the expert, and I look forward to getting out and stretching my legs a little after being cooped up for so long. Anything else? Over."

"Yeah. When you get to Lookout Springs, let yourself in and give us a call from the phone there. That way we'll know if the problem with the line is between here and there and not between the guard station and you. Over."

*And you're hoping it is so my day in the rain will have been have been a useless exercise, aren't you, Bert?* That's what I thought to myself as I keyed the transmit button. But what I said was "Good idea. I guess that's why you get paid the big bucks. Okay, I need to get started, so if there's nothing else, Item Seven-Three will be ten-seven for the rest of the day. Item Seven-Three out."

And as I put my hands on the small of my back and arched it into a stretch, I heard Bert's "Item Seven-One out."

I thought about his snide comment that I was an expert on phone-line repair. "Probably not an expert, but certainly more knowledgeable than anyone else in the District," I said aloud. "Especially you, Bert." And that was definitely true as far as the line from Lookout Springs to Squaw Mountain was concerned. On that line I *was* an expert.

\* \* \*

I had begun working for the Forest Service at age sixteen, planting trees on weekend crews in the fall and spring. But I didn't qualify for summer work until I reached eighteen.

My first day on the job, I met Johnny Groves at the District warehouse. Johnny was the District Assistant, the person in charge of all work crews, maintenance, firefighting, and everything else involving grunts like me and most of the men working in the field. He was, in essence, if not in pay scale, the second most important person in the District. Only the District Ranger himself held a more responsible position. In addition, Johnny Groves never asked a man to do anything he himself was not willing to do. We didn't simply work for Johnny. We worked side by side *with* him.

When Johnny was bumped upstairs to the Supervisor's Office in Portland, his replacement was Bert, a hire from another district. I'm sure stepping into the shoes of a man like Johnny Groves accounted in part for Bert's hostile attitude toward all of us.

He had replaced a man we admired, and he seemed to have set out to prove his job could be handled without currying the favor of anyone he bossed. In addition, his only appearances in the field occurred when he occasionally arrived unannounced, sniffed around a little, climbed back into his pickup, and drove away. Otherwise, no one was really sure where he spent his time. People could seldom find him when they needed him. But most of the time, people tried *not* to need him.

That first day on the job, Johnny introduced me to Little John Boyle, who, unlike the Little John in *Robin Hood*, was actually little. Around five-three and 130 pounds. Little John and I were destined to spend that summer on a crew that had not before existed in the District. "It's going to be called the maintenance crew," Johnny explained. "You'll have a lot of fun because you'll be working on all kinds of different things." He flashed his lopsided grin as he explained, "Little John, here is the foreman. And you, Bob, are the crew."

All the time he gave me this abbreviated explanation of my new job, we loaded gear into his pickup. This included climbing spurs, boxes of glass insulators, coils of telephone wire, pruning poles, and heavy leather belts weighted with hatchets, pliers, and hammers.

Fifteen or twenty minutes later, as we drove up the Clackamas River Road, Johnny, who had said absolutely nothing about what we were going to do that day, gave me a sideways glance and asked, "So, Bob, have you ever climbed with spurs before?"

"Not yet," I answered. It was the kind of response he liked. From that moment we weren't simply boss and employee. We were friends.

The job that first day and for several days later turned out to be repairing the winter damage suffered by the telephone line between Lookout Springs Guard Station and Squaw Mountain Lookout. So, yes, after that summer, I had had more experience with telephone-line repair than anyone else still working in the District. And while I might not have been an expert in everything required on that job, I was certainly an expert on the four-mile stretch of telephone line I was about to work once again.

But those days with Johnny and Little John had been sunny and warm. What I faced this day was rain, wind, mud, and cold. Maybe Bert had this in mind from the beginning of our radio conversation, but I couldn't help thinking he had hit upon this plan to back up his claim that someday my mouth would get me into trouble. If so, that made twice in one day Bert had been right. And *that* had to have been a record for him.

\* \* \*

I had stepped into my pants and was pulling a tee shirt over my head when I felt a warm body rub against my legs. I looked down into the brown eyes of Tinker, my peach-colored spaniel. When she had my attention, she moved to the door and looked back at me.

"Okay," I said, moving toward her. "But I warn you it's raining cats and ...well, dogs out there. I'll let you out, but you have to go down the steps to do what you have to do. I don't want you peeing on the catwalk. Understand me? I don't want you peeing on the catwalk."

When I opened the door, she took a step outward, stopped, stared into the downpour, and began backing into the lookout. "No, you don't," I said, putting a bare foot against her tail end and pushing her forward. "You need to go, so go. But remember what I said about the catwalk."

She looked back at me as if to say, "I don't see *you* going out there" and then bounded forward to disappear down the five concrete steps leading to the outcropping of granite upon which the lookout had been built.

"Good girl," I encouraged and, leaving the door slightly ajar, turned back to finish dressing. I felt somewhat hypocritical over my stern warning that Tinker go down the steps to relieve herself because frequently I had gone out that door in the middle of the night and made my way barefooted to the southeastern corner of the catwalk, the corner that hung over a cliff far above Squaw Meadows. There, using the reflected moon in the meadow's string of small lakes as a target, I performed the operation I had warned Tinker not to do.

*But,* I rationalized to myself, *I pee into the valley, not on the catwalk.* Nevertheless, I knew it was not a distinction Tinker would appreciate.

As I searched through my clothing box for my rain pants, Tinker pushed open the door and padded inside. Though she had been out only a few minutes, her coat dripped water as she entered. She gave me a look as if to say, "You asked for this" and began a slight squirming motion with her rear end.

"No," I shouted. "Don't shake! Don't sha …" Too late. Water from the vibrating dog sprayed in all directions, puddling the floor.

"Oh, well," I shrugged, "that's okay. When we return this afternoon, we're going to bring in so much mud and water we'll have to scrub the floor anyway." I reached for a towel and, wrapping it around her, began to rub vigorously. She squirmed in delight, and when I had reduced her soaked coat to soggy damp, she jumped onto the bed, performed her obligatory three turns and flopped down into a curled ball. In a few minutes, her eyes closed and her breathing slowed as she slipped into sleep.

I reached down and stroked her head. Behind one of her ears, I fingered a couple of small mats. Speckled mud coated the front paw under her chin. *Good,* I thought. *That's how a dog is supposed to look.* Only a couple of years before, this would have been an unheard-of condition for Tinker. In those two years, Tinker had become my special project. I had changed her from some kind of woman's accessory—like an expensive pair of earrings brought out only on special occasions—into a real dog.

My first wife's father was a master sergeant in the U.S. Army, and his wife *should* have been. When I met them, he was stationed at Fort Lewis, Washington. They lived in a tidy suburban home near the base. I take that back. *Tidy* isn't strong enough. *Obsessively tidy* is definitely better.

The interior of the home was coldly immaculate. Everything in its place as if expecting a photographer from *Home and Garden* to arrive any moment. The lawns were groomed, every flower arranged according to size and equally spaced, every bush perfectly trimmed. In short, everything was shipshape, as if waiting for a general's inspection.

And Tinker, their dog, was no exception. Groomed daily, nails clipped short, teeth regularly brushed, Tinker was simply another adornment to the home. I had never seen a dog's teeth brushed before.

I have read since that vets consider this a good thing. I grew up with dogs that would have taken the hand off anyone who presumed to brush their teeth. Dogs that gnawed bones and chewed leather—usually the soles of shoes carelessly left out for grabs—to clean their teeth. If Tinker occasionally had the audacity to chase a squirrel through the bark dust or heaven forbid! dig in one of the flower gardens, she suffered an immediate bath and heavy spraying with perfumed disinfectant.

I had never seen a dog more in need of being rescued.

When my wife's father was transferred to Germany, we inherited their furniture and Tinker—strictly on a loan basis, I might add. Everything was to be returned when they came back to the States.

The furniture I could do without. My wife and I lived in a small furnished apartment in southeast Portland, a complex that did not allow pets. To accommodate our sudden furniture-and-dog acquisition—albeit on the aforesaid temporary basis—we were forced to move into an unfurnished apartment in north Portland.

At the time, I was working for the Forest Service four days a week and attending college the other three days. My job took precedence on Tuesdays and Thursdays as well as weekends. Mondays, Wednesdays, and Fridays, I attended classes.

These were the weekends I worked as foreman of tree-planting crews made up of teenagers. Tree planting is a tough job. Clear-cuts in the Mt. Hood National Forest are never on level ground. They invariably cling to steep slopes fading into canyons. Crews line out at the top of these clear-cuts and work their way down into the canyons. At the bottom they line out again and work their way to the top. Every eight feet along the way, they swing heavy hoedags, pull back a foot of dirt, insert trees, chop in dirt from the side of the holes, and stomp the trees into place. Over and over and over again, up and down the mountain. It is a job assiduously avoided by full-time Forest Service employees. Thus, the use of money-hungry teenagers with strong backs.

The first weekend after our inheritance of Tinker, I declared she was going with me on the tree-planting job. "She can't," my wife objected. "She doesn't know anything about the woods. What if she gets lost or hurt or something?"

"What if she does?" I answered. "It would be the highpoint of her life so far."

And it was. Not getting lost or hurt, but the freedom of running up and down the mountainsides, chasing chipmunks, digging into mountain-beaver holes, pursuing the tormenting taunts of blue jays. Tinker had been introduced to the wild.

\* \* \*

The next morning she awoke so stiff and sore she could hardly move. "It's okay," I sympathized. "You were great yesterday. Better you take the day to rest up. We'll do it again next weekend."

But when I returned from the kitchen with my lunch bucket in hand, she lay at the door, waiting. She had dragged herself there. "Okay, you can come," I said, bending to pick her up. You'll probably have to spend the day in the crummy, but you can come."[12]

She did not spend her day in the crummy. By the time we had reached our job site, she had regained mobility, and while she didn't exactly charge down the mountain, she showed a remarkable recovery in her step as she slipped into the hidden recesses of the canyon. I knew at that moment she would be my dog even after my wife's parents returned. She was no longer some kind of peach-colored creampuff. She was my kind of dog, and she could never go back.

Tinker accompanied me on every job after that. On fire patrol while I drove the back roads of the District, my coworker had to hold her hind legs because she loved to snap through the open window at the brush of narrow roads. Without question, she would have leaped from the cab of the pickup to snatch a prize limp if he had not had a firm hold on her. On slash crews, we piled bush beside forest roads while Tinker chased through the clear-cuts above the roads, sometimes scaring up deer, which bounced down the hill and leaped across the road to plunge into the foliage below. She played while we worked. And when it came time for me to man Squaw Mountain Lookout, she was the perfect partner quiet, energetic, and a good listener, never merely acquiescing to my rambling comments but ready to acknowledge their validity whenever I was clearly in the right. In short, I could not have spent the summer with a better friend.

---

[12] "Crummy" is the term for any vehicle used to haul crews and their supplies into a forest setting.

\* \* \*

As I toyed with a breakfast of cereal, coffee, and sourdough bread, I thought about my radio conversation with Bert. It had been a highly unprofessional exchange, and I was as guilty as he. Bert had started things by suggesting I had intentionally turned off my phone to sleep in. But he was an easy target. In over his head as District Assistant, his buttons were easy to push, and I had pushed them.

The Forest Service directive on radio transmissions forbade personal conversations, and our conversation had become personal. I thought about all the lookouts, guard stations, and District home offices listening in as I goaded him. The lookouts would have cheered me on. The others—not so much. I wasn't proud of myself.

As I idly used my spoon to push Cheerios under the milk's surface, I thought about the directive not to have personal conversations on the radio. Clearly, no one in the Supervisor's Office listened to radio transmissions in the evening. The night came alive with frivolous chatter as lonely lookouts reached out for company. During this particular summer, an obvious romance had developed between a male on one lookout and a female on another. A version of online dating before anyone had ever heard of online anything.

My favorite evening call came from the rhino man. Every night, exactly at eight o'clock, he came on with this single line from an Ogden Nash poem: "The rhino is a homely beast." With no sign-in or sigh-out, he remained anonymous the entire summer. At first, I use to check the clock every time he clicked in with his strange sentence. Later, I merely rested assured it was eight o'clock on the dot. In fact, I and I assume others became annoyed if the star-crossed lovers carried on their flirtation through the eight-o'clock hour. On those nights the rhino man never clicked in. Instead the rest of us—because we weren't allowed to turn off our radios—were subjected to our own version of *As the World Turns*.

"Enough of this stalling," I declared, rising to rinse out my cup and bowl. "Tinker, get up. We've got a job to do." And as if that had been all she had been waiting for, she jumped from the bed and rushed to the door, watching me impatiently as I checked to see that everything was in place before pushing open the door and stepping into the rain.

* * *

Tinker and I made our way along the rocky path from the lookout to the end of the steep road that climbed the side of the mountain. When I approached the lookout's combination storage/woodshed and worked my key into its large padlock, Tinker began circling in anticipation.

The shed was one of Tinker's favorite places. Our first day on the job, while I put away gear along the shelved walls, she scared up a mouse. The resulting chase took her over and around boxes, along the base of the walls, over jumbled coils of wire and rope, and through scattered chips around the woodpile and chopping block. Eventually the mouse disappeared, probably through whatever hole had allowed it entrance in the first place.

Tinker never accepted the fact that the mouse may have permanently vacated the premises, and whenever we entered the shed, she began a new search for her elusive adversary.

While she checked her inventory of potential hiding places, I loaded a backpack with everything I might need to repair the phone line, including glass insulators, nails, staples, pliers, a hatchet, a hammer, and a small coil of wire. There were no climbing spurs in the shed, but I did have a pruning pole with a six-foot handle. With that I could take care of problem limbs up to ten or eleven feet overhead. Anything higher would require a return trip with spurs.

I had to call Tinker a couple of times before she reluctantly gave up her search and joined me outside the shed. From there we followed the road around a tight hairpin turn and headed down the mountain. The turn had taken us directly into the wind, and I lowered my head as I walked into the heavy rain drumming my hard hat.

Tinker seemed oblivious to the rain as she slipped into her normal routine, darting back and forth across the road, running ahead, and turning back to make sure I was coming before dashing off again. *You'd better pace yourself, girl,* I thought. *We have a long day ahead of us.*

I leaned into the wind, a double-bitted ax in my left hand and my right hand holding the handle of the pruning pole balanced over my shoulder. Somewhere high above the cut bank on the left side of the road perched the lookout, but I would not be able to see it or the phone line running up the mountain for at least fifty yards or more until the road lost some of its pitch.

When I reached that point, I clawed my way up the muddy bank and stood in waist-high scrub brush, looking up the mountainside. From this vantage point, I could sight along the phone line from cedar pole to cedar pole all the way to the lookout.

These poles were unusual for Forest Service telephone lines. Under normal circumstances, we strung the lines from tree to tree, usually somewhere between ten and twenty feet above ground level. However, since the lookout was above the timberline, the last two hundred yards had to be strung on poles.

When I had first worked this line, I hated the poles. Trees were much easier and safer to climb with spurs. But this time I appreciated them. Because they stood above the huckleberry bushes blanketing the final slope to the lookout, I could check the line without having to backtrack up the mountain.

Satisfied that the final stretch of line had no problems, I half climbed, half slid down the bank to the road, where Tinker anxiously waited. From the mud matting her legs and belly, I suspected she had tried to climb the bank without success. "It's okay," I said, reaching down to scratch her ears. "You didn't miss anything up there."

When we reached the timberline, I had to slow the pace and gain a sharper focus. Something as simple as a single waterlogged branch lying across the line could short it out. Walking along the road was easy enough, but in a couple of places where the road doubled back on itself, the line took shortcuts, running downward into gorges and back up the other sides.

By the time we had climbed out of the second of these, Tinker had slowed. She stayed with me but seemed to welcome the rest every time I stopped to clear brush from below the line or reach up with the pruning pole to cut high limbs overhead.

* * *

When I let myself into the guard station at Lookout Springs, I had an uneasy feeling I had not found the problem. I would have much preferred to find a major break in the line, a snag lying across it anything that would have definitely been the cause of the phone outage. But nothing like that had presented itself.

I left Tinker outside, much to her disapproval, because I didn't want to mess up the place any more than necessary. However, I did leave the cabin's door open so that she could watch me through the screen door. When I lifted the phone from its hook, I hoped for a dead line. That would mean the trouble lay between the District headquarters and Lookout Springs, taking the responsibility out of my hands. If not, I knew Bert would insist I walk the line again the next day.

I cranked the handle twice, the code for the Headquarters office. Almost immediately, the District clerk answered. "District Office. Lenny, here."

Keeping disappointment out of my voice, I said, "Hey, Lenny. It's Bob. I'm at Lookout Springs. Bert around?"

"Nope."

"Good. When he comes in, tell him I checked the phone line, cleaned up all possible problems, and am now on my way back up the mountain."

"Gotcha. I'll tell him. Oh, by the way, some good news. The weather is supposed to clear later this afternoon."

"Great. So maybe I could have run the line tomorrow in decent weather instead of slogging through the rain and mud today."

"Seems reasonable to me all right," Lenny agreed.

"Well, anyway, I'll call you from the lookout when I get back up there. Hopefully, the phone will be working."

"Right. Good luck."

I searched through Matt's cupboards for something to eat. Usually I'd feel guilty getting into his food, but I knew he'd be bringing up fresh supplies when he returned from his time off. I left him an IOU for a peanut-butter sandwich and an apology for the muddy tracks before rejoining Tinker outside.

After we had shared the sandwich, we began hiking back up the road. Lenny had been right. By the time we reached the lookout, the rain had stopped, and the clouds were breaking up. We were both tired, Tinker so exhausted she didn't even bother to go on her mouse hunt when I returned the gear to the storage shed.

When we reached the catwalk, I unlaced my muddy boots and kicked them off. Inside, I picked up the same towel I had used on Tinker that morning and rubbed her as dry as I could. Finally I turned toward the phone. I didn't want to check it. I hadn't really found anything significantly wrong with the line, and if I hadn't corrected the problem, I'd have to call Bert on the radio. He would relish ragging me, the so-called phone-line expert, on my inability to fix my own telephone. This with the entire Mt. Hood National Forest listening in.

Reluctantly, I lifted the receiver from the phone box and held it to my ear. No static. I gave the crank a couple of turns and listened again. Nothing. The phone was as dead as it had been that morning. Replacing the receiver, I looked down at Tinker and shook my head. Frustrated, I looked for ways to stall before making the radio call.

Using Tinker's towel, I knelt to the floor and began wiping up her muddy footprints. As I moved forward, I jarred the lightning platform leaning against the wall, and as it fell toward me, I reached out to keep it from banging against the stove.

Like all lookout personnel, I depended upon the building's lightning rod to protect me from strikes. But, in addition, my training stressed taking other precautions during a lightning storm, including turning off the radio and telephone, avoiding contact with metal objects, and standing on the lightning platform, a heavy piece of plywood approximately three feet long and two feet wide with four glass insulators on its underneath side.

I had tried standing on one in the first lookout I had manned. Even with no one else in the lookout, I felt self-consciously silly, a little like a bashful model posing for an art class. I decided I could follow the rules on everything else but only a really scary storm could make me take refuge on that Mickey-Mouse contraption.

I propped the platform back into place and sat back on my heels, thinking about the other lightning-storm precautions that had come to mind: avoid metal objects, turn off the radio, turn off the telephone... A disturbing thought struck me. *Turn off the telephone. You don't suppose... No, that couldn't be, could it?*

I rose to my feet and looked through the windows at the final telephone pole before the line reached the lookout. Halfway down the pole, a metal box contained the line's turnoff switch. A handle on the side of the box activated the switch. Pushed up, it turned the phone on. Pulled down, it turned the phone off.

In keeping with the warning not to touch any metal objects during a storm, a nylon rope trailed from the handle to the upper railing on the lookout's catwalk. A rope that looked for all the world like a neighborhood clothesline. To shut off the phone without touching the box, I merely had to make my way around the catwalk and pull the rope.

And because the rope looked like a clothesline, that's exactly how I had used it. All summer I had hung my laundry on the line. A day before the recent storm, I had washed most of my socks, the socks now hanging on the line, socks that had begun as crew socks but, after two days of heavy rain, had become tube socks, soaked with water and stretched to unbelievable lengths. The nylon line from the shutoff box to the catwalk bowed under the weight of the socks. And that weight had turned off my phone.

I went outside and pulled on my boots again. From there I walked down the steps and made my way around the lookout to the rope. Having removed the socks, I reached up and pushed the turnoff handle to the on position before returning to the lookout. Once again inside, I paused to plan my strategy before lifting the phone receiver and cranking two long rings.

"District office. Lenny, here."

"Hey, Lenny. It's Bob."

"Hi, Bob. Sounds like you fixed it."

"Yeah, I did. Has Bert shown up?"

"Haven't seen him."

"Well, when he does, could you change my earlier message a little? Tell him I found the problem early. It was something that would be easily overlooked by anyone without my experience in telephone-line repair. But I went ahead and worked the rest of the line to Lookout Springs because I enjoyed the opportunity to get out of the lookout for a while and stretch my legs. Can you tell him that for me?"

"I'd love to. Word for word just the way you said it. Anything else?"

"Nope. That's it."

"Right. Talk to you in the morning."

I hung up and looked over at Tinker, curled on the bed. "*What?* Don't give me that look. Sometimes a little white lie is good for the soul."

I walked to the food locker and took out a box. Shaking it at Tinker, I asked, "How about a milk bone? You deserve a treat after the long day you just put it."

I approached the bed, where she had come to her feet in anticipation. But I held the treat back, looking sternly down at her. "And by the way," I said, "what happened today, that's to be our little secret. Understand? No one must ever hear of the wet socks on the turnoff rope. Agreed?" I held the milk bone high until she reached upward, pawing the air. "Okay, then," I said, reaching down with my free hand to shake her paw. "I'm glad you see it my way." I dropped the bone on the bed and watched her nose it a couple of times before she began eating.

I had just brushed the crumbs into a pile so that she would clean up her mess when a sonorous voice filled the lookout. "The rhino is a homely beast." Smiling, I checked my watch. Eight o'clock on the dot. Just twelve hours ago, I had been pulled from a nice dream by the radio, and now the rhino man's soothing voice reminded me how tired I was.

"It's been a long day, Tinker," I said, pushing her over to make room for me on the bed. "A long day, this day of the long socks." I lay on my back, hands behind my head and closed my eyes. Tinker curled into my side, her body heat adding another touch of comfort. "I'm just going to rest my eyes for a moment," I said to her, "and then I'll start dinner." I felt her shift, and then her breathing slowed as she drifted into sleep. *I wish I could remember that dream*, I thought to myself. *I'm just going to rest my eyes for a moment, and then ...*

And then I, too, drifted into sleep.

# FRAGMENTS FROM AFRICA

## A COLLAGE OF FAST-FORWARD MEMORIES

In 2006 I fulfilled a lifelong dream with a trip through seven countries in Southern Africa. The day after I returned, I attended my writing class, suffering jet lag but happy to be back. My classmates, however, expected me to have written something about the trip.

I had never intended to do that, but because I didn't like disappointing them, I promised something for the next class.

Six days later I had written nothing. Despite all my traveling, I don't write travelogues. I write stories. For a week I had struggled to find a narrative, a story with a beginning, a middle, and an end. Finally I realized my time in Southern Africa could not be captured in such a narrative. I had lived every day in the moment with no thoughts about the day before or the day to come.

I woke each morning to the sounds of Africa. Every evening I looked to the brilliance of stars overhead, stars so much brighter and seemingly so much closer than those in the light pollution of our industrialized world. I treasured each moment of this experience. And because I did, I couldn't separate those moments into a straight-forward narrative.

When I let myself go—not trying to corral these moments into something I could control and organize—I allowed events, people, and scenes to flash through my mind in a chaotic jumble of memories. Eventually, I realized I didn't want to organize these memories. I wanted them to come to my reader just as they came to me. And that's the way I wrote it.

* **I stand on Table Mountain,** panoramic views of Cape Town behind me, a long stretch of the Cape of Good Hope ahead. The Cape has long been considered the point where the Atlantic and Indian

Oceans collide.[13] I somehow half-expect a dividing line, gray Atlantic water boiling over into a turquoise Indian Ocean. But there is no such demarcation. Blue waters with tinges of turquoise near the beaches extend in both directions from the Cape.

* I hike down the Cape in a torrential rainstorm. So many mariners in earlier centuries anticipated rounding this point. Those sailing east eager to leave the stormy Atlantic for the warmer Indian. Those sailing west elated, knowing soon they would turn north and head for home and family in Lisbon, Amsterdam, London. Homesick sailors returning in ships fragrant with spices from Java and points east.

* I visit Robben Island Prison, South Africa's Alcatraz. I stand in the hall outside the eight-by-seven-foot cell where Nelson Mandela spent the first eighteen years of his twenty-seven-year imprisonment. The cell contains a small bench. On the bench are a tin plate and cup. A lidded bucket in a corner served as a toilet. On the floor lies a sleeping mat with a padded wooden block for a pillow. I stand outside the door of the cell to take a photograph because I am unable to take the shot inside the cell. It is so small I fill it up when I enter.

* I visit the lime quarry, where Mandela served his sentence at hard labor. Here is a cave used as a makeshift lavatory by the prisoners. Because of the stench, the guards would not enter the cave, making it a sanctuary where prisoners could speak freely and teach each other. The motto of this illicit educational system: "Each one teaches one." The cave functioned as a classroom for a number of former prisoners who later serve in the South Africa government.

* In Johannesburg I experience more of the evils of apartheid. The largest Catholic Church in Soweto is scarred with bullet holes, reminders of the police raids to break up political addresses disguised as sermons. The police fired into crowds of people fleeing the bullets and tear gas. These police assaults occurred not once or twice but

---

[13]   Geographers have decided the two oceans actually meet at Cape Agulhas, a point to the southeast of Cape Hope. For centuries, however, navigators considered the Cape of Good Hope the place where these oceans meet. What sounds more romantic and uplifting—Cape Agulhas or Cape of Good Hope? Sometimes these researchers take things from us that we don't want to lose.

innumerable times as the resistance movement gained strength in the face of this country's repression.

* I travel east to the Africa that drew me on this trip. On my first morning in a game park in Zululand, I awaken to grunting, scrapping sounds on the other side of my bungalow's wall. A female warthog and her two youngsters root along the foundation, rubbing their scaly, semi-bald sides against the building. The mother's formidable tusks keep me at a distance. I enjoy these bristly relatives of Porky, Petunia, and Salomey.

* I spend a day in a Zulu settlement. I walk along a road that narrows into a trail on my way to visit a secondary school. There teenage girls in school uniforms sing and dance for their visitors. That strange Zulu dance. On every fourth or fifth beat, the dancer lifts a leg high, knee locked, foot at chest level, then brings it thunderously down, stomping the ground.

* In game camps over dinner, Zulus in warrior garb, spears in thrust position, dance at night by firelight. I see again the raised leg, the stomp that would shatter my ankle if I tried it. The Zulu Stomp.

* I go on game drives in open-sided Toyotas with tiered seating for ten passengers. At five o'clock in the morning, we see both the night predators and the early risers. It's cold. I did not expect cold in Africa.

* On these game drives I see the animals that brought me to Africa: elephants, rhinos, giraffes, cape buffalo, zebra, wildebeests, baboon troops with young riding the backs of mothers, panthers casually draped in the limbs of trees, antelopes of all types.

I sympathize with the graceful but woefully overworked impala. One dominant buck herds a harem of thirty or forty does. He spending all his time corralling them, moving them, chasing them, and fending off the surreptitious advances of young bachelors who move in their circles just outside his domain. Eventually weakened by his lack of rest and inability to take time to eat, the dominant buck becomes vulnerable and is chased away by an enterprising bachelor, who is a bachelor no more. But then *he* has to defend his new harem. And the cycle continues. Ah, the travails of love.

* And because this is nature in the raw, not a zoo, not a Walt Disney movie, sometimes the sightings are not so pleasant. A baby impala is trapped in the muck of a waterhole by a pack of wild dogs. The dogs frolic around the edges of the waterhole, chasing each other, rolling

in the sand, biding their time. Our group leaves before seeing what following groups see: the dogs pretending to go away but merely hiding in the bush, the baby struggling to the shore, the kill, the feast.

* Two lions feed on a giraffe brought down just hours before we come upon them. Blood streaks cross the road where they dragged the body into the bush. Angered by our intrusion, the larger male snarls and, tail twitching, walks away into the high grass. The second lion dismisses us, returning its bloody muzzle to the gaping hole in the giraffe's belly.

* I join a game drive at night. We stop in the middle of a hyena pack cavorting on the road. Beside our rig, a mother nurses several young. Others lie on their backs, four feet waving in the air. A hyena ballet.

* An ugly puff adder slithers along the shoulder of the road. Looking down on it, I shudder. A holdover reaction from my days in Pakistan, I suppose.

* With three other adventurers, I go on a rhino trek. Accompanied by two park rangers armed with powerful rifles, we set out on foot to track these reclusive animals. I learn more about animal dung than I ever hoped to learn. I can tell the difference in rhino dung, elephant dung, and hippo dung. I become a dung expert.

Dung piles turn out to be a sophisticated form of rhino post office. The dominant rhino returns again and again to several large piles strategically placed around his territory. He scrapes his feet through each pile and walks through the bush, spreading the word in this case, the smell that here he rules. It seems rhinos can identify each other by individual smells. His ever-growing piles warn others, and they respond according to their intentions.

Subservient males leave their own piles near but never on the dominant rhino's pile. He then allows them to graze in his territory. An interested female urinates on one of his piles. He checks it. "Yes, I remember her." And off he goes, looking for love.

But when another dominant male arrives, he defiantly uses the first rhino's pile. The challenge is cast. More than a gauntlet has been thrown down. They search each other out. One will rule this dung-defined territory. One will be driven away.

Today's gang graffiti? Just a human version of rhino dung.

We find a family of rhino and approach to within twenty-five yards. We take a good vantage point behind some high brush. We watch the slow movements of a grazing male, female, and baby. Rhinos have notoriously bad eyesight, but their hearing and sense of smell are excellent. We are able to get this close only because we are upwind. The lead ranger tests this just as the great white hunter in the movies tests the wind. He holds up a handful of dust and lets it drift through his fingers.

We return to our Toyota. As we begin the drive back to camp, the rhino family emerges from the bush ahead of us. "Not to worry," cautions the ranger. "They ignore vehicles. Vehicles have never threatened them. Just stay sitting. Don't put your hands or feet outside the rig, and you'll simply be part of the vehicle. No threat, no fear."

The family makes its way slowly toward us, grazing on grasses and pulling leaves from low brush. Twenty yards from us. Ten yards. The big male strolls across the road directly in front of our rig. The family follows. I breathe again.

*I visit a village of children near our game camp. Over one hundred orphans live under the care of a single woman chief. Most have lost their parents to AIDS, the scourge devouring Africa. The average life expectancy in these South African countries is in the thirties, a figure skewered by the number of children and young adults succumbing to this disease.

The children greet us with smiles and song, grasping our hands in the traditional three-movement African handshake. They dance for us. And dance *with* us, giggling at our lack of rhythm. They are happy. And one of every five will suffer the same death as their parents.[14]

*I travel on to Zimbabwe and Zambia to walk along Victoria Falls. Over a mile of raging water cascades into a zigzag ravine. Perfect double rainbows arch overhead. Clouds of mists continually hover above. From a distance, the mist looks like the smoke of a major fire. In the local language the falls are called *Mosi-oa-Tunya,* "the smoke that thunders."

I travel above the falls by helicopter. If only David Livingston could have seen his magnificent falls from this viewpoint.

Victoria Falls is David Livingston country. From the helicopter, I see the small island where Livingston camped the day before he saw the

---

[14]  As I mentioned in the introduction, I wrote this piece in 2006. Now, in October, 2014, the World Health Organization reports that the Ebola outbreak in Africa has orphaned 3,700 children. The names of these scourges may change, but for the children, the results are the same.

falls for the first time. I spend time in a village that has existed in the same place for hundreds of years. Here I shoot the breeze with a group of young men in the shade of the same tree under which Livingston, in 1885, sat while he awaited an audience with the village chief.

The village has no running water, no electricity. But these enterprising young men have set up a solar panel to power their radio. They listen to the latest in Zambian pop music.

*I travel into Botswana for a game drive and a trip in a small boat up the Chobe River. We come near a pod of hippos, the larger adults opening their mouths in what appear to be yawns of boredom. "Not yawning," says the ranger guiding us. "Posturing. It's a warning. We have come as close as they will allow."

Hippos look so cuddly cute. In reality, they account for more human deaths than any other animal in Africa. They trample people who get between them and the water. They swamp boats when angered or threatened. The bigger hippos open their mouths in a four-foot-wide gape, revealing canine teeth over two feet long.

We do not move closer.

As we marvel at the herds of elephants on the banks of the Chobe, our ranger suggests we try to count them. "See if you can," he challenges. Most of us give up early as we try to track the babies moving under the bellies and around the feet of the adults. But others count over two hundred elephants before they resign themselves to the impossibility of the task.

Crocodiles sun on the banks of the river. They, too, are open-mouthed, jagged jaws hinged wide as if caught in a stop-action pose. It's not a challenge this time, however. The crocodile is yet another animal without sweat glands. Open mouths give off heat. Also, closing the mouth, grabbing something and holding on, takes muscle. An open mouth is simply crocodile relaxation.

Time to leave Africa. I come away with sensory overload.

The sounds. Animals crying out in the night. Fear? Anger? Mating? All of the above? The lilt of South African English, not quite British, not quite Australian. Always a surprise coming from the mouths of young children. The absolute silence on an early morning game walk.

The smells. The putrescence of a crocodile kill stashed in the marshes of a lake to "season." The medicinal odor of insect repellent applied daily in malaria country. The heady fragrance of a camp kitchen after a long day in the bush.

The tastes. Ostrich (both raw and cooked), boar, crocodile, kudu, eland, shark. I try it all.

The feel. Everything is prickly in Africa. Thorns as long as my thumb on low-lying brush. Twisting upward through the trees, a massive vine with lethal-looking barbs aptly named the thorny rope. Nasty little quill-like stickers hidden in the grass. After a game walk my pant legs look like the scene of a pygmy porcupine orgy. In the African wild even plants have to devise defense mechanisms in order to survive.

And, above all, the sights. Blood-red sunrises and sunsets. On one of my last evenings, I travel down the Zambezi River aboard *The African Queen*. The setting sun, a blaze of red fire reflected in the water, the shoreline moving into shadow, the predators already on the move.

Blood-red. So appropriate a color for this land with its violent, life-at-its-essence nature interwoven with its raw beauty and siren call. This land called Africa.

# LAST WILL AND TESTAMENT

In the twenty-eight years we've been married, Sue has become an intrepid traveler. She had no qualms about visiting the DMZ in Korea. While floating in a small boat on a dark night in China, she giggled as we watched trained cormorants, streaking through lantern-lit waters, deliver fish to a fisherman on his bamboo raft. When we were caught in a snowstorm while visiting Dracula's castle in Transylvania, she thought the experience was great fun.

But when the trip through Southern African came up, Sue refused to accompany me. She had some kind of strange premonition about this trip. In fact, she was so concerned, she pointed out I had never prepared a will. She insisted I do so before leaving. I said I would. But, of course, I didn't.

The day before I was leave, she asked if I had taken care of the will. When I admitted that it had skipped my mind, she cut me no slack. In spite of last-minute packing, I had to find time to write a will. She demanded it be a legal document, not simply something I scribbled on a piece of paper.

So I sat down at my computer, composed a beautiful will, and took the time to have it notarized. Following is a copy of that exquisite document.

## LAST WILL AND TESTAMENT OF
## ROBERT FOX CHRISTENSON

**Be it known** that I, Robert Fox Christenson, being of relatively sound mind (depending upon whom you ask) do hereby declare that if I bite the dust in Africa, everything I own—material goods, financial holdings, copyrights, etc.—shall go to my wife, Susan Valerie Christenson, to do with however she wishes.

As for my remains, anything of value to donor programs is up for grabs. The body should not, however, be donated to a science lab or medical school. I refuse to be a formaldehyde-dipped cadaver worked over by a couple of med students with names like Bunny and Tiffy, giggly little twits who have given me an equally obnoxious nickname and treat me like a pickled prop. After all, I *have* seen the movie *Gross Anatomy.*

Anything left over should be shipped home for burial. Cremation is out. It might be cheaper, but I'll probably be in flames soon enough without jumping the gun.

As for services, I want to be buried without a ceremony. A month or so later, a memorial may be held if enough people can be conned into attending. The purpose of the wait is to do away with all the emotional drain usually found in these services. The memorial should be upbeat. Only one song may be played: Willie Nelson's *On the Road Again.*

On the other hand, if I don't *quite* bite the dust but end up in a vegetative state from which there is no hope of return, a state in which my future looks no brighter than my being used as a gigantic paperweight or third base in a baseball game (the base, not the player), the plug should be pulled. This decision is in the hands of my wife, Susan Valerie Christenson. If she says "Pull," someone should pull.

However, if I return in fine form (my intention, by the way), my wife, Susan Valerie Christenson, owes me a bottle of twelve-year-old Scotch. This condition has been inserted into this document as punishment because she insisted I engage in this nonsense before leaving.

Sincerely,

Robert Fox Christenson

Affixed with my indecipherable and, therefore, forgery-proof signature on this date in the year of our Lord Two Thousand, Six, A.D.

---

(Indecipherable and, therefore, forgery-proof signature)

---

(Date)

> By the way, when I returned home, a bottle of Chivas Regal awaited me on the dining table.

# TITHING

**I stood in** the hot, steamy locker room, my grass-and-blood-stained football jersey at my feet. From the showers came the yells and laughter of my teammates celebrating our win. We had earned the right to play for the state championship the following week.

Guys were already leaving the showers, eager to dress for the after-game dance.

I was always among the last to shower. I loved the accouterments of football: the pads, the jersey, the pants, the helmet. For home games, I arrived early, dressed, and found a quiet place to still the butterflies that had been building throughout the day. And with the game over, I delayed removing my uniform as I came down from the adrenalin of football.

"Hey," Stan shouted, flipping a towel at me. "Get a move on. The girls are waiting."

"Yeah, well," I replied, "I'm worth waiting for."

"Right," he grinned, snapping the towel hard this time.

Turning away to avoid the sting, I saw him—my father standing just inside the door. With a half-wave as if embarrassed to draw attention to himself, he walked toward me.

I watched as he crossed the room. He was still in his work clothes: red felt hunting hat pushed back on his head, a faded blue work shirt, top two buttons undone, over baggy, ragged jeans. He owned two—maybe three—of these blue shirts, distinguished only by different patterns in the holes ripped by guardian brush surrounding trees he brought down. Always worn partially buttoned with rolled-up sleeves, the shirts smelled of my father: tobacco, sweat, and especially sawdust.

The mill did not release him at day's end. It came home with him as hidden sawdust in the band of his hat, in his pockets, even in his navel. Sawdust worked through his clothes to his stomach as if seeking the very core of this creator of the sawdust itself.

As he neared, he grinned the lopsided grin that signaled a long stop at the tavern. I realized why he had been so late he didn't have time to change his clothes before coming to the game.

I noticed teammates looking our way. They weren't watching us because of his work clothes. Many of us were loggers' and farmers' sons. It was the fact he was there at all. None of us had ever seen a father come into the after-game locker room. I would have never imagined *my* father would be the one to violate this taboo.

He stood in front of me, hands in pockets. "I just wanted to say, 'Good game.'"

"Thanks. Did you come right from work?"

He grinned. "No, not quite. Don't tell your mother, though. She thinks I did."

"I doubt it," I replied.

"Me, too," he smiled.

We laughed, both knowing he would catch hell later.

Then he pulled his right hand from his pocket. In his fist, he held several crumpled bills. "Here," he whispered. "Have a good time tonight."

"You don't have to," I said. "I'm okay."

"No, I want to. Have a good time tonight."

The bills were in his mutilated hand. Covered with scar tissue, one finger gone, another useless, a knuckle missing, the hand was colored pink with transplanted skin. Four years before, a slip near the big saw had left him with this patched-together hand. "You work in logging long enough," he said, "and you're bound to lose some parts. A finger? If I lose only that, count me lucky."

He stood there, holding the bills out to me. As I took the money, he squeezed my hand. "Well, then," he said. "Have a good time tonight." He turned and walked to the door.

In my hand were four crumbled dollar bills, probably the change he had crammed into his pocket as he left the tavern. He would have been hurried, cutting it close. He hated missing the introduction of the starting lineups. He liked hearing my name—his name—announced.

I stood there, looking at the bills in my hand. Four dollars. Four crumpled one-dollar bills. On a good day he might clear forty dollars. He probably had worked ten hours that day. And the last hour, pushing through fatigue, he would have earned the four dollars he gave to me.

*Ten percent,* I thought, looking at the bills. *It's like tithing except not to a church. It's like tithing ten percent to a son with all the opportunities the father had been denied as a boy.*

\* \* \*

My father watched me play football one more season. In the spring of my senior year, the mill, not satisfied with merely taking parts, took the rest of him.

We had eighteen years together. I should have memories of other times when we came close to saying what we felt. But I do not. My father and I tithed in our conversations with each other. In coded speech, we each gave ten percent of what we meant.

"Good game," coupled with four crumpled dollars, meant "I'm so proud of you."

"Thanks" added to "You don't need to do that" meant "I understand. No need to say it."

\* \* \*

Fifty-nine years later, I break through the code. I place an unmanly rose on his stone. "I know how much you loved me," I whisper. "And I'm sure you know how much I loved you. We couldn't talk then, but we can now. I'm going to tell you about the feelings of a boy in a locker room who sees the father he loved walk toward him."

I look across the river at Mt. Hood, emerging from an early morning mist. I look down at the rose across his name—my name—and I begin to speak.

"Sometimes you win. Sometimes you lose. Sometimes it rains."
Ebby Calvin "Nuke" LaLosh

# ACKNOWLEDGEMENTS

**I wrote** *Into the Wild with a Virgin Bride* and most of *Sand, Sawdust, and Scotch* while attending a Portland Community College class entitled *Write Your Life Story*. The class is taught by Eva Gibson, an accomplished author of twenty-three books and an excellent teacher, who, through encouragement and gentle guidance, brings out the best in her students. The class is unusual in that students who sign up for what they believe is a one-term course keep returning. Some stay a few terms, and others attend for years. They hone their own writing skills and serve as excellent sounding boards for each other. If not for Eva and my fellow students, I would never have written these books.

I know most readers skim through acknowledgements in books. I certainly do. So if you were not in these classes, feel free to check out now. But if you were, I want you to know how much I appreciate the positive comments and sense of direction I received from all of you. Thank you for sharing your joy in writing with me.

Skip, whose encyclopedic memory astounds us all
Yildiz, our Turkish delight
Pat, whose book *Lost* should have been put on the market
Mark, fireman, writer, and seekers of oddities
Golden, the man with the golden voice
Gladys, whose homey narratives make us wish we were part of her family
Two Sandys, one of Stayton and the other of the School of Hard Knocks
Louise, intrepid trekker in the mountains of Nepal
Nancy, who not only has a talent for critiquing the writing of others but
    also can mimic a barking sea lion better than anyone else I know
Bob, whose family left post-war Japan to seek a wilderness refuge in
    southern Oregon
Chris, whose detailed stories will be so important to her family
Terry, who has a talent for introspective writing

Elizabeth, poetic artist with both the brush and the pen, who also shared
  Frank's writing whenever he skipped class to work the stock market
George, whose book *Somehow, We'll Survive* should be on everyone's
  bookshelf
Mary Lou, who brought Montana to Oregon and shared Harl with us.
Mae, who wrote of the tragic injustice suffered by her family and other
  Japanese-Americans removed to internment camps after the Pearl
  Harbor attack
Joanne of the Skinner Ranch
Gerry, gentle student of Buddhism
Marie, our knitting scientist
Margaret, who made our mouths water with her description of Polish
  cooking
Rosanne, whose family has the unique distinction of having ordered a
  complete house from Montgomery Ward
Cookie, whose enrollments in the class were spaced seven years apart
Bill, who flew an airplane thirty minutes after his first flying lesson
Kate, who dropped in because her exercise class had been cancelled and,
  to our good fortune, decided to stay
Dee, who takes such joy in good writing
Cheri, who should be writing tourist brochures for Alaska
Emma Jane, who wrote simple, straight-to-the-point reflections of a
  time past
Barbara, who encouraged me to submit to literary journals
Alishia, who dropped out just when she was finding her voice
Paul and Clare, who welcomed me into the class my first year,
  entertaining me with their classic husband-wife interplay
Anja, who shared her single year in the U.S. with us
Another Pat, this one a bank teller who dreamed of an anti-theft device
  button under her counter designed to deliver a blow to a would-be
  robber's knee (or regions higher up) when he tried to rob the bank

And those we'll all miss:

Mac, who at ninety years old, was often the youngest person in the room
Kate, who introduced everything she wrote with "This is just a bit of
  fluff" before proceeding to knock our socks off

Harl, who rubbed elbows with the big dogs in Oregon yet seldom dropped names in class, instead entertaining us with delightfully humorous stories of his boyhood and his early years in law
Frank, who had an unbounded enthusiasm for life
Maureen, our Welsh poet, who was such a joy in her quiet way

To all of you, including the people I've no doubt missed, thank you. You made this book come to life.

Bob Christenson
October, 2014

# WHERE AND WHEN

## *WASHINGTON*

1937 - 1938: Hoquiam
1938 - 1943: In and around Copalis Beach
1943 - 1944: Aberdeen

## *OREGON*

1944 - 1946: A farm outside Estacada
1946 - 1956: Estacada
1956 - 1959: Portland
1959 - 1964: Clackamas

## *WEST PAKISTAN*

1964 - 1967: Baral Colony

## *OREGON*

1967 - 1969: Oak Grove
1969 - 1971: Portland
1971 - 1979: Damascus
1979 - 1993: Clackamas
1993 - Present: Tigard

**Bob Christenson grew** up in a small Oregon timber town. By age fourteen, he worked in his family's sawmill. At age sixteen, he began employment with the U.S. Forest Service, a job he held for ten years to help pay for college and augment his salary as a young English teacher.

In 1964, Bob accepted a teaching position in Pakistan. Three years later, he returned to Oregon, hooked on international travel but certain he would never again live outside the Pacific Northwest.

In 1993, Bob retired from teaching. Today Bob and Sue share a condominium with Tahnee and Baxter, two cats they rescued from a nearby shelter. They continue traveling the world. When home, Bob reads, writes, and goes fishing whenever he needs a forest fix.

Edwards Brothers Malloy
Thorofare, NJ  USA
January 7, 2015